"Tyranny, like hell, is not easily conquered;
yet we have this consolation with us,
that the harder the conflict,
the more glorious the triumph.
What we obtain too cheap,
we esteem too lightly:
it is dearness only that
gives every thing its value."

Thomas Paine

The Greater The Honor

A Novel of the Barbary Wars

WILLIAM H. WHITE

ISBN 1-888671-44-0 (Hard Cover)
ISBN 1-888671-20-3 (Soft Cover)

Cover art © 2002 Paul Garnett
Ships left to right, USS *Constitution*, a fishing smack, USS *Argus*, USS *Enterprise*, USS *Syren*
Illustrations © 2002 Paul Garnett

Graphic design and production by:
Words & Pictures, Inc., 27 South River Road South, Edgewater, Maryland 21037

Printed in the USA by:
Victor Graphics, 1211 Bernard Drive, Baltimore, MD 21223 USA

Questions regarding the content of this book should be addressed to:

TILLER Publishing

605 Talbot Street, Suite Two
St. Michaels, Maryland 21663
410-745-3750 • Fax: 410-745-9743
www.tillerbooks.com

DEDICATION

This book is for the ladies to the south,
Felicity, Missy, Lizzy, and Sally, with love.
And for Andrew who joined us in September, 2002.

ACKNOWLEDGEMENTS

D uring the course of researching and writing this novel, I was assisted by several people whose efforts contributed accuracy and wisdom to my efforts. I would be remiss were I not to thank them publicly.

At the USS Constitution Museum, Charlestown Navy Yard, Boston, MA: Margherita Desy, Curator, who provided access to the brilliant new research library there and, more importantly, recommendations for titles, papers, and logs that would prove invaluable.

Kate Lennon, Librarian, patiently explained to me the intricacies of the microfilm reader and printer, then sorted me out when I got in trouble with it, and provided microfilmed logs from the USS *Constitution* during that ship's involvement in the Barbary Wars.

At the Massachusetts Historical Society: William Fowler, PhD, made available to me countless sources about the practice of dueling, and provided a read of the manuscript to ensure its accuracy as well as his fine introduction.

At the Gibraltar Tourism Office, Gibraltar: Tina Gache, who offered voluminous historical information on "The Rock," including its early development from first settlement to modern times, and responded to my many emails with patience and alacrity.

At The Chipstone Foundation, Milwaukee, WI: Nancy Sazama, provided a photograph of the splendid contemporary engraving of the August 3rd 1804 bombardment of Tripoli and allowed its use in this book.

Donald Petrie, writer, historian, and expert in prize law, helped with issues concerning prize law and a complete read of the manuscript with an eye toward its historical accuracy. His suggestions were invaluable. His lovely wife Mary offered her enthusiastic endorsement of the literary aspect of the book.

Others include:

Bob Paulus, my friend and mentor, has the most remarkable collection of esoterica regarding the formative days of the U.S. Navy and an unstinting willingness to share it.

Joe Burns, friend and sailing pal, was always available to discuss a plot concept, provide a read with suggestions, and offer continuing encouragement.

Deborah Bowles, a legal secretary in Washington, DC, stumbled across a wonderful, long out-of-print book in a used bookstore in Maine and sent it to me. It became a significant source which proved accurate to a fault.

As always, my sister, Linda W. Wiseman, an independent scholar of the decorative arts, way of life, and interior design of the early days of the Republic, was available with minutiae about life in the 18th and 19th centuries including food, music, and customs.

My editor at Tiller Publishing, Jerri Anne Hopkins, was helpful in making the text more readable and grammatically accurate; and patient with my sometimes obstinate reluctance to amend a grammatically offensive passage.

And Jay Benford, Publisher, willingly took a chance on an untried writer some years ago and has a continuing appetite for my yarns.

Of course, Paul Garnett, artist extraordinaire, provided his splendid and creative cover and inside sketches. While we're not supposed to "judge a book by its cover," we do, and an eye-catching illustration is surely a help in attracting attention!

Last, but surely not least, I could not have found a more supportive family than my wife Ann, sons Skip, John, and Josh, and daughters-in-law Felicity and Missy. Your encouraging words and love were inspirational.

If I have succeeded in making this story interesting, exciting, or historically accurate, it is in no small measure because these good folks were unstinting in their willingness to help. Thank you all for making me look good.

William H. White
Fall, 2002

INTRODUCTION

Novelists, like historians, are storytellers. Unlike historians, however, they find the elements of plot and suspense not in libraries and archives but in their own imaginations. Bill White is one of those few novelists who is comfortable both in the world of imagination as well as amongst books and dusty manuscripts. In *The Greater the Honor* he weaves an imaginative tale of young men in war set against an historical background that is accurate in nearly every detail.

Young America was a sea minded nation. In the early years of the republic, merchants in Boston, New York, Philadelphia and a dozen other ports sent their vessels to sea instructing their captains "Try All Ports." These ships were venturing into a hostile world where few nations wished us well. Nowhere was the danger greater than in the western Mediterranean where the Barbary Corsairs waited to pounce upon our trade.

For centuries these North African Corsairs had made their livelihood preying upon merchant vessels sailing in the western Mediterranean. Nations that wished to pass through these waters had either to pay or fight. Most decided to pay—it was cheaper. Our new nation did not have the means to do either. Our government had neither the money to offer tribute nor the resources to build a navy. Not until 1797 did we finally launch fighting ships. "Old Ironsides" was the first but others soon followed, and in 1801 during his first administration, President Thomas Jefferson dispatched an American squadron to protect our trade against the "Barbary Pirates."

The year is 1803, and young Oliver Baldwin arrives in Boston to take his berth aboard the newly launched United States brig *Argus* commanded by Stephen Decatur. *Argus* is bound for the Mediterranean to join Commodore Preble's squadron.

Baldwin and his shipmates are in for a rollicking adventure. Under Decatur's careful eye the young men serving under him learn to hand, reef, steer and fight!

William Fowler, Ph.D.
Director, Massachusetts Historical Society

The attack made on Tripoli on the 3rd August 1804 by the American Squadron under Commodore Edward Preble to whom this Plate is respectfully dedicated by his Obedient Servant John B. Guerazzi. Courtesy Chipstone Foundation. Photo Gavin Ashworth.

Full Rigged Ship (Frigate)

Gunboat

Tripolitan Galley

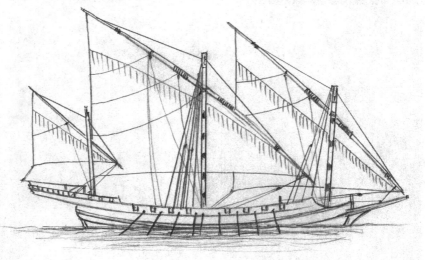

Brig

Ketch

Schooner

CHAPTER ONE

"Excuse me, sir. Perchance can you direct me to the ship *Argus*? I have been told she was to be found at this wharf." My voice broke, an embarrassment to my effort at maturity, raising further sweat on my brow, which immediately trickled down my reddening cheeks. I had hoped not to be taken as a mere boy. The heat of the August afternoon could easily be blamed for my flushed countenance and the sweat that now ran freely. Indeed, it was a sweltering day, even for August; it seemed of late as though each day was determined to be more uncomfortable than its predecessor.

The fellow—a bit of an unsavory character I thought after he had turned to give me his attention—looked me over top to bottom and scowled at me from under a beetle brow trimmed in bushy eyebrows. He took in my forest green suit, white shirt, now wilted and travel worn, and low boots, taking time in his appraisal. He then fixed his rheumy gaze upon my youthful face. His very look made me blanch, but there appeared no opportunity to make my escape. And I didn't think it would do to insult or irritate this fellow. His countenance looked for all the world like I imagined the demons to look, the ones my father spoke of so often while reminding me of the unwholesomeness of the world beyond Philadelphia.

I could not help but notice that his dress was akin to what I would associate with a drayman at home, a none too prosperous one at that. He wore a plaid shirt of indeterminate color covered by an unbuttoned waistcoat that had perhaps been fawn-colored but was now stained with so many colors that its original shade was lost forever. It was unbuttoned, not because of the heat of the afternoon, but due to a complete lack of buttons. Trousers of canvas marked him a sailor to all but me. Topping off this costume was a tarpaulin hat that had long since seen better days covering greasy black hair which, judging from what stuck out under the hat, was some unruly. His voice, when I finally heard it, was raspy and nasal, nearly a snarl.

"She ain't a ship, boy; she's a brig. An' just what would a lad of your stripe be wantin' with the *Argus* brig?" He stopped and again took my measure. When I met his gaze and remained silent, he added, "She be lyin' yonder in the roads." He pointed in a generally seaward direction where, following his outstretched arm, I was able to make out several vessels lying to their anchors in the shimmering haze.

"I thank you most kindly, sir. I shall endeavor to get myself out there on the morrow. I am, you see, assigned in her. Midshipman, I am, and ordered to that *brig*, Lieutenant Stephen Decatur commanding, by Mister Robert Smith;

he's Secretary of the Navy. Signed my Warrant with his own hand, he did." I dispatched him neatly with the practiced words I was sure would leave him suitably impressed. Hoping I had, indeed, put the gentleman (I am only assuming that he was indeed worthy of that distinction) off with my brusque manner, I turned about, relieved that my voice had not this time failed me and, again shouldering the chest I had earlier set down, stepped off for a house I had earlier espied which advertised 'rooms.'

"Heave to, there young sir. I had no idea I was bein' spoke to by such as yerself. Where are ye bound under such a press of canvas?" His scowl had disappeared, replaced by what I imagined to be a smile, and his brow lifted inquiringly as he spoke.

"Why, I am going to secure for myself a room for the night and some supper, I suppose. There." Now I pointed and he looked. "It seems convenient." Maybe I had proven my independence to him.

"That's a place seamen gather. Right rowdy they are, they been drinkin'. Ain't no place for a young lad to be by hisself. I'd be pleased to accompany you and give you a good steer."

"I am fourteen, sir. I would reckon to be able to take care of myself." I didn't savor the thought of spending any more time than I had already with this fellow and I again started toward the hotel. With him at my heel.

As I approached the building that I had selected as my shelter for the night, a quick glance to my rear assured me that, yes, he was still following and apparently determined to provide me "a good steer" whether I needed one or not. That I had little idea of what he meant by "a good steer" concerned me only slightly as I stepped through the front door trying to look as if I weren't staggering under the weight of my seachest, and that I knew exactly what I was about. I managed to bang it more than once against the doorjamb and, upon setting it down, with some considerable relief, checked it carefully for dents and scratches. The words on the front were undamaged and, as I read them for the thousandth time, I felt the same rush of pride I had felt when first I had gazed upon them: *Midshipman Oliver C. Baldwin—United States Brig Argus.*

I took stock of my surroundings: a narrow stair rose in front of me, disappearing into darkness somewhere on, I assumed, the second storey. To my right, a door stood closed. It held no indication of what lay behind it, but from the sounds issuing forth, I gathered, correctly, it was the taproom and pushed the door open.

The noise of twenty or more men talking and laughing and trying to be heard over their own din assaulted me, and I very nearly tripped over my self-appointed escort as I stepped backwards. I regained my footing and peered into the room. Through the gloom, it seemed to be longer than it was wide by about twice and was filled with tables surrounded by ladder-back chairs. None, that I could discern, appeared particularly stable; many were missing slats in their backs, and even several of the unoccupied ones seemed to teeter precariously on uneven legs.

Certainly not furniture from the Baldwin shop of Philadelphia! I mused silently.

Lanterns gave off a sickly yellow glow in a dismal effort to augment the waning daylight that struggled in through the narrow, grime-covered windows; the shadows created by the smoky lamps danced grotesquely in an exaggerated imitation of the gestures and movements of the room's inhabitants. The fog of tobacco smoke and the black oily emanations from the lanterns hanging from the ceiling beams brought tears to my eyes and constricted my throat. The resulting coughing fit made my eyes run even more. I know not whether it was the noise I was making in my attempts to breathe or the rush of clear air into the room, but most eyes turned to me and conversation stopped. The sudden silence was startling.

I hesitated, not relishing the thought of entry into that atmosphere, and reconsidered my decision to spend the night in this place. My friend from the wharf gave me a none-too-gentle shove, propelling me unceremoniously into the room. The noise began again with renewed vigor, in recognition that no personage of consequence was entering. Without a word, my friend guided me through the palpable air, around tables and chairs, mostly unseen by me, to an unoccupied table. These ladder-backs at least had four legs of equal length and more than a few of the slats from which their name arose. He waved a hand and, as if by magic, two brimming tankards appeared on the table.

You'll not be wanting to taste strong drink, Oliver. And while you'll be getting a regular ration, half, I believe on account of your youth, aboard ship, you'll do well to avoid it. Whiskey and rum are the devil's own creations and most certainly not for young gentlemen from Philadelphia. My father's words of only a few days ago drifted through my head, surprisingly clear. I fancied I could hear his voice saying them, even over the din of the taproom. A tap on the shoulder brought me back to the present, and I turned to find a large gentleman in a none-too-clean waistcoat over what might have once been a white shirt standing with his hand out.

"Pay the man, lad, so we can get on with it. You've money, I collect?" My friend from the wharf prodded me and I withdrew my purse from its place within my jacket. I produced some coins that disappeared from my hand, and the publican with them, so quickly I myself was not even sure they had ever been there.

"I am not sure this is where I want to spend the night. Perhaps some other . . ."

"Nonsense, lad. This here's a fine place and I reckon ye'll be as well set here as any place. Now drink yer ale and tell me yer name. And what you're about. Mine's Langford, Edward Langford. From right here in Boston. Doubled the Horn twicet and shipwrecked inta the bargain." He took a long draught from the pewter in front of him and, setting it down noisily, looked at me with raised eyebrows.

"I'm Oliver Baldwin, *Midshipman* Oliver Baldwin. From Philadelphia—that's in Pennsylvania. And I am to sail with Captain Decatur in the brig *Argus*. Captain Decatur is a Philadelphia man, also, you know." Mister Langford nodded attentively and I continued.

"It is interesting that your name is Edward; I have a brother, older than me by some six years, whose name is Edward. He is also in the Navy, a lieutenant in the frigate *Philadelphia* under Captain Bainbridge. I am given to understand that the *Philadelphia* has only recently left for the Mediterranean Sea and will be part of the squadron with *Constitution* and Commodore Preble." I fairly yelled to be heard over the noise, and Mister Langford leaned forward to catch my words.

Lest there be any doubt in his mind of my part in this mighty armada, I added, "And *Argus* will be joining the squadron as soon as she has completed fitting out. She is just finished building, you know." I knew this, and it was about the extent of my knowledge, from a letter we had received from my brother, Edward, posted just before *Philadelphia* sailed a month back.

As I stopped, he took another long draught from the tankard and pushed mine toward me, nodding to indicate I should drink. Since this was ale, according to Edward Langford, and Father's admonition had mentioned only *strong* drink, I lifted the pewter to my lips, swallowed my first taste of the bitter brew, and grimaced, albeit involuntarily.

Mister Langford laughed and encouraged me to try again, which I did. And again. And again. He signaled the keeper for more, for which I again paid, and mid-way through the second, or perhaps it was the third, tankard, it appeared we had become quite good friends. We talked at some length; I told him about my cabinet-maker father and about my brother who was to have been the only one of us to join the Navy.

"So what are ye doing here, *Mister Midshipman* Baldwin? I would reckon yer're s'posed to be learnin' the wood butcherin' trade."

"Yes, sir. That was Father's intent. But it turned out I could not be around the wood chips and dust created by the process of manufacture. Made me sneeze and teared my eyes so badly I could barely see. Father thought it best for me to go to sea and, since he and Lieutenant Decatur are friends, he prevailed on him to secure a midshipman's warrant for me. It was Lieutenant Decatur's thought to have me in his vessel should I be able to get myself to Boston in time to make her sailing." I recalled that it had been Father who thought it best for me to be at sea. Mother had bitterly opposed his decision and I remembered many tearful arguments between them when they thought I was out of earshot.

He offered comments, the content of which I am afraid I took little note, and I became aware that the din of the room had receded to a swirling buzz in my head. In fact, from time to time, I could have sworn that the room itself was swirling, and I gripped the table to keep myself from falling out of the chair. I discovered that I had a bit of difficulty forming words I had used all my life; my lips seemed to have a mind of their own.

I have little recollection of the remainder of the evening or our conversation, save that we laughed a great deal and that, at some point, he guided me up the stairs. I know this only because when I awakened the next morning, I was in a small room on a rank mattress that quite literally crawled with vermin.

A most unpleasant odor assaulted my nostrils. I found its source to be a disagreeable and still wet puddle of vomit, apparently mine, next to the bed. The sour smell and its proximity inspired me to alight from the cot to distance myself from it, but as soon as I gained my feet, the room spun and swirled around me. I put my hand on the table for support and carefully returned my bottom to the bed. Smell and vermin be damned!

I closed my eyes in the hope that my head would stop its incessant reeling. *I have taken a fever from the heat yesterday. That or the noxious atmosphere in the taproom last night, the smoke and all.* I rubbed a hand over my face and tried tentatively opening my eyes again to take stock of my surroundings. My gaze fell upon my seachest standing open by the door, and I smiled again as I read the name on its front.

"Open . . . it's open. Shouldn't be open." The words fought their way through the fog in my brain and, I believe, some actually found their way out of my dry and evil-tasting mouth.

I flew, or rather staggered, across the room. Though it was only two steps, it seemed to take a long while. All thoughts of my churning stomach and pounding head were gone. I dropped to my knees, steadying myself on the chest, and peered into it. Pieces of clothing hung out of the upper compartment. A dear little book put in by my mother was bent and crushed in a corner. My quadrant and books on navigation were still intact in their locked cubbyhole, and the drawer under the shelf still contained my linen, neatly folded and obviously untouched. Who possibly could have rifled my belongings in such a manner?

I poked around, pulling things out and trying to puzzle out what might be missing. Uniforms, hats, both dress and undress, dirk, linens, some papers of food and teas and some bottles of medicines which stood in their own small compartment. Yes, it appeared that everything was still there, albeit in considerable disarray. In the haste of whoever had wreaked havoc among my belongings, a paper of some powder, the purpose of which I could not call to mind but which none the less smelled evil and potent, had burst and managed to distribute itself liberally over the contents of the chest. Whatever it was that someone had been seeking remained a mystery to me. With the distraction of the rifled chest gone, the incessant pounding in my head returned.

I sat on the floor for a long moment considering what to do. I half-heartedly brushed at the specks of blue-green powder from the burst medicine paper which seemed to cling tenaciously to many of my garments and were, of course, most easily visible on my snow-white breeches. I rearranged the clothes in my chest, clothes which Mother had so painstakingly folded, in a manner that I am sure would have caused her to frown and cluck, but so that at least I could close it. That effort alone took some time as I had to stop repeatedly to quell the heaving that had a firm grip on my poor stomach. The aroma of the spilt medicinal potion compounded my distress. The pounding in my head, the terrible thirst I suddenly realized I had, and the pain behind my eyes all the while gained strength. All I wanted to do was to lie back down, anywhere, and keep my eyes closed. That seemed to make the pain ease some.

When I finally gained the courage to again get to my feet, I realized I had no idea of the time or even whether it was morning or afternoon. I had to get myself out to the ship. I spied my green coat on a rickety chair and grabbed at it, seeking the watch my father had given me on my departure.

"It must be in another pocket," I told myself as I felt around for the heavy timepiece.

But it was not and I realized, with increasing alarm, neither was my purse. Panic took hold of me and I sank to the floor reeling from the knowledge, certain that I was doomed. My first experience away from the neat house on Held Street and my parents' protective and comfortable circumstances had ended in disaster only a few days from its beginning! What was I to do? I was penniless and quite obviously dying of some distressing malady. My family would never know what happened to me, beyond the fact that I never reported to my ship. I could see Mother wringing her hands and repeating, "I told you, Edward, he was too young to go off by himself." The tears stained her face, and my father could only shake his head in sadness. I felt a tear start down my own cheek as my panic gave way to the horrible certainty that what was to be a wonderful adventure, and my start down the road to manhood, had died a-borning.

CHAPTER TWO

It must have been some hours later that I awoke on the floor, my green coat, now devoid of my possessions, clutched to my bosom and my cheeks salty with dried tears; I was stiff and thirsty. My head and stomach were only slightly improved, but my resolve had strengthened. With the realization that my only likely source of help lay in the *Argus* brig, I managed to struggle into my dress uniform, resting often during the process. Quitting the cubicle with its foul smells and worse memories, I made my unsteady way to the taproom in search of the proprietor to explain my unfortunate circumstances.

There I found a woman, the owner, who seemed to know me (she explained that the evening before I had spoken to her about a room) and who felt some measure of pity for my bad luck. She handed me a mug of water and directed me to the landing where the boats from the naval vessels arrived, suggesting I might find a boat from *Argus* that would carry me to the anchorage for no charge. My room was paid. She mentioned that a man fitting my recollection of Mister Langford had settled with her last night.

"And no favor he's done me! It was with my own money, he did!" I wondered aloud whether it was after he had robbed me.

"Oh my, young sir. I wouldn't imagine such a thing would go on in *my* establishment! The men who frequent the Horn and Musket would most certainly not be of such low character. You must have misplaced your belongings when you . . . well. Surely you wasn't robbed here! Now hurry yourself down to the landing so's you don't get left ashore again." Barely were the words out of her mouth when she turned and hurried off.

After watching her retreat into a back room, I carefully fitted my cocked hat onto my pounding head and made my way to the street door. When the full force of the mid-day sun hit my eyes, the pain almost made me cry out. Knives in my eye sockets could not have been more painful. Tears streamed forth and rolled down my cheeks. My whole head felt as if it were squeezed in one of the vices Father used to hold a board and my stomach continued to churn and roil. But despite my surely serious, perhaps fatal, illness, I was resolved to get to my ship.

I found the landing the woman had mentioned barely one hundred yards further down the quay from where I had met Mister Langford yesterday and carefully lowered my chest to the rough stones. There were four boats—I learned quickly they were three cutters and a jolly boat—secured to a ring set in the stones. Two sailors guarded each and chatted quietly without regard to my approach. I shifted so as to cast a shadow over the ones in the nearest boat and tentatively cleared my throat.

This interrupted the conversation, and all eight of the sailors now looked at me with gazes ranging from hard to merely curious.

"What can we do for you, sir?" The sailor in the nearest boat stood and faced me.

"I am Oliver Baldwin, midshipman, and assigned to the USS *Argus*. Can you take me to the brig?" I was not going to show my ignorance by referring to the *Argus* as a *ship* again. I smiled hopefully.

"Well, now. A young gentleman for Cap'n Decatur." The sailor grinned and shot a glance over his shoulder at another man in the boat farthest out from the steps. He raised his voice. "Looks like this one's one o' your'n, Tom." He turned back to me. "That ugly fellow yonder, the one for'ard in the jolly boat there. He'll be off'n the *Argus*. You'll have to ask him, I reckon."

Well! What a stroke of luck. Here was a boat from my ship and sitting right at my feet waiting to take me to my new home. I looked inquiringly at the man now standing in the front of the boat; he didn't seem terribly ugly to me, though it did appear that his eyes were uneven on his face and his mouth turned down on one side. He wore a hat of varnished straw with a red and blue ribbon tied 'round its crown, and a short pigtail showed below the brim. I bent to take hold of my seachest, but before I even got a satisfactory grip on it, the man, Tom, spoke.

"You'll be wantin' to heave to there, sir. This here's Cap'n Decatur's jolly boat, and, while I am sure he would certainly not mind waitin' in this hot sun while we rowed you out yonder and then rowed back to fetch him, I would think you might be wantin' to find yourself some other way out to *Argus*. No tellin' when the cap'n'll be back." He looked at me hard for a moment. "You sick, young fella? You look some peaked."

"I am quite fine," I said, trying with all I could muster to sound and look better than I was feeling. My ride to the ship had evaporated in a cloud of sarcasm as quickly as it appeared. I was no closer to getting aboard than I had been an hour ago and felt nearly as bad on top of it.

"Aye, sir. I am glad o' that. You walk just a ways down the quay there, maybe a musket shot is all, and you'll come onto the landing where the wherrymen pick up they's fares. Reckon one o' them'll take you out to *Argus* and glad of the fare."

"But I haven't . . ." I realized that my complete lack of funds was of no interest to these sailors and stopped. As I again took hold of my chest, I sensed a presence behind me and noticed that the men in the boats had all stood up, assuming a position of attention.

"What have we here? A new young gentleman for *Argus*, perchance?" The voice was kindly, almost amused.

I turned, swinging my heavy seachest around and squarely into the midsection of a perfectly turned out lieutenant in the Navy. I recognized the single epaulette (I recall Edward had called it a 'swab') on his shoulder as the mark of that rank and remembered when my brother had so proudly shown off his own same uniform a few years back. Edward had let me touch the gold on his swab, which he wore on his left shoulder. But this man was wearing it on his right. As my addled brain struggled with this twist, I heard Edward's voice bragging that "As soon as I get a command of my own, this shifts to starboard." So the man, the lieutenant in front of me, whom I had just about knocked over, was captain of a ship! What had I done?

"Oooof!" He stepped back and caught his wind. "Watch where you're swinging that chest, sir. You very nearly put me on my stern end!" He studied me briefly, then glanced at my seachest, still carried by its ends across my own midsection. He scowled, thinking. Then the scowl evaporated as he took in my new uniform, spotless save for a few tenacious bits of blue-green powder on one leg of the snowy breeches and the opposite stocking, and returned to look at my blushing face.

"It's Oliver C. Baldwin of Philadelphia, I collect. We've not met, but I am well acquainted with both your father and brother. I am Stephen Decatur." He smiled and stuck out a hand.

I, of course, still held my seachest and stood rooted to the spot unable to shake his hand, doff my hat in a practiced and proper salute, or, in fact, so much as speak. My brain, in its weakened state, quite refused to function. Finally, and with some effort, I managed to gather my wits and again set my burden down.

"Oh, yes, sir. I am glad to make your acquaintance, sir." I shook his hand and then reached for my hat. Instead of doffing it as I had practiced a hundred times in front of my long-suffering but patient parents, I simply knocked it to the ground, where it bounced once and slid neatly down the slime-covered steps toward the water below.

A sailor who had watched the preceding from one of the boats, calmly reached out and scooped up my new hat a scant inch before it would have hit the waters of Boston Harbor and, with a smirk, held it out to me. Retrieving it required me to go down several of the slime- and seaweed-covered steps, each slipperier than its predecessor; even with the caution I exercised, I very nearly wound up in the same water my hat had only just escaped. Only by dropping onto one knee was I saved from the ignominy of falling into the water before I had even so much as *seen* my ship. Of course, my knee breeches and stocking paid the price.

"Thank you, sir." I uttered as I took the proffered hat and placed it firmly back on my head. So far, this day had not gone well at all; I collect it could have been somewhat worse, though how, exactly, quite eluded me. I carefully made my way back up the slippery stones; I could feel my face flushing to an even deeper crimson than it already was as I heard the suppressed laughter of the sailors behind me.

Captain Decatur was still smiling, whether at my antics and obvious embarrassment or just because it was his nature, I knew not. "You needn't call the men 'sir,' Oliver; it's *you they* call 'sir.' Since you're quite obviously heading out to the brig, I should be happy to offer you a lift. Save you the expense of dealing with those thieves in the wherries. They would likely try to take advantage of a young man like yourself and overcharge you for your passage." He looked to his sailor in the jolly boat. "Lockhart, where is your crew? Get them rounded up, if you please, and let us depart as quickly as we may. There is much to be done aboard."

The sailor, Tom Lockhart, touched his forehead with a knuckle and, stepping through each of the other boats with nary a false step, scampered up the same stones I had found so troubling. He headed for a knot of seamen I could see some distance, (perhaps a musket shot?) down the quay.

With his crew at their positions, Captain Decatur sharing the back part of the boat (I quickly discovered it was called the *sternsheets*) with me, and my chest tucked away in the front, we set out for the anchorage. So intently was I watching the men as they pulled their oars in perfect rhythm, fascinated by the ease with which they maintained the cadence of their stroke, that I became aware that the captain was speaking to me only after he had raised his voice some and repeated my name.

"Oh! Sir. Yes, sir. I am sorry, Captain. I didn't realize it was me you were speaking to."

"All I said, Mister Baldwin, was 'I trust you saw your parents well when you left Philadelphia?' I have not seen your father in quite some time, though I did have a pleasant visit with your brother on board of *Philadelphia* some two weeks before they sailed—'bout a month ago I recollect it was. You'll be pleased to learn he was well and quite looking forward to getting into this scrap with the Pasha."

"Yes, sir. My father was in fine health when I left, as was Mother. She was more than sorry to see me off to sea, I think, but otherwise in quite fine fettle. Father has been commissioned to build the Cabin furnishings for a Navy vessel currently laid down in Philadelphia. I think he is quite pleased to again be manufacturing furniture for ships."

"I have seen his work and am indeed sorry that the Department of the Navy decided to build *Argus* here in Boston rather than in Philadelphia; it would have pleased me no end to have had Edward Baldwin's handiwork in my Cabin and the wardroom."

I smiled at the compliment, though it was to my father and one I had heard many times before. Since Captain Decatur seemed to have returned to his private thoughts, I said no more and began to look at our surroundings as we made our way through the calm waters of Boston Harbor.

There was scant breeze and, while there were a great number of ships which seemed to be heading in every direction possible, none was having much luck in making forward motion. They seemed to float, motionless, above their own reflections. I noticed that even the men who peopled these ships seemed motionless. The sails hung limp without the hint of a breeze to even ripple the canvas. The heat of the day had built, and just sitting still in the boat caused me to perspire copiously. I noticed that the captain seemed untroubled by the intemperate weather; his brow remained dry and there were no tell-tale trickles making their way down his cheeks.

I also noticed that, with the passage of time, the effects of the malady from which I had been suffering seemed to abate. My head no longer pounded, the pain receded to a dull ache above my neck, and my stomach seemed to have settled itself to some degree. Food certainly held no interest for me, but I thought that should I be in a position to eat something, I would, at the least, be able to keep it down. Perhaps I had been too hasty in determining the ultimate course the disease might follow.

As we passed among ships both anchored and not, I could distinguish the cries of what I assumed to be officers issuing orders, using words that were quite foreign to me.

"Man t'gallant halyards and sheets. Step lively, you lubbers! Clap onto the sheets and weather t'gallant braces."

"Lay out, men. Loose t'gallants! Let fall. Hoist away, lads! Haul taut."

Other shouts meant just as little to me. Some I had heard my brother Edward utter, but I could see that I would have to learn an entirely new language to survive this employment. Hopefully, I watched to see what action the orders brought and was rewarded to observe a sail, two above the large lower sail which was already set, tumble and drop from its folded position along the pole to which it was tied, while ropes attached to the corners of the canvas pulled it down. Men were stationed along the pole high above the deck, their feet on a length of rope running along under the pole. Then the pole itself began to climb up the mast to the chanting of a large group of men on the ship's deck as they hauled, sweating, on another rope. All this effort seemed to accomplish little as the sail, now fully deployed, just hung slack from its pole, not stirring a whit, to the apparent chagrin of somebody on the deck who immediately began issuing more orders in an increasingly agitated voice. Then we were by the ship, and I felt it imprudent to twist myself around in the confines of the sternsheets to continue my observations. I contented myself with watching the seagulls dive after fish, each crying out in delight when successful. With one part of my mind, I was thinking about the vast amount of information I would have to learn. Would that I had listened more attentively to Edward!

"Well, Mister Baldwin. There she is. That's your home, for a while anyway, perhaps two or three years. What say you?" Decatur looked away from his vessel and smiled at me.

Ahead of us I could see there were five ships anchored. A pair of them were quite substantial while the other three were progressively smaller. I was uncertain as to which of the vessels the captain was referring but unwilling to display any greater ignorance than already I had. After all, I was sure that the captain would think that since I have a brother in the Navy surely he must have taught me something—at least the difference between a brig and whatever else the other ships were!

"Oh, sir!" said I. "She's quite lovely. And how tall are her . . . masts. Surely you must be very proud to be captain of such a splendid ship." My eyes darted wildly around the anchorage trying to pick out the one he captained. I quickly settled on the largest and, even to my untrained eye, most beautiful of the five. I hoped my enthusiasm would cover my complete and utter ignorance.

"Oliver, you're looking at the wrong ship. The one you're looking at is *Constitution*, a frigate. A splendid ship and true, she is, and a fair piece larger than my little *Argus*. There, Oliver, more to your right hand. The one with but two masts . . . there, just to the left of the two little ones. Look this way! You see?" Decatur pointed at his ship, hiding well the dismay he surely must be feeling that one of his officers (indeed, only a midshipman, but an officer nonetheless) is incapable even of recognizing a brig!

"Oh, yes, sir. I see now. Sorry, sir." I could feel the color rise in my cheeks again and resolved to keep silent until I could speak with some assurance that I would not blunder.

I studied the *Argus* brig intently, taking in everything I could see. My first reaction was how small she appeared! And I was to sail all the way across the Atlantic Ocean and into the Mediterranean Sea in that? The thought flashed through my mind that perhaps I had been better off in the rooming house: sick, destitute and lost, but at least on dry land! I had heard stories in Philadelphia—stories of harrowing adventures in storms and with enemy ships in the late unpleasantness with France. And I knew my brother would not make these up. Nor would the men whom I had overheard telling my father of monster waves and enormous winds, and iron balls shot right through one side of a ship and out the other! What was I doing here? Suddenly it seemed to get even warmer. I could feel sweat trickling down my neck and back. The symptoms of my malady had reasserted themselves; my stomach lurched and heaved, and my head was back in that vice again.

Gradually, we drew closer. As the boat came around the back of the ship, *Argus* suddenly looked huge. I craned my neck and peered up at the glazed windows in the back wall that looked out over the harbor. From having been once with Father at the Philadelphia Navy Yard while he was building furniture in a ship under construction there, I knew that this apartment belonged to the captain. It boasted protruding windows on each side as well. I remembered my father calling them *quarter galleries* and that inside them would be seats similar to the ones he had fashioned on a vessel in Philadelphia. The boat turned to go along the side and, from where I sat, it looked a long distance indeed to the forward end where the bowsprit protruded at a rakish angle quite a ways into the summer sky. Perhaps my new home was more substantial than I had first thought. *Yes*, I decided, *this will do nicely.*

Then, at a command uttered by Tom Lockhart, who was steering (I heard the captain call him *cox'n*), the men rowing suddenly stopped and, as one, stood their oars on end as the boat drifted into place under an opening in the rail above us. It was timed perfectly, and we stopped below, and in perfect line with, a series of boards that had been afixed one above the other to the gleaming black side of the ship. Two ropes, thick as a man's wrist, hung down the side. Extending along the side in both directions and just below the edge of the deck were open square doors where I could see the snouts of guns peeking out from within.

Somebody on the ship threw a smaller rope down into our boat, and it was caught by a sailor and tied to the front. Then Decatur stood and, grasping the thick ropes, one in each hand, stepped onto the horizontal board just above the boat's side. He marched right up the ship's side as easily as though he were walking up a staircase. I heard a flurry of activity above me though I was unable to see what was happening. While I was taking this all in, I realized that the cox'n was looking at me expectantly. Finally he spoke, only a little exasperation showing in his voice.

"You'll be wantin' to step carefully, sir. I'd reckon this'll be yer first time up a ship's side. Clap onto them manropes there, and just walk right up them battens and right onto the deck. Easy as kiss my hand, sir. We'll send your chest up right quick." He didn't smile at me, but neither did he glare at me. I stood and tentatively grabbed onto what I assumed to be the nearest manrope. Fortunately, I was right and, grabbing the other, put a foot on the lowest batten. My hands were slippery with sweat. The day had only gotten hotter, and I was sure Decatur's hands had been just as—well, perhaps not. I put my weight on the batten and brought the other foot up, so as to stand on it, then repeated the process.

As my head cleared the edge of the ship, I saw several pairs of legs, some covered in stockings and breeches and some in canvas trousers. I paused, realizing that were I to slip now and fall, I would become instantly a laughing stock. Reflexively, I tightened my already nervous grip on the ropes. But I hardly had time to think about this before a hand reached out and, grabbing my right arm, practically lifted me to the deck.

"You can let go the manrope now, sir. You're here." I looked up and met the source of the quiet, kindly voice: an older chap with a ring in his left ear and warm, smiling eyes. A long pigtail hung down his back, and the mahogany-colored skin of his face was lined and weathered. A short blue jacket over a dirty white shirt pulled taut over an ample belly, and canvas trousers completed the image. "Anderson's the name, sir. Bosun. And welcome aboard USS *Argus.*"

Remembering my manners, carefully drilled into me by Mother, I smiled and stuck out my hand. Bosun Anderson took a step back and knuckled his forehead. With a red face, I returned his salute by, this time, properly doffing my hat. I mumbled something that resembled "Sorry, sir" before I remembered that Captain Decatur had only an hour ago remonstrated me for calling someone 'sir.'

"Mister Baldwin, should you have a moment when you have completed your conversation with Bosun Anderson, perhaps you'd be good enough to step over here." Decatur's voice, while quiet, carried a quality that inspired me to nearly fall over myself to respond.

"Sir?" I said, stepping to where the captain and several officers stood. I noticed one of the men was dressed like me, in a blue cloth coat with a stand-up collar decorated with a small diamond-shaped bit of gold lace. His breeches and stockings were white (mine had become quite soiled as a result of my morning's activities and the spilled blue-green powder), as was his vest. The other two lieutenants (I saw from their single left shoulder swabs) eyed me in open appraisal.

"Gentlemen, meet Oliver C. Baldwin who, as it happens, is also from Philadelphia. Mister Baldwin has only recently received his Warrant, and we—and the *Argus* brig—are to be his teachers and schoolroom. I suggest we will all manage quite nicely in our respective roles. His brother, whom I have known from my own youth, is third lieutenant in *Philadelphia* with Bill Bainbridge. I am sure that *our* Mister Baldwin will take to his new employment as quickly as did his brother." Decatur then turned slightly and made a sweeping gesture to include the three with him, then introduced them by name. I was still struggling with the position Captain Decatur had placed me in by his reference to Edward when he began to introduce me to his officers.

"This is Mister Judd Devon. He is the senior midshipman aboard and will show you to the midshipmen's berth below. You will meet your fellow occupants of the berth in due course, I suspect. These gentlemen are Lieutenants Cutler and Morris. Lieutenant Cutler is first lieutenant and is in charge of almost everything aboard—including the midshipmen. Another lieutenant, our surgeon, and our Marine officer have not yet reported, but I have no doubt you will meet them in due course." Decatur smiled at what I took to be a private joke. He turned to Devon. "Take Mister Baldwin below, if you please, and see that he gets his bearings."

Devon and I saluted, doffing our hats (I thought mine was smarter), and he led me toward the back of the ship.

My guide was taller than me by nearly a foot and, I suspect, more than a few years my senior. He had a look of experience about him, confidence at what he was about, perhaps, and seemed to be comfortable with the nautical trappings that surrounded us. Suddenly I felt all the hopeful bravado and outward confidence that had been my mainstay since beginning this adventure falter; I was again the smallest and youngest. And with so much knowledge to gain! In the academy I had attended at home for some five years, I was generally the weakest and smallest of the boys and as such, frequently bore the brunt of the physical pranks played by the older boys. I had hoped not to be cast in the same role in the Navy, or at least, that my fellow midshipmen would be more of my size and age.

"Your chest will be down directly, I should imagine. Your first time in a Navy ship?" Devon talked to me over his shoulder as he hustled to do the captain's bidding.

I hurried along behind him trying to avoid the boxes, crates, barrels, kegs and huge coils of rope that lay scattered about the deck. The disarray was certainly not what I had expected to see. At the same time, I was doing my best to take in everything I saw and guess its purpose.

My eye picked up movement above me. I looked up to see some men and, it appeared, boys, perhaps younger than I, scampering about in the tangle of ropes, masts, and the other trappings high above the deck. They seemed quite at home up there, carelessly leaping from one place to another with complete disregard for where they would put their feet, or hands, for that matter. They danced with grace and agility through the web of ropes that could only have been woven by a huge and careless spider. I had stopped to study this amazing feat of derring-do when I realized that my guide had also stopped and was calling my name rather insistently.

"Mister Baldwin . . . OLIVER! Come along now. I just asked you was this your first time on a Navy ship?"

I tore my eyes from the spectacle above and hurried after him once again while I considered my answer. "Of course not!" I responded, recalling my visit to the Philadelphia Navy Yard and the ship Father had been furnishing at the time; it must have been two or three years ago.

"Well, that's a relief. When I was with Commodore Morris in the *Chesapeake* frigate last year in the Mediterranean, we had a midshipman, about your age he was, I reckon, who had never been on a ship 'til he arrived aboard. What a fool he was, by God! Had to explain everything, orders, duties, even where the head was, and still he missed half of it."

"You've already been in the Mediterranean? How long have you been in the Navy?" I inquired. I had just assumed that all the midshipmen would be beginners like myself.

"Aye. Sailed with Morris something over a year ago. We just got back beginning of July." Judd stopped, waiting for me to catch up, and lowered his voice conspiratorially. "He wasn't much interested in fightin' the pirates belongin' to the pasha—Commodore Morris, I mean; seemed like he spent more time in Malta and Gibraltar havin' fancy dinners than ever he did dealin' with those rascals in Tripoli! Heard the Navy was fixin' to court martial him."

I was quite agog at my colleague's vast experience and knowledge. He had already stepped off again to wherever it was he was leading me, so I hurried to catch up to him, nearly losing my footing over a coil of rope that I had failed to notice until I had already stumbled.

"Here you are, Oliver. Right down this ladder and then another beyond it. I will be right in your wake."

In front of me was what amounted to a square hole in the deck with its cover standing open. Below it was the ladder Judd had mentioned. It was quite dark down there, even in the middle of the day. I stepped over the edge of the hole onto the ladder, which was quite steep, and went down, albeit carefully. When I felt the deck beneath my feet, I stopped, and Judd quite ran into me.

"Damme, Baldwin! Don't stop at the bottom of a ladder when it's dark like this. Step away if you must stop. Here, hold this." The senior midshipman thrust a small tin into my hand and picked up a burning candle that had been resting on a small shelf behind the ladder. I had missed seeing it, coming as I had, from the brightness of the day above. Suddenly a small flame arose from the tin I held and, in its light, I could see a smaller candle in its center.

"That's what we call a purser's glim, Baldwin. You'll need that to see where you're going on the next deck down." Having spoken, Judd stepped to our right and disappeared from sight. I barely had time to register that he had mentioned yet another deck down; surely they didn't make people live in the very bowels of the ship!

I could make out the glow of his candle and the flickering shadows as he descended the second ladder into even more profound darkness. I hurried after him, trying to show more confidence than I felt. Then we were there.

I stepped through a doorway without its door, noticing that my guide had found it necessary to duck his head and, in the light of by Judd's candle, my glim and a single lantern hanging from the low ceiling, cast my eyes on my home for the next two or three years, if Captain Decatur was correct. I was shocked. I certainly didn't expect an apartment like the captain's, but this! That anyone would be expected to survive, let alone sleep, rest, eat and work in such privation . . . well, words failed me. I stood and stared. Devon seemed not to notice my dismay.

"This is the cockpit—the mids' quarters. That'll be your cot in there." And he stepped around a small and necessarily low table to hold his candle into a compartment, more a cupboard, to my reeling mind, barely larger than a coffin. It contained a cot attached at either end to the walls and a minuscule writing desk mounted opposite. "And we eat here at the table. You'll put your chest out here to sit on. Keep your belongings in it as there won't be any spare room when the last of you shows up." He smiled at my shock. "I know it's right small, but you'll get used to it; we all do."

"How . . . how many midshipmen share this . . . apartment?" I inquired still staggered from the almost physical blow of surprise.

"Oh, just four of us. Not bad considering some ships have as many as eight mids. There were seven of us in *Chesapeake*. And in not much more space." He grinned, relishing my obvious discomfort, and added, "And we might get a marine officer if the gunroom gets full. There's two or three more lieutenants and at least one marine officer to show yet. That's besides the other two midshipmen. 'Course, *Argus* isn't even in commission yet, so there's no telling when they'll report aboard. Captain Decatur was telling me . . ." He was verbally strutting and, as I lost interest, his words became a quiet buzz, then faded from my consciousness.

This was to be my home, along with three and possibly four others! I felt as if I had been punched in the stomach. I gripped the doorjamb to steady myself as my head reeled with the knowledge, certain that I would never survive three weeks in this . . . this box, let alone three *years*! As I looked around the minuscule compartment, I imagined other boys sitting on their chests at the table, jammed in like herring in a barrel. As I watched the vision, more boys appeared and crowded themselves into what little space there had been around the table. Then still more hung out of the openings of the sleeping cupboards and shouted to each other that, as he was the youngest, Oliver would have to surrender his place at table. Someone, a boy with a scarred face, added with obvious relish that Oliver would also have to share his cot with . . . I shook my head to clear the image. Maybe sawdust, sneezing, and running eyes weren't so bad after all! And Midshipman Judd Devon was now, I realized, talking about the rules.

" . . . share of the mess rations. We all pay on joining the mess and every month after." His words jerked me back to the tiny room. *Pay? Pay who for what?*

"Uh . . . excuse me, sir," I stammered. "I didn't get all of that. Pay what? And how much was it you said?" I thought of my complete lack of finances. I had assumed the Navy provided food for everyone, even the midshipmen. If I had to pay to eat here, what would become of me? I would have to beg for my food!

He answered my questions, and I realized that it didn't signify whether the charges for eating were twenty cents or twenty dollars; I had nothing. And I would not begin drawing pay until the ship was commissioned and then at the rate of nineteen dollars per month. Of course, when we went to sea we stood a possibility of catching enemy ships and then everyone in the ship shared in the spoils—prize money. I had less than a dim understanding of how this worked, and that only from Edward's passing comments, but thought it a grand idea. But that was for the future; I was expected to pay my share of the food we consumed, now, in advance. I suddenly noticed how stifling the midshipmen's quarters had become.

We passed a sailor with my chest as we made our way back to the open space on the deck above and then emerged into the sunlight, blinking like rats out of the hole.

"Er . . . Mister Devon, sir. I have a problem, I think. I have no money. Not a penny. You see, sir . . ."

He cut me off mid-explanation. "First off, you don't have to call me Mister Devon; Judd'll do just fine 'less there's sailors at hand. Then it has to be more formal. And I really don't care what your problems are; you got to sort them out for your own self. Now I got work to see to. Why don't you find the first lieutenant and tell him your woes, and mayhaps he'll find you a job to do." He strode away forward without a backward glance.

CHAPTER THREE

My dire financial straits ended quickly enough as soon as I explained to Lieutenant Cutler the circumstances that had conspired to cause my difficulties. At the mention of Edward Langford's name, his eyes narrowed slightly and I saw him bow his head in a barely perceptible nod.

"Do you know of the gentleman, sir?" I queried.

"Aye. That scoundrel has been hangin' about the waterfront here for a while now. Since *Argus* was laid down, I collect. He's famous, or perhaps I should say in*famous*, around the harbor. Preys on anyone he thinks might have a dollar he can get his miserable paws on. I would reckon you'll cross tacks with him again before the ship is done fittin' out and sails. I'll let some of the lads know to keep a weather eye out for your Mister Langford. Might be he could answer a question or two with a bit of helpful persuasion."

"That he took advantage of my illness and weakened state was quite unfair, I think. Had I not been feeling so poorly . . ."

"Oliver, you were drunk. And yes, I agree that he took advantage of you bein' drunk, and gettin' you drunk to start with. But that's how he works. And the 'illness' you had when you woke up was nothing more nor less than the result of your overindulgence. You are making way, slowly, on the course to manhood! You must try to give nothing to leeward and drive on." Cutler smiled at me.

I was stunned! Drunk! I was not sick at all, but suffering the effects of my own actions! Exactly what Father had warned me of. A small part of me had stood a little taller when the lieutenant mentioned "making way on the course to manhood," though I had no idea at all what he had meant by "give nothing to leeward," and yet, at the same time, I wondered briefly why, if feeling the way I had was the result, men took spirits at all. I was quite sure I would think twice the next time! And I began immediately plotting my revenge on that rascal Edward Langford, should our "tacks cross" as Lieutenant Cutler had predicted, though again, I was not completely sure of his meaning.

Before the day's end, when the bosun piped the hands to 'spirits up' and then supper, I had met with a Mister Nathan Baker, the ship's purser. And right as ever was whoever named him to be in charge of the finances and provisions, from food to clothes to money and even gunpowder, of *Argus*. A flinty old curmudgeon, he was, who wore spectacles on the end of his long, pointy nose and focused a hard-eyed stare over them at whoever had the misfortune to be standing across his table. Why, his very look brought to mind the tight-fisted denizens of the few counting houses into which I had ventured in the company of my father. Unfinished gray hair touched his collar and fell over his furrowed brow nearly to his eyebrows.

"And that is what happened, sir. Lieutenant Cutler told me to see you to advance me against my pay," I concluded as I again went through the tale of my mis-adventure. I did not mention that I had lost my watch into the bargain and was decidedly vague about how it had all come to pass. I had no idea how much money I should seek, were he to ask, which he did at once.

"Uh . . . well . . . I am not sure, sir." I fumbled. I should get enough so I did not have to repeat this interview, but I knew also that I would have to pay it back out of the pay I received from the Navy, presumably in the person of Purser Baker, and was hesitant about asking for what might be thought of as too much.

"Well, Mister Baldwin. How much was it you lost?" He seemed to put extra effort into the last word.

"Sir, it was twenty-five dollars I had when I left Philadelphia. I might have used two or perhaps two and a half. I do not recall how much was in my purse at the alehouse nor how much my room . . ."

He dismissed my further ruminations with an impatient wave of his hand. "I have little interest in how much your father gave you nor in how much you squandered away in your foolish pursuits. As a midshipman, you are to be compensated at the rate of nineteen dollars per month, Mister Baldwin. In the interest of leaving you with something when you do finally draw some pay, I will advance you five dollars." He reached into a canvas bag which he had drawn from a cupboard beside his table and produced five dollar coins which he stacked carefully on the table.

"Sign this." He shoved a piece of paper which was covered for half of its length with legal-sounding words penned in a flowing hand. At the bottom was drawn a line upon which I was instructed to afix my name. I took the proffered pen from his ink-stained, gnarled hand and, after dipping the quill carefully in the ink pot, wrote my name in my best penmanship.

He sprinkled the paper with sand, blew off the excess, and pushed the small stack of coins toward me. "I would suggest you be some frugal with that. No tellin' when you're likely to get what's left of your allowance. Ship won't likely be in commission for another two or, mayhaps, three weeks."

I thanked him profusely for his generosity and advice and escaped the confines of the purser's office to retrace my steps to the upper deck, which I had only recently learned was called the *spar* deck.

"Are you planning to scamper about the ship for the remainder of the day in that sorry excuse for a uniform, Mister Baldwin?" The first lieutenant greeted my return to daylight.

"Uh . . . no, sir. I will change it for my other now, sir." I turned to head *aft* to the same hatch I had used with Judd Devon, figuring that the familiar route would be the one least likely to get me lost in the bowels of the ship. In my haste, I tripped over a rope stretched ankle high between a ring in the deck and a piece of equipment, I know not what it might have been, and fell full length at Cutler's feet.

"Mind where you step, Baldwin." Cutler turned away. Even in my fully developed embarrassment, I noticed the smile playing at his mouth. It served only to add further to my discomfort.

The days passed and became weeks, and gradually I became more comfortable with my surroundings. I was learning the proper names of parts of the ship and could use them correctly. I enjoyed trying them out, seeing how they fit my mouth, and found that most, with a little practice, rolled off my tongue with an ease that might, one day, be mistaken for comfort. Within the first week, I had even learned my way about the ship. With the exception of the *magazine* where the gunner stores the powder for the cannon, I had seen the insides of the entire vessel from the *fo'c'sle,* where the more experienced hands worked, to the Cabin, where Captain Decatur lived and did his work when he was not on deck overseeing this or that in the preparations for completing the fitting out of his ship. I had even penetrated all the way down to the *orlop* deck, the very bottom of the ship, where cables and ropes and all manner of things were stored (even the cockpit seemed less confining).

Then Bosun Anderson took me aloft. Apparently, when I first came aboard, he had decided to make my education his project. Whenever he had the time or when he was supervising his bosun's mates in a task, he would seek me out to watch and carefully explain whatever I didn't understand, which, early on, was nearly everything!

He taught me the names of all the rigging and much of the equipment on deck. I learned to distinguish a sheet from a halyard, a clewline from a buntline and how to tie several knots. Now it was time to see the rest of *Argus.* My teacher had scolded me, with respect of course, when I balked at climbing into the rigging.

"Mister Baldwin, you cain't learn what's aloft from the deck—or out of one o' them books, neither. Now get yourself into them ratlines afore I hoist you up there by the seat o' yer brand spankin' new trousers!" His eyes twinkled as he threatened me, and I knew he would not make good his threat. But nonetheless, I feigned fear of his wrath, which acted nicely to cover my fear of stepping onto the bulwark and then into the rigging, and did as he asked. Once I had climbed, with his constant encouragement, about halfway to the maintop, the first place one could actually stop climbing and sit or stand on a platform, he followed me and directed my movements. When we got to the maintop, I found there to be a landing, of sorts, with a low railing around it and hole in its center where the top of the lower mast and the bottom of the topmast were joined.

"This is the fightin' top, and where they'll station Marines with muskets when we actually do battle." Anderson leaned casually against the mast and watched me, closely I thought, for some reaction to being this high above the deck. I was surprised and impressed at his most indifferent demeanor; he was not even lightly holding on to anything! For myself, I kept my strong grip on a conveniently located shroud and, with some trepidation while still maintaining a strangle hold on the tarred rope of the shroud, I carefully stood erect and looked around me.

I gazed at the maze of ropes and spars and, putting to us the knowledge I had acquired about halyards and lifts, sheets and braces, began to see order instead of the cobweb of ropes that I had observed when first I came aboard *Argus*. Screwing up my courage, I carefully shifted myself so I could look down at the deck. What a sight! I could see most of the ship's spar deck and the men moving about it doing their work. I was thrilled, my earlier fear completely forgotten, and I slackened my grip. I, Oliver C. Baldwin of Philadelphia, was *aloft*! I reveled in my accomplishment. Then down on the deck, I spied a familiar face.

"Judd! Judd Devon! Look up here. See where I am!" I called out to my friend and fellow midshipman, and I released my grip to wave frantically to him.

"Hush now, sir. You don't wanna be callin' out like that." Anderson quickly admonished me. I was further convinced of the veracity of his instruction by the look of fury on Devon's face when he looked up in response to my shout. Later, when we came back to the deck, I was further chastised by the senior midshipman. The bosun, however, did not mention my misstep again; there was enough other instruction and wisdom he wanted to share and the more important of those, he did repeat.

If he told me once, he must have told me a dozen and more times, "Mister Baldwin, the men appreciate an officer who can show any foremast Jack his duty. Lets 'em know that the officer understands what it takes to get a job of work done. That's what you want to be—that kind of an officer. That's what Cap'n Decatur is, and that's what you will be if'n you learn good what I'm teachin' you."

It sounded like good advice. From what I'd seen of the captain, he was most certainly the kind of officer I wanted to be.

And so, I learned. I studied my books at night in the confines of my sleeping 'cupboard' and by day, I watched and studied what Devon and Bosun Anderson did. I became quite agile aloft and had, one quiet afternoon, actually *touched* the very top of the main t'gallant mast and stood on the footropes of the t'gallant yard. There was no place higher on *Argus*! The swaying of my perch bothered me a little at first, then I became accustomed to the movement and found I could move from the mast all the way to the yardarm at the end of the yard with ease. I discovered that the footrope for the last six or so feet on the yard was called a *Flemish horse*, which I found most hilarious. To my surprise and joy, it seemed to me I had taken to my new employment and surroundings quite as naturally as a duck to the water. I was becoming a sailor!

It seemed a very short while, though, in fact, it had been nearly a month longer than I expected, before the *Argus* was finished and ready for sea. Sails had been afixed—*bent*—to the yards and stores loaded. Shot and powder were brought aboard under the watchful eye of Purser Baker and our gunner, a giant of a man who walked with a stiff leg and whose roar, when provoked, could be heard at the masthead. The excitement aboard was palpable and I think everyone from the lowest idler to Captain Decatur was as eager as ever could be to get to sea and take our part in the fight with the pirates of the Barbary coast.

Argus was ready, I knew; but was I? I worried that even with all that I had learned, it would not be enough. In my cot in the dark hours, I imagined events in which I would be completely out of my depth. But now time had run out; whatever I had yet to learn about the ship and the Navy would have to be accomplished at sea. And that was where we would head. But first, there had to be a commissioning and then a party.

Flags were stretched throughout the rigging from the tops of the masts and down each of the yards, and salutes were fired and answered across the harbor as *Argus* became a commissioned vessel in the United States Navy, earning her the letters 'USS' before her name. The guns sounded like thunderclaps as their echoes rolled across the harbor. I can't believe there was any aboard more excited by the goings-on than I. We fired our own guns, responding gun for gun to each salute fired by the Navy vessels present.

Captain Decatur had all our sailors dressed in their most perfect uniforms and sent many of them into the rigging to stand on the ratlines and, higher up, on the yards. It was a fine sight they made, and the midshipmen, all but one of us, were likewise stationed in various parts of the rigging, which gave us a splendid view of the proceedings. The spectacularly loud and rousing celebration laid a pall of thick white smoke tinged with lavender across the roads of Boston Harbor. Through it, from my perch on the foreyard, I could make out on the shoreline colorful flags floating lethargically in the easy breeze and many small boats rowing or sailing around the fleet while their occupants offered *huzzahs* and good wishes to our handsome vessel. It was a heady time for all aboard, even the more seasoned; I think even Judd Devon, standing in the mainmast fighting top, was, for all his vast experience, quite nearly as thrilled as I.

And that night, Captain Decatur gave a party for all the officers in the harbor as well as a host of important men from Boston, even the midshipmen had been invited. The captain was resplendent in his finest full dress uniform of a blue coat lined in blue with a standing collar and long tails above knee breeches and stockings of the purest white. Gold lace and delicate embroidery adorned the coat and, of course, a gleaming gold epaulette graced his right shoulder while a brilliantly decorated sword hung in its hanger on his left side. He greeted each guest by name as they stepped aboard. One of us midshipmen, also in our finest (or cleanest) full dress uniform, complete with the small dirk allowed us by virtue of our rank, escorted each of the ladies aft to the quarterdeck while the gentlemen trailed in our wake. The bosun had sailors lined up on both sides of the entrance to salute the dignitaries to the whistling of a bosun's mate's pipe as boats came and departed, first bringing the guests, then later, taking them home. The Marines, also in their finest uniforms, with their shining bayonets mounted at the ends of their muskets, were stationed in ranks throughout the ship. As each guest arrived on the board, the Marines stood to a rigid attention with a great stamping of booted feet.

A canvas, also festooned with flags of every color, had been rigged over the quarterdeck and a festive air, brimming with anticipation and excitement filled the guests and the ship's company. The evening rang with toasts and laughter and the pleasing lilt of ladies voices as all joined in singing patriotic songs. A band played, and many of the officers, both ours and those from other ships in harbor, invited the ladies to dance. The midshipmen, of course, only watched and listened as Judd Devon pointed out the more important men and the prettier of the ladies. Judd had actually purloined a bottle of wine that, when offered to me, I declined; the memory of past experiences was still quite fresh. The party lasted well into the evening, and it was not until the men had been called for the middle watch that the last staggering straggler was placed in a chair and lowered into a boat to be taken on shore.

The following morning I sprang out of my cot and hastily dressed in duck trousers and cotton shirt, eager to play my part in getting the USS *Argus* underweigh at last. Imagine my dismay when I stepped out of the hatch onto the spar deck to find the entire vessel cloaked in a shroud of white; I could not even make out the bowsprit and trying to catch a glimpse of the t'gallant masts or even the topmasts was quite fruitless. I knew there were ships anchored near us—I had been watching them come and go for more than three weeks—but the fog had quite swallowed them up as well. Lieutenant Morris appeared from the mists as a wraith heading aft and, with one look at my face, became sympathetic to my disappointment.

"Rarely does the fog last in these waters for more than a day or two, Oliver. We'll be underweigh soon enough. We'll be needin' a fair breeze as well and would be waitin' on that in any case. You watch and see if I'm not right." The third lieutenant smiled his consolation and continued aft to the quarterdeck where I could just make out his form as it disappeared into a scuttle there.

I cast another look about the ship, all that I could see of her, taking in the dripping rigging as it faded into nothingness aloft and the spar deck guns, black and glistening in their wetness. I noticed that each successive one became more indistinct as my eye traveled forward. With disappointment shrouding my very soul even more than the fog shrouded the brig, I returned below to take some breakfast with my fellow occupants of the cockpit.

The three of them were seated on their chests around the table: Judd at the head, as befitted his position as the senior among us, and flanked by Tom Wheatley on his left, or larboard, side and the round-faced, and bodied, James Stevens, the youngest of us at just thirteen, to his right or starboard hand. My place at the foot of the table had been left open, and Riley, our steward, stood, or rather stooped, as he was nearly six feet in height, half in and half out of my 'cupboard.' They all looked up upon my entrance. Wheatley, whom I had quickly grown to dislike, spoke first.

"Well, Baldwin, it don't feel like you've done a respectable job gettin' us underweigh. I'd warrant we're still swingin' to the hook, just like we been doin' for the two weeks since I come aboard and before. Decatur squeamish 'bout goin' to war?" His tone and words rankled, and, remembering Mother's counsel, I took a deep breath before answering.

"There's thick fog over us and not a breath of wind, Tom. And I'd bet my last dollar that *Captain* Decatur is more eager and ready than any aboard to get his ship to sea and into the conflict with the Bashaw."

"Oh, yes. I quite forgot that our captain is also a *Philadelphia man* who wouldn't be squeamish about anything." Wheatley tried unsuccessfully to imitate the accent of an educated person. He did it frequently as a last effort at insulting any who spoke clearer English than he, but it served only to heighten the disdain his target felt towards him. Judd Devon spoke up in an effort to extinguish the smoldering embers of animosity before they could burst into the full flame of hate and disrupt the camaraderie of our quarters.

"Fog, huh? Well, I would guess we'll be swinging to the hook for at least another day or two. Once it comes in to these waters, it'll generally hang about for a couple of days, though I have experienced a fortnight of unbroken fog myself right here in Boston." Judd too had little use for Wheatley and directed his comment at me. A week and more back, after Thomas Wheatley had joined our mess, Judd had mentioned privately to me that he had taken the opinion that "Our newest member comported himself with an arrogance ill-befitting his experience and talents." I noticed Devon had put on just a bit more of the aristocratic air than normal and took it as a response to Tom's jibe at me. Tom, for his part, said nothing, but it seemed as if his whole lower jaw thrust even farther forward from its normally defiant cast.

Young James took it all in and, when the comments concluded, looked at me with close-set eyes and then at Judd while he asked, around a half-chewed mouthful of burgoo, "So, did you find out when we really will leave, Oliver? I wonder if there would be time for me to get ashore once more." He smiled hopefully at Judd and, releasing the cheekful of breakfast, chewed with renewed enthusiasm while he awaited a favorable answer. The cheek, recently the repository for the contents of his mouth, remained puffed out, as did its mate opposite.

"I would think so, James. But you likely ought to ask Lieutenant Cutler 'bout that. Seems like you've been ashore quite frequently in the last week or so. You've got some business there, I collect?" Judd knew full well that the lad had no business ashore, but rather he was scared to death about going to sea, having been sent to the Navy by his widowed mother as one less mouth to feed.

To my knowledge, James Stevens had made no effort to learn anything of the ship or her workings; in fact, he seemed to close his mind to any assistance offered by any of us in that direction. On one occasion, the rotund youngster had admitted tearfully to Judd that he wanted no part of the Navy, Captain Decatur, or the *Argus* brig. In keeping with his obstinate attitude, he also quite refused to even pick up the navigation book we had been assigned to read preparatory to learning the practical aspect of the art, nor, to my knowledge, had he even opened any of the other books on seamanship or naval etiquette we all had been required to read. However, in spite of his distaste for the Navy and our ship, he seemed to have developed a great taste for the offerings of the midshipmen's mess, and, at least once, had secured for himself an invitation to the Gunroom to dine with the officers. Even Thomas Wheatley had joined our quiet wager as to whether or not the invitation would be repeated!

Now, however, Wheatley directed his bile at our youngest and weakest shipmate. "He likely wants to go cry to his mama one last time. What have you to go ashore for, you little worm? You'd better spend your time learning how to be a midshipman, 'stead o' runnin' off to your mama every chance you get. We had a youngster like yourself in the *Norfolk* brig; didn't last the year. If he wasn't seasick or whining about missing his mother, he was just underfoot. I think I can take the credit for his not being in the Navy any longer! You might take a lesson from that, Little Jimmy."

"Wheatley, leave the boy alone. What James does is none of your concern." Judd, his tone hard-edged, had a look on his face that would brook none of Wheatley's bullying, and the strength to enforce it should he need to.

Wheatley, chastised, glared at Judd for a moment and then returned his attention to his food, chewing with unnecessary fervor. For my part, I remained silent, and then the moment had passed, assisted by Riley, who noisily cleared and replaced dishes. When he spilled a dollop of burgoo into Wheatley's lap, incurring a predictable invective including the mention of a flogging, our mess returned to a more normal tone, albeit with an undercurrent of tension.

As the ship was ready for sea in all respects, there was little to do in the way of further preparation. The mids, along with much of the ship's company were allowed to spend the day in private pursuits, studying, mending clothes, or skylarking on deck. For my own self, I had found a seat on the capstan while Bosun Anderson expanded my education of knots and splices, patiently demonstrating each to me until I could repeat it flawlessly.

Shortly before 'spirits up' was piped, James Stevens rushed up with his familiar waddling gait, quite red in the face from his exertions, and announced in his squeaking voice, "Oliver! I've been looking all over the ship for you. Lieutenant Morris wants you in the Gunroom quick as ever you please. You'd better . . ."

"James, James, calm down. I am sure it isn't a crisis. Did he happen to mention what it was he wanted me for?" I slid off the capstan head, handing the piece of rope I was splicing back to the bosun.

"Why would he tell me anything, Baldwin? He's likely not even aware I'm part of the ship's company; that or he thinks I'm just a messenger. I don't count for nothin' here."

"Were you to do something to change that, such as read the books we're supposed to, learn your lessons, and try to get on with being a midshipman, he, and the other officers, might not think you 'count for nothing' and help you." I could not hear him whine without I offered him my—and others'— thoughts on his position. He merely looked at me and wandered over to the bulwark to stare into the water through the still swirling fog.

I found Lieutenant Morris sitting in the Gunroom with the first lieutenant and the captain of marines, Lieutenant Trippe. Another lieutenant, William Hobbs, who had only recently joined the ship, stood in his cabin doorway quite involved with a sheaf of papers. I remained silent and was unnoticed at the open door for a moment and took the opportunity to observe my superiors as they continued their conversation.

The Marine lieutenant, whom I had only met once before was a man of about twenty-five years, short and heavily built with quite broad shoulders and a thick neck. His voice seemed to rumble from somewhere deep within him. His face, what I could see of it, as he was partially turned away from me, was almost square with wide-set eyes and a flat nose. He wore a mustache and bushy side-whiskers and looked to me as though he were one who would brook no nonsense.

In contrast, Lieutenants Cutler and Morris were lanky men with long narrow faces. Each appeared to be about thirty. Cutler had small eyes which seemed to penetrate that at which he peered, while Morris's were friendly and often showed the beginnings of a smile. Lieutenant Morris had an aquiline nose and full, almost feminine, lips. Neither wore a mustache, but both wore long, square-trimmed sideburns and unbound hair which just touched the collars of their blue jackets.

Lieutenant Hobbs was an older man, thirty-five and more, were I to chance a guess, who wore spectacles most of the time. Even with the lenses before his eyes, he found it necessary to squint in order to see, which gave him a decidedly sinister look. His height was not much greater than my own, but his build was considerably more robust. His weathered face indicated some considerable time at sea. Indeed, I had heard from Judd Devon that Mister Hobbs had sailed against the French in the short war America had fought at the end of the past century. He had signed on as second lieutenant.

Lieutenant Morris looked up, catching me openly staring at him. I looked immediately away and felt the color rise in my face. He smiled at my embarrassment.

"Oh, yes, Baldwin. I presume young what's-his-name . . . Stevens? Yes, Stevens discovered your hiding place! I have something here that I am told belongs to you." Morris reached into his pocket as my face went pale at his remark about a "hiding place."

"Oh, sir. I was not hiding at all. I was right in plain sight at the capstan with Mister Anderson for the past turn of the glass and more. I don't have a single idea as to why Mister Stevens was unable to discover my whereabouts. But I surely was not hiding!" I thought it sounded, even to me, a trifle whiny. *Hold your tongue, Baldwin. You won't do yourself any favor acting the child.* I took my own advice and stopped my protestations.

"Indeed. I am sure you were not. Must have missed you in the fog, I reckon. In the event, might this be yours?" Morris thrust out his hand at me and laid on the table a silver watch—*my* silver watch!

"Oh, my, sir. Yes, sir. It surely is my watch. If I may inquire, sir, how did it happen to come into your possession?" I couldn't believe my eyes! The watch that had been stolen from me even before I reported on board *Argus* was right there in front of me, ticking happily on the table. I stepped closer and, fearful that it might only be a mirage, tentatively reached out my hand.

The timepiece did not disappear; indeed, it did not even move. I picked it up and, turning it over carefully, almost reverently, examined it for signs of abuse or perhaps a clue as to where it had been. Each of the several times I had been ashore on one or another of the errands necessary before departure, I had kept a "weather eye" out for that scoundrel, Edward Langford. I had even revisited the alehouse where I had met with my misadventure and walked the length of the pier where I had first encountered him. All to no avail. He was nowhere to be found, at least in my wanderings limited by the time afforded me by whichever of the missions I was on. Of course, I had made no plan of action or even thought much about what I would say beyond youthful bravado and boast. Perhaps it was just as well we never "crossed tacks" as Lieutenant Cutler had predicted. But the lieutenant *had* been right about the return of my watch.

"The gunner picked it up from a fellow ashore in a taproom. Likely your friend Langford. He was tryin' to sell it to raise a few dollars for whiskey and offered it to Gunner Tarbox. Lieutenant Cutler had mentioned some weeks ago you'd been robbed of your property and the gunner recollected what he'd heard. You owe him five dollars, I might mention. That'd be the amount he paid Langford, or whoever it was selling the watch, and it wouldn't be right for him to be out of pocket on your account." Morris, having offered his explanation of how my timepiece had found its way back to me, turned back to Captain Trippe and quite ignored my slack-jawed stare.

I was both blessed and cursed in the same stroke! Here was my watch safely back in my possession, but I was expected to repay Gunner Tarbox the money he had expended on the assumption the watch might be mine! The problem, of course, was that I had only three of the five dollars Purser Baker had advanced me, having spent two of my precious coins for, among other things, my ration allowance in the Midshipmen's Mess. I did not fancy returning to the flinty-faced Mister Baker for a further advance on my pay! I noticed when I lifted my eyes from the timepiece that Lieutenant Cutler was watching me closely; I guessed that he had suspected my dilemma.

"Was there something else, Mister Baldwin?" he queried. A smile was forming on his thin lips and even in the dim light of a pair of lanterns, I could see an uncharacteristic sparkle beginning to form in his eyes as he waited for my response.

"I . . .uh . . . well, sir. Uh . . . no, sir. I reckon not." I couldn't bring myself to admit that once again I was in the straits of financial difficulty.

"Then you are dismissed. I would suggest you find Mister Tarbox and thank him for capturing your watch by refunding the investment he made on your behalf. Likely he'll be in the magazine or not far from it." Cutler's eyes bored into me, then, seeing nothing of further interest in me, returned his attention to his colleagues.

"Aye, aye, sir. I'll do that exactly." I turned and left the Gunroom, my joy at the return of my timepiece offset by my dismay at having to come up with five dollars that I did not, and would not for a month and more, have.

The gunner, a warrant officer of indeterminate age, was a towering figure who, without any effort at all, could frighten all but the most seaworthy of sailors, not to mention young midshipmen. As I searched him out (my heart was not in it), I tried to determine what course I would follow when indeed I did "cross tacks" with him. As I stepped off the ladder just aft of the magazine, I spied Mister Tarbox just removing the carpet slippers from his feet (they were required in the magazine so as not to cause an unwelcome spark). He looked up at my approach.

"Yes, Mister Baldwin? Is there something I can do for you?" In the confines of the lower deck, his voice was overpowering.

"I . . . uh . . . yes, Gunner. That is . . ." I still had not decided on what to say. I hesitated, collected myself, and pressed on. "Actually, Mister Tarbox, I wanted to thank you for recovering my watch." *That was a good start*, I thought. "My father gave it to me before I left home and I was some dismayed over its loss. Lieutenant Morris returned it to me just now and gave me to understand that I was in your debt for having recovered it." He had no idea just how in his debt I was about to be!

"Aye. Shifty-eyed fellow it were, in some alehouse near the piers, what had it. Sailor he were, if'n I was to wager on it, and ashore not by his own hand. Offered it to me for some whiskey money, I reckon. Since the first lieutenant had told most of the hands that we might keep an eye open for it, I figgered to take it off'n him and see if'n it might be your'n. If'n it weren't, I'd gotten my own self a fair watch at only a few dollars. Probably worth more'n twelve, I'd warrant." He continued putting on his shoes without looking further at me, until I remained silent, thinking.

"Was there something else, Mister Baldwin?" Tarbox stood up as straight as the low overhead, or ceiling, would permit and fixed me with a questioning stare. His forehead was furrowed and his balding scalp was sweating quite freely in the confined, but strangely cool atmosphere of the lower deck. He wiped his great hands on his already dirty canvas trousers and, putting the just-doffed carpet slippers in their cubbyhole, waited for a response.

"Well, yes, I thought . . . that is to say . . . I . . . uh . . . I should repay you for your trouble on my behalf." *Actually, Lieutenant Morris thought I should.*

"That would be welcome, sir. I was five dollars out of pocket to secure your timepiece and I'll be glad to have it back." He actually smiled at me! Then he stepped around me and headed up the ladder without a backward glance. His stiff leg necessitated a one-step-at-a-time gait, but he accomplished the ascent with the practiced ease of one who had dealt with his handicap for some years. I followed him all the way to the spar deck where the bosun was enjoying a pipe at the rail. Tarbox slipped into place beside his fellow warrant officer and pulled out, lit, and took a great puff on a cheroot.

His back was to me, and I suppose I could have made off right then and there without further conversation. I had not been taught to run from a problem; best to confront them straight on. So I stayed, shuffling my feet while I thought of something to say.

Tarbox and Anderson turned to face me. I looked from one to the other until the gunner broke the silence.

"Was there something else, Mister Baldwin? I figgered we was done below."

"I want to pay you your money, Gunner, but I am short until I start drawing my pay. I certainly will not cheat you; I was brought up right and would never do that. But if you can wait a bit, I'll see you get the five dollars quick as I get it." My voice quavered a trifle, so I stopped and watched his lined face for an indication of how I was doing. No reaction. "I'll let you hold my watch until I pay you. As a bond for my word, if you like." This last quite slipped out. I had had no intention of offering him my watch. Who knew what might happen to it in his care?

"I think I can trust you, Mister Baldwin. Where are you gonna go anyway? We're gonna be gettin' the barky sailin' quick as the fog lifts and less'n you take to swimmin', ain't much chance of you gettin' away from me! 'Sides, you're an officer, or almost one, and, I reckon, a gentleman." As he made this wondrous proclamation, his expression never so much as changed a whit! I had survived yet another financial crisis! My joy knew no bounds!

"Thank you, Mister Tarbox. I promise I will pay you straight away on getting my money from the purser. And you needn't worry about my 'taking to swimming,' sir; I was never much for it. And thank you for understanding—and for finding my watch." I smiled as he nodded and turned back to the rail. I started aft and could hear him, as likely could any other on deck, telling Bosun Anderson of our encounter.

CHAPTER FOUR

Two days later, as predicted by Lieutenant Morris and Judd, the fog did, in fact, lift, replaced by a brilliantly clear late September sky. The breeze that blew out the fog remained, and Captain Decatur pronounced it fair for getting *Argus* to sea. In a cacophony of thumps, groans, clatter, and shouted commands, we began the process, sending men to their stations, pulling sheets and halyards from their racks, and securing loose items around the decks. With my knowledge, recently acquired through Bosun Anderson, I was quite pleased to be able to make sense of the activity surrounding me.

From my vantage point on the quarterdeck, the frenzied activities of the men carrying out the orders shouted by, first, the sailing master, and then relayed by the bosun and his mates, appeared as something less than a ballet of precision and efficiency of effort. The topmen, the most experienced of our hands, were sent aloft to cast off the brails holding the furled sails to their yards; the anchor was hove short and, on the bellow from the deck "Layout and loose!" the brails came away. That was about the last part of getting *Argus* to sea that went smoothly.

Immediately, the sailing master shouted, "Man tops'l halyards and sheets. Stand to the weather braces! Hoist away the fore and main tops'ls. Haul taut and sheet 'er home! Hoist away the jib and fore stays'l. Lively, there, step lively."

The response to these commands, heard by some of the seamen for the first time ever, was not inspiring, even to me. I thought briefly back to my ride with Captain Decatur in his jolly boat when I had first heard many of these commands from another ship and how utterly nonsensical they were to me then and sympathized with the *landsmen* (first-timers) who scurried about in utter confusion. Many could not tell a tops'l halyard from a jib sheet, having not had the benefit of Bosun Anderson's tutelage as I had. With a great amount of cursing, kicking, and shoving, the proper lines were picked up and hauled, and the fore and main tops'ls, gleaming white in their newness, tumbled out of their furls and were pulled around to catch the breeze. Forward, the jibs snapped as they shivered, ready to be sheeted home to help haul the ship's bow off to leeward. I stole a glance at our captain; his look was one of utter despair, and I noticed he shook his head more than once at the efforts of his crew.

When things had settled down once more, Captain Decatur waved his hand which brought a shouted command from the bosun. And the thirty men manning the capstan bars "put their backs into it." Stepping in time to the beat set by the Marine drummer, they marched the capstan around, their progress measured by the click of the pawls on the capstan's base and the movement of the continuous messenger line that hauled in the dripping hawser. The great hempen rope, actually three ropes braided together, disappeared into a hawse hole in the deck and wound up on the orlop deck where a half dozen idlers carefully laid it out so it could be used again quickly. As Anderson leaned over the ship's bow to watch, the anchor was hauled clear, dripping great gouts of black ooze that splashed into the sparkling waters of Boston Harbor, leaving a dark cloudy stain on the surface as the only mark of *Argus* having spent some five weeks and more in this place. As the great bower became visible, it was, this time, the bosun who waved toward the quarterdeck. Sailing Master Chase ordered the jib and stays'l backed, and I felt *Argus* stir to life.

A quietly spoken command from Decatur to the quartermasters at the wheel brought the ship's head around. The brig paid off on the larboard tack heading for the open sea. The sails filled with a *whoomp*, and gradually we gained speed.

I was thrilled! Nothing I had seen or experienced in my time in *Argus* had prepared me for feeling her come to life under my very feet! It quite literally took my breath away and, at the same time, made me want to shout out in glee. The energy and glory, the grace and dignity, and the power of *my* ship actually going to sea, to fight the pirates of North Africa, left me in awe. I was transfixed and drank in everything around me much as a thirsty man might gulp his life-saving elixir.

"Oliver, your mouth is hanging agape!" First Lieutenant Cutler spoke quietly to me from his where he stood at the weather rail. While I could not see his face—he had turned back to observe the progress of the ship—I was quite certain he was as close to a smile as he was capable of. And I closed my mouth.

I tore my eyes from the men aloft and stole a glance at Captain Decatur as he studied his vessel's performance. We were moving slowly and, I thought, majestically. But apparently not majestically enough for the captain. He was frowning as he studied the sails and our progress, his eyes shifting from the dazzling white aloft to the dazzling white of the streamers of foam pushed away from our hull.

"Mister Church, you may set the courses and the spanker, if you please. And we'll have the main tops'l and t'gallant stay'ls as well." Almost to himself he added, "Now's as good a time as any to see how she feels under a press of canvas."

"Aye, sir. Courses and spanker it is. Stay'ls as well, sir. Larboard watch, stations for making sail for'ard. Starboard watch, stations for making sail aft! Topmen aloft! Let's look lively now, lads." Church fairly bellowed his orders and then enlisted Bosun Anderson to assist him in shoving, kicking, and dragging the poor sailors to their posts. The men still seemed quite confused and, amid the milling, shuffling gangs of seamen, Anderson and Church stood out; their voices were clear above the cacophony of the chaos. I saw Judd Devon and Tom

Wheatley both assisting the warrant officers with their task. I stepped forward to take a role myself.

"You just watch, Baldwin. You don't know no more'n most of these lubbers, your own self. Maybe by the time we get into the action over yonder, you'll know the difference 'twixt a brace and a sheet." Wheatley had moved away from his own task to greet me in a voice that, had there been less noise about the deck, would have been clear to any hand on the spar deck. I noticed that his true accent, the one that had no hint of education mixed into it, had come through. Without waiting for a response and, I thought, to demonstrate his authority to me, he turned away and grabbed a sailor, shoving him toward the main weather brace and telling him to "Clap onto that sheet, sailor, and heave around when you're told."

As it happened, I knew the sailor was an experienced hand who well knew the difference between a "sheet" and a "brace." The man simply stared for a moment at the midshipman, then headed aft to assist in setting the spanker as he had previously been directed. I decided aft was a better choice for Oliver Baldwin as well and followed.

It was not long, or so it seemed to me, before *Argus* was tearing across the waters of Massachusetts Bay on a heading that would take us clear of the dangerous shoals off the tip of Cape Cod and into the broader reaches of the Atlantic. The cloud of dazzling white canvas aloft strained to contain the wind that drove us; I could not tear my eyes from the spectacle and again reviewed my knowledge of the sails, lines, and spars gained from the hours I had spent in the dizzying heights with Judd and Bosun Anderson. My joy at realizing that I could name all the sails and their associated ropes, tackles, and lifts knew no bounds! I smiled as I shifted my gaze to the sea astern and watched the white feather of our wake laid straight as an arrow on the deep blue of the Bay, the sole mark of our passage.

The cool breeze felt good as it ruffled my hair and puffed out my jacket. I stood by the main backstay on the wind'ard side, but well aft, of the quarterdeck (I had early learned that the wind'ard side of the *quarterdeck itself* was the exclusive domain of the captain and, on occasion, the watch officer) and watched the white tipped waves march towards us and lift the stern gracefully as we sailed east. The late morning sun glinted off the sea in a blinding effulgence. I felt like dancing, it was so exciting and exhilarating. Never in my wildest dreams had I imagined anything so wonderful. I could hardly believe that I, Oliver C. Baldwin of Philadelphia, was here, at sea as an officer in the United States Navy, and headed off on a grand adventure!

The brig settled into what would quickly become her 'at sea' posture: one watch on deck tending to the chores necessary to keep her on course and moving swiftly through the seas, and the other below or taking their ease topside, busying themselves with personal chores or just, in the case of the landsmen, enjoying the spectacle as much as I. I heard the pipe and drum sound the call to 'spirits up' and, a short while later, dinner; the weather deck became quickly crowded with sailors who queued up for their ration of whiskey mixed with water and then, the noon meal.

Our meal in the cockpit would not be served for another hour, and I contented myself with roaming the deck, chatting with the watch and getting used to the feel of the motion of *Argus* as she flew past the tip of the Cape, visible only as a low spit of land well to our south.

As I made my way forward, I caught sight of James, our reluctant midshipman, standing at the bulwark by the foremast shrouds on the windward side of the spar deck. His two-handed grip on the thick tarred hemp and the chalk-white color of his face when he turned at my approach spoke more eloquently than any words could of his condition. His new varnished straw hat was gone, presumably over the side. He seemed not to notice or at least, to care.

"Is this not the most terrible feeling, Oliver? How can you just walk about so carelessly, without bracing yourself against this tossing and rolling? I can't imagine how dreadful it will be when we get farther from land! Why Captain Decatur had to leave Boston in the middle of a storm is beyond my ken. I should think one would have to hang on just to keep from being hurled over the side!"

"Oh, James, it really isn't so bad. And we surely are not in a 'storm' or anything like one from what I've heard of them from my brother. Try to move with the motion. It doesn't seem to bother me even a little. You should . . ." Before I could finish the sentence, Midshipman Stevens turned away from me and poured out his breakfast. It was immediately caught by the wind blowing in our faces and returned to him, the bulwark, and the deck. It would have covered me as well had I not stepped away as he turned.

"Oh, my Lord! I think I will die! I can not do this. And what a mess!" Stevens turned back to face me, wiping off the front of his newly decorated jacket. His eyes streamed with tears, whether from his recent upheaval or frustration or fear I knew not. His countenance remained as white as his shirt should have been.

"I would suggest, James, that the other side of the deck would be a better place to stand, should you feel that coming on again!" I smiled encouragingly at the poor boy and pointed at the leeward side of the ship. "Dinner will be set out in the cockpit shortly. You might want to change before we eat." I added with some, I am shy to admit, pleasure.

"Oh, God! Even the thought makes me . . ." He turned and, with less to offer this time, repeated his earlier performance, with much the same result. I patted him carefully on a dry spot and left him to his misery.

I continued my tour of the deck and delighted in the spray that *Argus* flung over her bows as she flew with the wind. The waves, rollers, actually, that greeted us came from far out in the Atlantic, and the swift little brig rode up and over some, while she brushed aside the smaller ones with her stout bow.

The spray that occasionally showered the fo'c'sle deck caught the sun and made miniature rainbows that sparkled for a moment and then vanished, only to be replaced by another and then another. I was captivated by the wondrous display and cared not a whit that much of the spray managed to wet my canvas jacket and trousers. I laughed aloud as a particularly large wave smacked thunderously into the bow, causing the ship to shudder as she pushed the offending impediment to our progress aside and pressed onward, her pace unslack-'ed. The wave was gone, but in going had sent a great deluge of water straight up into the air. Much of it landed on me and suddenly I was wet to my skin. I had had no idea that going to sea would be this much fun. No wonder Edward loved it so much!

"Mister Baldwin, have you nothing better to do than stand here in the bows getting wet? I should think you would be better used learning your responsibilities while we are underway!" First Lieutenant Cutler had approached me unseen and caught me quite unaware.

"I . . . uh . . .oh, sir. Yes, sir. I will do so at once!" I stammered a reply, my face feeling hot and flushed at having been caught acting more like a child than an officer in the United States Navy.

Quite abashed, I made my way on the rolling deck toward the quarterdeck. I could see Captain Decatur standing near the wheel on the windward side. As I approached, he shifted his gaze from the t'gallants to me, taking in my bedraggled appearance. A smile started on his lips, a sparkle in his eyes.

"Enjoying your first day at sea, Mister Baldwin?" The smile grew broader and his eyes crinkled.

"Oh, yes, sir! It is quite exciting. I am exhilarated by the whole of it!" I could not contain myself. I, too, smiled broadly.

"Aye, that it is. I have always enjoyed the feeling of a fine vessel and a good wind. And over the past month and more, I have been chafing to get shed of the dirt and stagnant air of the harbor. *Argus* is everything Mister Hartt promised me she'd be." Decatur noticed my blank look; it was apparent that the name meant nothing to me. He added, "He also built Preble's *Constitution*, you know. As fine a swimmer—for a '44'—as ever one could hope for. Sailed in her myself a year and more back. We will make a splendid crossing, I should imagine!"

We continued to chat, well, perhaps *chat* isn't quite right; Decatur spoke and I listened, about the sailing characteristics of the brig and others until Lieutenant Cutler appeared and stepped with the captain to the windward side of the deck. I remembered my place and remained where I was. The wind carried bits and snatches of their conversation down to me.

" . . . quarters . . . afternoon?" Cutler was saying.

"Aye. Can't start training 'em too . . . powder and shot . . . hand weapons . . . tomorrow . . ." The captain's words, most of them, were carried away and I wondered what was in store for us.

"Mister Baldwin, tell your fellow midshipmen that we will be beating to quarters after dinner, if you please, and find Mister Devon. I'll be needing a word with him directly." The first lieutenant threw the words at me over his shoulder as he stepped forward toward the waist. "And put on some dry clothes!"

"Oh, yes, sir. I had planned . . ." He was gone, not expecting or needing a reply to his orders. I set off in search of Judd and the ordered dry clothes.

Even before I had stepped off the ladder into the passageway leading to the cockpit, I could hear Tom Wheatley's voice, raised in anger, from within the midshipmen's apartment.

"Just who the devil do you think you are? You got no right ordering me to do anything. You think just on account of you been out with Morris and passed through Gibraltar once or twice you got some kinda God-given right to lord it over me acause I ain't? Lemme tell you something, Devon, I may not always talk like you *educated* ones, but I know people. I can tell what they's thinkin' just by lookin' at 'em. I got *insight*! An' you're thinkin' you're better 'an me— that I'm some kinda pond scum what don't belong . . ."

Judd's voice remained controlled and calm; he stopped Wheatley's tirade with a voice as sharp-edged as a knife. "I would not judge you by your words, Tom, but by your actions. Same as with the sailors. A man's got to be able to hand, reef, and steer to gain their respect; I feel the same. We don't have to be friends, but if you're able, I will most surely respect you." He paused. Thomas muttered something I couldn't make out, then Judd continued.

"And I am senior to you. It's not just that I've got more experience than you; I have more years in the Navy than you, or any of the others, for that matter. And I spent three years at sea in merchant traders before that. That is why I am, at least partially, responsible for you as well as Baldwin and young Stevens. I expect all of you to listen to me and follow . . ."

"You ain't got no right to order me anywhere, Devon. I'll take orders from Cutler or Decatur or them others in the Gunroom. But not you. You're no better 'an me, by God!" Tom was getting more and more exercised. I stepped through the doorway.

The two stood facing each other, their faces mere inches apart. Wheatley's jaw thrust forward defiantly, and I saw that his hands were balled into fists. Judd, while flushed with the heat of the argument, remained outwardly calm, his hands clasped behind his back. Both turned at my entrance to the cockpit.

"This ain't no concern of your'n, Baldwin. Get yourself gone whilst *Mister* Devon and I finish this business!" Wheatley spoke without looking at me; his gaze had returned to Judd and he took a half step back, measuring the distance between them. His rancor and defiance had increased, and I knew instinctively that he was a powder keg that any little spark might ignite.

I shifted my astonished gaze from Wheatley's red face twisted in anger to Judd's calm and, outwardly at least, restrained look. Even their bodies were at odds; Tom was tense, rigid, and coiled, ready to strike. Judd, by all appearances, could have been chatting with a friend about nothing more consequential than the weather.

"No, Oliver. You may stay. Our conversation is concluded. Tom, here, has made his position clear, as have I. We have little further to discuss." Judd still kept a wary eye on Wheatley.

"Beggin' yer pardon, sirs. Got your vittles, here." Riley, our steward, stood in the doorway directly behind me, his arms laden with our "vittles."

I stepped out of his way and he set his burden on the table. The confrontation had ended, but tension hung heavy in the air. I side-stepped around the table and opened my chest to find some dry clothes. I suddenly remembered that the first lieutenant had sent me; I looked up at Judd Devon.

"Oh, Lord, Judd! I very nearly forgot; Mister Cutler sent me to tell you he wanted a word with you quick as ever you please."

Devon nodded at me and, stepping around the unmoving and still flushed Wheatley, left the confines of the cockpit with an admonition tossed over his shoulder to "Save me a ration!"

"I'll weather the bastard next time, by God!" Wheatley muttered ominously as he shifted his gaze to me. "What happened to you, Baldwin? Fall overboard? And where's your fat little friend?" Thwarted in his attempt to best our senior, and biggest, member, my repugnant shipmate turned his bullying sneer to me.

"We took some spray over the bow, Tom. It was quite exciting. I reckon I got taken with the moment and stood a bit too long. But there were little rainbows and the water was sparkling. I was enthralled by the whole of it." I smiled, hoping to show that I was no threat to him. I had met many of his stripe in the Academy, usually to my sorrow. I wanted none of that here. "James is feeling poorly and will likely not be here for dinner." I felt momentarily guilty at my earlier lack of feeling for him and added, "He seemed quite ill. And even a little afraid." Wrong words, I realized too late. Tom would use any weakness to make Stevens' life even more miserable than it already was. I tried to pass it off lightly. "I am sure it will pass. Soon's he gets used to it all." The wolfish smile told me my efforts were for naught. James would bear Wheatley's invective at the first opportunity.

"Oh, that fat little mama's boy ain't likely to miss a meal, no matter how sick he is! You mark my words, Baldwin, your little friend'll show up when there's food to be had!" The grin had been replaced by an all-too-familiar sneer, and Wheatley took his place at the table, looked around our diminutive quarters, taking in Riley and me. Then he stood and shifted his seat to the one at the head of the table. His nasty smile challenged me to comment, but I kept my own counsel.

"I believe, sir, that the seat you've taken is Mister Devon's. I 'spect he'll be wantin' it when he returns for his vittles." Riley continued setting out our food and utensils. He spoke without looking at Thomas.

"You just set out our food, Riley, and I'll worry about where I rest my arse. 'Sides, *Mister* Devon ain't here, now is he? No tellin' when he'll be finished with the First and with him gone, I guess I'm the senior and got a right to set myself anywhere I like." The flippant manner with which Wheatley brushed aside the steward's remark told of the midshipman's regard for any beneath him. His jaw assumed its defiant thrust, daring the older sailor to challenge his self-pro-claimed authority.

Dinner was a quiet affair, quite a departure from our usual boisterous meals. Even Riley seemed moved to make no noise as he shifted dishes and brought additional elements of the meal to us from the pantry he shared with the Gunroom stewards. Of course, it was just the two of us. Then Judd appeared in the doorway.

He stood for a moment taking in the scene before him, and particularly, Wheatley seated at the head of the table. "I'll have my seat now, Tom. You may shift over to your usual one." Judd took a step toward the head of the table.

I could see Tom quite literally thinking over his choice; would he acknowl-edge Judd's authority or would he challenge it? The tableau remained for a heartbeat and more. Then Lieutenant Hobbs appeared at our door and Tom stood with a thin smile.

"Of course you shall have your seat, Judd. We weren't sure when you would return. I sat here merely to make it easier for Riley to get around the table."

Riley snorted, but said nothing.

Without further word, Judd took the vacated seat, Riley put a plate before him, and Lieutenant Hobbs spoke, directing his words to all.

"Cap'n Decatur has let out the word that we'll be exercising the great guns immediately all hands are fed. You lads're going to have to see that your divi-sions are mustered when we beat to quarters and then stand ready by your guns for Mister Tarbox to give you and your crews instruction. Lieutenants Morris and Cutler will be making rounds as well, should you have any questions." Hobbs raised his eyebrows which, with his head down as he peered over his spectacles, gave him a curiously owlish look. His gaze went from me to Judd and finally settled on Tom. "You all understand that we have only the time of our crossing to prepare for fighting the Bashaw. We have half the crew as lands-men; you and your crews must learn fast and be able to stand up to anything those piratical bastards can think of. Cap'n Decatur will tolerate no foolishness nor skylarkin'. Be clear on that!" He spoke to all of us, but his eyes had fastened on Tom Wheatley.

"Aye, aye, sir. You can surely count on us doin' our duty. Yes, sir!" Wheat-ley's ingratiating tone fooled none of us, but save for a brief hardening of his stare, Hobbs merely nodded and left the cockpit.

"Where's James?" Judd glanced quickly around our tiny quarters and directed the question to me.

Tom answered before I could even take a breath and, as though his earlier effort at civility was too much for him, had again become antagonistic. "Oh, little Jimmy is feeling poorly and misses his mama. He didn't care to join us for dinner, so I reckon the poor dear really is feelin' low; it's not like fat James to miss a meal!"

Judd shot a glance at him, then at me.

"Aye, Judd. He was on the spar deck earlier and sick. I think he might have been a mite bit scared as well. I suspect he'll get used to it before long, and he will be fine." I smiled at our senior midshipman.

"He's going to have to do his work whether he feels poorly or not. What Lieutenant Cutler wanted me for was to give out the assignments for each of our gun batteries." He stopped and consulted a piece of paper he had withdrawn from his jacket pocket. "Oliver, you'll be in charge of the forward three carronades, twenty-four-pounders, they are, larboard and starboard. That's six guns. Tom, the next three aft larboard and starboard. I have the aftermost battery on the gundeck, and James will be in charge of the long twelve-pounders on the spar deck. When I finish my dinner, I will find him and so inform him."

"I'll lay a wager right here and now that my crews will out-shoot any of yours in the first competition. And you can pass that on to young James 'in charge of the spar deck long guns' as well." Wheatley's challenge dripped with rancor and bravado. Neither Judd nor I felt moved to comment, and our meal was finished peacefully, albeit quietly. For a change, there was none of the banter and horseplay in which we usually indulged, which caused Riley no end of frustration.

My own thoughts were consumed with the notion that we would be *exercising the great guns!* I barely chewed my food, so anxious was I to get started with this, the most exciting and, I was sure, the most rewarding part of my new employment. This was what we were all about! No sooner had I finished the last morsel of my dinner than I stood, asked permission from our senior member to be excused—even in my excitement, I remembered the rules of the cockpit so carefully drummed into my head—and dashed headlong out the door and up the ladder. In my haste, I missed most of the derisive comment that Thomas Wheatley threw after me. I thought, as I tore up the second ladder to the spar deck, that firing the guns would be a perfect tonic for poor suffering James. And I wanted to be the one to tell him of Captain Decatur's plans for the afternoon!

I reached the top deck and immediately headed forward to the spot where I had last seen the boy hanging breathlessly over the bulwark. As I made my way up the windward side, I wondered idly whether he had taken my advice about moving to the leeward side. I hoped that the move might not have been necessary and that he was through with the seasickness.

He still looked pale, though less so, I thought as I studied his face, and the soil on his jacket seemed to have dried, perhaps because he had not been sick again, since he still stood exactly where I left him at the weather fore shrouds. He still clung tenaciously to them.

"We're going to fire the guns, James! And you're to be in charge of the long guns right here on the spar deck." I pointed excitedly at the sleek cannon forward and vaguely motioned to the other aft of the quarterdeck.

He stared at me, glassy-eyed and uncomprehending.

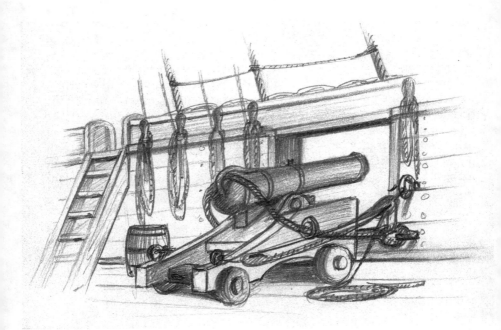

CHAPTER FIVE

"Them salutes we fired back in the harbor was only half-charges o' powder, Mister Baldwin. And you're right; they wasn't turrible loud." Gunner Tarbox stood with me as the three forward guns in the larboard battery were swabbed out and loaded yet again. I had jumped back at the first discharge and covered my ears for the next two. I suddenly understood why Tarbox's natural voice was so loud; most men could hear little immediately after the discharge of cannon, and the gunner's employment required him to give orders all during firing. I noted that his voice came through the ringing in my own ears with a quite natural sound. But I have gotten ahead of myself.

Within half a glass of my sharing our good news with James, the Marine on the spar deck began beating his drum. It was echoed by another on the gundeck as the ship was called to quarters. Remembering my assignment was on the gundeck, I dashed for the ladder, leaving the still-sick midshipman where he stood. The deck was in turmoil; men ran about, shouting at each other; questions, curses, and the din of confusion filled the air. The gundeck was little better.

Tarbox and Judd stood amidships shoving sailors fore and aft, urging them to quiet and alacrity as they stumbled to their assigned stations. I pushed through them and stood by my six charges waiting expectantly for my three gun crews to arrive. A petty officer who seemed to know what he was about was first on the scene. He acknowledged me with a cursory nod (it might have been a form of salute) and immediately began to check over the guns. I watched in rapt attention as he uncoiled the breeching tackles and laid them carefully on the deck. He then pulled a curious instrument, one that put me in mind of a nail with a kind of loop in one end, out of a pouch slung over his shoulder and, with the concentration of one who has seen the result of slovenliness, pressed it into the hole atop each cannon, larboard and starboard. He looked up and caught me watching.

"I'd reckon you'll be Mister Baldwin." He waited not a moment for me to acknowledge his accuracy and returned his attention to the task at hand while he continued. "Bradford, gun cap'n. I'm makin' sure the touch holes is clear on these pieces so the powder'll run down to the charge when we load 'em. Powder don't get through, gun don't fire. Simple as that." He looked up at me again as he moved to the next twenty-four-pounder carronade and repeated the operation. "Johnson and Parker'll be the other gun cap'ns. Don't know where they got to, but they's good men. Shipped with 'em in that business with the French.

In the *New York* frigate we was. You been to sea afore, sir?" He still hadn't looked up, so intent was he on the matter at hand.

Why did everyone want to know if I'd been to sea before? "No, this is my first ship, Bradford. I want to learn as much as ever I can about these guns and how they work. That's why I'm watching you so carefully." I got a glance (was it approving?) as he moved to the next behemoth in the line.

"Right simple, it is, sir. First thing we do is pull the tompions," he pronounced it *tomkins*, "out o' the barrels. They's in there to plug up the ends and keep the water out. Powder charge goes in first, rammed in tight, then the ball an' wad. Ram 'er again so it's all nice an' tight in there an' then I pierce the cartridge with the priming iron—that's this." He held up the nail-like implement he had been using. "Then I pour some powder into the pan and the touch hole—that'll be this here what I'm clearing—and when the order to fire is given—that's your job—I lay the hot end of the linstock into the powder here, and *boom*, off she goes. Simple as that, like I said." He returned to his work, satisfied that he had told me everything necessary about the ungainly-looking, short-barreled guns.

Fortunately he was not looking at me when he uttered the words ". . . that's your job" or he would have seen me blanch in the sudden and horrifying realization of my awesome responsibility. My thoughts raced ahead to our firing and flashed through my brain like bolts of lightning. *How would I know when to give the order to fire? Who would tell me, or would I have to determine it on my own? And what would happen if I gave the order to fire at the wrong time?* I suspected that determining at what I was to fire would be evident. Suddenly, my great anticipation and excitement at exercising the great guns seemed to lose some of its luster!

During the time Bradford had been talking about his guns, most of the other sailors assigned to me for my three gun crews had shown up. The other two petty officers, I recalled their names as Johnson and Parker, or Perkins, or something like that, were organizing the men at each gun, assigning them to tasks. I heard him mention 'train tackles' and 'breeching tackles' as well as 'handspikes.' And suddenly, there seemed to be order—at least around *my* guns. The men were quiet and listened, as did I, to Bradford as he explained to them what was expected of each. I noticed Lieutenant Cutler heading for us from somewhere aft. As he passed Wheatley's battery and the confusion that still reigned there, he stopped and spoke a few words with Tom. From the look that crossed Tom's face, I knew Mister Cutler had not been offering praise. Then he was at the aftermost of my carronades. I stepped forward to greet him with a crisp salute and, as I lifted my hat off my head, it hit the low beams of the ceiling (I quickly learned it was properly called the *overhead*) and flew out of my hand. I heard a few of my sailors snicker as I bent to retrieve it and felt my face flush with embarrassment as I straightened to face our first lieutenant.

"Well, Mister Baldwin. I see . . . well. Are your guns manned properly and ready to fire?"

I shot a glance in Bradford's direction and received a barely perceptible nod.

"Yes, sir. They are ready. And so are the men." While I really had no idea as to this last, I didn't think it would hurt to sound confident, and it might cause him to forget my clumsy salute.

"It is customary to send a man to the quarterdeck to report when your battery is ready, Mister Baldwin. Since this is our first time beating to quarters, I shall excuse it. But remember your duties." He scowled at me, paused, and continued. "Either Lieutenant Hobbs or Gunner Tarbox will be along directly to oversee your firing. Kindly wait until one or the other arrives before you load." He looked over my shoulder at the carronades and squinted his eyes.

"With what, exactly, were you planning to load them, Mister Baldwin?" he said.

"Why, sir, with a powder cartridge and ball, sir. Ram down a wad and then pour some powder into the priming hole and touch it with the linstock!" I smiled, knowing I had impressed him with my complete grasp of the art of naval cannonading. I refrained from adding, "Simple as that, sir!"

"And what were you planning to use for 'powder cartridges and balls,' Mister Baldwin?" Cutler, his eyebrows raised and a tiny smile working at the corners of his mouth, studied me for a reaction.

"Lieutenant, sir. If I may." Bradford was coming to my rescue! "I have sent the boy to the magazine for the cartridges, sir. I reckon it'll take him longer than it might on account of this bein' our first firin' an' all. Our shot is stacked right yonder in the shot rack, sir." Bradford stood straight and tall; there was no hesitation in his response. "Mister Baldwin didn't have a chance to send for our charges since he was busy assignin' the men to they's stations. So I took care of it." The gun captain stood just out of Cutler's line of sight and winked at me.

"Very well, then. You may load and fire when Mister Hobbs or the gunner gets here. And, Baldwin, send a man to the quarterdeck to let us know when that will be." The First turned and headed back the way he had come, his gaze locked onto Thomas Wheatley's still disorganized and quite voluble crews.

"Oh, my goodness! Bradford, you saved me there, and I thank you! It never occurred to me that I was supposed to send someone after our powder. I shan't forget next time, you may be sure!" I offered a most sincere smile to the gun captain, who merely nodded his acknowledgment.

In a few minutes Gunner Tarbox showed up and, in his booming voice, inquired as to our readiness. The boy (Tarbox corrected me, calling the boy a *powder monkey*) Bradford had sent for the powder charges had not yet returned, but otherwise, we, and the carronades, were ready. Tarbox explained the exercise to the men, admonishing them to go slowly at first so "no one gets 'emselves hurt." Serious nods and furtive glances at the three behemoths pulled back from the gunports for loading was the only response, and then our *powder monkey* staggered up with an armload of charges, each charge amounting to six pounds of powder wrapped in a flannel bag. He set them down carefully where directed at each gun and I summarily sent him to the quarterdeck to inform Cutler, and, I suppose, Captain Decatur, of our readiness to fire. I wanted our guns to be the first!

Bradford and his fellow gun captains laid out charges and shot by each gun and made sure the rammers and swabs were in their places on the bulwark by each. They each ran through the loading procedure with their crews again, and this time actually had them clap on to the side tackles, haul the heavy monsters toward the bulwark so their snouts poked out of the ports, then back by way of the train tackles. Of course, he explained, the guns wouldn't have to be *hauled* back; they'd each get back to the ". . . limit of they's breechings quicker 'an kiss my hand when they fired. . . an' woe be to whoever be standin' too close." More serious looks from all and nods from the more seasoned hands.

Our powder monkey had returned. "Lieutenant Cutler says we kin go ahead an' fire whenever you're ready, Mister Baldwin. Long as Gunner Tarbox is here." He tugged on a piece of hair hanging from the front of his hat by way of a salute.

"Sail handlers to stations for shortening sail! Topmen aloft!" The cry came through the gundeck. And about half of my men summarily left their posts at the guns, joining others in the dash for the spar deck. I was suddenly quite confused. How was I to fire my guns, for which permission had just been granted, when the quarterdeck took my sailors to shorten sail? I looked at Tarbox and Bradford.

"Usual part of firin', sir. Got to shorten the barky down so's the cap'n got better control over her. They'll be furlin' courses and royals quick as ever they can. Leave her with a spanker, tops'ls, and a jib. Called 'battle sail' it is. When we's actually fightin' the brig, it helps not havin' all that sail aloft. Keeps it from catchin' fire as well." The gunner explained in a voice loud enough for the whole forward end of the gundeck to hear. "I reckon Mister Cutler wanted everyone mannin' the guns first so's they'll get used to runnin' up yonder and then back. Generally though, we'll shorten down afore we're ready to fire, soon as they beat to quarters. The men what ain't needed to handle the sails would make the guns ready, just like you seen here."

I could feel *Argus* slowing down as the ponderous press of canvas aloft was reduced. From the sound of the feet over our heads, the task was completed with less confusion than accompanied its earlier setting. They —and I—were learning our jobs, and only one day out!

I listened attentively while Tarbox and Bradford discussed our firing. The gunner impressed upon all three of my gun captains that this "drill is just to get the men familiar with the firing itself. Ain't trying to hit nothin.' That'll be for the next time, likely tomorrow, dependin' on the cap'n's mind." And then the sail handlers and topmen returned and we once again took our stations.

"Mister Baldwin, when you're quite ready, if you please!" Cutler's voice floated down the ladder from the spar deck. I, in turn, quite unnecessarily, after receiving a nod from Tarbox, responded.

"Aye, aye, sir!" I shouted back, quite pleased with my quick and seaman-like answer. More quietly, though I suspect that in my excitement it may have been a good deal louder than was necessary, and with an unspeakably dry mouth, I cried to Bradford, standing by the forward-most gun, "FIRE!"

Gunner Tarbox spoke softly (for him). "Sir, we ain't loaded 'em yet nor run 'em out. Better to do that first *then* order 'em fired!"

"Load, Bradford, and run 'em out," said I, hoping my face was not as flushed as it felt. Fortunately, the men were now busy and none looked my way, though Perkins, or Parker or whatever the second gun's captain called himself, did smirk as he also began to oversee the loading of his gun. I couldn't let it bother me as, consumed with fascination, I watched Bradford's crew perform the slow dance of loading a twenty-four-pounder carronade, knowing that with each successive time, the dance would become faster.

One man, called a *sponger,* picked up a flannel bag containing the powder and jammed it into the breech—the open end—of the gun, forcing it all the way down with a *rammer.* Bradford called out, "Home!" indicating it was all the way in as he felt it touch his priming iron. Immediately another sailor picked up one the twenty-four-pound iron balls and pushed it into the yawning muzzle, where it disappeared to join the powder cartridge. The sponger shoved his rammer in behind the ball. When he withdrew it, the same man who had loaded the shot pushed a wad down to be rammed home on top of the ball.

On Bradford's command, four men on each side of the big gun clapped onto the side tackles and heaved around, hauling the gun into the bulwark so that the muzzle stuck out the side of the ship through the open gunport. Immediately he poked his priming iron into the hole atop the carronade's barrel to puncture the cartridge and poured a careful measure of black powder into the touch hole and the pan.

"Ready, sir!" Bradford held the smoking linstock before him and blew gently on it, causing the slow match it held to glow a bright orange. Then he looked at me for the order to fire, which command I gave quickly and, this time, properly.

I watched as he blew once more on the match and then touched the brightly glowing brand to the powder in the carronade's pan. The powder sputtered and smoked and, in less than a heartbeat, had burned down to the cartridge.

BOOOM! The gun fired with a thunderclap, shooting a yard and more of flame and a cloud of choking lavender-tinged smoke out the end of the barrel. Instantly, the massive gun bucked back in recoil so quickly that all I saw was a blur. Then the barrel and its slide came to rest against the breeching tackle, ready to be sponged and reloaded. Even though I had known that the gun was going to fire—had not I myself given the order?—I was unprepared for the deafening roar it had let out. The only sound I could hear was the ringing in my own head! I could see the men gesturing and knew they were shouting, but it was quite beyond my ability to make out a word of what was said. Seeing Parsons blowing on his slow match, I covered my ears in anticipation of the next onslaught.

BOOOM! BOOOM! Both guns fired and jumped back in quick succession. This time I was ready. While my head still rang, it seemed that the bellow from these two was less painful to my poor ears, protected as they were behind my hands. The cloud of smoke generated by all three of the guns' firing blew back upon us, tearing our eyes and obscuring our vision. My mouth tasted like sulfur as I breathed in the choking fumes.

Then there was silence; profound silence. I looked questioningly at the gunner and shook my head to stop the din within. My question to him about the intensity of the noise had likely been expressed with more force than I had intended, but his answer, spoken in his booming voice, penetrated to my brain quite easily.

I could see that many of the men, the landsmen, were quite as confounded as I at the tumult we had created. Then Bradford and his colleagues were shouting orders and pushing their sailors this way and that in an effort to prepare the guns to be fired again.

I shot a glance at Wheatley's battery to see if he was ready to fire. He was not. Indeed, it appeared that one of his men had dropped an iron ball. Since we were firing from the windward, or high, side, Mister Newton's laws of gravity prevailed, and the shot rolled across the deck with two of his sailors in pursuit. They were encouraged by Tom's frenzied shouts. Gunner Tarbox, a grim look of determination on his face, left my battery with the admonition to "Be careful, sir. And try 'er again, slow-like." He headed to the next three carronades aft which belonged to my thoroughly agitated messmate.

BOOM! From overheard I heard the roar of the forward twelve-pounder. I recalled it, and the one aft, were under the command (if such a lofty word could be used) of our star-crossed, suffering young mid, James Stevens. The sound of the cannon's wheels rolling back in recoil directly over our heads caused some of our men to duck involuntarily, myself included. It sounded like thunder, the worst and most ferocious thunder I had ever heard. But, in my joy that James' gun was ready and had fired before Tom's were even loaded, I quite dismissed the noise and looked again at Tom's three charges still at the limits of their breechings. Both Wheatley and Gunner Tarbox were red in the face. The men I took to be the gun captains were exhorting in chorus their men to "get them damn charges rammed home, you damn lubbers!"

And so the afternoon went. Of course, all the guns were fired, most several times, even Wheatley's. I knew from my books that these guns, despite their girth and weight of metal, could fire a ball barely one thousand yards. I had tried in vain to view the fall of our shot, but with my sight restricted to only that provided by the gunport, I was unable to catch a single one.

Midway through the exercise, when we had loaded, fired, sponged and reloaded some four or five times, there came a bellow which turned quickly into a scream of agony from my aftermost carronade. I had been standing forward of Bradford's gun and shouting into the gun captain's ear when gun three fired and the bellowing began. One of Parker's sailors, a man assigned to the side tackles, had been too eager in his employment. When the monster fired and bucked into recoil, his foot had been all but severed as the one-ton slide-mounted carriage rolled over it. Blood squirted from the wound in a pulsating fountain of crimson as some of his mates dragged him clear, and the screaming continued.

Lieutenant Hobbs, who happened to be nearby, ran to the stricken sailor. He grabbed the man's handkerchief from around his neck and tied it quickly and expertly over the gushing foot. The sailor was carried below to the hospital, his screams diminishing both from his increasing weakness and the increasing distance between us. I remained rooted to the deck, transfixed by the spectacle, and stared at the glistening pool of gore that remained on the deck and gun slide.

"Usually only happens first time they're fired, Mister Baldwin. Less'n someone gets too eager. Reckon that fellow's not going to get in the way again, if he don't lose that foot, or bleed to death." Hobbs had spoken to me calmly— quite matter-of-factly, I thought, considering the cruel wound the man had received. "You can continue your firin.' Give you a chance to work short-handed. And see if you can reload some faster. A crack crew should be able to fire three times in five minutes." Our second lieutenant then turned and moved away to observe us.

I was not sure, barring another accident, why I would ever have to fire 'short-handed' as he put it and doubted our ability to meet the goal of 'three times in five minutes.' I said as much to Parker.

"You gots to remember, sir, most times they's gonna be someone shootin' back. And here's where they aim; the guns and the top hamper to take the rig down, us, too. And rare it is when both vessels don't suffer terrible losses of men and guns. And when they's folks shootin' back at us, it sure makes the lads want to get her loaded quick as ever they can. You can be sure of that!" Parker's tone was patient, but his eyes were focused on his task, that of rearranging his men to make up for, not only the wounded one, but the two who had carried him below as well.

Here was yet another piece of news that I had never considered. Of course, it seemed completely logical when I thought about it, but that didn't change the fact that this employment might not be as exhilarating as I had imagined! I thought he was likely right about the inspiration provided by another ship's return fire.

By suppertime, we were done. The guns had been swabbed out for the last time, their side tackles hauled taut so their muzzles, tompions securely in place, were snug against the bulwark, and the gunports closed tightly. We were all, officers, midshipmen, and seamen, exhausted. Even the normally animated queue for grog was subdued as the men filed by the cask to receive their due, well earned this day!

As I prowled around the decks, most of what I overheard from the men centered on what had happened to their fellows hurt in the afternoon's firing. It soon became apparent to me that Carlson, my heaver on gun three whose foot got crushed, was not the only casualty by a long shot. Indeed, I heard talk of other crushed feet, hands mutilated and burned, and one (though I suspect the speaker might have been making more of the hurt than was the case) who was smote blind by an excess of powder in the touch hole. I imagined that the surgeon, a man whose skills were regularly maligned by most, would be hard pressed to breast the steady flow of injured arriving at his hospital, which I later discovered was the mess table in the cockpit. I heard precious little of the excitement and eagerness that preceded the drills. Even my own, though still smoldering in my breast, was remarkably subdued as I made my way to the quarterdeck to take my watch with Lieutenant Hobbs.

"Well, Mister Baldwin, what say you of our shooting this afternoon? Not quite what you expected, I'd warrant." Hobbs greeted me as I reported my presence by saluting him and the quarterdeck.

"It was quite . . ." I hesitated, not sure of what word might suitably express my excitement, awe, and shock at the power and deafening noise. ". . . loud, sir. But I believe that our men might be more used to their employment now." I desperately wanted to report that my crews, at least, had attained the goal Hobbs had set out for me, but in truth, we fired at nearly the same rate at the end of the drill as we had at its beginning. I said as much.

"You more 'an likely will gain your speed by the time we raise Gibraltar, Baldwin. And o' course, no matter how fast you are in practice, those lads'll fire faster than even they thought possible when someone's shootin' back at 'em!" He smiled and looked at me over the top of his spectacles. "And we'll be continuing to exercise at the great guns, as well as small arms and boarding weapons, all the way over. You'll get your chance. Tomorrow you'll be tryin' to hit a target."

That's the second time I've heard about someone shooting back at us! I thought again about the carnage we inflicted on *ourselves* and wondered what horrors lay ahead of us when an enemy broadside found its target in our hull.

The brig continued her southeasterly rush, once again under full sail to the t'gallants. And I began to learn the task of the watch officers as Lieutenant Hobbs patiently explained to me about recording our speeds and courses on the slate, trimming the sails to gain the best advantage of the wind, and steering a proper course, or more properly, ensuring the quartermasters handling the big double wheel did. It seemed only a few minutes, rather than two hours, had passed when Lieutenant Morris and Thomas Wheatley appeared to relieve us for our supper. While the two lieutenants discussed the state of the vessel, our course, and other points necessary to a proper watch, Wheatley glared at me from across the quarterdeck, finally stepping close to growl at me.

"Only reason you and your fat friend beat me on the guns today was on account of the imbeciles they give me for my crews. Lieutenant Cutler's gonna swap around some of the men and I aim to see that I get the best ones. You and your little fat friend better watch yourselves tomorrow, Baldwin! I don't like bein' beat at grown-up business by children. It ain't gonna happen again; you mark my words."

"Thomas, I don't think they'll change anyone, save replacing the ones who got hurt today. I heard you had more than a few who got taken to the hospital. I imagine those are the replacements Lieutenant Cutler must have had in mind."

"Not on your life, Baldwin. I aim to get that gun captain—what's his name? Bradford? Aye, he's the one! Then we'll see how good your guns look! Tarbox told me he's the best gun captain in the ship. Seems only right he should be workin' for me." Tom stopped growling his threats and stared at me, waiting for a reaction. He wore that smug look that made me angry even when it wasn't directed at me.

"Mister Baldwin, have you passed on to your relief the information necessary for him to assume the watch?" Lieutenant Hobbs spoke from where he and Lieutenant Morris stood by the wheel.

"No, sir. He has not yet had the time, bein' busy as he's been lordin' it over me on account o' his guns was faster than mine this afternoon. I am still waitin'." Wheatley's voice was smooth and held no rancor; he put his hand on his hip and raised his eyebrows as he returned his eye to mine. A slight smile worked at one corner of his mouth.

"Wha . . . how dare . . . you can't . . . why do . . ." I sputtered and stammered, rendered speechless by this bald-faced lie. I could barely contain my outrage, but managed to give him the scant essentials to the ship's condition through clenched teeth. Having done so, I turned and left the quarterdeck. I knew my face was red. I could feel the heat it created as the blood pounded through my head, but this time, it was not because of my own misstep. Lieutenant Hobbs stopped before entering the hatch.

"What was going on there, Baldwin? Is there a problem between you and Wheatley?"

"No, sir. What he said was not . . . that is, I had not given him the information, but not on account of . . . well, I guess I was wrong, sir. I will see that it doesn't happen again, sir." There seemed no future in expecting the officers to deal with my problem with Wheatley; we would have to sort it out for ourselves. I decided, with the same resolve I used to get myself out of that unfortunate situation ashore, that I would do so, one way or another.

Supper in the cockpit was quietly pleasant. Judd, James and I enjoyed each other's stories about the afternoon's events and, with Thomas on watch topside, there was no rancor. Even James seemed to be feeling better, and his attitude showed marked improvement as a result of his part in the exercise with the great guns. I must confess that I and, I think, the others, took a certain unstated pleasure in the absence of our colleague. Even Riley seemed to be less surly and did not once slam a dish or cup on the table.

I took to my cot early, intending to study some before succumbing to the arms of Orpheus, but quickly fell into a dreamless sleep until I was awakened to assume the watch at midnight.

CHAPTER SIX

On the following day, our exercise at the great guns, as promised, included actually firing at a real target. The carpenter and his mates had cobbled together a sort of raft consisting of barrels and other jetsam that was put overboard. Once the ship, reduced again to her battle sail, had maneuvered into position, we were instructed to "Fire as you bear," meaning that each gun should shoot when we could train it around to "see" the target. The results were dismal. Both Gunner Tarbox and Lieutenant Hobbs were at their wits' end trying to combine the elements of speed with accuracy, but by the end of the day, it appeared that only one of the two would be attained. It did not help that the seas were up from the day before. In spite of the skill of the gun captains, timing the discharge of the gun with the roll of the ship and firing quickly seemed quite beyond our grasp. To further confound the gun crews, each battery was expected to fire in sequence and immediately following its predecessor, offering a minimum interval during which we, or rather our sailors, had to sponge, load, run out and train the guns onto the target. After each pass, Captain Decatur wore or tacked *Argus* around so as to bring the batteries on the opposite side to bear while the gun crews ran across the deck to load, run out, train and fire in sequence.

At the conclusion of the firing exercises, the officers seemed subdued and spent some considerable time talking among themselves both on the quarterdeck with Captain Decatur and off it with Gunner Tarbox and some of the gun captains. After the noon meal, some of us had the opportunity to alter the officers' perception of our skills.

Small arms and boarding drills were conducted by watch on the spar deck. We midshipmen were taken as a group by Gunner Tarbox, who stood at the bulwark amidships with a box of pistols, several horns of powder, and a small cask attached to a lengthy piece of thin rope. The sailors, meanwhile, learned the use of the cutlass, pike, halfpike, and hatchet, or as some referred to it, the tomahawk.

"Who among you has fired a pistol before?" Tarbox studied each of our faces as we stood mute before him. James and I exchanged glances; his eyes were big and I suspected the thought of a pistol in his own hand made him uncomfortable. For my own part, I thought it might be fun! Then Judd stepped forward.

"I am familiar with the use of a pistol, Gunner. Fired one regular on our last cruise with Commodore Morris and before, when I was in the merchants."

Tarbox nodded, and I stole a glance at Wheatley, surprised he had not spoken up right off, given his year of service already as a midshipman. He was not looking at me, but glaring at Judd, the familiar thrust to his jaw and clenched fists a clear indication of what would be coming next. He did not keep us in suspense for long.

"I've fired pistols before, Gunner. Ain't nothin' to it. I even hit what I aim at. I was among the best on the *Norfolk* brig down to the Chesapeake." He shot a glance at Judd, then fixed his glare on the gunner.

There it was! We all knew well of his time in the brig, since he mentioned it often enough in the cockpit and elsewhere, comparing us to his mates there. His remarks usually centered on how much James and I had to learn and how poorly *Argus* compared to his former vessel.

"Well, then, sir, why don't you just take one of these and show these other young gentlemen how to use it?" The gunner handed Tom a pistol and stepped back.

Wheatley took the proffered gun and turned it this way and that as he studied it. I wasn't sure he knew what to do next, but I was proven wrong when he pulled back the hammer with its flint and then released it slowly so that no spark was created. It seemed to me that there was a slight tremor in his hands as he held the weapon.

"Where's the balls and powder at, Gunner? Pistol ain't nothin' but a cudgel without it's loaded." He suddenly turned the weapon in his hand and, grasping it by its barrel, swung it down toward the bulwark so that the heavy brass knob on the pistol's butt made a *thud* and a dent in the wood. He smiled wolfishly at James and me. The smile broadened as I heard James draw in his breath.

"Here now, sir. Ain't no need to be beatin' on the barky. You'll want to save that for them piratical bastards over yonder when we get there. For now, here's your ball and powder." The gunner pointed to a pouch and horn hanging from the bulwark. "Show your fellows how to load it and then we'll see what you can hit with it. Aside the bulwark." Tarbox's last remark made all of us except, of course, Wheatley, smile.

Wheatley fairly snatched the offered powder horn off its peg. He angrily poured some powder (it seemed like quite a lot to me) into the muzzle and stuffed a wad in quickly. He yanked the ramrod from under the barrel and thrust it into the opening. His jaw had returned to its defiant cast, I noticed. He said something under his breath and, though I was unable to make out clearly what he muttered, it sounded like "beside the bulwark, indeed." He shifted the gun to his right hand and sprinkled a few grains of powder into the pan atop the barrel.

"He didn't put a ball in, Oliver!" James whispered. His glee at seeing our tormentor about to embarrass himself again was barely contained. Even with his complete lack of familiarity with a pistol, James had noticed this oversight.

I looked at Gunner Tarbox to see if he would step in. He did not; in fact, he picked up the small cask, uncoiled its line, and balanced it on the bulwark right next to the quite obvious dent Thomas had just made.

"Well, Mister Wheatley, if you're happy with your load, let's see what you can hit with it." Tarbox stepped forward and, with a mighty heave, pitched the cask over the side so that it ran immediately to the end of its tether and then started in toward the ship's side. "There's your target, sir. Fire when you will."

Tom stepped to the bulwark, aimed his pistol and pulled the trigger. James and I held our breath as the flint struck the steel, making a spark which touched off the powder in the pan. The fire sputtered and smoked and then with a *crack*, the pistol spat out a foot-long flame and the wad Thomas had so energetically rammed down the barrel. The end of the barrel split with a squeal that followed so closely on the sound of the discharge as to be almost indistinguishable from it. Thomas dropped the pistol and cried out in alarm. Tarbox and Judd smiled. James and I laughed aloud. The pistol clattered to the deck, and, since we were standing on the leeward side, slid toward the waterway under the bulwark where there was nothing to stop it from continuing into the sea. And continue it did, in spite of the gunner's shout for Thomas to retrieve it.

"Well, I reckon it wasn't no good for doin' anything with, save using it as a cudgel, like you showed us, Mister Wheatley. Blew the end of her clear off, you done, by God! And didn't even load a ball!" Tarbox didn't raise his voice or even look distressed; his tone was matter-of-fact and probably angered Wheatley even more than had he been more severe.

"Pistol hadda been split when you gave it to me. Wouldn't have done that—opened up the barrel like it done—less'n it was already split. You were trying to get me hurt, and probably intentional it was, too. I ought to bring you up on charges to the captain for what you done." Wheatley's invective, now that he had recovered from the shock of the explosion in his hand, was issued in a voice loud enough to cause some of the men nearby to stop their cutlass training and look at our group. Tarbox ignored him completely and, picking up another pistol, spoke quietly, for him, to all of us. I noticed that Tom was flexing the fingers of his right hand, shaking it from time to time, as if trying to restore it to sensitivity.

"I will now show you how to load, prime, and fire a muzzle-loading pistol. Observe, if you will, sirs, that I am pouring a *measured* amount of powder into the barrel; the end of the horn, here, will do that for you if'n you don't tip it up too much. A wad's next, rammed down tight with the rammer, here, and then, Mister Wheatley, a ball goes in." Gunner Tarbox looked right at Thomas, a sparkle in his eyes the only indication of his jibe at the midshipman. "Ram her down nice and snug, put a small amount of powder, like you done, sir, in the pan, and pull the hammer back." He held up the loaded and cocked pistol for all to see. Was it my imagination, or was it more in front of Thomas' eyes than any others?

He handed the pistol, butt first, to James. It might have been a venomous serpent from the way James took it into his chubby hand. The look on his face was one of wild-eyed horror.

"Don't be scared of it, sir. It ain't gonna do you no harm less'n it's pointed *at* you. Just grab aholt of the butt like you done and aim her out yonder. When she settles down in your hand, just pull the trigger—and hang on to it!" I thought this was more for the benefit of Thomas than anyone else, but James nodded seriously at the advice and raised the gun at arm's length in front of him.

The rest us of watched as James waved the loaded pistol around, the barrel describing circles that seemed to get wider and wider in the air. We all, even Gunner Tarbox, took a step backward.

"Never mind yourself about the target, sir. Just try to hit the water for now." Tarbox had been through this before, and his patience and humor would see him through yet again.

Bang! The gun jumped up as it fired; James yelped in surprise, but he hung onto it. A little cloud of gray smoke hung momentarily over the gun and then blew away in the steady breeze. And I saw a tiny geyser shoot up in the water some fifty yards from the ship. James' face split into a big smile.

"I did it! And I didn't drop it overboard!" His exclamation brought smiles to all of us, save Thomas, who glared at the young mid, muttering something about "hitting the water."

"All right, sir. That was just fine. Now *you* load it and try it again." Tarbox handed him the powder horn.

James was caught up in the excitement of his success. He slowly poured some powder into the muzzle, rammed home a wad and ball and looked expectantly at the gunner. Tarbox was hauling in the cask and, when he had retrieved it, stepped forward in his peculiar gait, balanced it on the bulwark, and looked back to James.

"You let me know when you're ready, Mister Stevens, and then we'll see about hittin' something."

"Aye. That'll be a joke, him hittin' something asides the water!" Wheatley mumbled his invective, but we all, including James, heard it quite plainly.

"You just watch, Thomas. At least I got a chance of hitting the cask; there's a ball in the gun!"

James must be feeling better, I thought. *He's actually standing up for himself!*

"When you young sirs are through a-visitin', I'll heave this overboard." *Was Tarbox losing his patience?*

"I'm ready, Gunner." James raised the heavy pistol to arm's length again and, while it still made circles in the air, they were smaller, I thought.

The cask flew out from the ship, splashed in the water and immediately began to drift aft as *Argus* continued sailing on her course.

Thomas Wheatley gave James a shove at exactly the moment James pulled the trigger. The little geyser was nowhere near the cask, which continued to move quickly aft.

"Damn you, Wheatley! You did that on purpose. You made me miss!" Tears welled up in the young mid's eyes as he glared in frustration at his tormentor.

"Now, little Jimmy, you know Cap'n Decatur don't allow no cussin' aboard his ship. If you apologize for 'damning' me, I won't have to mention it to him. Probably save you from gettin' mast-headed, it will. And don't cry." Thomas smiled benignly at Stevens who stared, quite uncomprehendingly, at him. I'm not sure James even knew what 'mast-heading' meant; I knew that I didn't.

"You go to hell, Wheatley. I'll take whatever Captain Decatur gives me. But I will not apologize for what I said unless you apologize for pushing me."

This was a new James, standing up for himself. Judd once again assumed the role of peacemaker.

"All right now, gentlemen. Let us not waste Gunner Tarbox's time with squabbling. Thomas, leave James alone. You'll get your turn to show us how good you might, or might not, be. James, load the pistol and take one more shot at the cask. No one will bother you . . . this time." This last was accompanied by a sharp look at Wheatley and received an equally hard look in return.

And so the pistol practice continued. We each took several turns at loading and firing the gun. While only Judd actually hit the cask, the rest of us got quite close with a few shots. I think mine might have been closest! Of course, Wheatley's misses were accompanied by a host of excuses including being pushed, losing his balance from an unexpected roll of the ship, and the cask bouncing on a wave at an inopportune moment.

As we broke up to go about our respective duties, I saw Judd take Thomas aside and, while I could hear not a word of their conversation, I could imagine what was said just by their postures and the looks on their faces. I knew the incident was not yet over.

The sailors were still at their cutlass drills. I watched for a moment as two parried and thrust at each other. The heavy swords clanged as they met, accompanied by the grunts of the men and the occasional epithet as one or another succeeded in a move. Of course, blood had been spilt, and once again, the surgeon was busy sewing up gashes in arms and legs made by the overzealous combatants. I was glad that we midshipmen had been given pistols to use! The thought of a cutlass in Thomas Wheatley's hands was almost too much for me to imagine!

That evening the midshipmen received word that we were to dine in the Cabin with Captain Decatur for dinner on the morrow. Judd had told me that a captain often invited the other officers and even the occasional midshipman to his table, but when Harris, the captain's steward stepped into the cockpit with the invitation, I couldn't believe my ears. I was going to eat in the captain's Cabin! I think James was more nervous than even I was, thinking about how Wheatley had threatened to tell Decatur about the cussing incident.

"Do you think he will, Oliver? I wouldn't know what to say if he did actually tell the captain." James furrowed brow and round eyes suggested that, despite his brave words earlier, he really was afraid of Wheatley and what he might do or say.

"Oh, I don't think he'd do that, James. That remark was just said to scare you. Besides, Captain Decatur might not even care." I wished I believed my own words as much as I wanted James to. I knew the captain had a firm policy that was intolerant of any swearing aboard his ship.

The evening's meal passed without the usual boisterous skylarking in the cockpit, and, as usual, Thomas sounded the only discordant note by defending his poor performance with the pistol while, at the same time, denigrating our own. Judd, the only one among us who had actually *hit* the target, smoothed his ruffled feathers with a droll remark about all of us needing practice, which we were bound to get as long as Tarbox maintained his patience and sense of humor.

The evening watches were stood, and the day following dawned red and fiery. I had the morning watch and observed it with great delight until Mister Hobbs mentioned that it likely signaled a change for the worse in the weather. The day continued with practice at the great guns. This time both Tarbox and Hobbs noticed some improvement. When the crew was piped to 'spirits up' and dinner, we mids scurried to the cockpit to change into appropriate uniform for our dinner with Captain Decatur.

At the appointed hour, the four of us, in our best uniforms, which consisted of our *cleanest*, but with well-blackened boots and polished brass, stood outside the Cabin in the close passageway while the captain's Marine sentry knocked, announced us, and then nodded us into the Cabin.

We filed in, Judd, then Thomas, me, and James. Captain Decatur stood in the larboard quarter gallery talking with Lieutenant Cutler and Mister Wakefield, our surgeon. He excused himself and stepped forward to greet us with a smile and a welcoming handshake.

"How nice of you young gentlemen to join me for dinner. I thought it might prove a good opportunity for us all to get to know one another better since we're to be shipmates for some time, should Providence smile on us. Please, let us all take a seat. Mister Cutler, here on my right, if you please, Mister Wakefield, there on my left, and Mister Devon next to Mister Cutler. Mister Baldwin, you'll sit next to Mister Wakefield, if you would, please, and, Mister Wheatley, there, and you, Mister Stevens, right there next to your colleague, if you please."

The table fitted us all quite comfortably and had been set with a white linen and lit by candles in plate holders. Glasses (real crystal, I think) were at each place and in front of the captain's place was a large decanter filled with wine. The light from the candles sparkled and reflected in the glassware, shooting little sparks of brilliance around the room as the flames flickered. Never had I dined in such splendor! As we sat, I thought fleetingly of our mess in the cockpit and how it would never seem quite the same.

"We've not been formally introduced; I am Reliance Wakefield, sir, and I know you are Mister Baldwin, of Philadelphia, if I recall correctly."

"Yes, sir. Oliver Baldwin, sir. I am most pleased to make your acquaintance." I stuck out my hand, turning awkwardly to offer it to the doctor, who shook it heartily and smiled at me. Almost at once, he poured my glass full with the dark, aromatic wine from the decanter handed to him by the captain.

"I'm a Marylander, myself, near Baltimore. Been up to Philadelphia many times. Fine city, it is. Pity it's no longer our capital; served very well, 'ceptin' for the outbreaks of yellow fever that seem to spring up every summer." He smiled, whether at me or the recollection of times in Philadelphia, I don't know. Then he continued, still smiling. "Our captain tells me you have a brother sailing with Bainbridge in *Philadelphia*. I collect they left sometime before us, even before the commodore did, I believe. Bad business, this mess with the Bashaw. I hope this fight will settle that scoundrel's account once and for all. Should've been done back in '92 or '93 when those pirates first acted up! All of 'em together, Tripoli, Algiers, the whole lot of 'em!" The smile was gone, replaced by a thin line of bloodless lips and a pair of vertical lines emanating from his eyebrows over his nose. He shook his head, then, pulling a delicate white handkerchief from his pocket, proceeded to blow his nose noisily.

"Oh, sir," I said quickly. "I do hope so! I am not aware of the details of the difficulties with those piratical bast . . ." I instantly blushed, having caught myself in language ill-suited to the Cabin and this august company. Too much time with the gunner and bosun was beginning to color my language. Recovering a little of my poise, I continued, "those . . . em . . . *corsairs* of the Bashaw. But I have heard that they quite routinely stop American merchant ships and demand tribute to their king and, should the money not be paid, seize our ships, and our sailors. Surely, we can not allow that to continue. I am proud to be part of Captain Decatur's crew and part of Commodore Preble's squadron who will bring them to heel!"

"For one so young, you seem to have a firmly made up mind on the subject, Oliver, if I may be so informal. However, in spite of *my* feelings about our activities yonder, I would think a more moderate posture might suit better for a young man as yourself. Sometimes thinking—and talking—are the better route to obtaining your desires and needs, rather than fighting." Mister Wakefield said this quietly and completely without rancor, and I took no offense at his bluntness. Now it was my turn to smile, which I am sure, he attributed to the "wisdom" of youth. The clear ringing sound of a knife tapping a crystal glass silenced the conversation and drew our attention to Captain Decatur.

"Gentlemen, if I may. Raise your glasses and drink to the success of our cruise and a speedy end to the tyranny of the pasha of Tripoli. Let us finally make the Mediterranean Sea safe for our merchant fleet!" Decatur, seeing that the decanter had made it 'round the table, had hoisted his own glass on high and was waiting for us to do likewise. We did and then tasted our wine with varying degrees of enthusiasm ranging from sips to gulps. Still cautious, I sipped mine and enjoyed the taste greatly.

"To a speedy passage. Fair winds and easy seas!" Lieutenant Cutler now had raised his glass, and we all drank again. *Was this going to go all the way 'round the table? Would I be expected to offer . . . no, surely not a midshipman!* I decided I would be guided by what Judd did, which, to my great relief, was nothing.

"To our distinguished captain! We could be in no better hands than those of one on his third cruise to these hostile waters. Gentlemen, Captain Decatur!" Mister Wakefield raised his own glass and we all, except, of course, the captain, dutifully followed suit, drinking again. Apparently only the officers were expected to offer salutes.

Harris chose this moment to make his entrance with a large covered platter (like the candlesticks, it also appeared to be plate), which he placed in front of the captain, removing the domed lid with a flourish upon Decatur's nod.

A smell such as I had yet to experience aboard *Argus* immediately filled the Cabin and reminded me of walking past some of the wonderful kitchens near our home in Philadelphia. Rich and heady, the aroma removed any thought that had not to do with eating, and instantly I found myself swallowing the wetness that built without restraint in my mouth. I saw that James, across the table to my right, was so entranced by the meal that he had neglected either to swallow or wipe the drool from his chin.

"James . . . James!" I hissed at him. When he finally tore his eyes from the head of the table to look at me, I wiped my chin with great gusto hoping he would do likewise; instead I got a quizzical look, briefly, and then was ignored in favor of the platter of meat. The line of drool stretched, until Mister Wakefield also noticed it.

"Young man! Yes, you. Mister Stevens. Be so kind as to wipe your chin before we have a flood here. Wouldn't do to have to man the pumps every time food was brought to the captain's table!" From my perspective alongside the good doctor, I was unable to determine whether or not he was smiling, but I suspect that he was enjoying James' discomfort.

A flushed face received the attention of first, the midshipman's sleeve and then, on consideration, his napkin. He mumbled, "Thank you, sir," and James' eyes went back to the food. More had come to join the first offering.

As Decatur began to serve out the brilliantly roasted lamb, Harris brought in a great tureen of soup, covered, but with the handle of a ladle protruding from under the lid, a platter of fish quite obviously recently caught, and several dishes of vegetables. Several of the newly arrived dishes were placed around the table and, when the table would bear no more, on a sideboard behind us. Never had I seen so much food! Several more decanters of wine in varying shades also stood on the sideboard in a kind of rack that would keep them from sliding off the polished surface should *Argus* roll or lurch.

"While I'm sure that fresh food is not yet a treat for you young gentlemen, I assure you, it will be soon enough. Since we are barely three days out, Harris has provided us with a fine repast which I hope will satisfy your palates, and your appetites. And he himself caught this splendid fish only this morning. Eat hearty, gentlemen!" Decatur smiled at all of us and, lifting his fork, signaled us to commence eating.

We all did so with vigor. The Cabin became quiet, the only sound that of utensils scraping on plates. It was Judd who broke the silence when, around a mouthful of fish, he addressed Decatur.

"Mister Wakefield mentioned this would be your *third* cruise to the Barbary Coast, sir. I knew you had been in Morris' squadron. Indeed, I myself was there last year with Commodore Morris, but I was unaware of a previous visit. Would you tell us about it?"

"There is not much to tell. I was first lieutenant in *Essex* with Captain Bainbridge, the very same commanding *Philadelphia* and Oliver's brother as we speak." I colored at being singled out, and Decatur continued without noticing. "Richard Dale was commodore, and we sailed from Hampton, Virginia, with the whole squadron in early June of the year one. We had the same kind of passage across I am hoping for this time, about thirty days and no trouble. And we found action at once; we had barely cleared Gibraltar when we stopped two Tripolitan corsairs from getting out into the Atlantic. I suspect we saved some American vessels from an unhappy experience by that!

"The commodore found through his sources that we were indeed at war with Tripoli. In fact, on May tenth, even before the squadron left the United States, the Pasha had cut down the flagpole bearing our flag that stood in front of the American consul's residence, clearly an act of war, according to Commodore Dale. He sent *Philadelphia*, she was under Captain Samuel Barron then, to cruise in the Straits and stop any Tripolitan cruisers he found. *Essex* convoyed the ship *Grand Turk* to Tunis, with whom the United States was, at that moment, at peace, and thence sailed to Europe to bring our merchants through the Straits. We did put in—or rather sailed off and on—near Tripoli, but there was no scrap as the corsairs were elsewhere.

"The only one of us to see any action was my friend Andrew Sterrett, who had the schooner *Enterprise* mounting twelve long guns. He managed to take one of the rascals after a three-hour fight at close quarters. The pirate actually surrendered three times before Captain Sterrett finally took him; each of the first two times that scoundrel struck, he attacked with renewed vigor as quickly as *Enterprise* ceased firing. Finally, according to David Porter, first lieutenant of *Enterprise,* the polacca was in such dire straits that the crew had no choice but to strike their colors once and for all. Sterrett lost not a man, but the pirate had quite a sizable butcher's bill; as I recall, it was fifty men killed or wounded, including their captain. I have often thought how wonderful it might have been had I been with Andrew that day. Oh! The action, and the glory!"

This last was uttered almost under his breath as if not meant for us to hear, and I noticed a curious glint in his eyes as he spoke, one that became more intense as he dreamed aloud of his own participation in the event. It would not be for some months that I discovered the reason.

"Shir . . . whaff's a *polacca*?" James asked around a mouthful.

"Young man, should you wish the captain, or anyone, for that matter, to understand you, I would suggest you swallow your food *before* you speak." Mister Wakefield looked at Stevens with a glance both bemused and stern. He received a muffled, but contrite, acknowledgement.

"A *polacca*, Mister Stevens, is a low slung vessel of seventy to one hundred tons which sports, generally, two masts, lateen rigged. Some of the smaller ones have but one mast, also lateen. In either case, they also have six to eight sweeps, oars, if you will, on a side which they frequently use when going to weather. They are equipped with up to six cannon, some as heavy as eighteen-pounders. You might also hear them called *polacres* as well. And they are crewed by as rum a bunch of cutthroats as most have ever seen, all dressed in white robes." Decatur looked at James and raised his eyebrows.

"Thank you, sir." Very clear and completely intelligible, this time.

The captain continued his tale.

"Where was I? Oh, yes, Sterrett's victory. Congress voted him a sword and his crew a month's extra pay." Decatur, the fire in his eyes now gone, smiled at the good fortune of his friend, while we midshipmen all thought of the glory and wonders of a month's pay.

"Did Captain Sterrett take the pirate's vessel, the *polacca*, as a prize, sir? There couldn't have been much left of her after the action you described." Devon had stopped eating and was riveted to the captain's tale.

"Oh, not on your life! President Jefferson wouldn't allow it. Our orders *then* were to disable the vessel so as not to allow it to commit further crimes against our own ships and to turn it and the crew loose. It wasn't until early in the next year that the Congress approved us taking prizes." Decatur, pleased with the question, looked for a moment at Judd, taking his measure, then spooned himself another portion of fresh vegetables.

"What about the other Barbary States, Captain? Did they interfere with the blockades of Tripoli or our ships there?" I had heard from some of the men aboard that, when an American ship-of-war appeared in the Mediterranean, the enemy could turn out to be Algiers, Tunis, Tripoli, or Morocco. Gunner Tarbox had told me they were "all a bunch of piratical bastards what can't even get along with each other, let alone any other country! If it ain't one of 'em goin' to war, it's another, by God."

"Most of the time, no, Oliver. We had established treaties, at some considerable expense, I might add, with all of them by 1800. Even Tripoli, for that matter. Difference was, the others all stuck with the treaties but the pasha of Tripoli thought he might get a better 'tribute' if he started again. And he did that by declaring war on the United States. I heard that the Bashaw actually told Captain Bainbridge that if he had no one with whom he was at war, he had no employment for his corsairs! To him, a clearly intolerable situation. And things were no better when we went back in the Fall of '02. I was in the *New York* frigate then under Captain James Barron."

"Whuff's a 'tribufe,' sir?" James had stopped eating long enough to mumble a question around a mouthful. After receiving a sharp look from Wakefield, he swallowed and repeated, clearly, "What's a 'tribute,' sir?"

Reliance Wakefield pounced on James' question before the captain could even draw a breath. "These scoundrels, all of them along the Barbary Coast, are so imbued with their own self-importance that the only way they will enter a treaty with another country is by payment of treasure to the pasha, or the Dey, or the Bashaw depending on which rascally one is at war. This treasure could be money, jewels, weapons, ships, or more likely, all of it. And how much depends on how many prisoners and ships the scoundrel holds of the unlucky nation seeking only to protect their trade in those waters. I happened to be witness to some negotiations with the Dey of Algiers in the late century and was astounded to learn that that overbearing . . . *person* actually demanded *and got* a frigate as part of his 'tribute' from the United States. Aye, indeed. Called *Crescent* it was, and a fine vessel to boot." He shook his head ruefully at the memory.

"Our esteemed surgeon has been abroad, as well, gentlemen, and he has a different approach to negotiations than do I. Would you not agree, Mister Wakefield?" Decatur barely glanced at the doctor, but I could see he was smiling as he asked the question.

"The difference is slight, Captain; I would only negotiate up to a point. Then I'd offer 'em *tribute* delivered from the working end of our twenty-four-pounders. Once I had their attention, I suspect the *negotiations* might go some different!" He paused, as if determining how far he might go. "Not like that mealy Morris. He'd likely give 'em anything they asked for just to avoid a fight! Fine way for a Navy captain to behave, you ask me!"

"Now, now, Reliance. Morris wasn't like that at all. I know he wanted to bombard Tripoli with the squadron late in '02, but that *mistral* blew in and kept us all off shore far enough that we might as well not have even been there. One of the hazards of the north coast of the African continent during the winter months. That wind blows right down from Europe and turns that coastline into a most dangerous lee shore. And even then we had no significant number of vessels of sufficiently shallow draft to get close enough to their fortifications to offer a proper *tribute*," he smiled as he intentionally used the surgeon's meaning. "That water along the harbor is nothing if it ain't shallow. Treacherous in places, it is."

Harris was now picking up our dishes and removing the scant remains of the lamb, fish, soup, and vegetables—to the dismay of our youngest diner. I think James would have continued to eat until he overflowed! He was quite obviously cured of his earlier bout of seasickness.

James' dismay was soon turned to joy as the white linen, now quite spotted with a veritable rainbow of colors, was removed and, with some fanfare, Harris stepped from the pantry with the biggest platter of duff I had ever seen. I glanced at James to see if he had begun again to drool, but while his eyes were alight at the prospect of sharing in this rare treat, his chin remained dry.

Several decanters of wine had been drunk, and the current decanter, only about halfway down, was removed, and a different one, dark and rich looking, took its place in front of the captain. Decatur began serving out the duff and handing the plates to Harris to place in front of each of us.

James, immediately his bowl was in place, grabbed up a spoon and began to consume his portion with great gusto.

"Ooof! Thomas, get your elbow outta my ribs!" James plaintive whisper carried nicely to both ends of the table, causing all of us to look at the young mid.

"If you showed some manners, and respect to the captain, I wouldn't have to nudge you, Jimmy. You're s'posed to wait 'til Cap'n Decatur eats before you climb like a fat little piggy into the trough!" Even in the Cabin, Thomas could not restrain his invective. His whisper, too, was louder than necessary and, I suspect, intentionally so.

"That's quite all right, James. Harris' duff is enough to make us all forget our manners. But I believe we're all ready to enjoy it now." Decatur smiled at Stevens who smiled eagerly back even as he again took up his spoon. Wheatley simply glared at his neighbor and then focused his attention on his own dessert.

"Mister Wheatley, you've certainly been quiet. Why don't you tell us about your experiences aboard the *Norfolk* brig. I would be interested in how you think she compares to our own *Argus*. You were out of Baltimore, were you not?"

"Yes, sir. *Norfolk* sailed out of Baltimore!" Wheatley laughed alone at his little joke and I realized, with a start, that my fellow midshipman had participated in the wine somewhat more than might have been propitious. "A sharp vessel, she was, and a fine sailor. Carried *long guns*, not carronades like some are being fitted out with these days. Ten six-pounders and four four-pounders she had. I would like to have seen her with bigger, but that's what they gave us. Didn't seem like she'd be much good in a fight with them little guns, but it never did signify anyway. Never fired 'em, 'ceptin' in practice. I s'pose we woulda just run away had there been the occasion to cross tacks with a Frenchie. Didn't seem like Cap'n Maxwell had much stomach for fightin.' Likely a good thing we never left the Bay and . . ." Wheatley stopped when he noticed the effect his little speech was having on the group. Decatur's eyebrows were up and a half smile played at his mouth. Lieutenant Cutler looked aghast. From what I could see of the surgeon's face, it bore the same expression I had seen when he spoke of the "piratical rascals of the Barbary Coast."

"Would that have been Captain Jack Maxwell with whom you served, Thomas?" The captain spoke in a flat tone, giving away nothing.

"Aye. Cap'n Jack Maxwell. Actually, a lieutenant he was while I was aboard the brig. Not much of a fightin' man, I collect. And probably the reason the Navy give him command of a vessel they knew wouldn't leave the Bay." Wheatley nodded and, after swallowing the remainder of his wine, spooned in another mouthful of duff.

"I collect you and Captain Maxwell didn't see eye to eye on things, Thomas. Did you ever speak with him about his employment previous to taking the *Norfolk* brig?" Again Decatur's tone gave nothing away.

"Oh, I never asked. And he wasn't much on invitin' his mids to dine with him. I'm not sure he would have cared much for my opinion, in the event. So, no. We wasn't encouraged to *share* our thoughts. Pretty much kept 'em in the cockpit or on deck away from the captain."

"Jack Maxwell's a good friend of mine. Mister Wakefield knows him as well. We were together on my first cruise against the Barbary Corsairs. Do you recall the mention I made of Andrew Sterrett and his *Enterprise*? Lieutenant Maxwell was in *Enterprise* with Sterrett. Contrary to what you may have been led to believe, Maxwell is a first-rate fighter. Fought like a badger, he did, with Sterrett in that action against the Tripolitan polacre. There was talk after *Norfolk* was scrapped last year that he was going to be assigned the *Syren*, but I guess Charlie Stewart got the nod over him. But don't assume that Jack Maxwell isn't a fighter because he drew a command that didn't see action. Besides, when you were in his ship, the United States was not in a declared war with anyone. And certainly not in our home waters." Decatur's tone had hardened noticeably. I took unrestrained pleasure in watching the expression on my colleague's face change from arrogant disdain to confusion and then, finally, to horror as the realization of his gaffe struck home.

Then Wakefield added, "And, young man, were I you, I would consider quite seriously holding my opinions within, especially when those opinions have to do with your superiors."

I was unable to discern Thomas' answer as it was mumbled around a mouthful of duff, but I suspect it might not have been as contrite as it should have been. Even though it would have pleased me to watch the captain's reaction to Wheatley's remark, it was apparent that he, like me, had not heard it. Cutler's face, however, darkened perceptibly, a clear indication that, though he said nothing, he surely heard whatever it was Thomas had said.

The conversation, what little there was time for as we savored our duff, remained trivial. Finally even James refused an additional helping, and Harris cleared away the wreckage. A decanter of Madeira appeared and was shared out to each of us. I noticed Captain Decatur and Lieutenant Cutler deep in conversation, but carried on in undertones and quite inaudible to me, across the table and one removed from them.

". . . from your brother before we sailed?" Mister Wakefield was studying me closely, I realized with a start, waiting for an answer. So intent on eavesdropping on the captain's conversation that I had quite missed what it was he had said.

"Excuse me, sir. I didn't hear all of that. Would you mind . . .?"

"I merely inquired as to whether or not you had heard from your brother before we sailed. Of course, a letter could not have reached Boston yet from Gibraltar, as I am sure they have only recently arrived there."

"Oh, sir. Yes, he did leave a letter for me with Captain Decatur, I collect you knew they were acquainted, which the captain was kind enough to give me shortly after I reported into *Argus*. I am hoping to see him in Gibraltar when we arrive. I s'pose it's possible—likely even—that they will already have sailed when we reach there. Perhaps he will have left a letter for me, should that turn out to be the case." Even as I spoke, I kept my ear cocked to pick up any morsel of the captain's conversation.

"Mister Baldwin, I suspect that, should Captain Decatur wish to include you in his conversation, he would have invited you to join him and Lieutenant Cutler in a glass." The surgeon's reproach caused me to color, and I could feel the heat rise up my neck. I quickly turned my eyes to meet his and saw the sparkle that belied his tone.

We chatted about Edward and my family in Philadelphia and sipped our Madeira. I noticed that the Cabin had become intolerably warm since we finished our meal and thought some fresh air might serve to clear my head, which, as the heat rose, had become a little muddled. I felt a trickle of moisture making its way down my cheek and brushed at it half-heartedly. My stomach suddenly seemed a little uncertain as well. Quickly I made to stand up, realizing as I did so that the room seemed to move in a way unrelated to the motion of *Argus*. I steadied myself with a hand on the edge of the table.

"Have you the watch, sir?" Wakefield questioned me.

A perfect excuse! How better to hide my discomfort. "Indeed, I do, sir. I just heard eight bells chime and should be on the quarterdeck even now." I stood all the way up, trying not to sway beyond that caused by the motion of the ship. I knew most of the blood had drained from my head and realized I must look poorly.

"You must ask the captain's permission, Oliver," the surgeon whispered at me as I steadied myself.

"Sir," said I. "Captain Decatur." He looked up from his conversation with the first lieutenant. "Excuse me, sir, but I must be on deck, er, the quarterdeck, sir. I think the next watch is mine, sir. Thank you for a splendid dinner, sir. May I be excused?" It sounded reasonable to me, and I missed the quizzical look from Decatur and the smiles from the good doctor and the lieutenant.

"Of course, Mister Baldwin. Wouldn't do at all to miss your watch. Punctuality is the hallmark of a good naval officer. Hurry along now." Decatur stood and smiled as I turned and took my departure. As I closed the door behind me, I caught a burst of laughter that was cut off as it began by the door.

Thankfully, I had only one ladder to navigate and emerged into the fresh air and daylight blinking and still quite unsteady. My stomach, apparently sensing that relief was close at hand, began to churn most disturbingly.

"About time you showed up, Mister Baldwin. Promptness to take a watch or a meal is one of the captain's . . ." Mister Hobbs stared at me over his spectacles and as he spoke, I realized that I needed to be close to the leeward bulwark. My stomach, having spent sufficient time merely churning, now lurched and heaved. My mouth was quite wet, causing me to swallow repeatedly. Without hearing another word Lieutenant Hobbs uttered, I fled to the rail and offered my splendid dinner to Davey Jones.

"Are you ill, Mister Baldwin?" Hobbs called to me as he witnessed my undignified behavior.

"No, sir. Just fine, now, sir. May I get myself some water, sir? And then I shall return to stand my watch." I hoped my voice sounded stronger to him than it did to me.

I walked as steadily as I could to the scuttlebutt amidships and ladled out a measure. Some I drank and some I spilled down my neck, which felt quite good. My head was clearing. Wiping my face on a sleeve as I returned aft, I smiled at the second lieutenant and assumed my position near the wheel, trying to look more competent than I felt.

"I would bet we're due for some weather, Mister Baldwin. The clouds seem to be filling in and the wind is moving toward the east. Likely won't be pleasant during the night watches." He paused, cast a glance aloft, and added quietly, "Or tomorrow, neither, for that matter."

I cast a look at the sky and noticed that the brilliant blue sky we had enjoyed for several days had turned white. Puffy gray clouds were superimposed here and there and seemed to be moving toward the sou'west at a considerable pace. I recalled the fiery sunrise and Mister Hobbs' comment that it foretold bad weather only that very morning.

Staring at the heavens made my head swim. I quickly looked down at the binnacle, trying to regain my balance. As I did so, I noticed the slate on which the quartermaster or the watch officer had written our speed and course at each turn of the glass. Our speed had been steadily increasing from the leisurely five knots around the noon hour to nearly ten knots at the last reading. Our course seemed to be more southerly than I recalled it had been earlier. I commented on it to Lieutenant Hobbs, hoping to distract myself from the dizziness and renewed churning in my belly, as well as impress him with my sharp seaman's eye.

"I just told you the wind was hauling to the east, Mister Baldwin, and rising. Of course we're making better speed and, on account of the barky being unable to sail *into* the wind, we must adjust our course to the south so as not to put ourselves in stays." He made no attempt to disguise any of the disdain he felt at having to explain such a basic fact of seamanship.

"Aye, sir. I should have figured that out for myself, sir." I stopped, chastised, and, hoping that doing so would not cause me further discomfort, looked aloft at the straining sails. We were still rigged to the t'gallants, and each was as taut as could be. The braces had been hauled around to allow the sails to catch the less-than-favorable breeze, and I could see that they and the sheets were pulled tight and shivering under the strain.

"Will we be shortening down, sir? Should I call out the watch?" I shifted my gaze to meet the watch officer's. Maybe *this* time he would think I had become more seamanlike.

"Not right away, I think. But I would reckon the captain will order some reduction within the next glass or two." Hobbs looked at me again with the same intensity that had met me when I returned from the leeward rail. "Are you quite all right, Oliver? You look some pale. You're not getting seasick, are you?"

"Oh, sir, no. I don't think it's that at all. Perhaps I ate too much at dinner with the captain and it's not sitting well. I shall be quite fine soon." *I hope*, I added silently.

"Drank too much is more likely, I'd think." Hobbs' comment was under his breath, but quite audible to me, standing directly in front of him as I was. Louder he added, "Perhaps you might like to take a position closer to the rail there." He motioned with his chin to leeward, and I thought it prudent to take his suggestion.

The remainder of the watch passed without incident or further offerings to the deeps. Before I was relieved by Thomas Wheatley, I thought I might be beginning to feel better again. It occurred to me that my relief was somewhat subdued when he appeared to take the watch, but it didn't signify immediately. There was none of the rancor in his voice when he announced himself, and, until I noticed his chin thrust forward, I had about convinced myself that he would be pleasant. In spite of my misgivings, he said nothing designed to anger or intimidate me. In fact, he said very little, save, "Thank you, Mister Baldwin; I relieve you."

I doffed my hat in a perfunctory salute and stepped to the break of the poop as I made my way to the hatch leading below, looking forward to crawling into my cot even though four bells had only just sounded, signaling 6 o' clock in the evening.

But it was not to be, at least not immediately.

My messmates greeted me at the door to the cockpit, each grinning from ear to ear; James, particularly, was fairly dancing with excitement about something. I had only to wait a moment before he grabbed my arm and, still grinning, poured forth a torrent of words at such a rate that I had trouble understanding what he was saying.

"Oliver! You missed it! You left before Mister Cutler and the captain each gave Thomas a full broadside!" James continued his dance of joy as he spoke and, while his words didn't seem to make much sense to me, I did notice that he was using naval terms, and correctly.

"Shortly after you left—were you feeling poorly, Oliver?—Wheatley asked Cutler to join him in a glass." Judd took over and began to relate the story more calmly. I simply nodded at his question.

"James and I, as well as the captain and Mister Wakefield, were still at table chatting quite amiably about not much of anything. Since I was sitting just to the other side of Cutler, I could hardly help but overhear their conversation. I think Thomas might have had a trifle more wine than he should have, and his voice carried some beyond Cutler's ears. He started out by saying, 'Perhaps, sir, were it not too bold of me, I might suggest some small changes in the gun crews on the gundeck carronades which might serve to improve our speed and accuracy, two elements I know both you and Captain Decatur hold dear to your hearts.' I saw he had Cutler's attention right off and, out of the corner of my eye, I caught the captain cock his head slightly so as to better hear the conversation." Judd smiled as he recalled the incident. "So Cutler looks this funny look at Thomas and nods his head, I guess telling him to go on."

James, having gained some measure of control over himself, jumped in and picked up Judd's story. "Thomas went on in some detail about how the changes he wanted would help his battery and, 'after all, was not the midship battery the most important in the ship?' so he should have Bradford and two or three others from *your* guns. I think he wanted one or more of my men also." In spite of this revelation, James continued to grin.

"Decatur, I reckon, heard all of this, likely including the part James didn't mention about how bad some of his gun crew was, especially one of the captains," Devon continued. "He stared at Wheatley with a look like none I ever saw before. Scared *me* a little, actually, and it wasn't even aimed at me. The silence was long, and I saw Thomas get a little red in the face, like he knew what was comin'! But he didn't, not by a long shot! None of us did.

"Captain Decatur stood up and leaned forward onto the table, so his face was close to Wheatley's. Looks him right in the eye and, almost *growling*, says, 'I will not countenance your denigration of the crews assigned to you for their poor performance. Your gun captains are among the more experienced in the ship and, with proper leadership, would easily exceed the performance of the other crews. I recommend, sir, that you look to yourself for the explanation of their less-than-acceptable cannonading.'

"Well, Oliver, I can tell you Wheatley was stunned, stunned as if he'd been knocked on the head with a belaying pin. He just sat there, getting redder and redder in the face. His mouth hung open and he started to sputter a little. Then Mister Wakefield leans across the table and says, real quiet-like, 'I would suggest, Mister Wheatley, there is little to say at this point. You had best keep your own counsel and go about your duties.' Thomas looks at him, his expression never changed, and stands up, turns about, and leaves the Cabin."

"Judd and I looked at each other . . ." James started out, and the senior midshipman interrupted him.

"And then you started to titter, like a little girl. It was all I could do to keep a serious face, but James, here, he didn't even try. Just busted out giggling and laughing and carrying on 'til Cutler says, 'I think you young gentlemen may be excused, now, to see to your duties.' We both stood, made our bows to the captain, and left. But what a show! Wouldn't have missed it for all the world! Reckon Wheatley's going to be some nicer, or perhaps he'll be even worse. But he sure ain't likely to offer any more suggestions to the first lieutenant!"

I smiled at my messmate's misfortune, feeling better just from hearing about his encounter with our two most senior officers, either of whom had the ability to end his career with a word. And I suddenly understood Wheatley's subdued behavior as he took over the watch a few moments earlier.

My general lack of goodwill for Thomas Wheatley overshadowed my fleeting guilt at enjoying the suffering of another. I uttered some words of restrained joy at our good, and Wheatley's ill, fortune as I made my way to my cot.

CHAPTER SEVEN

"Mister Baldwin! Mister Baldwin, sir! Wake up! They've called out all hands and yer wanted on the quarterdeck." It was late into the middle watch when I was roused from my dreamless sleep by a seaman sent by the watch officer. As I swam up through the depths of my slumber to consciousness, I became aware that the attitude of the ship was different than it had been; the cot was swaying back and forth quite vigorously and, when I set foot upon the deck, I discovered that standing upright was impossible. *Argus* was heeled over to a degree that had me reaching for a handhold as I struggled one-handed into my clothes. After completely losing my balance as the ship shuddered violently several times, I finished dressing and staggered out of the cockpit to the ladder. Already I could hear sounds of men shouting, feet pounding, and the louder sounds of the ship herself, groaning of the rig, creaks and squeals as lines ran through blocks and fairleads, and the banging of a line or block as a sail was adjusted. They were sounds to which I had become so accustomed in the days we had been underway that I barely acknowledged them. Now they demanded notice. This cacophony was set in counterpoint to another symphony, one which I had never before heard, a roaring quite unearthly and ferocious in its intensity. Even from where I stood, hanging on to the ladder, it seemed to overwhelm my senses.

As I started up the final ladder to the spar deck, a gout of water cascaded down on me, soaking me quite to the skin and bringing me, with startling suddenness, to a state of full wakefulness. With a new clarity of mind, I grasped quickly that we were either sinking or were about to. In some distant part of my brain I wondered why I had not been awakened sooner. With mounting horror at what surely must be a dreadful finish to my naval career, I renewed my efforts at ascending the ladder. At least if I could get myself topside, I should not perish unseen and unheard in the bowels of the ship.

On deck, I saw quickly that we were not about to sink, at least not yet. Rain lashed at me with stinging force; the wind threatened to blow me right over. Salt water swirled around my feet and flew through the air, thrown up by waves that rolled *Argus* down with each new onslaught. I barely had time to take it all in before I felt a strong hand grip my right arm and turned to see Lieutenant Hobbs, hatless, his tarpaulin coat soaked, hair plastered down to his forehead, and water streaming off his cheeks and nose. He thrust his face close to mine, and I noticed that, for the first time since I had known him, he wore no glasses.

"Get aloft on the foremast with your men, Baldwin, and get the forecourse off her. Then see to short reefing the tops'l." Hobbs, though only inches from my face, had to shout the words to be heard over the high baritone scream of the wind. Wind, that not only drowned out his words, tearing them away so that I caught only some of them, but tugged and whipped our clothing and, indeed, our very beings, threatening to carry us away.

The thought of climbing into the rigging and then onto a yard, while the ship lurched and the seas rolled her onto her beam ends and the wind tried with all its considerable might to rip my hands from the shrouds and my feet from the ratlines, struck me numb with fear. I stood, rooted to the deck and quite unable to direct my feet to carry out Hobbs' order.

The rain stung my face, each drop the size of a teacup but felt like sand as it struck me. I half expected to find blood on my hand when I wiped it across my eyes. The rain mixed with the salt spray as it ran down my cheeks and into my mouth, giving it a curiously brackish taste rather than the sweet, fresh taste I had always associated with a heavenly offering.

"Get a move on, Baldwin. Don't think about it, just get it done. Half your men are already up there. You don't get that sail off'n her, we'll blow it out for sure!" Hobbs screamed into my ear, all the while propelling me forward with a strong grip. He left me to make my way to the weather foreshrouds with a final shouted admonition, ". . . hand . . . lifeline . . . careful." The wind took most of what he said, but I assumed he had cautioned me to hold on to the lifeline recently rigged fore and aft for the full length of the ship. He would not have to worry about me carrying out *that* order!

As I made my way slowly and carefully forward, I took stock of the conditions surrounding me. To wind'ard, the seas reached high over my head; even in the blackness of the night, I could make out the ghostly spume and foam writhing at the tops of their towering crests as they roared down on us, sending torrents of water crashing onto the deck as one after another met the resistance of *Argus'* strong oak hull. Water swirled as high as my knees before it ran off astern to leeward and was quickly replaced by more as wave after wave hammered us. The ship rolled with each one, sometimes as far down as to dip her main yard in a retreating sea, then struggled back up to where only her leeward bulwark touched the water. Each time, she shook herself and staggered onward. Some of the waves merely washed under us, heaving the vessel upward with a suddenness that caused my stomach to lurch, then dropping her, heeled unnaturally back to windward, with equal force and precipitousness. Part of my brain idly wondered how long the brig could stand this punishment. A further thought about *our* surviving the wrath of Nature flickered into my consciousness, and I pushed it away, not wishing to dwell on such a horror.

As my hand felt the rough hemp of the foreshrouds, I released my grip on the lifeline and clung with both hands to the thick, tarred rope. A wave broke over the bulwark, and, for a moment, I was sure its fury would tear my grip loose. I was underwater, gasping and sputtering, feet off the deck, but hanging on with both hands for dear life. After what seemed an hour, the water passed on. I struggled to regain my footing and, finding a brief lull in our pounding, stepped onto the bulwark and then into the ratlines. Still with a death grip on the shrouds, I was able to take a breath only when I turned my head away from the force of the wind-lashed rain and spume.

It occurred to me as I climbed that someone had made a poor choice in naming this part of the rigging after something so closely associated with death. *Shrouds, indeed! Not good, thinking that way. Keep climbing and hold tight!* After perhaps ten or fifteen laborious steps, I realized that the waves were no longer breaking over me and the wind was, in fact, pressing me into the ratlines rather than trying to tear me out of them. I increased my pace and quickly reached the fighting top where some six of my division were waiting to move out on the yard; another half-dozen were already on the yard, their feet swaying drunkenly in the footropes as we, the mast, the yard, and the fighting top traced wild arcs through the rain-drenched, wind-riven night sky.

Faintly, and likely only because of its higher pitch, I heard Bosun Anderson's whistle from the deck. It was the signal to clew up the straining canvas of the forecourse.

"Get ready, men. They're hauling up the clews." I screamed at the sailors clinging to the yard over the big sail. The yard was braced around, barely adding to the motion. With a thunderclap, the course began to shiver, then flog itself as the wind caught the windward edge no longer held taut by the bowline. At the same time, the men on deck began to heave around on the clewlines, dragging the corners of the sail up toward the center of the yard. I could picture those poor souls on deck, straining at their task, soaked to the skin under the deluge of water, both salt and fresh, cascading over them as they struggled desperately to keep their footing and, through sheer strength, haul up the wildly thrashing sail. But my task, and that of my men, was up here, and I strained to make out what was acting with them.

The sailors on the yard, each with an arm through a becket and their feet on the wildly swinging footropes, grabbed handfuls of wet canvas, trying to contain the sail between their bellies and the stout spar. It was a slow and torturous task; each time they made some progress, a particularly vicious gust would rip away the canvas already gained, and slowly, laboriously, the men would struggle to recapture the sail.

Eventually it was done. The men worked their way in from the yard, inching slowly along the footropes until they reached the relative safety of the top. With my heart in my mouth, I saw the last man to come off the yard, Welch, I think it was, lose his footing just as he made for the platform of the fighting top. It was only through his own instinctive grab at the rail and the quick thinking of the captain of the foretop, who caught at Welch's jacket and, with the help of two others, hauled him up to the platform, that he was not cast into the sea. It would have been certain death had he fallen.

I noticed, when I had regained my composure after that near accident, that *Argus* seemed to be moving less violently. I glanced aft at the mainmast, through the pelting rain and stygian blackness, and I was able to make out the main course furled to its spar. The men were moving further aloft to reef the topsail. I remembered that Lieutenant Hobbs had wanted not only the course furled but also the tops'l short-reefed, and I shouted through the wind to my sailors, barely a foot away from me.

"We've got to reef the tops'l. Lieutenant Hobbs . . ." The wind blew away my words and, in my effort at making myself heard, my voice cracked. This was no time for embarrassment and I screamed my orders once more. The captain of the top nodded at me, at least I think he did, and motioned his men up to the next yard. Again, faintly I heard Anderson's whistle and saw the tops'l yard move as it was hauled around to spill some of its wind, then was lowered slowly. The sailors repeated their performance, but only to the extent of gathering in the sail to the lowest reef points, and then it was done. The yard was braced around again, and *Argus*, her heel less and her motion through the seas easier, careered through the night. The foretop crew and I descended to the deck; the maelstrom of sea and rain there seemed only slightly diminished. On deck, I noticed that many of my sailors had suffered some considerable damage to their hands in our, *their*, struggle with the wet, flogging canvas; several had lost fingernails, while most of the others wiped blood from knuckles, fingers, and forearms.

As I made my way slowly, hand over hand on the lifeline, aft toward the quarterdeck, I made out a dim shape in the lee of the cutter, which was securely lashed to the booms. Stretching one arm out while the other held tightly to the lifeline, my hand almost reached the boat's lashings. Timing my move with the ship's roll, I cast off the security of the safety line and plunged headlong a few feet to crash into the side of the upturned cutter.

"What are you doing here? Are you hurt?" Putting my face close to the man, I peered through the blackness and pelting rain at the form huddled by the boat's stern, his arms hooked through the after lashings. The man's face turned up to me. I made out the angular lines and thrusting jaw of Thomas Wheatley. His eyes were wide, and I noticed that I saw mostly their whites as he stared at me. Like everyone else who was topside, he was soaked; his face streamed water and his oiled tarpaulin jacket seemed to offer little protection from either the driving horizontal rain or the waves that sent seawater swirling around the deck.

"We're . . . die . . . know it. Nothing . . . live through this . . . I . . . just a . . . time . . ." His soaked hair was plastered to his head and, where it fell across his face, offered a strange sight indeed. Had our circumstances been different, I would surely have laughed, or at least smiled, at this apparition. The wind snatched the words from his mouth.

"I'll help you to the lifeline. Give me your hand!" I screamed into his face and reached out one hand to take ahold of his arm.

"Get away . . . nothing . . . us." The arm jerked back, and he clutched even more tightly to the rope lashings. He seemed, as near as I could make out through the elements, to shrink down even further. He was resolute in his determination to remain where he was, or at least to maintain his death grip on the cutter's lashings. I left him cowering and, pushing off from the side of the boat, made a successful grab for the lifeline and followed it to the quarterdeck.

I discovered a knot of forms—impossible to determine officer or seaman through the rain-lashed darkness—on the quarterdeck and made my uncertain way carefully toward them.

Near the wheel, attended by four strong quartermasters who struggled in a fierce battle with the seas to maintain control of *Argus*, I could make out, in the flickering glow of the binnacle box, another cluster of forms: Captain Decatur, Lieutenant Cutler, Lieutenant Morris, and Judd Devon. Sheltering behind them, in the limited lee offered by his superiors, was Midshipman James Stevens, equally wet and disheveled despite his efforts at avoiding the fury of the storm. I stepped, or more accurately, staggered, up to the group.

"I'd warrant . . . first . . . at sea. This . . . up . . . suddenly. Wind . . . stronger." Cutler shouted into my face as I got close to him. " . . . job get . . . sail off her. She's . . . easier."

I had little idea of just what he was telling me, but nodded in his direction, hoping he could see me through the rain. James poked his head out around Judd's side and looked at me, his eyes wide, and I noticed that the hand that hung onto the quarterdeck railing was trembling. Though he certainly must have been as cold and miserable as I, it occurred to me that the tremor in his hand was more a manifestation of fear than the climate; I didn't know if the others were afraid, but I certainly was, so I assumed James was also. *But at least we weren't cowering in the lee of the boat,* I thought with some satisfaction.

Captain Decatur pointed aloft and had his face close to the first lieutenant's. I followed his outstretched arm and made out, through the rain and darkness, the main tops'l, reefed close as it was, straining at its buntlines, which stretched across the belly of the sail. As I watched, the wind'ard edge of the sail curled inward, sending a quick shiver through the sail.

"Wind . . . coming 'round more. Bring . . . down . . . point. Can't lose . . . sail," Decatur shouted. The four men on the wheel forced the ship's head off and away from the wind. The main tops'l filled with a *crack* that resounded even over the screaming whine of the wind. Then Decatur grabbed Cutler's arm and pointed below. He motioned to the rest of us to follow.

In turn, we each made our way, save for Lieutenant Morris who had the watch, down the scuttle and into the sudden stillness of the passageway outside the Cabin. Stillness is, perhaps, overstating the conditions; the deck under our feet still heaved and rolled, the creaks and groans of the ship and her rigging persisted, and the screaming of the wind, though reduced to a more manageable roar, continued to fill our senses.. But the rain did not follow us below, and, in the light of a swinging lantern hung from the bulkhead, I could make out the faces and features of my fellows. Water streamed off our clothes and limbs, pooling on the deck below our feet before running off into one or another corner with each roll of the ship.

"This come on so sudden we're some lucky we didn't lose a sail or worse, part of the rig. You gentlemen were valiant in your efforts at shortening down. Likely saved us from gettin' cruel hurt. And I thank you. But, I suspect, this is a long way from over; the way the wind is moving to the east and south makes me think we'll be in for it for a while, well into the morning, at any rate. Should it get much worse, we may have to run off before it, but I hate to give up the distance we've made to weather that would cost us. At least now, we're still more or less heading toward Gibraltar, even though I've had to bring her off in a more southerly direction than I would normally wish." Decatur seemed more concerned about being late at Gibraltar than about the dangers of the storm. He smiled in the dim glow of the lantern that cast grotesque moving shadows over us and the passageway as the ship rolled and bucked.

"*Argus* is well-found, strong, and solid," he continued. "Long as we manage her well, she'll stand up to this. Most of the men, now, have found their sea-legs, as, I assume, have you young gentlemen." The captain broadened his smile encouragingly; his glance seemed to linger a touch longer on Judd and myself. I certainly took some heart from his own confidence. Judd Devon nodded, his concerned look still in place. James, still wide-eyed with fear, clung to the rail of the ladder we had just descended behind the captain. Even in the yellow glow of the lantern, I saw he was quite pale. I knew that my earlier diagnosis of the tremor in his hand had been correct. I imagined that I myself might look a trifle pale, maybe even wide-eyed, as well.

"What about these huge seas, sir? Seems we're takin' a fair amount of water aboard." Judd spoke for the first time, saying what was on all our minds; certainly it was on mine.

"Mister Hobbs is, as we speak, with the carpenter sounding the well. I expect I should have his report in due course. In the meantime, we will continue as hard on it as we can and hope that the wind moves no farther to the south. And keep your men, those that aren't necessary to manage the ship, off the deck. No sense in unnecessarily losing a man overboard. You may return to your duties, or cots."

'*Unnecessarily?*' *When is it necessary?* The thought flashed unbidden through my confused brain, but I held my tongue. I turned to step to the next ladder which would take me to the cockpit, following close astern of Judd.

"Mister Baldwin, have you, perchance, seen your colleague about the deck, or below, in the cockpit?" Lieutenant Cutler stopped me short with his question.

He could only be talking about Thomas; Judd and James had been quite visible during our time on deck and after. The words sprang to my lips telling him of the circumstances under which I had seen Wheatley, and then I stopped, turning to face him. "No, sir. When I came topside, Lieutenant Hobbs sent me straight away to the foretop and then I came aft to the quarterdeck. I didn't notice whether he was in the cockpit when I left. I certainly hope nothing unto-ward has happened to him." *How easily that lie rolled off my tongue!*

"Very well. You may get what little sleep you might before you take the watch." Cutler turned, more suddenly than I thought he meant to when the ship took a particularly violent lurch and roll, and started up the ladder. I, with-out a look backward, started down the other, trying to understand what it was that had made me answer his question as I did.

By the time I returned to the quarterdeck, the wind, if anything, was stronger. *Argus*, stripped down to a pair of close reefed tops'ls and a forestays'l, fairly flew, flinging seas into the air to be blown back aboard by the tempest before they could return to their rightful place. The rain seemed to have eased a trifle, at least it no longer stung when I turned my face to the wind. The air was very nearly as wet as it had been, but much saltier. A glance at the binnacle told me the wind had continued to veer farther past east into the southeast and the ship was heading now in the wrong direction, in fact, *away* from Gibraltar.

Even I could see that eventually we would have to tack, a prospect that held a specter of dread. Bringing the ship head-to-wind, head-to-seas under these conditions was perilous, holding the potential for being caught in stays and then overpowered by the wind and sea. Lieutenant Hobbs voiced my thoughts.

"Mister Baldwin, it is apparent that we will have to tack the barky. Step below, if you please, and fetch Captain Decatur. Messenger, roust out the hands and ask the bosun and sailing master to step aft." Hobbs, bedraggled and soaked from his exposure to the elements, looked to me some concerned; his brow fur-rowed and, even in his giving orders to me and the messenger, he seemed dis-tant, preoccupied. His glance shifted, squinty-eyed from the effort to see with-out his spectacles, between the compass, bathed in the flickering yellow glow of the binnacle lantern, to the main tops'l. *If he is concerned, then I reckon it's proper that I should be scared.* I left him and made my way to the scuttle.

My knock was answered immediately; I doubt the captain had been asleep.

"Mister Hobbs' compliments, sir. He sent me to tell you he feels the ship should be tacked as the wind has veered farther to the south." I was conscious of the puddle I was making on the Cabin deck as I stood as much at attention as the motion of the ship permitted.

"Thank you, Mister Baldwin. What course are we making now?" He had sat up immediately on my entrance and now looked at my sodden countenance with alert eyes, his brain obviously fully awake.

"South sou'west, a quarter west, sir. When she steadies on anything."

"Very well, then. Please convey to Mister Hobbs that I shall be on deck directly. I collect he has called out the hands?"

"Aye, sir; he has. Only just a moment ago the messenger was sent to fetch the men as well as Bosun Anderson and Mister Church."

The captain had pulled on his boots and was shrugging into his still wet coat as I took my departure. He appeared behind me on deck only a moment after I had reported back to Mister Hobbs.

I could make out little of the detail, but I knew Decatur would be studying the set of the scant sail we carried, taking in as much as he could see through the darkness and spray. Then he peered at the compass and, as the glow of the light in the binnacle glanced off his face, I saw a frown form followed by a shake of his head. Decatur, still frowning, stepped away from the binnacle box and made his way to the taffrail at the stern. I could see him standing there, his back to the ship, pondering; his legs were spread against the cant of the deck, and his hands rested on the taffrail. Indistinct forms began to appear forward, seeking what shelter could be found from the elements. Mister Church materialized out of the night and approached Mister Hobbs.

"Time to tack, sir? The men are about all rousted out. Mister Anderson is with 'em amidships." Church shouted into the wind and I made out an acknowledging nod from the second lieutenant.

"No, Mister Church. Mister Hobbs, I believe we shall wear and then head-reach to the nor'east. At least that will move us, slowly to be sure, but move us indeed in a direction more suitable to our needs." Captain Decatur, back from his taffrail ruminations, had made his decision. Though I had no idea what *headreaching* meant, I was sure that even in his zeal to reach Gibraltar as fast as ever possible, he would do nothing to endanger either his ship or his crew.

"STATIONS FOR WEARING SHIP! STEP LIVELY, YOU MEN!" Church's bellow caught me unawares, and I started visibly.

"Mister Hobbs, what is *headreaching*, sir? And what would you want me to do?" I raised my voice enough to be heard by the second lieutenant but, I hoped, not by the captain. It wouldn't do, I thought, to trumpet my short-comings to him!

"Soon enough you'll find out, Oliver. Let us get the barky worn around first and then we'll take the next step." He turned forward again and shouted at the retreating back of our sailing master. "When you're ready, Mister Church. We will bear off first."

Shouted commands, fragmented by the wind, drifted aft. I could hear orders being issued which included "braces" and knew Church would have men stationed at the lee and weather braces to haul the tops'l yards, fore and main, around as the ship turned to bring the wind, and seas, more aft. For a short while, we would be running off before the tempest, then hauling the yards around to bring the wind on the other side so as to head in a more northerly direction.

And that is exactly what Mister Hobbs did; *Argus* fell off, sailing large with the wind blowing over the stern. As she did so, the waves began to come from aft of the beam, first rolling her down so as to dip the mainyard into the sea and later, lifting the stern as they swept down from behind us and rolled on, leaving the brig wallowing momentarily in a trough. Then the next wave would sweep down and the motion would repeat.

"Mister Church, I think preventer braces on the foretops'l yard would be in order." Decatur bellowed forward and a faint "Aye" acknowledged his instruction.

"There will be a sudden and violent strain on the yard when we cross the wind, Oliver. The preventers the captain just ordered will take up the shock and, with luck, save the yard from breaking or parting its tyes or parrel." Hobbs, his eyes never leaving the hands amidships who were rigging the preventers, shouted his explanation of the captain's orders in my direction. "Go and have a look, if you will, and see they're getting it right. And clap on to the lifeline. We'll be wearing in a moment."

A glance at the monstrous waves rolling down on us from astern, their tops foaming white as they crested, then tumbling down into the darkness, quickly overcame my natural reluctance to leave the quarterdeck and the relatively safe haven it offered. Even though I was quite certain that Mister Hobbs was making sport of my insufficient knowledge, here was another opportunity to expand on what Bosun Anderson had already taught me.

I took hold of the safety line and carefully, slowly, made my way to the waist where the men, under Anderson's supervision, had rigged additional lines to the foretops'l braces and were just now setting them up. The ship, even though alternately lifting her stern then bow to the action of the waves, was drier here than before; seas were not breaking over us and sending great gouts of green water down the deck. I suspected the men welcomed the change.

"READY, SIR!" Church shouted aft and waved his arm, likely unseen by Hobbs. But he had been heard and almost immediately came Hobbs' voice back, suddenly loud, carried forward by the wind.

"Helm is up. Stand to your braces!" *Argus* moved slowly to take the seas and the wind on her opposite quarter.

With a great crash, the tops'ls were shifted, their yards braced around, and *Argus* sailed off before the storm on the other tack. Now all we had to do was *headreach* to the nor'east. I made my way back to the quarterdeck, noticing the orange cast on the horizon to the east, a harbinger of the new day and, apparently, a continuation of the same devilish weather.

" . . . have the main stays'l set as we bear up. Move smartly; I am loath to make this westering any longer than necessary. We are giving up much of what we gained to the east last night." Decatur was issuing further orders to Hobbs and Chase, who had somehow beat me back to the quarterdeck.

Orders rang out, carried forward easily by the wind, and men clambered into the rigging to set the stays'l Decatur wanted. The helmsmen, under the guidance of Lieutenant Hobbs, began to ease the bow of the ship closer and closer to the eye of the wind. The nearly exhausted men amidships adjusted our well-reefed canvas and the yards to keep the sails drawing. *Argus* became, once again, close-hauled on a nor'easterly heading, just as the captain had predicted she would. I learned that this, sailing close-hauled under severely shortened sail in a storm, was *headreaching*. While not making a great deal of progress forward, we rode more easily, drier, and were in less danger of being overcome by the elements. Had we hove to, we would have made no progress at all, clearly an unacceptable option to our most determined captain.

As the day brightened, and the sky become visible, so also did the seas and the clouds racing across the slate heavens. Great black, puffy clouds they were, with their edges shredded by the gale. Lightning streaked from one to another now, something we had not seen during the night. But the seas in the increasing daylight were even more awful and terrifying to behold.

Huge, towering waves bore down on us from the weather bow, the wind blowing their tops asunder and leaving white trails of spume on the surface of each one. Spray filled the air and stung the eyes. Every so often, a particularly large wave, some looked as high as our main yard, would crash against the wind'ard bow and spend itself, dumping a great deluge of water down the length of our deck. Others would roll us onto our beam-ends, making *Argus* stagger and shake herself as she fought to regain her proper attitude. I thought *not* seeing these waves and the effects of the gale on the water's surface was less troubling. Would that it were still dark!

But, we managed to survive and actually made some progress, scant though it was, toward our destination. Though the galley fires had been extinguished by the storm and the men were forced to eat cold food, all hands performed admirably, according to both Captain Decatur and Mister Cutler. By nightfall, the wind had diminished, and an easier sea soon followed. A brilliant sunset, with streaks of red and orange, gold, yellow and purple, turned the sea into a garish and gaudy artist's palette with hues that, Lieutenant Morris assured me, bespoke a fine day on the morrow. The galley fires were relit, the men given an extra tot of whiskey, and, as the wind blew fresh and clean from the southwest over our starboard quarter, the *Argus* brig flew through the diminishing seas toward Gibraltar, to the unmitigated joy of our captain.

CHAPTER EIGHT

" Land! Land ho! Fine on the larboard bow! Deck there, land on the larboard bow!" The lookout's cry brought most of the hands and all of the midshipmen not already there to the deck. Some, myself included, leaped into the rigging to catch a first glimpse of what we hoped was Gibraltar. From the fighting top of the foremast, I squinted into the sun, still low on the horizon as the morning watch took the deck, and made out a faint smudge, darker than the sea and the sky, separating the two. Our joy and excitement knew no bounds; even some of the older more experienced hands had trouble hiding their delight at reaching our destination.

But we had not; the land, I discovered when I returned to the quarterdeck, proved to be the coast of Spain just south of Cape St. Vincent. It would be necessary to sail another several hundred miles southeast along the coast to Gibraltar, which we did in a fine fair breeze under brilliant, deep blue skies, finally passing through that most famous narrows and into the harbor there on All Saints Day, the first of November, 1803, some five weeks after departing Boston.

The harbor on the west side of that distinctive peninsula was bustling; ships, most showing the British ensign, swung to anchors while long boats, cutters, and yawls stroked to and fro between the quay wall and the ships. As we rounded up, searching for both an American flag and a place to set our anchor, we fired a salute which was promptly and noisily answered by a British two-decker anchored just off the quay.

"You know, Mister Baldwin, Gibraltar has not always been a British possession; it was, as recently as the last century, owned by the Kingdom of Spain. It only became British by the Treaty of Utrecht. Of course, after thinking on it for some considerable years, Spain tried to take it back by force of arms, once in the 1720s and again in the late 1770s. They were unsuccessful both times, and Britain remains still the undisputed owner of the Rock. We Americans are here only through their forbearance." Decatur spoke, peering intently through a long glass as he searched the assembled vessels for any he recognized. Lieutenant Morris held the deck and stood by the helm, guiding the brig through the anchorage. I was on the quarterdeck, and at the captain's side, by virtue of now being Morris' junior watch officer. Our rigging was alive with sailors ready to hand the sails on orders from Mister Church as we prepared to come to our anchor.

"Can you make out *Constitution*, Cap'n?" Morris also studied the fleet, but without the aid of a glass. For myself, I wondered whether he could identify *Philadelphia*. I longed to see my brother and share with him the adventures I had experienced on my "course to manhood" and see whether or not he would opine that I had "given nothing to leeward" as Lieutenant Cutler had instructed.

"No, Mister Morris, I can not. An easier vessel to spot I could not imagine, but she does not appear to be in." Decatur paused, making another swing of the glass through the harbor and, as if reading my mind, added, "Nor does Bainbridge. I can make the schooner *Enterprise* and a few of the other smaller vessels . . . in fact, I believe I see Charlie Stewart's *Syren*, just there." He stretched out his arm, pointing, and muttered something under his breath. I didn't catch all of it, but Decatur's tone sounded as if the captain was disappointed or angry that his friend Charles Stewart had beaten us across the sea. Oh! how that man longed to get his ship into the action!

My own disappointment knew no bounds. I had rehearsed in my mind greeting Edward in proper naval tradition before even we were halfway here, and now, *Philadelphia* was not to be seen. I would have to settle for a letter left for me and my hopes rose on that happy thought. *Would that he had!*

Barely had we set our best bower into the sandy bottom of Gibraltar's harbor when a boat put out from the nearby *Enterprise* bearing none other than her captain, Lieutenant Isaac Hull. After being welcomed aboard with due pomp and ceremony, he and Decatur disappeared to the Cabin to be joined by our first lieutenant as quickly as he had got the ship put to rights. The midshipmen discussed in some detail what the meeting would offer, to us, mainly, and debated at some length what *Argus* would be doing over the next several months.

"I don't need to guess; I *know* what we'll be doin' quick as the ship gets set aright, and we get more food an' such aboard." Wheatley's smug expression of certainty stopped our conjecture dead in its tracks. We all turned to him expectantly. James asked the question Tom was awaiting, like a cat watching a bird get closer and closer, and, like the cat, he pounced on young James.

"What do you think, stupid? We're gonna go kill pirates. We're gonna be sent to Tripoli, and *Argus* is gonna pound them rascals into matchwood, them what we don't take as prizes, that is." He smiled, daring Stevens, or any of us, to contradict him. I had noticed a gradual decline in Wheatley's effort at speaking properly, and the unvarnished Thomas seemed to show through more and more.

"That's certainly a safe bet, Tom. I believe that's why we're here in the first place. Doesn't take a gypsy to figure out that sending *Argus,* and us, after almost daily gun drills all the way across, to some friendly port, there to partake of the pleasures offered, would answer at all." Judd's tone was friendly enough, but the slow shake of his head told more eloquently how he felt about Thomas' prediction. "It's my bet that Preble either has, or will soon, throw up a blockade across Tripoli's harbor. Whether or not we go in and 'pound them rascals into matchwood' will depend on the success of a blockade. 'Sides, *Argus* is one of the few vessels shallow enough to get into the thin water close to shore, where we can do some good."

I noticed James break into a grin as he added, albeit quietly, "And Judd's been here before. 'At's more'n you can say, Mister Know-it-all!"

Wheatley's jaw assumed its forward thrust as he acknowledged James' comment with barely a glance, then scowled at Devon. "You remember I tol' you all I could 'read' people and know what's actin' with 'em? Well, this is one o' them times. I watched Decatur with that lieutenant what come aboard a while ago and managed to catch a few words of what they was sayin' afore they got into the Cabin. And I know I'm right 'bout this. You mark my words!"

"Tom, why don't we wait 'til Cap'n Decatur comes out of his meeting with Cap'n Hull? Like as not, he'll let us know what the future holds for *Argus* and all of us." I offered my thought with as pleasant a tone as I could manage.

"Well, Oliver, I guess we ain't got a choice, now do we? So I reckon we're stuck with doin' just that; but you," and here he looked at each of us for a moment before continuing, "wait and see if'n I ain't right on the mark on this." And he stood, turned and left the cockpit without a further word.

"What's acting between you and Wheatley, Oliver? Seems like the last few weeks, he ain't once come after you the way he does Judd and me. You two aren't becoming friends, are you?" James grinned at his joke, and I caught a smiling Judd nodding in agreement as he spoke.

"I surely haven't an idea, James. But you're quite right; he has been more than civil to me for quite a while. Almost friendly, in fact. I really hadn't taken notice of it 'til you mentioned it now, but as I think on it, he has been laying off me for some time." James' comment made me think back on what might have caused the shift in Wheatley's attitude toward me and not either of the other two. *Unlikely it is*, I thought, *that he might have decided that we should be friends; and if it is so, why me and not the other two?* I pondered the question while James and Judd discussed Wheatley and the assignment *Argus* might draw when the Commodore returned. Then it struck me.

It was several days after I had found him hiding behind the cutter during that frightful storm that he changed the way he treated me. While I hadn't said a word to anyone, and had even lied to Lieutenant Cutler about his where-abouts during the storm, Tom didn't know that, or that I wouldn't. He must think that by not picking on me he could ensure my silence. That had to be it! He was ashamed of his behavior and *afraid* of me, or rather what I knew and what I might say! *There* was a twist; a bully afraid of me, the butt of pranks from people like him most of my life. I was sure he had figured out that, at least 'til then, I had not spoken of his cowardly behavior.

My father had drummed into my head that being a tattle would do me no good at all, rather only serve to antagonize those who might make my life mis-erable. I struggled to remember this advice when, shortly after the weather calmed, I heard Tom tell any in earshot of his heroic efforts on the main yard. That, after he heard Lieutenant Hobbs mention to the first lieutenant my own role in shortening sail that night. When first I heard Wheatley telling this tale, I was stunned; surely he . . . well, I guess he *did* expect any who heard to believe him. It was so dark and impossible to see anything that night, who might say otherwise? And the maintop was, indeed, his station. If his lack of animosity toward me was the result of my silence, well, so be it. I hadn't planned on mentioning it in any case. But, by the time we had set our anchor in Gibraltar, the final ember of goodwill that might have flickered in my breast for Thomas Wheatley had been extinguished, and I felt nothing but enmity toward him. While I would go nary a step out of my way to court his friendship, neither would I speak ill of him; it seemed quite fruitless. Whenever possible, I simply ignored him.

The mid-day ritual of 'spirits up' was just being piped when Harris, the captain's steward, poked his head into the cockpit and announced that all officers and midshipmen were wanted in the Cabin, if you please, sirs, and the cap'n would brook no delays. The three us of stood at once and made our way up and aft, as bidden.

"Harris, you might want to have a look topside for Mister Wheatley. No telling where he might have got to, but he should be told." Judd suggested to the sailor before he withdrew from our quarters. Harris nodded, knuckled his forehead, and left, presumably in search of the missing mid.

"And where is Mister Wheatley?" Captain Decatur asked no one in particular after we all, save Thomas, had pressed into his Great Cabin. The silence was complete 'til, feeling a responsibility to speak for his messmate, Judd responded.

"Sir, he was not in the cockpit when Harris fetched us here. If you like, I would be pleased to have a look for him."

"That won't be necessary, Mister Devon. Harris, did you look anywhere beside the cockpit for Mister Wheatley? Well," Decatur continued after receiving an affirmative nod, "pass the word for him, Harris, if you please." Even in the Cabin, we could hear Tom's name move about the ship as the 'word was passed.'

After waiting a moment or two with no appearance from our missing messmate, Decatur faced us and spoke. "I have been informed that Commodore Preble has left orders that Isaac Hull and I are to exchange commands; he is senior to me and as such, is entitled to the larger vessel. Captain Hull will be taking *Argus* out quick as she's got her rigging set up taut and stores aboard. Since he will bring his officers and midshipmen with him, I will be taking you gentlemen with me to *Enterprise*. I can not offer you the accommodations you enjoy here; you will be most assuredly cramped on the schooner, but each of you is welcome to come. Mister Wakefield has already indicated to me he will join me. I have sailed in *Enterprise*; she carries twelve long twelve-pounders, and she is a sprightly and well-mannered vessel, built on the Eastern Shore of Maryland. You may recall that it was *Enterprise* under Andrew Sterrett that captured the Tripolitan polacre back in August of the year one."

As with one voice, each of us expressed our willingness to transfer with our captain to the smaller vessel. I suspect each of us had our own reasons for going. For my part, I trusted Decatur and felt that, with his previous experience with these 'piratical bastards,' he would do well by us.

"I will see how many of his officers Hull is bringing and will act—and choose—accordingly. I will also take Gunner Tarbox and Bosun Anderson as well as my cox'n, Lockhart. Since I, as commanding officer, can select some men to go with us, are there any who you would suggest might be helpful in our new assignment?" Captain Decatur paused and, since he seemed to be looking directly at me, I spoke without a thought.

"Bradford, sir. Gun captain on the forward carronades in my crews." Realizing I had likely spoken out of turn, I colored and felt the heat rise in my neck, then make its way to my hairline. But none in the room, including the captain, so much as glanced my way. The captain nodded and made a note on a piece of paper he took from his desk. Several other names were offered for the new crew, and then we were excused.

"Judd," I called after our senior mid had started up the ladder to the weatherdeck. "What do you make of that?"

"Only that Hull is senior and *Argus* is a bigger, newer ship. Decatur ain't entitled to such a vessel when they's others senior to him on smaller older ones. Simple as that."

"Then why wasn't Hull given the command of *Argus* in Boston?"

"On account of the fact that he was still here, in the Mediterranean. As was *Enterprise*." Judd had picked up a glass and was studying the shore, particularly the area around the dockyards. He lowered the glass and turned. Seeing James by my side, he studied him for a moment, then, when Stevens was beginning to color under the scrutiny, he spoke. "Did you say you'd go to the schooner with the rest?"

"Uh . . . aye. I did." James hesitated before answering, unsure of where Judd was taking him.

"Why?"

"Uh . . . well . . . I guess . . ." He suddenly looked square at Devon. "You and Oliver said you was goin' so I figured I'd go too. We get along fine and I thought maybe Wheatley, since he wasn't there, mightn't be asked."

"Have you done any of the book studying you were assigned? Have you learned anything about navigation like you were supposed to while we sailed from Boston? I can not recall ever having seen you with a quadrant at the noon sights when we fixed our position each day." With each question, Judd's voice got harder, and James seemed to shrink further into himself.

"Some," he answered with as much conviction as he could muster. It didn't sound terribly convincing to me, but I was merely a bystander in this, and becoming more uncomfortable, perhaps in sympathy with James. I left the group, heading forward to speak with Bosun Anderson, whom I had seen amidships.

"Did you hear that we're moving, Mister Anderson? To the schooner *Enterprise* with Cap'n Decatur." I couldn't wait to tell him we would still be shipmates.

"Aye, Mister Baldwin. I heard exactly that. A scrappy little ship, that one is. I'd warrant you'll see some action on her, by God!" Anderson smiled at me.

"One of the only real shallow ones out here. An' the reason she ain't been home since the year one when first she come across. Them big frigates got a great weight of metal in their broadsides, but they can't get close enough to the shore to do any good over there on the Barbary Coast. Takes a right shallow draft to work in close an' catch them piratical bastards when they run fer the beach."

I met this news with some mixed emotions. One part of me wanted desperately to see action, experience the excitement and thrill of firing our guns at a real target, another ship, and boarding an enemy "in the smoke." Another part of my head was buzzing with uncertainty; danger, a ruthless adversary, and the likelihood of death at his hands kept my joy at the bosun's prediction at bay.

Adding further to my concern was something I had heard from Gunner Tarbox some weeks ago, in fact, just after he had accepted, with barely a smile, and certainly small comment, reimbursement for his five dollar investment in my timepiece. He mentioned, quite casually, that the pirates often take prisoners who then become slaves to the pasha, kept on short rations and used to build walls, buildings, and most recently, the beginnings of a fort right on Tripoli Harbor. As masters, the pirates were quite without equal in their ruthlessness and cruelty. That specter seemed, in my mind, some worse than death! It made my head reel. *What if we were unsuccessful in a meeting with the pirates and they captured us? Oh, dear!*

I made my way forward to ensure my division's responsibilities had been attended to and, as I returned to the waist an hour and more later, I encountered Stevens, a worried look contorting his round face to something less pleasant than its normal jovial, if slightly vacuous, appearance.

"What troubles you, James? You look ready to . . . I'm not sure, but . . ."

"Oliver, you've got to help me. Judd said he was going to tell on me to Mister Cutler that I wasn't doin' my book-studyin' like I'm s'posed to. Said Cutler wouldn't let me go with you and Decatur to that other ship; I forget which one he said." His eyes began to well up.

"Well, have you?" I had suggested to him countless times since Boston that he should be learning about navigation, seamanship, and tactics, all of which were contained in the books we had, but, to my knowledge, he had opened nary a one.

"No. Well, a little. But I can't make hide nor hair out of that stuff. I don't understand any of it!" The tears were beginning to flow now, coursing down his cheeks, but mercifully, without the usual attendant sobbing and sniffling.

"Why haven't you asked Judd or me or even Thomas for help with it, if you don't understand it?"

"Thomas! There's a laugh. He wouldn't help me none; he hates me. And Judd's always too busy with this or that. And you, well, you're always doin' your own studyin' and I didn't want to interrupt you." I think it even sounded a little weak to him. Then he got angry. "I reckon my troubles're just that, *my* troubles! I don't know why I even thought you'd help me. Mister fancy-academy-educated Midshipman Baldwin!"

"Haul small, there, James. Whatever are you talking about? I have done nothing, nothing at all, to you. In fact, quite the opposite. Why would you think I would not help you? 'Sides, you haven't told me what it is you want my help with."

Stevens sniffed and wiped a sleeve across his eyes. I guess my tone might have been a trifle hard, but it served to have some calming effect on him. I could see him make an effort to stand straighter and get "ahold of himself" as my brother, Edward, used to say to me when I behaved badly.

"Teach me to read." He looked at his shoes and said the words so quietly, mumbled actually, that I almost didn't catch them. After he had spoken, he simply raised up his head and looked at me, square in the eyes.

I couldn't believe my own ears! I sputtered, stunned at this confession, for some moments and studied his earnest expression and imploring eyes. Suddenly so many of the events of the past few months, his attitude about learning his craft, studying navigation and seamanship, and even writing in the deck log when directed during his watch (he claimed his handwriting was so bad that no one would be able to read what he wrote) became clear to me. How he had managed to secure a midshipman's warrant would most assuredly be a topic of future conversation!

"You really don't know how to read, James?" I still had trouble believing what I had heard.

"Do you think I would have told you that if it ain't true? That I ain't got my letters? I didn't go to some fancy academy in Philadelphia like you. An' I had to take care of my Ma so I couldn't even go to one of the 'charity schools' like some done. My Ma helped me to speak acceptable, but she never got around to teachin' me to read an' write anything but my name. And some of my numbers. Will you help me? I'll work at it real hard, Oliver; you'll see. I know I can learn to do it, and then I can learn the stuff I'm s'posed to, and people won't be so mean to me—if I know things, that is. And maybe someday, I can take the examination and stand for lieutenant."

"Of course. But we'll have to start on something easy. We'll look when we go ashore. There must be a store that sells primers on reading." I stopped, seeing the smile break across his face; it was like watching the sun come out after a storm. The salty streaks his tears had left disappeared into the folds of his cheeks and jaw, so broad was his grin. He grabbed my hand and shook it so hard I finally had to break away from him. I turned to continue aft to the cockpit where I had been headed when James had intercepted me.

"You can't tell no one what we're doing, Oliver. Please. If Wheatley ever found out, it'd be the end of me." His last plea received a wave of acknowledgment as I hurried away, wondering how ever I would go about teaching someone to read and write.

To me, it felt like I had known how all my life. *Maybe he should have taken someone else into his confidence; Mister Wakefield, he'd be the one to do what James wanted. Aye, Mister Wakefield.* All of a sudden it seemed to me that I was the bearer of everyone's secrets, first Thomas' cowardly behavior and now James' revelation.

I was still pondering this weighty burden when I stepped into the mids' cockpit and found Judd putting on his finest uniform.

"If you get your shore-rig on quick enough, you can ride in with me. Got some dispatches and the like to take ashore and then I aim to have a look around, see what's changed since last I was here. And get dinner. I got it cleared with Cutler for you to go. If you want to, that is." He smiled at me without slowing his pace of dressing. "I'll show you around The Rock."

James' problem disappeared in my frantic rush to find a suitably clean uniform in my chest, blacken a pair of shoes to remove the white stains of dried salt water, and discover where I had stowed my cocked hat, put away since we left Boston.

"We have to ask permission to go ashore, Oliver. I will find Mister Cutler and ask for both of us while you finish dressing; meet me on deck quick as you can." And with that, he left, resplendent in what appeared to be a brand new uniform, but could not have been since he, nor anyone else, had not been ashore since we left Boston.

"Judd! Wait! Didn't you say you already got us both permission to go ashore? Why do you have to do it again?" I called after him as I feverishly brushed the accumulated mold and mildew off my coat.

"I just meant he said it would be fine for you to accompany me; but you have to have *permission*—we both do—to leave the ship. You ask just before you actually go. Now set some sail and get rigged out while I go take care of that." Then he was gone up the ladder in search of the first lieutenant while I rooted frantically through my chest for stockings that were both clean and structurally intact.

CHAPTER NINE

As I stepped out of the boat onto solid ground for the first time in over a month, I took in the warehouses, drays, wagons and their animals, great piles of stores, ropes and spars, and bustle that greeted me. Judd came up beside me on the quay and waited while I turned a full circle taking in the sights ashore as well as the breakwaters that protected the harbor from the sea. Then I realized that the stones beneath my feet were not moving.

Immediately dizzy, I put out my hand to steady myself; the nearest object happened to be Judd, who had his back to me while he instructed the boat crew to return to the ship. He caught himself before falling into either the water or the boat and turned, ready to berate me for pushing him.

My pale countenance and queasy expression made him change course and smile at my obvious discomfort. I was seasick! Standing here on *terra firma* and very nearly as sick as had James been leaving Boston! Between the waves of dizziness that made my stomach heave, I again felt sorry for the poor boy. But I could ill-comprehend my own problem, especially now I was on dry land.

"Oliver, you're swaying! Stand still. Oh, I know; you're *landsick*. First time ashore after a spell at sea, feels like the land should be moving but it ain't. Makes you dizzy. We all get it. It passes in a bit, and each time you come ashore, it will bother you less, just like bein' seasick. Remember how you had to find your *sea*legs where we first went out? Well, this is the same thing; you have to find your *land*legs, and you will!" He smiled at my blanched face as I tentatively took a step on the heaving quay. I quickly realized that I would not be sick. Judd was right, and this strange feeling would indeed pass.

"Come on, now. Let's walk up to the town. Walking some will help your problem. Besides, the dockyard area holds no attraction for us; there's nothing right on the waterfront but warehouses, ship-fitters and chandlers. I have only to stop at the port captain's office with this dispatch case, and then we're free to do what we will." Judd set off at a brisk pace, catching me gawking up the towering mountain above us. I had to hurry to catch up, and I was still hampered by my seeming inability to stop swaying. I discovered that my gait had taken on a rhythmic roll, much as if I were walking down the deck of a ship being tossed by the waves. Proudly, I decided I must look like the sailors I had noticed in Boston; now that wasn't so bad!

When Judd came out of the port captain's building, I pointed up the mountain. "Have you ever been up there, Judd?" I asked. "Doesn't look like it'd be easy climbing up *that*."

"Actually, I have. There are monkeys—they call them apes, here—up there and some ancient gun batteries carved right into the rock. We'll go up there later and you can see it yourself. But for now, the town and some vittles is my target." Judd spoke, never breaking his own rolling stride. I realized I would have to abandon my sightseeing while he 'had a target' in mind.

I will get up there my own self! And take my sweet time about it! I would like to see some apes, and the batteries.

We passed old buildings, many showing signs of considerable deterioration, while others we passed had been repaired to a fine degree of utility. All seemed to be in use, regardless of the condition.

"See that wall there? It was built on the ruins of a Moorish wall during the reign of Charles V." Seeing the puzzled expression that must have crossed my sweating face, he added, "Around 1550, Oliver. I thought you had studied history. Surely you heard about Charles V." Without waiting for me to defend myself, he went right on. "The original wall, the Moorish one, was built almost to the top of the mountain; they call it The Rock here. In fact, the Moors had built a pretty rugged seawall right to the south end of the peninsula, the point, down that way." He flung an arm in a generally southern direction. I looked, promptly tripped on a paving stone, caught myself, and resolved to concentrate on keeping up. There would be time later, I hoped, to wander about on my own, or with James. I decided that Judd was a better midshipman than tour guide.

Suddenly, we were in the town. It didn't start gradually like towns at home did with a few paltry stores giving way to more and more. It was just there; stores, alehouses, grog shops, and several restaurants. We continued up Main Street, bustling with passers-by. There were men in the uniform of the Royal Navy, both officer and seaman, though few of the latter, and men and women dressed in fancy civilian dress. All vied for space to pass, at the same time keeping out of the way of the horses, wagons, and coaches that seemed unlikely to stop for anything.

"Judd, why do you suppose there are so few Royal Navy sailors here? Seems like all the uniforms we've seen are officers." He had stopped to look into the window of a tavern and eating establishment and turned away from it to look about us as though he had not noticed the lack of sailors.

"I don't think the British sailors get leave of their ships. I remember being told last time we were here that they have a bad habit of running when they get ashore. Though where they'd run to on the Rock escapes me." He turned back to the window and added, "Hungry? Why don't we get a bite in here?" Without waiting for an answer, he pushed open the door and disappeared inside.

"You might consider finding a place for your lodging while we're here, Oliver. Most of the officers and mids do. It has been my experience" (*My experience? He's only been here once or twice before!*) "that there are several reasonable places where one might find comfortable lodging without running into debt. And where there are few prying eyes to despoil an evening's entertainment. If you take my meaning." Judd offered this advice around a mouthful of food and, while some of it was necessarily muffled, I thought I understood most of it.

"I have little in the way of funds, Judd. I took an advance on my pay because I was robbed in Boston and then had to pay back the gunner five dollars for my watch. I reckon I'll be sleeping aboard *Argus*, or should we move soon, the schooner Captain Decatur mentioned." I took another mouthful; it was quite delicious, and the ale washed it down nicely. *And this was not the 'strong drink' my father had warned me about . . . but then, neither was it in Boston.* I silently resolved to be restrained in my consumption of it.

"Very well, then. I shall point out a few places where you might find some amusement after we finish here and then I shall seek suitable lodging for myself. You can find your way back to the docks, I assume?"

I nodded, hopefully. *Maybe a chance to have a look around myself. Certainly I can walk at a more leisurely pace than did Judd.*

We finished our meal and, after fulfilling his promise by showing me the location of a coffee house and another eating establishment, Judd went off on his own errand. I quashed a certain uneasiness brought about by the recollection of being alone in Boston and headed back the way we had come, *strolling* this time, looking in shop windows and noticing the people and buildings I passed. Shortly before the shops ended, I discovered, behind a terribly dirty window, a seller of books. It was no wonder I had missed it coming in.

A place to find Stevens' primer! How fortunate. He'll be pleased I remembered.

A young woman of indeterminate age stood in deep shadow across the stacks of volumes littering the tables between us. When my eyes became accustomed to the gloom, I made my way toward her, noticing the dust and grit that seemed to cover much of her wares.

"Have you, perchance, a primer on reading?"

The girl looked up from the book she held and studied me, squinting slightly. As I could now make out more details of her dress and appearance, I decided she looked slatternly and fit in nicely with the surroundings. Her eyes were close-set and her nose quite large. Dark, stringy hair fell straight from her scalp and framed her face, giving it the appearance of . . . well, *horsey* came to my mind, and I hid my grin behind a hand as I coughed unnecessarily.

Her frock is filthy! And her face—it might be pretty were she to take some soap and water to it. I wonder her parents let her go out looking like that.

"I believe so, but I shall have to fetch me mum. Don't get much call for such a thing; wouldn't know where to look to find it anyway." She spoke flatly, didn't smile, scowl, or show any feeling whatever. Nor did she make a move to 'fetch her mum.'

"Is someone there, Rachel?" A shrill voice from somewhere above us.

"Yes, Mum. A boy here, in some kind of uniform, he is, is asking after a reading primer. Have we such a thing?" She raised her voice to answer, making it sound very much like her mother's.

Some kind of uniform, indeed. A midshipman in the United States Navy, you dolt!

"Of course, girl! Should be right on the table there, in front. Can you manage on your own or must I come down?" The voice, no less shrill, had an edge to it and did not sound as if coming down was likely.

"I shall look, Mum. Do you recall the price?" This conversation between the upper floor and Rachel continued at a level just below screaming. I tried to busy myself with looking at the volumes whose titles I could make out through the grime.

A few pence bought a very worn volume with most of its pages intact, and I escaped into the waning sunlight with the dusty volume held away from my clean white breeches. I blew at it, raising a small cloud of dust that swirled and shone as the individual particles caught the slanting light.

Hunter's English—Vol. 1. That ought to get James started. I hope he was serious about this. Wonder if I will be able to actually teach him?

I opened the book, reading bits and snatches of it as I walked down the hill. I bumped only a few people, mumbling "Sorry" as I continued scanning the pages, hoping I would find a clue about how to use the book. I could ill-recall my own need for such a volume, so many years ago it was that I had learned my letters.

By the time I reached the docks, it was quite dark. I looked around for some familiar landmark that might lead me to a boat landing.

Was this the place where Judd and I had started? Maybe over there a ways. Yes, I think that way, there. Do I remember that building? Seems different, somehow. Maybe just the dark . . . There was a pile of rope and spars right by the dock. Somebody must have moved it. But there's nary a soul to be seen. They all can't have left!

I looked out at the harbor. The lights of the ships anchored there glowed a warm yellow, showing disembodied details of the furnishings around them and making the dark places seem even darker. I studied the shapes carefully, trying to pick out *Argus* or at least one of the others I might recognize.

"Beggin' yer pardon, sir. Are ye lookin' for somethin' particular out there?" The voice behind me started me almost out of my shoes. I turned and came face to face with a young man of about my age.

His dress was not military, at least not any military I had ever heard of. He wore a plaid shirt of rough cloth, torn in several places and faded throughout. The sleeves came only to the middle of his forearm, allowing swarthy wrists and hands to hang out like stick arms on a scarecrow. His canvas breeches were similar to a sailor's and held up with a length of rope secured around his middle. Hanging on the make-shift belt was a knife of notable dimension in a well-worn leather sheath. He wore no shoes. His shaggy hair fell across his forehead, nearly covering wide spaced eyes which, I noticed, were assessing me quite as thoroughly as I assessed him. Thick lips over a jutting chin, just showing the start of a few wisps of beard, completed the picture. I wondered idly what he might look like in daylight! Surely like nothing military; a denizen of the docks, perhaps, and probably seeking a handout.

Not from me! My financial condition was so desperate that I could use a hand-out my own self. Stay calm and don't encourage him.

"I was trying to determine which of those vessels might be mine. And where they would land a boat were one to come to the dock." I held his gaze as I answered his question.

"And which one is your'n, sir?" He shot back.

"Well, did I not say that was what I was attempting to discern?" *This boy is a dolt!*

"Sir, what I was askin' was *what is the name* of yer vessel?"

I should have guessed that. No harm in telling him. "Why, it would be the brig *Argus*. We came in earlier. American. But I reckon you knew that."

"Oh, sir! *Argus* is over to the other end! You cain't see her from here. And I don't reckon they'd be likely to send a boat way 'round to this side." He pointed in a generally western direction.

How did I do that? I must have walked right past the place where Judd and I came out of the dockyards! Had my nose in that book I bought for James! No wonder I missed it.

"Very well, then. I shall just walk back to the other dock. I imagine there will be boats coming in there from the American ships. One will carry me out to *Argus*, I should think. Thank you."

"I can show you a short cut right through there, if you like." Again he pointed vaguely toward a dilapidated building.

"Oh, thank you. But I think I might find the proper pier on my own. I am grateful you told me where I should be." I smiled and started off on what I hoped was the correct course. I noticed my heart was beating a trifle faster than normal.

Just follow the edge of the pier, Oliver. He said it was this way. So all you have to do is walk along the water until you get there. Don't even need to go back up to the road. Simple as that.

He followed me, keeping up a steady chatter about this and that, most of which I missed completely, the rest I simply did not understand. I found my path blocked by a building which protruded right to the edge of the quay and turned to starboard to go around its landward end. Picking my way over loose stones, bricks, and bits of rubble, I moved slowly, carefully, as I followed the looming side of the warehouse which appeared only as a darker shape in the darkness of the night.

I noticed that I no longer heard my companion and his chattering. As I stopped to feel my way around something large in my path, I realized he was no longer in my wake.

"Just as well he's gone." I spoke quietly, but aloud, enjoying the comforting sound of a human voice, even my own, in this dark, unsettling place. "Made me a trifle nervous, he did. Had a look about him." I noticed that I still seemed to be breathing a bit faster than normal, maybe even faster than I had been before.

Just because you've been walking quickly. No reason to be nervous. No reason at all.

When I at last came to the end of the warehouse, I discovered a gap between that building and another. I turned to my larboard and walked confidently into the gap—and into an even darker passage. But one, I hoped, that would lead me to the far end of the pier, the place where I belonged, and where I would find not only the brig, but also American boats stroking between the fleet and the quay. I put a hand on the rough bricks as I moved, noting that the ground was less littered with debris than before.

Guess nobody comes back here, much. "Likely no reason to, being so far from the pier." This last I spoke aloud, though it came out as barely a whisper.

"Here now. You'll be smart to fetch up there. I'll be havin' yer purse, if ye don't mind, sir. And in the event you cain't see so good in the dark, I'm holding that knife you was eyein' when first we met."

That boy had returned. I knew there was something about him that wasn't just so! Now what? He said he held a knife, a large knife, and from the look of him, I would not doubt his ability to use it. A wharf rat just like Mister Cutler had called that fellow in Boston.

"I have no purse. I left it aboard the brig, where my messmates are awaiting my return. Likely wondering where I've gotten to and will be coming ashore to find me soon, I'd think." *That ought to give him something to think on!*

"We'll be done here afore they would ever find you. Just hand over the purse, and you can go on your way. No harm done."

"I told you, I have no purse."

"Yeah, you do. You musta paid money for that book you got, and it hadda come outta yer purse. Give it here. Else I'll be forced to gut yer like a fish!" I felt a hand prodding my midsection, whether for emphasis or in search of the purse, I knew not.

My eyes had become accustomed to the deep gloom of the area, and I could make out my assailant standing just in front of me at an arm's length away. He did hold the knife, I could make out the dull gleam of its blade, but it pointed down as his arm appeared to be hanging at his side.

Without thinking, I thrust out my arm and caught him squarely in the chest. As I did so, I stepped forward, adding more force to the shove and catching him unawares. I heard an explosive release of his breath as he fell back, lost his footing, and sat down hard. I heard the knife clatter to the stones—I hoped so, at any rate! I seized the opportunity to run as fast as ever I have run in my life, continuing in the direction I had started. I stumbled several times, catching myself and staggering for a few steps before regaining my stride. Then I saw some lights.

They glowed in muted but welcoming yellow splendor, gaining in intensity and size as I rushed pell mell toward the safety I *knew* they offered. People, sailors, officers, and *Americans!* I couldn't tell if the boy was pursuing me; I could hear no footfalls, but then I hadn't before, either. And I was not about to slow down enough to take a look astern. I convinced myself that I would be unable to see him anyway. Then I thought that I *could* hear the soft *plops* and scuffs of bare feet close aboard, inspiring me to a burst of speed toward the growing yellow glow. I picked out, in silhouette, a pile of debris perhaps, and very nearly dodged around it; I could feel my stockings snag and rip as I ran. But mercifully, I kept my footing and never even broke stride.

And then I was out—out from the pitch darkness of the building and into the dim circle of light offered by a pair of lamps set on posts. I slowed my pace a bit, savoring the embrace of safety and familiarity. This was where Judd and I had come ashore. I knew for certain. I chanced a look back the way I had run, seeking some sign of my antagonist, but either he was gone or remained hidden in the shadows and out of sight. My breath came in ragged gasps, and my heart tried to fight its way out of my chest, but I had made it! Supporting myself with a hand on the light post, I bent over nearly double as I struggled to catch my breath, which still came in great sobs. Gradually, the pain in my ribs subsided. I could stand erect, breathe almost normally, and my heart had stopped its clamoring to escape from the confines of my ribcage. I looked around, still reluctant to leave the security of my pool of light. But I had to find a boat, and there were none close at hand.

Necessity demanded I move. I walked cautiously along the edge of the quay, surveying the docks, the anchorage with its winking lights, the buildings farther ahead, and my wake to ensure my assailant was really gone. I stopped near a flight of steps that led to the water and happened to be right under a lamppost. Just a pistol shot away, I saw a boat bobbing alongside the quay, with its pennant affixed to a ring set into the stone. Quiet voices drifted to my ears and a closer look revealed a cox'n and four oarsmen, obviously waiting for someone to carry out to a ship. What a stroke of luck!

Now if I could prevail upon them with better success than I had found in Boston.

Taking several deep breaths in an attempt to regain my composure, I stood straight and marched quickly down to where they floated. After a moment's consideration of my request, the cox'n agreed to carry me to the brig. Perhaps the mention of Captain Decatur's name was helpful.

"You got it! You didn't forget! I thought when you and Judd went off together you would forget all about your promise to get me a reading book. Oh, Oliver! Thank you, thank you! Give it to me!" James had leaped to his feet the moment he spied me enter the cockpit and fairly snatched the book, none the worse for its harrowing delivery, from me. "You are going to stay and show me, aren't you?" He suddenly looked up from the open book, his eyes big and his brow furrowed.

I hadn't really thought about it, nor had I more than a passing notion of how I would go about 'showing' him. Quite obviously, Thomas was not in evidence. "Of course, James. A promise is a promise! But what about Thomas?"

In answer to my query regarding our comrade, James said that he thought Wheatley had gone ashore sometime after Judd and I did. Had not we seen him?

No, we had not, and that was that. We sat side by side at the cockpit table, the book between us, as I explained the intricacies of letter sounds and their names.

"I would have thought you lads would be ashore finding some mischief to get into with your colleagues, not sitting here reading books!" Cutler's voice startled us both, and James made a move to hide the book. I knew he was sure his secret had been discovered; I was fairly sure of it, myself.

"Cap'n Decatur wanted you to know that, tomorrow afternoon, the British are fixing a reception for the American squadron at some dandy's house in town, and *all* officers and midshipmen are expected to, no, *will* attend. Shouldn't be all bad; I hear they have no shortage of excellent food." James' eyes lit up at that. "And they're entertaining us with a music recital or some such." He stopped and looked from one to the other of us. "Where's Wheatley and Devon?"

"Oh, sir, Mister Devon went ashore. Something about dispatches or letters or some such, he said." I did not mention that I had been in company, though I was sure Cutler knew it since Judd had asked his permission for the both of us.

"I knew that, Baldwin! But he is not back yet? Did you not accompany him? I seem to recall he said something about you being with him."

"Oh, yes, sir. I did go. He delivered the dispatches and we had dinner. Then I returned aboard. Judd . . . Mister Devon said he had other business to attend to."

"Hmmmm. I'm sure he did. No matter. Tell him of our obligation tomorrow, if you please. And Wheatley? He is 'attending to business,' also?" Without waiting for an answer, which neither of us could offer, the first lieutenant delivered the rest of his message. "Four bells in the afternoon watch, dress uniform, ready to go ashore." Then he nodded, satisfied we understood our task, and left.

James looked at me, waited a few heartbeats, and pulled out his book from where it had disappeared under a rumpled shirt close at hand.

"Oh, Lord, Oliver. I thought for sure I had been found out! Thank God, it wasn't Thomas! I don't reckon Cutler might care, but Wheatley would make my life even more unbearable!"

I smiled at my student and remarked, "A dinner reception on the morrow; that sounds interesting. Might even be fun!"

"Oh, I doubt that. Except that part about 'excellent food.' *That* sounds interesting to me!" James almost drooled at the thought of the vittles he would find. If listening to some music was the price he had to pay, so be it! We got back to work on the book. His appetite for letters was even greater than for food, and it was not until the lantern guttered and flickered out that he would hear of stopping.

At muster the next morning, it was discovered that several of our men had not returned to the brig from their leaves. Their absences were duly noted, a petty officer and two seamen sent out to find them (or secure their releases from the local jail), and the day preceded without missing a beat. To my joy, none of the missing were mine, nor the did they include my two colleagues from the cockpit. Both Judd and Thomas were in attendance; the former smiling and talkative, the latter, quiet, scowling, and somewhat worse for the wear. A few chores to do, some work on the guns that we oversaw, and then it was time to get into our finest and go to the reception.

On the quay, when we disembarked, were the officers and midshipmen of several of our ships, and we marched more or less in company to the address above the town where the party would be held. Hardly had Captain Hull pulled the bell when the door was opened by a liveried servant. He acknowledged our presence and led us through a vaulted hall with well polished dark walls, then through an enormous double set of doors into a cavernous hall. The room had been fitted with a long table down its center, laid out with sparkling glasses, cutlery and plate. Paintings hung around the room depicting ships and men in naval garb. A few flags were draped high on the walls, and I was pleased to see an American flag displayed prominently among the British ensigns.

I could hear a sharp intake of breath as James took in the trappings of the establishment. I shot a glance at Thomas; he was dull-eyed and seemed to notice little of the splendor before us. Judd was chatting with Mister Morris as he took in the room; I suspect he would have us believe his being dined in this manner was not an unusual event. But, to my satisfaction, I did see his eyes become bigger and his attention to the officer waver as he viewed the opulence.

Candelabra placed down the length of the table—there must have been ten or a dozen of them, each fitted with six long white tapers—caused reflections of their flames to dance in the glasses and bounce off the highly polished plate. Around the walls of the room, sconces held more candles and, in combination with the sunlight filling the room through beautifully glazed windows and the candelabra, provided a bright and warm atmosphere for the festivities. James was overwhelmed.

"Oliver! Have you *ever* seen such a place in all your life? Look at the candles; they even got 'em lit in daylight! Ma would never do that at home. Candles were for night! What a place! Do you think someone actually lives here?" His hoarse whisper hid none of the excitement or awe that both he and I felt.

"Now aren't you glad you came? This is going to be better than anything we've done before, and I'd warrant the food will be better than anything either of us has eaten before!" I whispered back to him, still staring at our surroundings.

"Good afternoon, gentlemen." The voice came from the doorway behind us, and we turned as one to glimpse our host. "I am so glad so many of you were able to attend our little gathering. I am sure you are all consumed with your various duties and eager to be off to confront the heathens of the Barbary Coast, but we could not let our great friends escape without offering a small reception of welcome to you. I am only sorry your commodore—Preble, is it not?—is at sea and unable to join us. Likewise our own Admiral Nelson, currently en route to England.

"We are continuing a grand tradition this evening; we were privileged to offer our hospitality to Commodore Morris and his officers a year and more ago. I know some of you were here then as I recognize a few familiar faces. Which of you would be Captain Hull? . . . Captain Stewart? . . . Captain Decatur?" Each of the American captains nodded in turn.

A tall man with a kind face and smiling eyes, bordered above by unruly white eyebrows and below by an overlong nose and droopy white mustaches, stood comfortably in the entranceway. He wore the uniform of a Royal Navy admiral, complete with medals and a large medallion which he wore on a ribbon around his neck. He continued with his welcoming speech.

"I am Admiral Robert Barrett, Royal Navy, and, while not currently in command of anything," he smiled at his own disarming honesty, "I am able to enjoy the flexibility of entertaining my colleagues in suitable style. I hope you will make yourselves comfortable and enjoy that which my humble hospitality can offer you. Remember, this is Gibraltar, not London!" He walked, marched, actually, up to the three captains, extending his hand to each in turn and continued talking, but in lowered tones meant for them and not the rest of us.

Not a one of us would have paid a whit of attention in any case, as several ladies in splendid attire appeared in the doorway just vacated by Admiral Barrett and held, at that moment, our undivided attention.

Aware that our gazes had fixed upon the ladies, Barrett again raised his voice. "Let me introduce the members of my household who will, of course, be joining us for dinner, and with whom, I imagine, you will become better acquainted as the afternoon and evening progress." He stepped back to the door, bowed deeply to the wonderfully turned out damsels, took the first two, one on each arm, and stepped back into the room.

"On my right," he turned his head and smiled at the dark-haired beauty whose hand rested comfortably in the crook of the his arm, "is Lady Jane Parker. Lady Jane has lived here on the Rock for most of her life and can likely answer any of your questions, should any of you have one, about our lovely little peninsula." Lady Jane curtsied delicately and smiled demurely at the assemblage of Americans.

"And this is my sister, Lady Elizabeth Lovejoy, who has graced our household with her presence during the time her husband, Captain Sir Reginald Lovejoy, has been on the blockade with Admiral Lord Nelson." Barrett rolled the Rs in his brother-in-law's name so long, I supposed it must have included at least three of them! Lady Elizabeth curtsied a bit awkwardly and smiled, though somewhat less demurely, I thought, than did her friend. She was quite tall, whip-thin, and not unattractive.

The two women detached themselves from the admiral and moved gracefully into the van of the American officers, who parted like the Red Sea before Moses as they approached.

Their places were taken by two more ladies who were properly introduced to us, released into our midst, and immediately surrounded by several American officers who, elbowing each other more or less discretely, vied for their attention.

"And this, gentlemen, is my great good friend, Commodore Rodney Featherstone, late of Devonshire—he has arrived here only yesterday—who to his dismay, but my joy, is, like me, shore-bound!" Admiral Barrett smiled broadly again as he presented a distinguished-looking officer, who had even more pretty decorations and ribbons on his jacket than did his senior and who grimaced (was it good natured or not?) as he stepped into our gathering.

The Royal Navy certainly has a variety of decorations they give out! I wonder what he did to win all those?

I felt a sharp elbow in my side and turned to find Wheatley standing next to me, a wolfish grin on his still-pale face. "That fellow, the admiral, is what they call a "yellow admiral." Means he ain't got a command of any kind and likely won't. Put ashore for good, like laying up a ship in ordinary." His hoarse whisper blew a cloud of noxious odors in my direction, and I involuntarily took a step back. "And that other fellow, his 'great, good friend' is the same, I'd reckon. Not got much to do but go to parties." This last bit of intelligence was mercifully whispered into my ear.

"Oh? And how are you so sure of that?" I threw back sharply, also whispering, and received a disapproving look from one of the officers, one I did not know. He must have been in one of the other ships.

Thomas merely smiled at me; either on account of knowing something I didn't or my getting caught by an officer.

After a few more introductions (could they *all* be living here?), we were free to mix with the civilian guests. Of course, the ladies received much of the attention, especially from the younger members of our service, officer and mid alike. I separated myself from the throng, and a throng it had become, with eighteen or twenty Americans and some ten and more invited civilian guests as well as Admiral Barrett and his 'household.' I had found a painting, a most heroic image of a ship of the line engaged in desperate battle, and was studying it closely, more oblivious to the assemblage than not.

"Why do you not mingle with the other guests, young man? Do you not enjoy the art of conversation?" A woman, one to whom we had been introduced, stood at my elbow searching my face for some clue as to my behavior.

Forthright ain't in it! She—who is she?—speaks her mind plain as day!

I struggled to select her name from the several I had heard and after a moment decided on one.

"Oh, no, Lady Lovejoy!" I watched a smile play at the corners of her mouth; I must have gotten it right! "I am only taking the opportunity to enjoy the wonderful paintings in the room. Truly, they are splendid! Among the best I have ever seen." *Not that I had actually seen that many pictures of ships, but these several were grand.*

"I am impressed you remembered my name, but you should call me 'Lady Elizabeth' rather than 'Lady Lovejoy.' And isn't that just a marvelous painting? It is, of course, my husband's last command, HMS *Culloden*. A fine vessel she. This painting you are admiring was done in celebration of her glorious participation in the Battle of Cape St. Vincent against the Spanish. February 14, 1797, it was, and Sir Reginald sailed in direct support of Lord Nelson." She paused, squinted at the painting, withdrew a handkerchief from her sleeve, and stepped in front of me to wipe something she had spied from the frame. Though how ever she had seen anything on that magnificently carved and gilded piece of craftsmanship, I shall never figure. "That's better," she muttered as she stepped back to admire the painting and its now pristine frame. Then she smiled at me and continued, "The admiral, our host, was there with Lord Nelson on HMS *Captain*, you know. Took a notable role in the action."

"Oh, ma'am. Yes, I am sure I have heard of that!"

Lady Elizabeth had moved to a sconce in which the candle had dripped some wax onto the crystal stem. After eyeing it for a moment, she tentatively scraped at the offending wax with a fingernail and followed that with her handkerchief. The sconce gleamed in the wake of her ministrations. She was about to attack another when we were called to table.

"Ladies and gentlemen, may we be seated, if you please." Admiral Barrett stood near the middle of the long side of the table. He gestured to Lady Jane Parker to sit across from him, and a servant pulled out the appropriate chair for her. Lady Elizabeth, after dusting off the cushion with her napkin, took the seat on his right, refusing any help from admiral or servant alike.

The rest of us took seats at random, with, of course, the most popular being those adjacent to a lady. While each of us remained gentlemanly in our conduct, there were several times I waited, in vain, for a scuffle to break out as competitions for a particular chair were settled, first by size and then by seniority. I took a seat at the far end of the table, next to Lieutenant Hobbs. The other midshipmen found suitably distant seats and appeared as out of their depth as I as we considered what to do next.

While we had been chatting with our hosts, the table had been laid with an abundance of great silver warming dishes, wines in cut crystal decanters, water in pitchers, several great tureens of, I assumed, soup, and a great platter of cold meats that rested regally in the center of the table. Behind each chair stood a servant, ready to provide any of the dishes for his 'master' or replenish any glass that had gone dry. Never had I seen such splendor and grandeur.

I shot a glance at James, who sat several seats to my right, and saw him slack-jawed and glassy-eyed at the prospect of the meal spread before him. I sensed he was about to reach for a dish of some delicacy that was near to him and cleared my throat loudly. Unlike the meal in Decatur's Cabin on *Argus*, this time I caught his attention and stopped him with a tiny shake of my head. A worried look came over his face. I could almost hear him thinking that he would only be allowed to look but not partake of this array of gluttony.

I watched as our host and Lady Jane asked each of their respective servants to dish them up one or another of the selections set out. This, then, was how it was done. Gradually, and led by our host and hostess, we discovered that each of the dishes exceeded its predecessor in richness. The various wines (I heard mention of Madeira and Chianti and some Chateau or another) were heady, sweet or tart as appropriate, and in great supply. I watched in surprise as each measure of wine poured out was diluted with a smaller measure of water; apparently it was impolite to take your wine straight. Conversation was lively and, as the meal progressed, became more animated as comments were shouted, mostly by the American naval officers, from one end of the table to the other. The Englishmen and ladies among us maintained a quiet discourse confined to their immediate neighbor or the one directly across the table, and the behavior of their guests raised more than a few eyebrows.

As the more popular of the offerings became depleted, they were replaced with others. Ultimately, an entire roasted pig was carried in by two men and placed on a table alongside the one át which we sat. It was duly carved and portioned out to each of us along with further servings of vegetables and, of course, wine.

Hobbs had offered little in the way of conversation, preferring to engage the lady to his other side with his wit and wisdom. To my right, a gentleman, of greater years than I would have cared to guess, dozed fitfully, his head bouncing on his waistcoat as he dropped off, then caught himself. I wondered at first, horrified, if he had expired until he awoke with a start, a snort, and a fuzzy look around the table.

His skin appeared as parchment, stretched over the features of his face, exaggerating the bones and structure until I imagined I dined next to an elegantly dressed skeleton. A small pair of eyeglasses were perched in the middle of his significant nose, though why he bothered I could not imagine; they were so smudged and dirty that he could not possibly have seen through them. Unlike the other gentlemen in attendance, he wore no wig, and his sparse white hair fell to his collar from a fringe surrounding his bald pate. His voice, when he spoke to me, was thin and reedy, reminding me of the noise the crickets at home made in the summer. He told me his name was vander Muelen and his family had come to Gibraltar from Holland soon after the British had wrested it away from the Spaniards.

He studied me over the top of his spectacles. "I would imagine you know your history, young man? You were taught, I am sure, even in America, that the English could not have captured this fortress without the assistance of the Dutch? Indeed, it was an Anglo-Dutch force that finally took the Rock. A long and bloody battle it was, fought well before your own successful uprising in America. Skirmishes continued for nearly twenty years after." The cricket voice cackled as he thought of the role his forebears had played in the history of Gibraltar. "My own father was here. He was a young man, of course, and after the initial fighting died out, decided to remain. He sent for my mother and me at home in Holland to join him. I was quite young at the time, having attained barely five or six years of age. Stayed here ever since!" And he dozed off again.

I noticed that the room had become warm and wondered *could even so many candles create this much heat?* The servant behind me must have noticed my discomfort as well; he kept my glass of cool, though still diluted, wine full. James seemed to have a similar problem; I observed a trickle of sweat running unnoticed down the side of his face. Lieutenant Hobbs, on the other hand, seemed perfectly fine, though it did appear he was swirling a bit when I looked at him.

That must make it hard to eat. How does he do that and not fall out of his chair?

I resolved to keep my seat as well as a firm hand on the edge of the table which seemed to steady my world a bit.

Dessert was brought in by more servants (I think there were more servants than guests). While I think James might have managed to sample each and every delicacy, I was only able to test some four or five before I found myself completely incapable of eating another bite of anything. Fruit, compotes, cheeses, candies, little cakes called *petits fours,* jellies, and ice creams quickly disappeared, consumed by those with more foresight than I. My glass, still half full of one or another of the wines which had appeared in plenty, was removed to be replaced by another of a different shape; it was unthinkable that this new vessel should remain empty and indeed, the attentive servant behind me promptly filled it with a dark rich-looking wine, this time, without the water. A taste revealed incredible sweetness, too sweet, in fact, and I left the remainder of it untouched.

I had no idea how long we had been at this, but it seemed as if I had never been anywhere else. I sneaked a peek at my watch and discovered that over four hours had passed since we were invited to sit! And the candles, now much shorter, seemed to be carrying the burden of lighting the room.

I noticed a servant whisper into Admiral Barrett's ear; the latter nodded and rose. "Ladies and gentlemen, I have just been informed that our entertainment for the remainder of our evening has announced their readiness. So, if you would please to do so, let us move into the music hall. I am sure you will delight at what is in store for us there."

The admiral assisted Lady Elizabeth Lovejoy with her chair, winning a scowl from her in the process. Soon all were standing, some of us a trifle unsteadily, and our host led the way to the music hall. While smaller by half than the dining hall, it was more opulent and contained several sparkling chandeliers which threw the warm glow of their candles around the room. Chairs had been set up in ranks. In the front, four gentlemen, each holding an instrument, were already seated before music stands. There were no pictures on the walls, two of which were pierced in four places by windows draped in a rich, heavy-appearing material on which was depicted some kind of scene. On closer examination, the decoration was created by thread, much of it gold, woven onto the fabric.

We took seats, seniority still holding sway over the choice of where, and

Judd, Thomas, James and I found ourselves well in the back of the room along with a clutch of other midshipmen from *Syren* and the schooners.

"This might answer well, being near the door, Baldwin. Should one of us feel the need to escape what I suspect will be a sound akin to gutting a live cat, we can do so without causing a stir!" Thomas, ever the optimist, seemed to be feeling better than he had some four hours before. He eyed the musicians with a skeptical appraisal, as if he could discern their talent from their appearance.

Our host, the admiral, had stepped to the front of the room and stood among the musicians, who now had assumed a position of readiness. He cleared his throat and, in stentorian tones, addressed the assemblage.

"We are indeed privileged to have with us tonight the Royal Gibraltar String Quartet, who will play a selection of Joseph Haydn's compositions. You will, I am sure, know that this wonderful German genius has produced an abundance of operatic scores and has triumphed, as has his music, wherever people have listened, including in the Court of our own King George III. While some of the selections we will hear are familiar and quickly recognizable, others will not be. Indeed, we will be honored to hear the very first performance of a string quartet finished only this summer by Herr Haydn right here in Gibraltar. It is my most sincere hope you will enjoy this wonderful music." Barrett smiled at the man holding a violin to his neck, nodded, and sat down.

The gentleman with the violin tapped his bow on the music stand in front of him, then poised it over the strings of his instrument. On his nod, the group began to play. The song started out quietly with a repetitive melody; I had to strain to hear the notes. Then it built to a volume more readily heard and repeated the musical phrase several more times before moving on to a different melody, carried in turn by first, a violin, then the cello, and, finally, the last violin, which was played by the one I took to be the leader. It was pretty music, and I enjoyed listening, distracted only slightly by Wheatley's whispered comments and James' fidgeting in his seat to my left. I discovered I could concentrate more on the music if I closed my eyes and let it wash over me and carry me along with its rising and falling strains.

I awoke with a start and Wheatley's elbow in my ribs. The audience was applauding enthusiastically. With a scraping of chairs, many began to stand and yell out such things as "Bravo" and "Encore." I joined in the applause, though refrained from shouting out anything. I looked around, taking in the grinning faces of my colleagues, the guttering candles in the chandeliers and sconces, and the backs of the other guests. Then the evening was over, and we departed after effusive thanks and farewells to our hosts.

"I give you joy on your opportunity to put those heathen devils in their place, young man. Would that I could join you!" Barrett said with a smile to me and James as we shook his hand.

"Do be careful!" Lady Elizabeth offered, with great sincerity, to be echoed by Lady Jane Parker a moment later.

I have little recall of our return to the docks beyond that it was raining quite steadily, but as I stepped aboard *Argus*, Bosun Anderson, who had been left in charge of the brig, pressed an envelope into my hand.

"Delivered from the port captain's office, Mister Baldwin. A letter for you."

I took it and recognized my brother's familiar hand in which had been written, "Oliver Baldwin, midshipman, USS *ARGUS*" on the envelope. *How wonderful! Edward* did *leave a letter for me!* I tore it open and, holding the pages near a lantern, quickly began to read. I found only that *Philadelphia* had departed for the blockade of Tripoli, and that they had a new first lieutenant, a David Porter. Then the pages seemed to swim in front of my eyes and despite several attempts to decipher the words, I could make no sense of them. Perhaps the rain was blurring the ink! I carefully folded it, stuffed it into a pocket to read on the morrow, and went to bed.

The remainder of our time in Gibraltar was consumed with preparations for our imminent departure for Tripoli (would I see my brother there?) and transferring ourselves and our furnishings to the smaller schooner *Enterprise* while Captain Hull and his officers took over the brig. Several days passed before I recalled Edward's letter and had the opportunity to study it carefully.

CHAPTER TEN

"We will be escorting *Traveler* to Syracuse, and then likely will sail to Tripoli, there to join with *Philadelphia* and *Vixen*, currently maintaining the blockade of that harbor." Decatur addressed the entire complement of his new command, USS *Enterprise*. Next to him stood Lieutenant James Lawrence, our new first lieutenant since Mister Cutler had been struck, shortly after the lavish entertainment in the home of Admiral Barrett, with some unknown malady that had put him in hospital in Gibraltar. Also on the quarterdeck were Lieutenants Hobbs and Morris, Mister Wakefield, our surgeon, and the four of us midshipmen. Standing slightly apart were the warrants: Anderson and Tarbox from *Argus*, and Seth Cartee, sailing master, Patrick Keogh, sailmaker, and John Williams, our carpenter.

"Once off Tripoli, I fully expect that we will be given the opportunity to see action and, while this expedition may terminate in our sudden deaths or capture and slavery, I expect that it is more likely to result in our immortal glory. Every man aboard, officer and seaman, must possess the qualities of courage, obedience to orders, and love of country. It is those qualities that will see us through, and bring us to glory." Decatur stopped and, while the silence left in the wake of his stirring words rang, looked at every man he could see right squarely in the eyes.

Suddenly, a voice rang out from the men. "Three cheers for Cap'n Decatur!" The air was filled with lusty *huzzah*s as each soul aboard *Enterprise* was moved with the inspiration of the captain's words. Midshipmen included. I actually believe that James, for the first time, was pleased with his station and seemed eager for our commission.

For my own part, I, too, was caught up in the excitement and blood-racing anticipation of what was to come. Lurking in the back of my mind, and only occasionally making itself known, was my concern (fear?) at being on the receiving end of another's broadside. I knew our men could exchange shot for shot with any, but how would *I* react when the iron flew at *us* in smashing broadsides, any shot of which could clearly divide a man in two, or a long-leaf pine splinter, should the shot hit wood, spit him like a pig? I prayed, more frequently as the time for my baptism by fire drew closer, that I would acquit myself honorably.

Though we had only been aboard the schooner for something over a day, I had looked her over stem to stern, masthead to bilge and, with my limited knowledge, been unable to find her wanting. She was rigged with a big, gaff-topped mains'l on her after mast, to which, at the top, could be rigged a top-mast stays'l. Between the two masts, *Enterprise* carried a lower main stays'l, quite as large as might have been a normal fores'l, had she owned one. On the fore-mast, a square fores'l was topped with both a tops'l and t'gallant. Forward of that, attached to her rakish bowsprit and jibboom, stretched a pair of stays'ls and a jib.

She was armed with a dozen twelve-pounder long guns, more accurate and longer-legged than the carronades we had used on *Argus*, though her broadside carried not as heavy a weight of metal. She brought with her into the Mediter-ranean a fine record from the recent hostilities with France, where she success-fully engaged a Spanish brig and, later, a French Letter of Marque. More recently, as Decatur had mentioned at table (it seemed so long ago), under Captain Sterrett she had captured a Tripolitan polacre, suffering no losses in the engagement. I was sure she would continue to live up to her sobriquet of "lucky" *Enterprise*.

Most of the seventy seamen aboard had been in her for well beyond a year. While only about half were Americans, all seemed comfortable and capable. Bosun Anderson and Gunner Tarbox had replaced their opposite numbers, who had transferred with Captain Hull to *Argus*, and my gun captain, Bradford, and the captain's cox'n, Lockhart, were signed as additionals. While we boasted more officers and midshipmen than might have been normal on such a vessel, everyone seemed to "fit" together and enjoyed the common goal of bringing glory to ourselves, our captain, and our smart little ship. Mister Anderson had commented to me shortly after we reported aboard that he had known the other warrant officers, Cartee, Keogh, and Williams (though the last, the car-penter, he knew less well) for some years, and they were all well qualified and fine seamen. Even Thomas Wheatley had moderated his antagonism toward Judd and James—he had earlier declared a truce with me—and, while still dis-playing many of the traits we loathed, seemed willing to at least make the effort to curtail them based on his desire to share the camaraderie the rest of us enjoyed. A good thing, as the cockpit was stiflingly small, forcing the four of us to occupy about half the area we enjoyed in *Argus*. The gunroom and wardroom were equally tight, but it seemed to matter not a whit to any.

Two days later, *Traveler*, the supply vessel we were to escort, showed her signal that she was ready to depart, and depart we did, leaving Gibraltar on November 13, 1803, for Syracuse, a splendid harbor on the southeast coast of Sicily and only a few day's sail from Tripoli. *Argus*, we had been informed by the captain, was to remain near Gibraltar to attend to American interests in the Straits, while *Syren*, carrying former American Consul James Cathcart, had weighed for Leghorn, another British base well up the peninsula of Italy. We Enterprises were delighted, indeed, to be headed *toward* the action even if it meant heading first to Syracuse in the company of a dull sailer like *Traveler*. Some went so far as to gloat that our late vessel was reduced to a boring routine patrol far from the action. Not one of us midshipmen mentioned aloud Thomas Wheatley's earlier prediction, though I was quite certain the others, like me, had thought of it. In part, he *had* been right; even though *Argus* would not be sailing off to do battle with the pirates, *we* would be.

Our journey was uneventful. Had it not been for the opportunity to exercise the great guns on a daily basis, practice handing and reefing the sails, and setting the rig to suit both Bosun Anderson and Captain Decatur, it would have been dull to the extreme. James, his self-confidence growing with his ability to decipher his letters, seemed a new person and had neither complained nor shed a single tear throughout the ten-day voyage. He spent most all of his spare time pouring over the book I had secured for him in Gibraltar.

For my own part, I spent off-watch and off-duty time reading and rereading Edward's letter, which I had discovered shortly before we sailed. I had found it crumpled into a pocket, the ink somewhat smeared and blurred. In anticipation of what would be coming, I studied my books on seamanship, gunnery, and navigation. That is, when I wasn't secretly helping Stevens with his letters, a job of work that, while satisfying, had attached to it the onus of finding a place to work where we would be undiscovered by our messmates, especially Thomas Wheatley.

Edward, according to his letter, had enjoyed a quiet passage, unlike ours, from Boston to Gibraltar arriving at The Rock on 24 August. They had, he said, been sent out within a day in search of two vessels—Tripolitan cruisers, they were—which had been sighted off Cape de Gat. I checked our chart and found the place he mentioned somewhat east of Malaga on the south coast of Spain. They came across the vessels, which appeared to be a brig and a ship-rigged warship, during their second night out. The larger of the two had turned to be Moroccan with an order from the governor of Tangier to capture American vessels. The brig was its prize, a Boston ship named *Celia*, with Captain Bowen and seven of his crew confined below. Both the Moroccan and *Celia* were escorted back to Gibraltar, Edward went on, where the former became a prize of war. The Boston brig was restored to her rightful crew to continued their voyage, only slightly the worse for the wear.

My brother's letter had also detailed another less successful cruise into the Atlantic in search of yet another enemy warship, reported to be lurking near Cape St. Vincent. Unsatisfied, they returned to Gibraltar on 11 September. Since *Philadelphia* had no orders then except to wait on the arrival of the other ships in Preble's squadron, Edward had managed to find some time to explore the streets and alleys of Gibraltar, offering me some brotherly suggestions as to where I might find suitably safe entertainments. Some I had blundered across on my own, while others I made a mental note to discover on our return. Most of his offerings and wisdom for "getting along'" in my employment, including dealing with "difficult" messmates, officers and seamen, I had already discovered. His heartfelt concern for me caused me to smile, and I longed for his presence.

Philadelphia's respite lasted only a week and it was apparent that Edward fully expected to be away from The Rock for some time, or perhaps he expected the arrival of *Argus* was imminent, as he signed, dated, and sealed his letter mentioning only that *Philadelphia* would sail on 19 September in company of *Vixen* for Malaga, Malta, and thence to Tripoli to establish the blockade. He did add that Commodore Preble and most of the others in the squadron were heading off to "settle our affairs" with the emperor of Morocco, in the light of finding the Moroccan warship preying on the vessels of a country with whom they were supposedly at peace.

His letter gave me no end of joy, and I was bereft at having missed him in Gibraltar. I wanted to tell him of my own adventures, my progress in *our* employment, and enjoy his quiet camaraderie and friendship. I poured all my feelings, even those I could not share with Judd or James, and a description of Barrett's reception into a lengthy letter written over the ten days we spent at sea. Following his earlier lead, I deposited it on our arrival with the captain of the port of Syracuse, a charming and most accommodating Sicilian, who assured me he would *personally* deliver it to *Philadelphia* the very moment she set her anchor in his harbor.

Before even I had returned to *Enterprise* from my visit with the port captain, *Constitution* and the schooners *Nautilus* and *Vixen*, sailing in company from Malta, arrived in Syracuse, fired their obligatory salutes, and set their anchors. Almost at once, *Constitution* hoisted flags signaling, "All officers repair on board." I wondered idly why *Vixen* was here instead of on the blockade with *Philadelphia*, as Edward's letter had mentioned they were in company.

When we, along with officers from *Nautilus*, *Traveler*, and *Vixen* clambered up the boarding steps on *Constitution's* side, we found Commodore Preble in a high state of consternation and anxiety, pacing his quarterdeck like a caged lion.

"Gentlemen," he began even as the last of us stepped onto the quarterdeck, "I am afraid I have dreadful news for you; *Philadelphia* has been taken!" An audible intake of breath followed this statement, mine, perhaps, the loudest.

I felt as if I had been struck a mortal blow, and my knees began to buckle. I caught myself, grabbing onto Lieutenant Hobbs' arm. Philadelphia *taken! Edward was on that ship.* My mind reeled. I had only just posted a letter to him. *Were there casualties? Was my brother hurt, or heaven perish the thought, killed in the action? What to do now? What was I to do?*

" . . . allowed to keep her." The commodore was speaking again, after waiting a heartbeat or two for the news to register in each of us. I dragged my mind back to his quarterdeck and listened intently, desperate now for more details. "Those pirates must be deprived of their prize, regardless of the cost to us. Since retaking the frigate, or in some other way denying her use to the pasha, will be a perilous undertaking, I will ask only volunteers to undertake the comiss . . ."

Before even he had finished speaking, Captain Decatur stepped forward and, in a clearly audible voice, volunteered.

"I will attempt to get in to the harbor and cut out *Philadelphia*, sir."

"Your willingness to take this on, Captain Decatur, is most welcome. I accept your offer. You will pick your own crew to accompany you. Before anything further is decided however, let me tell you of the events surrounding her capture and where she currently lays, or at least where she was as of several days ago." Preble paused and looked off toward the mouth of the harbor for a moment. Out of the corner of my eye, I caught a glimpse of Decatur. He seemed to stand taller, and the hard look on his face had turned his normally pleasant mouth into a thin line. His brow was furrowed, and the muscles of his jaw worked, almost as though he were chewing. But his eyes were what demanded my attention; they seemed actually to glow with a fire I had not before seen, save briefly when he had mentioned at dinner some weeks past that his friend Captain Sterrett had been victorious in an action with a polacca.

"According to His Britannic Majesty's ship *Amazon*," Preble continued, "whose captain provided this distressing news, and corroborated by a letter from Captain Bainbridge himself, which *Vixen* brought from Malta and which I have only just completed reading, Bainbridge had sent Captain Smith on *Vixen* off in chase of two Tripolitan cruisers heard to be off Cape Bon." I saw Captain Smith, standing near the commodore, nod in agreement. "Some two days later, our frigate was driven to the eastward some distance by an unnaturally strong blow from the west. Within a day, the gale moderated and backed to the east again, allowing Captain Bainbridge to run back to his station on the last day of the month.

"When about five leagues east of Tripoli, the lookouts spied a pair of vessels, inshore of *Philadelphia*, making for the harbor there. Bainbridge immediately ordered his ship to give chase and, in seven fathoms of water, commenced firing on the hostiles. He found his fire ineffectual and was withdrawing to recommence his patrol blockade when the frigate took the bottom. He mentioned in his letter that she did, in fact, run onto rocks in twelve feet of water forward, seventeen feet aft.

"No feat of seamanship—and he tried everything imaginable, including, in a last desperate resort, cutting away the foremast—proved able to move his ship. At that time, the enemy gunboats returned to take advantage of the situation, firing on her from fairly close aboard for some four hours. Since Captain Bainbridge had pitched most of his cannon overboard in his effort to lighten and thence re-float the ship, they were powerless to drive them off. None of the remaining guns would bear in spite of his best efforts. When he observed reinforcements heading out from shore to assist the pirates who were, he thought, about to board him, he had little choice but to strike in an effort to save his crew. He mentioned that the gunboats' shots had mostly been aimed at his rig, though had they tried to hull her, many of the crew, he felt, would have lost their lives."

That means Edward might still be alive! Pray, unhurt as well. I grasped at this fragile straw of hope.

Preble continued, "His letter indicates that all signal books were destroyed and the carpenter had been sent to flood the magazines in an attempt to scuttle the ship. He was uncertain as to the outcome of that order, though as you shall soon learn, the effort was unsuccessful."

A murmur went through the assembled officers and midshipmen. Faces had grown dark, and I noticed many hands clenched tightly into fists.

"After the pirates boarded *Philadelphia* and looted everything they could carry off, the men and officers were taken ashore—the pirates, he mentioned, made the American sailors row the boats—whereupon the men were further humiliated as they were marched through the city to a prison, while the officers were taken directly to the pasha's palace. There, a Mister Nicholas Nissen, the Danish consul, made every effort to provide for their relief, but was successful only in procuring for them dry clothes, rags, according to Bainbridge's letter, and for the delivery of this letter." Preble stopped again and held Bainbridge's letter aloft. Then he motioned to Captain Smith of *Vixen* to step forward. "*Vixen*, upon returning to station and finding *Philadelphia* absent, sailed close enough to the harbor to see that the frigate was anchored in Tripoli Harbor and flying a flag we have all come to loathe. Needless to say, he was shocked and sailed immediately to Malta and thence to Syracuse with *Constitution*. Captain Smith, would you be kind enough to tell us how you found her, her condition, and level of readiness?"

All eyes shifted to Smith. The silence was complete; not one of us appeared to breathe, and even the perpetually screaming gulls had gone still, as if in recognition of the direness of the situation and the import of what we were about to hear.

"We managed to close with the mouth of the harbor enough to discover *Philadelphia* riding to a single cable some half a league from shore." Smith said. "The heavy nor'westerly we had on 2 November must have pushed enough water in to float her, allowing the Tripolitans to drag the hulk off the reef. Her foremast was still down, though it appeared to have been cut away from the ship's side. A few gunboats sailed off and on nearby and, upon noticing *Vixen*, made as if to come after us, firing a few shots, none of which told. From our observation, it appeared as if little, save towing the frigate into the harbor, had been accomplished. Captain Bainbridge's attempt at scuttling his vessel must have been imperfectly done as she seemed to be floating to her lines." Smith, finishing his report, stepped back into the rank of his officers.

What dreadful news! Where is my brother? How can we manage to free him, and, I added to myself, with a touch of guilt, *the other officers and sailors? What am I to do? Will those piratical bastards let their captives write letters? Perhaps, since they let Bainbridge send out his report to the commodore, they will. Maybe I will hear from Edward. Oh, please, let me hear from him that he is alive and unhurt!* My head continued to spin, and the rumble of conversation and outrage from the assemblage remained little more than a deep-throated humming around me.

How will I ever write this awful turn of events to our parents?

Commodore Preble was speaking again. "We will establish our base here in Syracuse, even though Malta is closer to Tripoli. The English there have little in the way of supplies and stores beyond their own needs, and, I am told, the ruler here might prove to be more amenable to helping us carry out our intentions in the area. In the meanwhile, I will attempt to find a way of contacting Captain Bainbridge. We will maintain a close blockade on the harbor at Tripoli and continue to carry out our mission of escorting American merchants, attacking enemy vessels, and assisting with communications between ourselves and our allies here in the Mediterranean." So wrapped in my own thoughts, it signified not a whit to me that he had uttered most of the last without benefit of a single breath.

Find a way of contacting Cap'n Bainbridge! My mind raced ahead of the commodore as he spoke those words. *If he can correspond with Bainbridge, then certainly I can send letters to Edward. That would be grand and likely relieve his loneliness in captivity. Perhaps he can even get letters out to me. I must write him quickly so as to be ready if there is a way found to get letters into the prison. Wait! The letter I left with the port captain; I must retrieve it at once.*

An elbow in my ribs brought me back to *Constitution's* quarterdeck once again. I turned in irritation to the owner of the elbow, James, who whispered, "Sorry about your brother, Oliver. Hope he's not hurt. Looks like Decatur is fixin' to take his leave. Reckon we should go with him."

Indeed, the meeting was over. Whether or not Preble had uttered any other words, or orders, to us I knew not. My head and body seemed still disconnected, one here and the other ashore in some pest-hole of a prison in Tripoli. As we approached the break in the bulwark to call in Decatur's boat, which had been laying off with the other ships' boats, I suddenly realized that Captain Decatur was speaking to me.

"Sad news, indeed, Mister Baldwin. I certainly hope that your brother, and my good friend, Edward Baldwin, is alive and unhurt. I can only imagine the concern you must feel; should my own brother, James—you perhaps noticed him with the officers from *Nautilus*—be captured or killed, I am quite sure it would be my undoing. We shall see this through, you may rest assured, though how we might go about gaining the release of our men is quite beyond me." Decatur paused, watching the boat draw alongside the frigate. Almost as if musing to himself, he added, "Doubt we can just storm the battlements with Marines. Mayhaps a lengthy bombardment will bring those rascals to heel!"

"Thank you, sir, for your sentiments. I certainly join in your hope. Did the commodore say anything about getting the crew released? My head must have been elsewhere, if he did."

"No, no. He did not. But I'd warrant he's thinkin' on it. I'd wager he'll try to contact that Danish consul—what was his name?—Nissen, I recollect. Aye, Nissen. Likely see if he can assist. But do not worry; I am confident this will work out satisfactorily, and Edward with it." Decatur put a hand on my shoulder in a paternal gesture of comfort.

"Sir, should you have need of a midshipman on your venture to recapture *Philadelphia*, I would be most pleased to be included." I spoke the words, surprised at hearing them uttered even as I thought them. *Oh, Lord! Oliver, you've got to think before you speak. You're just reacting foolishly to Edward's capture. After all, capturing that ship wouldn't help Edward; might even do him harm . . . pasha might take out his anger on the prisoners. And should anything happen to me, it would likely kill my parents to have one son a captive and perhaps, slave, of these piratical bastards and the other dead in a futile and ill-starred effort to rescue not the captives, but the lost vessel.* My shock at my utterance must have been visible to the captain; he smiled and again lightly touched my shoulder.

"Thank you, Mister Baldwin. Once a plan is decided upon, I will seek an appropriate number of volunteers from within our ship's company to carry it to fruition. You will certainly be considered." Decatur stepped down the side into his waiting boat, leaving me wondering what horrors I might have called down upon myself.

The remainder of November 1803 passed quite without any conscious thought on my part. I performed my various duties to both the vessel and James in a purely mechanical and perfunctory manner. We sailed for some weeks off and on the coast of Tripoli, with little success to record. The others were solicitous toward me; even Thomas Wheatley seemed to fade into a blurred background of blue jackets, white breeches, cannon, spars, sails, and a dazzling sea all set to a symphony of the groaning wind, slapping lines and canvas, and shouted orders. By early December we were back in Syracuse, loading stores and some additional spars for further forays toward the coast of North Africa.

CHAPTER ELEVEN

The seventeenth of December, 1803, found us close-hauled out of Syracuse in the company of *Constitution* on a southerly heading which would take us back to the coast of Tripoli. No news of any kind had reached us from the Bashaw's prison or Consul Nissen and, after my earlier hopes of communicating with my brother had soared with the possibilities offered by Captain Bainbridge's letter, the complete silence from that quarter now dashed into oblivion any remaining hope. I had visited the port captain in Syracuse to gain possession of my letter to Edward, and it sat, along with a new, as yet unfinished missive, in my chest. A poorly writ letter to my parents—barely begun and not yet to the point—sat in my tiny writing desk, blockaded by my own inability to know how I might break the news, devastating as I knew it would be, to them.

The port captain had been most solicitous, assuring me of his sincere desire to help in any way he might, but there was little even a man of his lofty position could do to ease my, and Edward's, plight. Oh! How I wished for the wisdom and advice of my parents, four thousand miles distant, they might as well have been on the moon, on what course to follow. Surely Father, at least, would know what to do. No matter how I struggled, I was quite unable to convince myself that I could arrive at a solution which would answer.

A week later, having been beset by either foul weather with contrary winds or flat calms, we approached the coast of Tripoli. The fact that it was only two days 'til Christmas weighed on my mind. I could not but worry what Edward was suffering at the hands of his captors. *Surely*, I thought, *they would permit no celebration for their 'infidel' prisoners*—a term I had only just learned from Bosun Anderson, to my further dismay. I was still no closer to arriving at a course of action or the completion of any of the letters I had begun. I had composed any number of weak and, to my mind, sniveling explanations to my parents, trying to break gently to them the terrible news of Edward's capture. Each was discarded as quickly as it was conceived. My mind reeled with combinations of words that would accomplish what I sought.

As the last rays of the sun turned the late day sky into brilliant shades of purple, orange, and red, I stood at the quarterdeck rail idly watching the commodore's ship, USS *Constitution*, as she breasted the light swell with her broad and powerful bow. The spray thrown up, as she effortlessly brushed aside a larger wave, caught the late sunlight and made it sparkle in a multicolored dazzle. Her sails, set to t'gallants, reflected the colors of the sky in muted tones and complimented her black hull with its distinctive ochre stripe. Had not my mind been elsewhere, I would have been struck by the magnificence of the spectacle; not only was I unmoved by the display, I was barely aware of its existence. So distant were my thoughts that it took a moment for the lookout's hail to register on my despondent consciousness.

"Deck there! Sail! Two points on the leeward bow. Deck there!"

When the sailor's words penetrated my brain, a glance at Lieutenant Hobbs, with whom I once again shared the watch, was all I needed to bring my head to the present and my body into the main shrouds to confirm the lookout's cry.

"Aye, Mister Hobbs. She appears to be ketch-rigged and heading just a trifle below our own course. Mayhaps heading for the coast. I make her to be about two or three leagues distant." My shouted confirmation of the lookout's sighting and response to Hobbs' request received a wave from the deck officer. Even before my feet touched the planks of the weather deck, I saw Captain Decatur emerge from the scuttle, hatless and without his jacket.

"Mister Baldwin, was that vessel showing any flag that you could make out?" The captain had that same glint in his eyes I had noticed on several other occasions. His glass was tucked under his arm, and he rubbed his hands together as if they were cold.

"No, sir. I saw none." Knowing Decatur would want all the information I could provide, I added, "And she didn't seem in much of a hurry. Unless she's just a dull sailer."

"Very well. Mister Hobbs, we will bear off half a point and see what reaction, if any, that provokes. Have the quartermaster show the appropriate signal to the flagship. And put up a British ensign, if you please." With that, Captain Decatur sprang into the weather ratlines and quickly climbed to the partners of the mainmast. As orders swirled around the schooner, the men became aware that something, a prize, perhaps, was afoot. The off watch began to appear on deck, craning their necks to see what had caused the excitement. Lieutenant Lawrence stepped onto the quarterdeck, slipping his sword into its hanger as he did. His eye took in everything around him: the fact that the schooner was eased from her earlier course and separating from the flagship; the signal flags whipping in the easy breeze; the British ensign; and, perhaps most importantly, that the captain was aloft. He stepped to the binnacle, peered in, then fixed our second lieutenant with his stare.

"What have we, Mister Hobbs? A prize in the offing, perchance?" I noticed that Lawrence had the same fiery gleam in his eyes as had the captain. I think we all had it in some degree, eager as we were for the opportunity to hurt the pirates as much as they had hurt us. There had been no chance whatever—in fact, this little ketch was the first vessel we had sighted in some time—to exact our punishment for the heinous deed that weighed so heavily on each man's mind, mine most especially.

"Can't say for certain yet, sir. Might be. 'Ceptin' accordin' to Mister Baldwin, here, she likely won't make us rich. Some puny from his description, she is." Hobbs peered over his glasses at Lawrence and then at me. I nodded silently in agreement.

"Signal from the commodore, sir." The quartermaster stood at the windward rail studying the flagship through a long glass. "'*Enterprise* to investigate vessel and engage if enemy.' " Then, as he lowered the glass, he added, "And he says 'good luck,' too, sir." The glass closed with a crisp snap and the sailor turned to Hobbs. "Any response, sir?"

"I would think none is needed, Taylor, save an acknowledgment. But keep an eye on them over there in case the commodore has more to say." Lawrence had glanced aloft before he answered; Decatur was still at the partners of the mainmast, the glass still at his eye as he studied the unknown vessel

The schooner increased her speed with the more favorable course. It wasn't long before we could see the strange vessel's masts from deck. With our superior speed and greater spread of canvas, *Enterprise* was within cannon shot range while there was still some light left in the sky. We could make out a lightly armed ketch of some sixty or seventy feet with a crew clad in the white robes of one or another of the North African nations. The captain had returned to the quarterdeck and paced as much as the narrow confines of the diminutive deck would allow, all the while, hammering a fist into his open hand.

"Mister Lawrence, we'll have action stations, if you please. And load the forward wind'ard twelve-pounder with a powder charge. We'll see whether he might heave to without a fight." The first lieutenant glanced at me, wordlessly sending me forward to carry out the captain's instructions. As I left, Decatur muttered something else to Lawrence, but, already heading forward, I was not close enough to him to understand what he said. Something about the men needing a fight, I thought.

The insistent beating of the drum was, for the most part, unnecessary as the crew, eager for action, had been at their action stations for the past glass and more. I, however, had not and hurried forward to instruct Bradford about loading the windward gun. I was pleased to see my two crews were at their stations, powder charges had been laid out as had shot, and all four of the forward guns for which I was responsible had been drawn back for loading.

"A powder charge only, Bradford, in number one, then stand by." I watched the quarterdeck to see when the runner I sent to report our readiness was acknowledged and saw Mister Lawrence look up, directly at me, and then wave his arm over his head.

"FIRE!" I shouted, quite unnecessarily as the decks were still calm and the men quiet. But even a powder charge could be thrilling when I knew it could lead to my first enemy action, as well as the first for many of my men. Thrilling and not a little frightening, I realized. The gun issued forth a mighty roar and a belch of flame from its muzzle. Acrid lavender smoke blew back across the deck, momentarily enveloping the gun crew in a sulphurous cloud, stinging our eyes, and causing the men to spit to rid their mouths of the evil taste.

"All right, you men, quit yer gawkin' and clap onto the breechings; that gun ain't gonna pull itself back." Bradford's crew had forgotten, as had I, that with no shot, the gun's recoil was insufficient to roll the carriage back for swabbing and reloading. Guiltily, I pulled my eyes away from the strange vessel and watched as the men swabbed out the bore and prepared to reload the cannon. I heard some muttering and comments that most likely were not meant for me, as the men worked.

"Hope they give us a scrap!"

"They won't quit that easy."

"Come on, you bastards, fire at us."

Clearly, the men were as ripe for a fight as the captain and first lieutenant were. For my own self, I wasn't sure yet; I did notice that my stomach suddenly felt like I had swallowed a bag of grape shot. A glance aft, where Tom Wheatley stood with his two crews and guns, told me that my colleague might be unsure as well. He seemed reserved in direct contrast to his men who, at the leeward guns, were glaring, shouting lewd challenges, and shaking fists at our intended prize.

A dull thud rolled across the water, diminished by the wind and our distance from the ketch. It was followed by a small geyser that shot up silently some one hundred feet to our leeward. At the same time, I noticed a tiny patch of color appear at the mizzen peak of the smaller ship. It was clearly a flag, but unidentifiable to my untrained eye.

"There it is, lads. They want to fight!" The two or three men who saw the splash shouted with glee; they would get their fight and the opportunity to begin to even the score with the 'piratical bastards.' Others on deck and aloft joined in enthusiastically. Their joy quickly rose to a cheer that resonated throughout the ship and, I'm sure, across the water to our quarry. Wheatley's tanned complexion seemed to have lost some of its color, and his hand nervously toyed with the butt of his dirk. For once, I shared something with him. I wondered if his stomach felt like mine did. Farther down the deck I could see James eagerly leaning over the bulwark, his hands describing what could only be our course to get alongside and board the enemy ship.

"Leeward battery, stand by. Load round shot. Battery commanders, fire as you bear!" Lawrence's voice carried easily down the deck, and the men turned to their tasks with a will. I could feel *Enterprise* bearing off and, as she did so, picking up speed. A quick look told me we were on a course that would cross the stern of our quarry and bring us to within pistol-shot range to his wind'ard. Our British ensign, a *ruse de guerre*, had been replaced by the American colors; we were going to fight!

My guns, given their forward-most position, would be the first to bear. My hands suddenly became moist, and I felt a trickle of sweat down the center of my back. My stomach felt no better. In fact, I kind of eased myself to the lee bulwark just in case. Gunner Tarbox appeared and stood silently by my side. Had he sensed my concerns or was he just making sure that Bradford was doing his job properly? He watched, his eyes shifting between the crews of both guns and our target.

The men loading the guns of my battery moved with precision as they swabbed the barrels, cleared the touch holes, rammed down a cartridge followed by a ball and wad, and hauled the carriage back to the bulwark. Bradford crouched behind the number one gun, watching for the ketch to appear in the narrow frame of the gunport. With trepidation and a glance at Tarbox, who nodded encouragingly at me, I peered over his shoulder. All the training and practice we had gone through had abandoned me without warning. I realized my mind was quite blank. I looked around hoping to see something that might help . . .

I noticed that Bradford was no longer looking down the barrel; he was half-turned, studying me. I could feel the gunner's eyes boring into the back of my head. *Why is he looking at me like that? He is waiting for me to do something . . . aye, that's it. But what?* As if to help me, he shifted his eyes back to the gun.

A quick glance down the long barrel of the twelve-pounder and out the gunport brought me back to the present. Looking as if it were balanced on the end of the cannon was the ketch. We were bearing to offer a raking fire to our target!

BOOM! BOOM! Two guns fired almost as one. But they weren't mine. Wheatley had beaten us to firing, even though I was sure only my two guns actually bore at the target. I looked at Bradford and received a nod as he blew on his match.

"FIRE!" I screamed. In my excitement, my voice let me down yet again, breaking into a girlish squeal. But fire we did. Bradford jammed his glowing linstock into the powder at the touch hole. It sizzled and sparked for a second. Suddenly that gun and, less than a second later, the next one aft, thundered, leapt back into their breechings, and lit the quickly darkening night with tongues of flame. My ears rang with the concussion. Once again, while I could see the activities of the men and knew there was noise, I could hear none of it.

The six guns along our leeward side spoke twice more before Lieutenant Lawrence waved his sword and shouted, "Cease fire!" Even with our diminished hearing, the mids and gun captains responsible for those pieces heard and stopped, peering through the smoke to see what result we had gained. I noticed Gunner Tarbox crouching by one of the guns, looking intently at our target.

I looked through the dissipating smoke and saw the ketch round up as she hauled down the bit of color I had noticed at the top of her mizzen. The top of her mainmast and what must have been a t'gallant yard hung at a crazy angle while crewmen, their white robes billowing in the dying breeze, struggled to control the wreckage.

"We done it, by God! They've struck their colors!" A voice floated forward; I recognized it as belonging to James. Before I could take in his enthusiasm, the entire crew joined in, echoing his cry. *Enterprise* eased her course once more, this time to go alongside our prize. My stomach seemed more settled, at least until I noticed the activity going on amidships.

Perhaps recalling the tale of treachery he had told us at his table, Captain Decatur had cutlasses, half-pikes, and hatchets issued to the men and pistols to the officers and midshipmen. If the commander of this vessel was of a like mind to his brother in arms who had surrendered three times to Captain Sterrett only to fight again when he tried to board, we would be ready. I gripped my pistol nervously, my hand sweating and slippery. With my other, I pressed gingerly at various points in my midsection.

The schooner seemed to fly through the water, even in the fading wind. It was now full dark, and we could see the lanterns rigged on our prize and the reflections of their light on the robes of the Tripolitan sailors; they did not look ready to repel boarders. nonetheless, I shifted my pistol to my left hand, wiping my right on my pant leg. My mouth, in contrast to my hands, had gone dry; I knew that if I spit, only dust would come out. Speaking was out of the question. I worked the lock on my pistol carefully, so as not to create a spark, and silently prayed that, should the need arise, I could fire it into a man.

I glanced around me. In the dim glow of our battle lanterns, the sailors looked a rum bunch of cutthroats; grime-covered faces under sweat-stained bandanas, cutlasses held in one hand, pikes or tomahawks in the other. Tom Wheatley stood some aft of me, fondling his pistol as his eyes darted about the ship. Gone, I thought, was the arrogant and cocksure midshipman who had pounded the butt of his pistol on the bulwark. Farther down the deck stood James, sweat running down his red face, his hat askew, and smudges across the front of his white shirt. He spoke with considerable animation to one of the sailors nearby. He was smiling; I could make out his teeth in the yellow glow of our own battle lanterns.

"Heave your grapnels, lads! Make fast!" someone, I think it was on the quarterdeck, shouted. Out of the corner of my eye, I saw a four-pronged hook fly through the space between our vessels, its hempen rope snaking out behind it. Two others were heaved and made fast, securing *Enterprise* to her capture.

"Get ready, lads!" Decatur's voice was decidedly closer this time. "Boarders away! Follow me, boys!" The captain brushed by me as he sprung onto the bulwark, sword held to the fore, pistol jammed into the top of his breeches. He leaped nimbly across the considerable gap of water still separating the ships and dropped onto the deck of our prize. Without thought, I followed him, pistol in one hand, dirk in the other.

In seconds, the enemy deck swarmed with American sailors; half-pikes and cutlasses waving in the air, horrifyingly close to friendly ears and noses. We pressed forward, then split, half of us working our way toward the quarterdeck of the little ship, while the others herded part of the Tripolitan crew forward in an effort to confine them around the butt of the long, rakish bowsprit.

The noise was awesome; the sailors of the pasha screaming at each other, or perhaps at us, in their own language while the American sailors shouted encouragement to each other and invective at the enemy with equal fervor. Strangely absent was the clanging of steel on steel or the sharp crack of discharging pistols.

Gradually, both the enemy crew and the Americans fell silent as Decatur's voice filled the night.

"She's ours, men. They've surrendered without condition. Disarm them and lock 'em below."

When we opened the hatches on the ship, we discovered her cargo. She carried female slaves, apparently in some quantity, and Decatur immediately belayed his order to lock the crew below. Instead, they were taken to *Enterprise* and put in the hold there.

"Mister Baldwin, Mister Devon will be sailing as prize-master to bring this vessel back to Syracuse. You will accompany him. We will meet you there within the week." When Captain Decatur, now back aboard the schooner, informed me that I was to be *second in command* of the prize, I am afraid I was only able to stare at him, slack-jawed and dumb.

"Get a seabag, boy, and step lively." Decatur, his hand firmly guiding my upper arm, steered me toward the aft scuttle to 'get a seabag.'

By the time I returned to the deck, a few hastily grabbed possessions thrown in a canvas seabag, the prize crew was aloft on the mainmast of our prize sorting out the damage and cutting away the t'gallant rigging so the spar could be lowered to the deck. Judd stood on the quarterdeck looking for all the world like a captain. I joined him, clambering over the bulwark of *Enterprise* and throwing my bag unceremoniously toward a small deckhouse on the ketch.

As I glanced backward, I saw Wheatley glowering in my direction. He stood next to a battle lantern which cast its pale yellow light on his face, leaving little doubt as to his thoughts on my selection. James, on the quarterdeck, waved at me enthusiastically, his still grimy face wreathed in a smile at my good fortune. I waved back. Then, on Decatur's orders, the grapnels were cast off, and the ketch and *Enterprise* separated, we to sail directly to Syracuse, and Decatur to report to the commodore on *Constitution*, then hopefully to join us in port.

I watched as the schooner's lights grew fainter and fainter then winked out altogether. Judd was busy giving orders and figuring our course to Syracuse, and I had my first opportunity to look around.

This vessel was some smaller than *Enterprise* and about half the size of *Argus*. She was narrow in her beam, about twelve feet, I thought, and actually quite sleek. She carried four carronades of about twenty-four pounds. She was also filthy and poorly kept. Part of this, I realized, could have been due to the brief skirmish, but most of the filth and disarray had long been in residence. I returned to the quarterdeck, if the slightly elevated deck aft where stood a helmsman at the long tiller could be so dignified, and approached Judd—Captain Devon.

"What do you think, Judd . . . I mean, *Cap'n Devon*? Will the rig hold?" I thought that sounded sufficiently intelligent.

"I expect she'll see us in to Syracuse safely, Oliver. And belay that 'cap'n' nonsense. Judd'll answer fine. Or Mister Devon. Perhaps you might have a look into the hold and see what shape our cargo is in. Likely scared and probably hungry as well, since these pirates aren't too concerned about their health. Takin' 'em to Constantinople, they were, slaves for the Sultan there. The vessel's named *Mastico*, by the way, and her captain, a Turk, it turns out, is still aboard—there, in the deckhouse. I got a man watchin' him, but I don't expect he'll give us any trouble. And he speaks some English, I discovered." Judd's smile was lit by the yellow glow of the binnacle light as he leaned over it to check our heading.

How proud he must be, this being his first command. I know how I feel and I'm only first lieutenant! Just thinking that title made me smile. I knew I wasn't *really* first lieutenant, but I might as well be, the only other officer aboard 'sides Judd. I made my way forward, stepping over indeterminate objects and piles of tangled cordage, stores, and an extra spar or two.

Amidships, the hatch over our hold was open, and two or three of our sailors were leering into the dark of the hold. I joined them to determine the reasons for the ribald comments they uttered, both to each other and down, into the hold. In the dim light cast by a shuttered lantern held below the coaming of the hatch, it quickly became clear. Our cargo of female slaves, packed into the confines of the hold, was each as innocent of covering as the day she was born!

When two of the men made to climb down into the hold, I stepped quickly and grabbed one by the shoulder. He turned to question who it was impeding his progress, and the curse that he might have uttered died on his lips when he saw my blue jacket.

"Just goin' down to give 'em some proper cover, sir. Ain't right, them bein' all nekked like that." I didn't recognize the sailor and assumed him to be one of the original Enterprises. He smiled hopefully at me as he tore his eyes away from the women.

"A fine idea, sailor." I thought fast, looking around me at the faces of his mates. They appeared none too happy I had spoiled their fun. "Some canvas would likely answer just fine. Perhaps the bosun will give you the t'gallant they just took down. He's just there." I pointed toward the mainmast where, indeed, Mister Anderson was overseeing the removal of the sail from the t'gallant yard. "You others, slide that hatch cover over, since you've nothing else to do." I continued on my way forward without a backward glance.

I did it! My first confrontation and I acted the officer! Oliver, you may just have a future in the Navy yet. You didn't get all red and flustered. I actually straightened my back and, as I made my way, smiling inwardly, toward the bow, might even have swaggered a trifle. I determined to include my small triumph in my letter to Edward. I thought it might make him smile in spite of his most awful circumstances.

Heading aft again, I passed the hatch; the cover was on and the men were sitting on it, the damaged sail across their knees. Each held a sheath-knife with which they cut wide strips from the canvas. Several pieces had already been carefully stacked on the deck, ready to be sent into the hold.

The same sailor I had stopped from joining the women looked up from his work. "I reckon it'll be all right to open this hatch enough to take this canvas down yonder, Mister Baldwin? I figgered to show 'em what we done for 'em."

"Yes, of course. But just open it and throw the strips down; I suspect they'll figure out what to do with them." I smiled and saw his smile fade to a scowl. I continued aft, still smiling.

Judd greeted me as I stepped onto the quarterdeck. "Mister Baldwin, looks like we might be going to get a bit of weather shortly. Have the bosun shorten her down to a reefed tops'l and single jib. We'll tie a reef into the mizzen later. I'd be willing to wager she'll manage some weather just fine, bein' as how she's French-built and not all that old. Cap'n Decatur told me before we parted company that she was built as a gunboat for Napoleon's attack on Egypt back in '98."

"Aye, Cap'n." I smiled in the dark, suspecting that, although he told me not to call him captain, he liked hearing it. Forward I went again to find the bosun and pass on Judd's orders.

Some considerable time passed before I returned to the quarterdeck. I had supervised, well, I watched, the shortening of our sails, and made sure that the canvas strips had been made available to our 'passengers' with due regard for their modesty. I also ensured that they got some vittles and water.

Judd was yawning. I could make out his tired eyes and furrowed brow in the light of our binnacle. "Why don't you take the watch for while, Oliver? I am dead on my feet."

I was speechless. I had stood countless watches with both Lieutenants Hobbs and Morris in *Argus* and again in *Enterprise*, but there was never a time when I was alone on the quarterdeck and 'in command' of anything. Judd had ordered me to relieve him with no more thought of my qualifications than anything. The weather was starting to make up. My brain raced, question after question surfacing faster than ever I could give them voice.

What happens if this storm comes in worse than you expect? What if the men won't follow my orders? Will I have to make any decisions? How long will I be "in command"? Where will you be? Will the rig hold up if the wind gets stronger? Should I shorten down some more? My God! How am I to manage the ship alone?

As matter-of-factly as if he were telling a story, and quite without regard to my own concerns, he told me the course we were steering and admonished me to check from time to time that the helmsman was, in fact, steering it. "And throw the log every turn of the glass and write down on the slate our course and speed. You'll need them to get our position tomorrow if the sun doesn't break through." Then he left. I barely had time to say, "Aye, sir," before he disappeared into the tiny deckhouse.

And here I am! Dear Lord, let nothing go awry, I prayed fervently, but silently. I noticed the sailor at the tiller was watching me closely. *Did I look* that *different from any other officer or midshipman he might have sailed with?* He was an older cove and not one of the men from *Argus* who had transferred with Captain Decatur. I either never knew, or could not, in my anxious state of mind, recall his name.

"Something wrong, sailor?"

"No, sir!"

"Then you'll be wantin' to mind your helm." I peered into the binnacle. "Looks like you want to come off some to hold your course. We're getting a trifle high." I spoke with no rancor and only loud enough for him to hear me. He looked once more, hard, at me then shifted his gaze to the compass and, muttering something that sounded to me like "children at sea," pulled the tiller to weather a bit. The French/Turkish/Tripolitan ketch eased off some and, even with her shortened sails, flew across the dark sea towards Sicily. At least I hoped it was toward Sicily. The helmsman's muttered comment did little to ease my own concerns. While I no longer considered myself a "child," I did recognize my lack of experience, especially at managing a ship by myself, and struggled to appear confident.

After a few hours, I began to feel the same bone tiredness that I guessed Judd had felt. I caught myself nodding off, even while standing. I moved around the tiny quarterdeck, feeling the wind in my face and the occasional splash of spray we threw up. My eyes felt as is they were full of grit, but rubbing them seemed not to help. *Keep moving, Oliver. You can't fall asleep if you're walking around.* The helmsman had been changed twice since Judd retired, and I was pleased to see the current sailor manning the big tiller was none other than Lockhart, Captain Decatur's cox'n.

"How's she feeling, Lockhart? Does she respond all right?" I thought some talk might revive me. Earlier in the watch I had been worried and, as a result, wide awake. Nothing had happened, my concerns had pretty well vanished, and now it became an effort just to maintain a proper watch.

"Yes, sir. Just fine." Lockhart knew better than I about officers, or mids for that matter, chattering with sailors on watch, particularly on the quarterdeck. He shifted his glance from the compass to the reefed main tops'l, watching for any sign of a shiver that would indicate a wind shift.

"Keep her full and by, Lockhart. I am going to take a turn around the deck."

I stepped forward with the thought of checking the watch, lookouts, sail handlers, and whoever else might be abroad at this hour. I found a clutch of men hunkered around the mainmast, sitting on the still closed hatch, and talking quietly. In fact, they did not hear my approach and started when I spoke.

"Everything all right up here, men?"

"Oh, yes, sir. Just fine. When do you figger to be back in Syracuse, Mister Baldwin? I collect that's where we's headed?"

I have no idea. Not a hint of when we'll be back in Syracuse. Can't tell them that, though. "Soon enough, sailor. And, yes, Syracuse is exactly where we're heading. Might even beat *Enterprise* and *Constitution* back." I was guessing, pure and simple. "Are you men supposed to be on lookout here?" *Always let them think you know what they're supposed to be doing.*

"No, sir, lookouts're aloft at the main crosstrees. We're here to relieve 'em and handle sails. Sir." I couldn't see who was talking even in the dim glow of the shuttered lantern, but thought it sounded a mite sharp. But I had asked, hadn't I?

"Very well. Stay awake and alert." I could think of nothing else and headed down the starboard side toward the quarterdeck.

"Light! Deck there! I have a light just for'ard of the beam to weather!"

Damn the luck! In another hour I could have turned the watch back over to Judd and gone to bed myself. Now there's something out there and more than likely, not a friend. "Aye. How far do you make it?" I called quietly back up to the man in the rigging.

"Cain't tell, sir. Might be a bit more 'an a league. Light keeps disappearing into the troughs."

"Very well. Keep watching it. Sing out if there's any change." I headed for the deckhouse and noted that the Turkish captain continued to sit quietly, occasionally glancing out the port. I made my way below and spoke softly to Judd, who was instantly awake and alert. He pulled on his boots, picked up his hat and a pistol and was on deck in a trice. After a quick look about the vessel to ensure everything was as it should be, he stepped onto the bulwark and into the main shrouds and climbed to the crosstrees with a night glass.

I suddenly realized that several lanterns were showing on deck and moved to get them extinguished without bellowing. I knew how sound carried over the water, even to wind'ard. While the wind was still up and pushing the waves to a height of several feet over the deck of the ketch, there was only a small chance the other vessel would see our lights; but, it occurred to me, we had seen *theirs* even with the waves.

By the time Judd had returned to the deck, I had ordered all our lights extinguished and cautioned the men to silence fore and aft.

"I can't make anything out of it, Oliver. Could be anyone out there. From the look of the lights, there are three of them. Whoever it is, is bigger than us and appears to be on a similar heading. Best we keep dark and quiet. No point in courting disaster." Judd sounded concerned. Maybe I was reading something into his tone, but I was concerned as well. Suddenly I realized I didn't seem to be tired anymore!

I pulled my watch from my pocket and squinted at its face in the dark. Nothing. I could make out not a single feature on the timepiece. Without thinking, I stepped to the glow from the deckhouse portlight and saw that it would be dawn in something more than an hour. And then I realized there was a light showing from the deckhouse, a very bright light.

I hurried around to the door and peered in. The Turkish captain was hunched by the window on the wind'ard side and was holding a lantern to it. The sailor assigned to watch him appeared to be unconscious in a chair.

"Here. What are you doing? Put out that light!" The Turk, startled, dropped the lantern and stepped back from the port. The crash and my exclamation had awakened the 'unconscious' sailor from his nap, and the three of us stared silently at one another for several heartbeats. The burning oil from the lantern crept across the deck, gaining strength as it consumed the woven carpet and the legs of another chair.

"FIRE! FIRE!" The sailor screamed as he leapt to his feet. The Turkish captain pressed himself into a corner, a smile playing at the corners of his mouth. He said something unintelligible, in Turkish, I guessed, and waved his arms in dramatic fashion, then pointed at the growing fire.

Judd, alarmed by the scream, headed into the cabin to determine the problem. He collided head-on with the exiting sailor, and the pair crashed to the deck in a heap. Devon was on his feet in an instant, issuing orders, the very ones which I should have issued even before he arrived. I had little time for self-recrimination, however.

"Buckets, get some buckets. And all hands on deck. Form a chain to the side." The men I had earlier spoken to appeared and moved swiftly to carry out Judd's orders. The light from within the cabin was getting brighter and brighter as the fire gained ground, fanned by the wind whipping around the corner and through the door. The wind'ard bulkhead of the structure was engulfed in flame. It would only be minutes before it burned through and then would threaten the whole ship. The Turkish captain was still in there, on the other side of the fire.

"Judd, Judd! The captain is in there. We've got to get him out!"

"Let the scoundrel burn, damn his eyes. He's the one 'at started this mess, tryin' to signal that ship out there." Judd snarled at me and shot a glance into the cabin where the Turk still huddled in the corner farthest from the flames. The features of his face shimmered through the heat, and I noticed that his smile was gone, while his eyes darted wildly from the flames to the doorway.

I was stunned! In the four months I had known Judd Devon, I had never heard him utter such venom, certainly not about another human being, not even Thomas Wheatley. For a long moment I didn't, couldn't, move, then a sailor returned toting a full bucket of water.

I snatched it from his hands and, stepping partly into the room, threw it into the hellish confines of the cabin. For a moment, some of the flames were extinguished. Tossing the bucket aside, I jumped farther in and grabbed the captain by his shirt front. With more strength than I thought I possessed, I dragged the man out behind the fire and into the night outside the cabin.

A bucket of water was dashed on his smoldering lower parts. He lay there on the deck simply staring at the activity around him. I caught my breath and joined the bucket line while the flames shot out the cabin wall and overhead.

Judd grabbed an axe and began crashing it into the burning wood, hauling pieces of it away from the rest with each bite of the blade. Another sailor joined him, wielding a hatchet, while a third, his hands wrapped in scraps of canvas, threw the smoldering, cherry-red bits they had cut away over the side. It was hot work, but quickly in hand. Soon the cabin was little more than a glowing pile of wreckage that all hands then pitched overboard. Each piece left a fiery arc and a trail of smoke in the darkness and landed in the water with a satisfying sizzle. Then the fire was out and the danger past.

CHAPTER TWELVE

I n the excitement of the conflagration, no one had thought to check on the other vessel. No one on deck, that is. The lookout had divided his attention between the progress his shipmates were making with the fire and the progress the strange ship was making—toward us, as it turned out. *One danger gone and another looming!* My joy at being selected as "first lieutenant" on this vessel was rapidly evaporating.

She was now almost within cannon-shot and Judd studied her from the deck with a night glass. He spoke in a low voice without taking his eye from the glass.

"Oliver, send the men to quarters; we may have to fight. I can make no colors on this vessel, and I am sure we must look like easy pickin's after that fire." Devon paused, and I headed forward to carry out his orders. "And make sure there are cutlasses and half pikes on deck; they may well try to board us if they think we still have problems. Get yourself a pistol as well." He studied the closing ship for another heartbeat, then added, "And see that some of the guns are double-shotted with ball and some loaded with grape or canister, whatever you can find. No telling what we might be in for, here." This last ominous comment was under his breath; he might not even have realized he spoke aloud. But I heard it, plain as day.

I hurried off, urging the men to their action stations. Most were already on deck and obviously shared Judd's opinion as to the likely outcome of a meeting with a strange vessel, making my words quite unnecessary. Bradford and another I recognized from one of Wheatley's gun crews had already bent to the task of loading our few cannon. I mentioned Judd's instructions as to their loads and, after issuing hand weapons to the others, saw that we were ready for a fight. This one, I feared, would not go as easily as our last.

I felt the ketch change her motion through the seas as Judd brought her bow higher to the wind; he was closing the distance to the stranger rather than trying to get away. Sails were braced and sheeted home and *Mastico* quickly picked up speed, toward a confrontation with the stranger. *Why would he want to get closer? We have only a few hands aboard to fight her and even fewer guns!*

"What ship is that?" The hail drifted down to us from the stranger, carried by the wind over the mile or less separating us. The accent was clearly English, but that was meaningless in these waters, I reminded myself.

I watched Judd to see what he would do. He continued to study the ship through his night glass and finally stepped onto the bulwark with a speaking trumpet held to his lips.

"We are American. The prize of the American schooner *Enterprise* and the frigate *Constitution*. Who are you?" Without moving the speaking trumpet from his lips, he shouted, "Blow on your matches, lads. Stand by!"

"He's lost his mind! We cain't fight with this toy of a ship!" One of the men crouching behind a carronade muttered to a mate. My thoughts, exactly. I realized that, once again, I had difficulty swallowing and found that my breathing seemed considerably faster than it had been only moments ago. In spite of the cool of the night, I realized my shirt was some wet and sticky.

After a short delay, a different voice, with a decidedly educated accent, answered, "His Britannic Majesty's brig *Amazon*. Lieutenant Throckmorton commanding. Are you experiencing difficulty? May we be of assistance?" The ship continued to close with us. Over my own exhalation, I heard a collective release of breath from the men near at hand.

"It would appear we have the situation under control, sir. But I thank you for your offer. We are directed to make for Syracuse to rejoin with *Constitution* and *Enterprise*. If you are headed that way, we would welcome the company."

"You are only a day or two from your landfall, captain. While we are only going as far as Malta, we would be pleased to give you escort that far. You may maintain a position under my lee." The disembodied English voice stopped. There was a bit of happy chatter from the hands as they realized there would be help at hand should it be needed. "Name your commander, sir, if you please." The same voice floated over the water, carried undiminished on the strong breeze.

"Midshipman Judd Devon of *Enterprise*. Stephen Decatur commanding." Judd's voice rang out quickly and must have satisfied Captain Throckmorton (or whoever on the British ship was our inquisitor) as the conversation ended, and we watched the dim figure of the ship change as *Amazon* bore up to continue on her original course. *Mastico* bore off to sail a cannon-shot off and in her lee.

"Stand down, men. Looks like we won't be fightin' tonight!" Even without seeing him, I, and I'm sure all the others aboard, could hear the relief in Judd's voice; indeed, we all shared it. Suddenly I could barely keep my eyes open. I staggered to the quarterdeck in the hope of relief.

"Aye. You've done well, Oliver. Go to bed. With *Amazon* standing by to weather we'll be fine. I managed to get a few hours' sleep, and now you should do the same." Judd's smile was accompanied by a hand on my shoulder. As I stepped toward the ladder below in the charred area of our deck where once the cabin had stood, he called quietly after me, "Have Wilson or whoever it is watching our Turkish friend there secure him to a chair, or the mizzenmast or anything else. We don't need him causing us any more troubles this night!"

I did so, barely noticing that the captain offered no resistance to the order. I was asleep even as I touched the cot, never removing my boots, dirk, or jacket.

The sun was up, indeed, it was quite high in a sky of the purest blue I had ever seen, when I returned to the deck, having been summoned by Captain Devon. The brightness of the day, the effulgence of the water, and having slept the sleep of the dead, all conspired to cause my eyes to squint almost shut for some minutes. Eyes shut or no, I could feel that the wind had eased to a pleasant breeze. Once again, *Mastico* was under her full sail. Judd laughed when he saw me.

"I am sure that Mister Cutler, were he here, or Mister Lawrence for certain, would have some suitably caustic comment on your appearance, Oliver. Did you not even remove your clothes when you retired?"

"Not even my boots, Judd. I have never been so fatigued."

"You'll find that the weight of responsibility can be tiring, Oliver. And while I can not apologize for dropping you headlong into that position last night, I was most pleased that you weathered it, and the other excitement we enjoyed, quite splendidly. You may rest assured that Lawrence and Decatur will receive favorable reports on your abilities." Judd seemed no worse for the wear. I doubt he had gotten any more sleep than I, yet he had the full weight of command on his shoulders whether he was asleep or not. But hearing that he would report to my credit put me in a happy state of mind. I caught myself smiling.

The men had been working to restore the ketch to a seaworthy condition, hammering boards down to replace the ones on the deck that had burned. I noticed a pair of unfamiliar faces in the group near where our deckhouse once had been. Their confident movements and the instructions they gave to the Enterprises working with them made them more than sailors, and I turned back to Judd. He anticipated my query.

"Captain Throckmorton was kind enough to lend us, early this morning, a carpenter and his mate, along with a few boards he felt they could spare. They'll be into Malta before the middle watch tonight, and, with the weather calmed down as much as it is, he didn't think the Royal Navy would miss them. The boards, of course, not the carpenters. Doing a fine job of fixing the damage, they are!" He smiled wearily at his little joke.

Indeed, except for the complete lack of the deckhouse, there seemed little to attest to our potentially disastrous excitement that just last night, or rather, early this morning, had looked so dreadful, even in the dark. A temporary chart table had been built on the quarterdeck to take the place of the one which had occupied much of the structure. Not only had the wind eased, but the seas were down considerably, and the ketch sailed on an easy reach with a pleasant motion to her. *Amazon* kept pace, now about a musket shot to wind'ard. *Mastico's* former captain, the Turk, dozed in the chair to which he was still secured, just for'ard of the mizzenmast.

"When do you figure we'll get in, Judd?" I looked all around the horizon and could see no land. Obviously, we were still some distance away, even from Malta where we would lose our escort.

"By my calculations, we ought to be seein' the southern point of Sicily about first light tomorrow and in the harbor by mid-day." He looked at me, the beginnings of a smile working at the corners of his mouth. "Why don't you see if you can get a noon sun line and work our position from that? See if you agree with me. Shouldn't be more'n an hour from now 'til noon, I'd guess."

The remainder of the day was spent putting *Mastico* to rights, returning the carpenter and his mate to the brig, with a jug of Spanish brandy Judd had found in the captain's cupboard by way of a thank you, and feeding the crew and our cargo. During the dark of the night, but before the middle watch began (I had relieved Judd shortly after our meager supper) a voice hailed from windward.

"Ahoy there, *Mastico*! We'll be taking our leave now. A safe passage to Syracuse to you! And thank you for the brandy. Right decent of you, that! And a glad Christmastide to you all."

"Thank you, sir, for the escort. And the assistance. And Christmas tidings to you, as well." I shouted back, hoping I sounded more like an officer than a fourteen-year-old midshipman. At least my voice broke into the higher registers less frequently now. To my joy, it held while I shouted through the dark to the English ship. As I watched them haul their wind and bear up to fetch Malta, I realized with a shock that we—the British commander and I—had just exchanged Christmas greetings—tomorrow would be that holy day. I could scarce believe it; the day had nearly arrived unnoticed! This exchange was the first thought I had had of Christmas, and I was startled by the suddenness. As long as I could remember, I had always anticipated the arrival of Christmas and all that it entailed. Now here it was very nearly upon me. My thoughts, as *Mastico* moved comfortably through the warm Mediterranean night, turned to Philadelphia and family, and the contrasts were inescapable.

This year for Oliver Baldwin, there would be no snow softening the hard edges of the streets and buildings of the city, no sleighs sounding the happy tinkling of bells as they carried red-cheeked and laughing families to and fro, visiting relatives and going to church, waving to the like-minded occupants of other sleighs they passed, and no fine dinner with family and relatives. Just warm winds, sea, this battle-scarred little ketch, and the monotony of watches, meals and the same faces. Faces that were familiar to be sure—and friends as well—but it would not be the same as being home. With an effort I hauled myself out of the sadness that washed over me and, with the realization that my brother's circumstances would allow even less, thought guiltily of Edward. He was even farther away, even though he was likely only a few hundred miles from where I stood this moment.

The poor man! I wonder if those piratical Arab scoundrels would even give the prisoners leave to acknowledge the day. Did the Philadelphia *frigate carry a chaplain? Was there anyone who might lead a service of some kind for the men? I know he must be lonely in his captivity. Anderson has told me of the conditions in those pest holes. I reckon he'll not be having a juicy goose with dumplings and a tasty duff for dessert, any more than I. And I am sure he would relish the 'monotony' of my life. His must be dreadful! At least I can see the sky and smell and feel the fresh sea breeze. And move about freely, even on this little vessel. I must finish my letter and find a way to get it to him. And one to my parents.*

Wonder if they'll do the same thing as every year, even though Edward and I are absent. This would be one of the only days in the year the shop will be closed for business. Father will have Martha hitched between the shafts of the sleigh, ready to pull him and Mother to church and then, afterwards, to visit with Aunt Sally and Uncle Jim and those noisome cousins of mine. Maybe they'll stay there for dinner, since there's only the two of them now, and Mother likely wouldn't want to fix a big dinner for just her and Father. And I'm sure she would be just as happy for the distraction of dining with her younger sister's family. Aunt Sally will make a fine dinner of a goose and dumplings and a wonderful plum duff for dessert. Oh! How I miss home. Even those cousins might not be so intolerable! Wonder if they'll think of me. I know they rarely spoke of Edward when he was away, a year and more at a time, when I was home, or within earshot. Maybe they . . .

"LAND! Deck there! Land just off the wind'ard bow. Maybe four leagues." The cry of the lookout jerked me rudely from my sorry reverie. I expected we would be coming onto Malta, especially after *Amazon* bid us farewell, but didn't think it would be this soon. I laid our track on the chart and extended it onward based on the numbers written on the slate.

Yes, that would have to be Malta. Sicily by dawn, just as Judd had predicted. My own earlier confirmation of his landfall was something less than exact and hardly confirmed his own calculations, though I had refrained from voicing anything beyond a vague agreement with his estimate. But what better proof could be had than our landfall at Malta! I looked forward to a return to my duties as midshipman on *Enterprise*; perhaps the responsibility of my temporary position was premature. I resolved to content myself with waiting until I had made further progress along the "course to manhood."

Judd appeared to take the middle watch and, after showing him our position on the chart and the dark smudge of land off our windward bow, I climbed down the ladder to the single cabin that we shared. This time, before climbing wearily into the cot, I stripped off my clothes and boots, anticipating another dreamless sleep, at least until I was called to relieve Judd before the dawn.

But it was not to be; my mind whirled and thrashed, first with thoughts again of home and, then turning once again to my poor brother. I pined for both, and wondered in my restlessness why I missed Edward so much when I was quite used to his long absences over the past five years and more. Perhaps, I decided, it was because of his nearness and the knowledge that I would not, and could not, see him. And because it was Christmas, a time of closeness and sharing for the Baldwin family.

Yes, that must be it. When he missed the holiday the first time, Father and Mother were quite beside themselves. Never mind that I was there, a mere boy of ten years. They tried to put on a good face and be jolly, but it was hollow, even to me. We did everything we had always done, visiting friends and family, attending services at the church, and sitting down to a wonderful dinner in mid-afternoon. But Edward's chair was empty, a sight that none of us could overlook. It cast a pall on the joy of the day and made Mother weep in spite of her efforts to avoid showing her dismay. Now both our chairs would be empty; what will Mother and Father be doing? I should have finished that letter to them. They should know that Edward is held captive. I reckon they don't even know where I am. Did Edward manage to get a letter out to them? Or to me? Oh God! Let there be some word in Syracuse when we get in!

I could not find a comfortable position in the cot. No matter how I turned, something poked into me or the motion of the ketch made sleep impossible. The cabin became close and hot, confining me. I lay in the cot, asleep, but, at the same time, aware of the sounds and motion of the vessel, sweating as images of Edward's prison, incongruously interlaced with memories of a snowy Christmas in Philadelphia, churned through my tortured dreams. Then they combined: Edward in chains and rags staggering in the snow down Held Street, the street we lived on, and me riding in the sleigh with Mother and Father laughing while my cousins threw snowballs at Edward. All of us, even Edward, singing Christmas carols. With a start, I awoke, sat up, and hit my head a resounding *whack* on the overhead. The blow jarred me back to the reality of the ketch, and I took in, as if for the first time, the cramped cabin with its single portlight, tiny table and chair, and my clothes strewn about. The scene was lit by the flickering light of a guttering candle I had left burning on the table. In spite of the scene's familiarity, it took me a moment or two to remember just where I was.

The cot was soaked with my sweat, as was my sleeping shirt. I could take it no longer. I stepped out of the narrow bed and donned my clothes. When I returned to the deck and the fresh air, I was surprised to see the first hint of dawn in the eastern sky, not more than a faint red glow, but the clear harbinger of a new day, nonetheless. To the north, a dark line on the horizon which could only be Sicily. *Home!* The ease with which I labeled this foreign, faraway seaport as 'home' struck me like a hammer-blow.

What is becoming of you, Oliver? I chastised myself. *Syracuse is not 'home' by a long shot. But won't it be grand to see James and Thomas again. Wonder how James is coming with his reading. I hope he's kept up even though I haven't been there to help him. He's a bright boy. I am sure he will attend avidly my tales of this adventure! Maybe even Thomas will. But whether he does or not, it will be good to see them again and learn what they've been doing. Hope* Enterprise *and* Constitution *are in when we get there. They certainly should be; that gale we struggled with would have been a blessing to them. Well, I reckon I'll find out soon. And whether there might be a letter from Edward. What a delight that would be!* I was rambling; my thoughts jumped from one thing to another without any conscious effort and were jumbled, almost as jumbled as my dreams.

"Mister Baldwin! How nice to see you up. I collect you're here to take the watch? I was about to send someone to awaken you." Judd's voice, quiet as it, was made me start and, grateful that the dark hid the flush as it started up my face, turned to see him, lit by a single lantern, smiling at me from the quarterdeck. So wrapped up in my thoughts of family, I had quite forgotten that Judd would be ready for relief. He leaned on the chart table, a pair of brass dividers in his right hand poised over the chart.

"Oh, sir. Yes, sir. That's it exactly. I came to relieve you so you could get some breakfast." I looked around the vessel, the horizon, the sea near at hand and saw none of it. Then I stepped aft to peer over his shoulder at the chart.

"We're just here. The land you no doubt noticed would, of course, be the southeastern tip of Sicily, here. Our course will continue just east of north as it has been, and you should be raising the harbor at Syracuse within a few hours. Wake me as soon as you have it, Oliver. We're almost in, and you should know you've done a fine job. You've come a long way in just four or five months!" Judd smiled at me and, I confess, I puffed up just a little at the compliment he offered. I agreed; I *had* come a long way!

Our breeze held nicely, and we tacked for the harbor at Syracuse shortly before the noon hour sounded. As we made our way in, I looked in vain for *Enterprise* and *Constitution*. *Nautilus, Vixen,* and several others I did not recognize swung to anchors near to the piers. A large British vessel of three masts and two decks of gunports showed the blue pendant of an admiral at her mast head and the church flag at her mizzen peak. As we passed by, I could make out the masses of men mustered in the waist for religious services. They were in dress finery, and the red coats of the Royal Marines stood out most clearly. Officers in their own full regalia stood or sat on the quarterdeck as someone, I assumed him to be a chaplain, spoke in stentorian tones, reading from a book he held before him.

"Stand by to fire the salute!" I shouted forward, pleased to demonstrate my alertness to Judd and continue to earn his regard for my performance.

"We won't be firin' a salute this time, Oliver. On account of it bein' Christmas and services are bein' held. Just head over yonder, and we'll drop the hook just there, to the east of *Nautilus*. Judd spoke quietly into my ear, but I caught the smile on Lockhart's face as he heard me corrected. I glared at the cox'n with as harsh a look as I could muster. The moment passed quickly as the need to navigate the vessel through the anchorage took all my attention, and Judd's.

No sooner had the best bower splashed into the placid waters of the harbor than I saw a boat pulled by four oars to a side making for us. It appeared to have come from *Vixen*. I took up the glass from the chart table and focused on the boat.

That's Captain Decatur in the sternsheets! What's he doing here? I must have spoken aloud because Judd responded, again quietly.

"I reckon he's coming to take possession of his prize. Probably has orders for us as well."

"But . . . How . . ." I sputtered for a moment, caught all aback. "How did he get here? Where's *Enterprise* or *Constitution?*"

"Well, the schooner there, the one the boat came away from, that'll be *Enterprise*. I have little idea of the whereabouts of *Constitution*, but perhaps Cap'n Decatur made a faster trip than the commodore."

Chagrined, I focused the glass on the schooner; sure enough, Judd was right. It was, with a more careful look, unmistakable as *Enterprise*. My self-confidence at being able to recognize ships of our squadron wavered. I recalled that day in Boston when Decatur had proudly pointed out his wonderful brig *Argus* to me after I had mistook the forty-four gun frigate *Constitution* for the smaller, two-masted vessel. *Well, at least* Vixen *and* Enterprise *are both schooners and about the same size!*

Judd interrupted my musings. "Are you going to hail that boat, Mister Baldwin? And since we know who it is, would not some ceremony at the side be in order?"

I covered my embarrassment and lapse by hailing the boat, then ordering the side manned with sailors and a bosun to blow his pipe. Then the captain was over the rail and smiling at us as he doffed his hat to the flag and us.

"You had an uneventful . . ." He stopped mid-sentence, looking around. "I seem to recall there was a deckhouse of some sort here."

We stood on the quarterdeck as Judd recounted the tale of our passage to him, the assistance provided by *Amazon*, the storm, but mercifully leaving out my inattention that allowed the fire to gain the hold it did. Then he asked about the human cargo we carried.

"I have arranged for a boat to take them ashore *post haste*, Mister Devon. And that Turkish captain as well. I suspect there are those, including the commodore, when he arrives, who will want a word with him."

"Sir, I thought *Constitution* would be in now also. Did you not sail in company with her after we separated?"

"As a matter of fact, Judd, the commodore went on to Tripoli to have a look around. He wanted to see firsthand what the harbor held and have a look at the defenses. I 'spect he'll be along in a day or two."

"Captain, sir, has . . . uhh . . . would you . . . ahh . . . has there been any further word from the Philadelphias since . . . well, since Captain Bainbridge's letter to the commodore?" I could no longer hold back. I had to know if there was any chance, any chance at all, that there might be a letter for me from Edward, even if it meant I would be chastised for approaching Decatur in this off-handed manner.

"Not a peep, Mister Baldwin. But I expect if Bainbridge did it once, he will manage to do it again. Don't despair or give up hope. At least not yet." Decatur smiled at me and, once again, touched me lightly on the shoulder as he watched my face fall in disappointment. "Right now, however, I think we have some work to do as the lighter I requested is soon to be here. And I want the prize moved alongside the schooner as soon as those poor souls in the hold, and that perfidious captain, are off-loaded. It is our hope, Preble's and mine, that the captain, the Turk, will be more forthcoming regarding the action of his vessel and the others of its ilk.

"I can tell you, the ketch's crew, those I had on *Enterprise*, have been no help at all, save one fellow who bragged, in very limited English, that they were present for the capture of Bainbridge's command. He took a great pleasure in describing, as best as his barely intelligible English could manage, how they rounded up the crew and marched them through the town." Decatur's eyes had become hard as he thought of the ignominy our officers and sailors must have felt; the smile was gone and his lips described a thin line. "I sustain myself with thoughts of re-taking our frigate and punishing the Bashaw to the fullest."

As he spoke, I noticed that his eyes grew bright, whether in fury over the capture of our ship or in anticipation of a bold and dangerous strike into the very heart of the enemy, I knew not.

CHAPTER THIRTEEN

James seemed to have grown up in just the few days it took Judd and me to sail the captured Tripolitan ketch into Syracuse. He stood straighter, looked you in the eye, and seemed not to whine any longer. It had been a week since our Christmas arrival, and there had been not a day that he had acted like the old James. And not a day had passed that he did not, with unrestrained enthusiasm, recount the brief battle in which we came to capture the ketch. His eyes grew bright, and his whole being became involved as he flew over each detail of his own role in the action, which he had taken to calling his "blooding," despite the fact that exactly no blood was shed—on either side. I chided him good naturedly as we stood in the bow, watching the activity in the harbor.

"Whether it was a real battle or no, Oliver, it was glorious! I have never felt such excitement over anything, not even when . . . well, never. And I can scarce wait until the next time!" His demeanor gave credence to his words. "And bein' able to read—or pretty much read—helps me a lot. I don't feel so much left out of things now. And I ain't . . . I mean, I'm not . . . afraid of Wheatley and his bragging any more. Knowing your letters . . . well, now I can make some sense of 'em, Oliver, I can see how important it is for a body to be able to read." He looked at me earnestly, and I knew I had been wrong to tease him. "And I don't reckon I need to tell you how grateful I am for you teachin' me." He smiled, and I recalled the delight he had exhibited at his new-found skill shortly after Judd and I returned aboard the previous week.

I had not been back in the cockpit for half a glass when James grabbed my arm and nearly dragged me out and up to the deck, where he proceeded to pull a copy of Bowditch's new book on mathematics and navigation out of the back of his trousers. Opening it, he read from it, haltingly, to be sure, but nonetheless accurately. To any noticing us, he might only have been explaining or discussing some elusive celestial concept rather than demonstrating his new-found ability. This was some different than reading from the English primer I had found in Gibraltar for him, and I told him so. He beamed and seemed actually to grow taller, straighter, before my very eyes.

We had returned to the cockpit, smiling with our secret, and Judd and I told of our adventures in *Mastico*, leaving nothing out. James hung on our every word, but Thomas seemed disinterested. It was not until Judd turned the conversation to the actual capture of the ketch that we discovered why.

"My guns fired, too, you know, Devon. Shots told, too. Fact is, if you recollect the *actual* events, my battery fired *before* either little Jimmy's or Baldwin's."

Wheatley's jaw thrust forward, daring any of us to contradict his statement.

"Thomas, I don't think any of us is questioning your participation in that skirmish; we—all of us—had a job to do, and we did it. That's what we're here for."

"Well, it ain't right that Fat James gets all the glory for firin' his guns. Like you said, we all fired. But I didn't see any of your shots tell; mine did. Fact is, I saw one of my shots take down their t'gallant mast."

I couldn't resist the opportunity. "Thomas, was it you who laid that gun yourself? I thought the gun captain did that. I know Bradford and Kelly sighted mine."

While he said nothing, Wheatley's jaw clenched and thrust farther forward. He glared at me with a killing look. Over his shoulder, I noticed Judd wink his eye at me. All of the bold talk from Thomas during our training had been as empty as his other boasts, and now he realized that we knew it.

"Wheatley's been some quiet this past week. Have you noticed it too, Oliver?" James changed the subject, and a smile formed on his round face as he savored the peace he had enjoyed.

"Aye. I think it's likely from knowin' we see him as nothing but a braggart. Either he's figuring a way to get back at us, or he's decided there's nothing to be gained from . . ."

"'Scuse me, Mister Baldwin." One the Marines who stood watch outside the captain's Cabin interrupted us, saluting smartly as he spoke. "Cap'n sends his respects and wishes your presence in the Cabin, sir." He turned at my acknowledgment, and James and I followed him aft and below.

"Do you want me to wait for you?" James inquired as we reached the door to the Cabin. A different Marine was posted there and came to attention, nodded at his mate, and knocked.

"I'll see you back in the cockpit, James; perhaps we can go ashore later for supper." Despite the changes that had come over James Stevens, his eating habits remained a constant.

"Oh, Mister Baldwin. Good of you to come." Decatur was seated at his table, studying a chart of the coast of Tripoli. "I have something for you." The captain fished around among some papers near at hand until he produced, with a flourish, several pages of foolscap covered in writing. Familiar writing.

My breathing seemed to stop at the same time as my heart did. My gaze fastened onto the papers he held, and I was unable to speak. *It could only be from Edward. Oh, thank God! He's alive. He did it! He got a letter out to me!* My thoughts swirled. *Give it to me! Don't wave it around like that. That's my letter. I can not wait another second for it.* Thank goodness, Captain Decatur could not hear my thoughts!

"How . . . where . . ." I stammered, not knowing what to say.

"You may have noticed that *Constitution* came in last night. Commodore Preble had stopped by Malta on his way back from Tripoli. Actually, the ship got damaged in a northeast gale they encountered, and he stopped there to do some knotting and splicing. The British had just received a communication from Bainbridge. Apparently, the Danish Consul—Nissen, I believe—delivered it to them, and in the letter were these pages which your brother, through Commodore Preble, asked be passed on to you. A messenger brought it this morning with a note from the commodore." He indicated another paper on his table. Decatur's smile was genuine as he extended his hand and the papers in my direction.

It took some considerable effort, but I took them like a gentleman rather than a starving beggar being offered a crust of bread. I glanced quickly at the fine familiar hand and then back at the captain.

"Take it and go, Oliver. I know how much that means to you. I am grateful my own brother, James, is free and with Dick Somers in *Nautilus*. I am sure that Bill Bainbridge's brother, Joseph—he's a lieutenant in *Vixen*, you know—feels much as you do. 'Course, he knew his brother was at least alive right from the start . . . ." I did not know Captain Bainbridge even had a brother, let alone that he was here in the squadron and very much in the same frustrating predicament as me. But right now, I could not have cared a whit for Captain Bainbridge's brother; I was interested only in my own and in the letter I held. Decatur's words drifted into the background noises of the ship as I furtively took a longer glance at the letter. When I looked up, finally coming to the realization that he had stopped speaking, the captain was still smiling at me. He waved his hand to the door, dismissing me, and I turned and, I'm afraid, in a not very officer-like way, stumbled out of his cabin to find a place where I could read undisturbed.

My dear brother, he began. I brushed the tears of joy from my eyes and the page jumped into sharp focus.

As you must, by now, be fully cognizant, the *Philadelphia* frigate has fallen into enemy hands, her crew, including the officers and yrs. truly, held in captivity by the Bashaw of Tripoli. The capture of that fine ship was through no fault of Cap't. Bainbridge; indeed, he did everything within his power to regain the deep water so near at hand. After jettisoning most of our great guns to no avail, he went so far as to order the foremast chopped off just above the deck in a final, and futile, effort to lighten the bow of our stricken ship so she might slide off the rocks which held her and back into the water. We held up under the almost constant fire of the pirates for nearly four hours with hardly a shot returned as we were unable to train our remaining guns far enough around to bear, a fact which the rogues in their small craft took full advantage of. When a further dozen and more gunboats came out from shore to assist their brethren in their piratical business, they all—the whole fleet of them—approached to board us. Cap't. Bainbridge took the only avenue open to him at that point; he struck. And I can tell you, my dear brother, it was with a great sadness that we all—officers and crew alike—witnessed the

Stars and Stripes hauled down to the shouting and cheering of our attackers. However only one man was hurt during the attack, and the cap't. was sure that, should the pirates board us in furtherance to their attack, many more would be cruel hurt and killed. David Porter, our first lieutenant, and I as well as the other officers, all agreed that he had little choice but to strike.

The blood-thirsty pirates—it seemed there were hundreds of them—scrambled aboard immediately, crying out in their heathen tongue with blood-curdling screams and their evil-looking curved swords, called scimitars, brandished aloft, and herded all the men into the waist and the officers onto the quarterdeck, while others in their number plundered our ship and personals without regard to decency or need. When they were quite satisfied that they had dis-covered all of any value (to them) we were put into the ship's boats and, under the gaze of an armed pirate in each, the men were forced to row us—their mates and officers—ashore. It was quite late of hour and nearly full dark by this time. They forced us overboard before we had reached sufficiently shallow waters, and each of us were soaked to the skin, head to foot. Our plight held no signifi-cance to them, save to further amuse them, and they marched us, wet and bedraggled, through the dark town, amid jeering and abu-sive citizens who held torches aloft, to a most daunting prison. Few among us thought we were in any particular danger of being put to death as we all had heard tales of merchant crews held captive until ransomed by their countrymen. We reasoned that we were worth more to these rascals alive than dead. But privation and torture held prominent positions in the forefront of most of our minds. With a sudden (to us) shift in attitude, the officers were not marched with the men into the prison, but rather forced to carry on to the palace of the Bashaw.

At that momentous place, we were herded into a splendid and opulent room of great proportion to wait, for what we knew not. After some hours, (I am sure it was well into the middle watch) dur-ing which we had nothing to eat or drink, we were marched into another chamber and forced at the points of scimitars to fall pros-trate before the most enormous human being I have ever beheld. He lounged on a proliferation of cushions and viewed us through hooded eyes. His clothes were of magnificently embroidered silk, and there was not a finger on either hand that did not hold at least one ring of enormous proportion.

Of course, this person—the Bashaw—spoke no English, pre-ferring instead the uncivilized and unintelligible tongue of his land and, after haranguing us for some time before coming to the realization that we understood not a word of the gibberish he spoke, he called into the room a Mr. Nissen, who is Denmark's consul in this hostile land and fluent in both Arabic and English.

After some lengthy discourse, it was related to us by Mr. Nissen that we would be provided some replacement clothes for our ruint ones and held, not in the prison with the sailors, but in an adjoining palace—ironically, the former residence of the American Consul here—nearby to the Bashaw's own. And he further procured for us some food, scant in quantity, but most welcome.

We are allowed no discourse with the world beyond our prison walls save for Cap't Bainbridge, who, through the good offices of Mr. Nissen, has won the privilege of corresponding with the Commodore and by whom I hope to ensure this letter's delivery to your hands. I would, in light of our difficulty in correspondence, ask that you inform our parents of my situation, begging them not to worry overmuch as my plight, while surely not of my own choosing, does not appear to be a threat to my well-being. And you, brother dear, take heart in that same fact and, while I would much welcome your thoughts and more particularly, your prayers, I would most assuredly not wish to burden you with concern for my situation. We are, at the present, comfortable and reasonably fed.

Lieutenant Porter has taken in hand the midshipmen and has them spending their time studying their trade and reading texts salvaged from the ship by our captors. They seem fully engrossed in furthering their understanding of the art of navigation and mathematics. As for the other officers and yrs. truly, we are, while surely not in positions we might wish on ourselves, not in any danger to our persons. As we have had no contact with our seamen since being separated from them those many weeks ago, I have no clue as to their welfare or condition.

As you reread this letter by the light of a candle and, perhaps choose to discuss it with our fellow Philadelphian, take heart in the knowledge that sitting idle will not answer and action will best occupy your mind and person.

With greatest affection, I am yr. Brother,
Edward Baldwin, Lt. United States Navy

I sat, the letter, twice read, in my lap, as I pictured Edward, dressed in the same rags I had seen in my dream, wasting away in his captivity. His brave words, and mention of his confinement in a palace, held little conviction in my mind. I was quite sure he had included them to allay my own concerns as well as those of our parents when I passed the grim news to them. I was certain he was held in a prison of dubious comfort and fed or not at the whim of his captors. I felt a tear starting again—indeed many of the words he wrote had been smudged by my own tears as I read and reread his letter. I felt drained, expunged of any will to do more than sit where I was and remember my brother in better times.

"Oliver! There you are! I have waited these hours and more for you in our cockpit, putting up with Wheatley's insults and abuse. What have you been doing? I was afraid Captain Decatur had mastheaded you when I couldn't find you. Are we going to get supper ashore like you promised?"

My thoughts of home and Edward shattered like a bottle dropped from the mainyard as James's interruption brought me, with breathtaking suddenness, back to the present and the foredeck of *Enterprise*. I blinked at James, recalling our earlier conversation (it seemed so long ago) and raised myself from the inboard end of the bowsprit, where I had been sitting. I folded my precious letter, placed it carefully into my pocket, and tried to smile at my young shipmate.

"Why are your eyes so red, Oliver? You've been crying, haven't you." It was not a question. "Did Decatur take you to task? What happened with him? What did you do?"

James's concern was genuine, and I could not help but be touched by it.

"No, James. The captain was not angry with me, and I am not in any trouble. In fact, he had a letter for me from Edward. From the Tripoli prison. I have been reading it this last hour and more. My apologies for having kept you waiting."

"How did Decatur get the letter? Why wouldn't your brother write directly to you? Is it because he and the captain are friends?"

"The letter was sent to the commodore with papers from Captain Bainbridge and, I collect, was more or less smuggled out of the prison. It came in on *Constitution* last night. I am some happy to have it, I can tell you." I smiled in spite of myself at his continued concern for my well-being. "Let us find Lieutenant Lawrence and see if perchance he will allow us leave to sup in the town."

As the schooner's boats were in the employ of others more senior to midshipmen, we managed to attract the attention of a passing craft which, for the consideration of several coins, carried us to the dock, just where *Mastico* rested. Her holds were open, presumably being aired out after their recent employment, and her sails neatly furled with tight, seaman-like harbor furls.

"Wonder how soon they'll be selling the ketch off. I don't imagine we'll see much in prize shares from such a small vessel, and since her human cargo was released rather than sold, I reckon there won't be but a pittance there either." I mused—more or less to myself—as we stood on the dock looking at my late home and scene of my 'first-lieutenancy' until James plucked at my sleeve, entreating me to 'hurry along.'

I am afraid I was less than an enthusiastic participant in our excursion in search of supper and, perhaps, entertainment. I mulled over Edward's letter while we walked, barely hearing James's excited comments over this shop or that coffee house. There was something about the words, or the things Edward had mentioned or something else, I could not put a finger on it, but I knew I missed something he had written. I was lifted from my thoughts by a booming and familiar voice.

"Here, you lads. Join me for a bite of supper, if you please." Mister Wakefield, our surgeon, stood in the doorway of a small tavern. A pewter mug of something was lifted aloft in one hand, while the other was extended in greeting to us. He had most obviously been eating; a white cloth napkin, far from spotless, hung from his collar, protecting both his shirt and his waistcoat. He wore no jacket. A welcoming smile split his broad face and caused his flushed cheeks to puff out.

"Oh, Mister Wakefield, sir. What a surprise to see you." James's enthusiasm at seeing a familiar in this foreign place burst out with his words. He turned to me. "Come on, Oliver. Let us join the doctor as he suggested."

I barely had time to agree before we were seated in the additional chairs brought quickly by an employee of the establishment on Wakefield's signal. In rapid and completely unintelligible Italian, the doctor gave instructions to the man, and moments later, food and drink appeared in front us. James immediately attacked it with the same gusto he had exhibited in Decatur's Cabin so many months ago.

"Well, boys. It is a pleasure to have your company this evening; you are most kind to humor an old man. How have you enjoyed your employment as naval officers thus far? I trust it has been to your liking? And Oliver, were you not involved with bringing in that prize ketch some days ago, the one we took off Tripoli? I heard she carried a cargo of slaves. As a gift for the sultan of Constantinople I was told. I'd warrant those poor souls are still giving thanks to whatever deities their heathen religion might dictate for their timely rescue!" The doctor beamed at us as he listened to my tale of bringing in *Mastico*, including the fire and the visit from the English brig. James, for the most part, remained involved in his meal and offered only an occasional grunt of agreement around mouthfuls of food. After a brief silence in which I, too, took advantage of Mister Wakefield's generosity, he spoke again.

"I heard you have received a letter from your brother, Oliver. I trust he is well, in spite of his unfortunate circumstances?" Wakefield smiled at me and took a draught of whatever was in his tankard.

"Oh, sir. I . . . that is . . . he says he is quite fine, sir, and not in any danger. In fact he mentioned the officers are being held in a palace nearby the Bashaw's own. He described their capture and what followed and said that only one man was hurt in the attack."

"Then why, pray tell, do you seem so disheartened? Knowing that your brother is safe and unhurt should lift a great burden from your young mind. You seem something less than pleased at the news."

"Oh, no, sir. It is not that at all. Of course I am greatly relieved that Edward is alive and unhurt and I am so pleased to have his letter." I smiled quickly at the thought. "But there is something about it . . . I don't know . . . just . . . it seems that there ought to . . . be something . . . something I should see, but am not." My concern over what my brother hadn't said caught the doctor's attention, and he frowned, then spoke very quietly.

"Perhaps, Oliver, if I should be allowed to see your letter, I might see what you think you have missed. Or perhaps there is nothing and your worry is for naught. Did you, perchance, bring the letter with you?"

I handed my prized missive over to Reliance Wakefield, who took it, smoothed it out on the table after pushing aside a plate recently emptied of his supper, and donned a pair of spectacles. He became solemn and quiet as he studied the papers with great intensity. His jaw worked from time to time as if chewing some last vestige of his supper, and lines formed in his forehead and around his mouth as he absorbed the words. I was sure that he was as caught up in Edward's descriptions of the tragedy as I had been earlier. I watched him in silence. James ate.

Suddenly the doctor looked up and, finding an employee of the tavern, called to him in Italian. The man disappeared and in the next moment was standing close at hand lighting a candle which he had thrust into a small ceramic holder in the center of the table. I was baffled by this addition, as the lantern sitting on the table augmented perfectly the light from other lanterns along the walls and the failing daylight filtering in through the windows.

"You were quite right, Oliver, to think there was something here you missed; there is, I am sure. It's the way Edward ends; you see, he says '. . . as you reread this by the light of a candle . . .'. That's the clue! Then he says, 'sitting idle will not answer and action will best occupy your mind and person.' He is telling us that we must *do something*! And he suggests that you should show this to Captain Decatur, your fellow Philadelphian. I am sure he has given us something here he would not want his captors to see. Watch!"

"How to rescue him . . . and the others, sir?" I asked. I noticed that James, caught by the doctor's animated tone, had stopped eating mid-chew. His cheeks puffed out in the familiar way that, at another time, I might have laughed at.

"I don't know yet, Oliver. Push that candle closer and let's see what shows up!" The mysterious smile and cryptic words caught my own attention fully, and I reached for the holder to edge it nearer to him. He selected a page of Edward's letter and held it toward the flame.

"Here, sir. Be careful, if you please. You will burn my letter!" I nearly shouted out my caution, completely forgetting my station, and the doctor's, in my horror of seeing the long-awaited sign of my brother's survival consumed by the flame.

"Do not fear, young Oliver. I have no intention of burning something of such great moment. To the contrary, indeed! Watch, if you please!" Wakefield held the page of writing near the candle, and, as I watched, more writing, a pale, rusty, brown this time, appeared between the lines of ink. I was speechless! I craned my neck to see more as he moved the page around the flame. Parts of the page became discolored as the heat from the flame built on the thin paper; then, to my absolute horror, the corner of the paper caught the flame and briefly flared before the surgeon quickly blew it out. The edge of my dear brother's letter was now charred and partially gone where the flame had touched it. Mister Wakefield seemed unmoved as he continued to move the page slowly across the flame, risking, with little regard for the future of the document, its complete destruction.

"Just as I thought. You brother has used his letter to you to communicate with us. This is likely important. We must go at once back to the ship and show this to Decatur, as Edward instructs us to." The doctor rose, threw a few coins on the table, grabbed his blue jacket, and sallied forth to the entranceway of the place. James, clearly horrified at the turn of events, looked up, a mouthful of food unchewed.

"Wait! I have not finished! Must we go now?" He chewed faster on seeing me rise also.

"Reckon we're going back to *Enterprise*, James. Mister Wakefield's likely halfway to the dock by now. And he's got my letter! Stay if you will, or not." I hurried after the surgeon and my precious letter and sensed that James, most probably still chewing his food, had rushed after me. To our great good fortune, one of the schooner's own boats was at the quay and, with Mister Wakefield's steady encouragement, carried us quickly to *Enterprise*.

"Captain! You will want to see this, I am sure. It appears we have received some most important information from Bainbridge. Or at the very least, one of his lieutenants." The doctor rushed past the Marine at Decatur's door, giving the startled man barely time to open it, let alone announce him. I followed more in keeping with my station, not wanting to lose sight of my letter, but also not wanting to barge into the captain's cabin without invitation. I had no idea where James had gotten to since our frantic run across the deck and down the ladder behind the agitated surgeon.

Decatur was as startled as the Marine had been at Wakefield's pronouncement. He looked up from the chart and other papers he had spread out before him as the doctor snatched up a candle stand from the shelf and set it squarely into the center of Decatur's table on top of the chart that, prior to our precipitous entrance, had held his attention.

The captain sputtered and fussed over the disruption to his study, but Mister Wakefield paid him no attention; he brandished the letter—my letter—with one page's corner charred and spoke as if Decatur had said nothing at all.

"Here, here it is. Look here." Wakefield held the first page of Edward's letter close to the flame; I moved around him so I could watch the magical letters as they appeared on this new page. With all my heart, I wanted to cry out a word of caution, but held my tongue as the captain became rapt, watching the paper darken slightly as the words, darker than the now discolored paper, began to appear.

Decatur's eyes grew wide as he saw them, and, while I suspect it was not in any surprise at their magical appearance, but more in response to the words themselves, he snatched the page from the doctor's fingers and held it himself, reading as the candle brought forth the hidden message. His hand seemed steadier than had the medico's and, while the paper as well as its writing became discolored, there was no flame or further charring, for which I was most grateful!

"Reliance, you are quite right! How did you determine that Edward Baldwin's letter might contain such intelligence?"

"It was Oliver, Captain, who actually figured it out." Now it was my turn to be surprised; I hadn't figured anything out. My face, having gone all slack-jawed, surely must have shown that the doctor's remark caught me all aback. But beyond a cursory nod and quick smile from the captain, I remained unseen, nearly as invisible as the writing in my letter had been. The surgeon continued, telling Decatur of our conversation in the tavern, while the captain shifted his glance from Wakefield to the letter and back again. Finally, the doctor showed Decatur the ending of Edward's letter with its cryptic instructions, the ones I had not understood. "And as you can see, sir, Lieutenant Baldwin suggests showing the letter to you, 'our fellow Philadelphian.' "

"Oliver, I want you to write down what I tell you. Here is paper, ink, and a pen. I am going to read aloud what your brother has written so I miss nothing when I tell the commodore." Decatur indicated the implements necessary to my new employment as scribe and began to read.

"*Philadelphia* frigate afloat approx. one cable from shore directly off Bashaw's palace. Appears fully manned with great guns restored aboard. Likely they are loaded. Gunboats patrol inner harbor." The captain paused, looked at me to ensure I was keeping pace with his dictation and, after waiting a moment, continued. "Shore batteries trained on harbor and frigate. One hundred fifteen long guns mounted. Manned around the clock. Nissen says twenty-five thousand Arabs. Nineteen gunboats, two galleys, two schooners, one brig constantly manned. Frigate must be destroyed at any cost. Suggest charter of local vessel to gain access to harbor without arousing suspicion, best done at night, and board with sufficient crew to overpower native crew. You will need several well-manned rowing boats to make good an escape after the enterprise has been accomplished. Suggest that it will be impossible to do naught but destroy *Philadelphia* as much as I would relish seeing her back under our own flag." Decatur stopped again, waiting as I hurriedly scribbled the last few of his words. "And it's signed, 'Bainbridge.'

"Well, gentlemen, it appears as if a solution to our problem of the frigate may be at hand. This is a fine piece of work, Oliver, and Reliance, and I am sure the commodore will be most grateful for it. Now, Oliver, give me what you wrote, and I shall return your letter to you. I must go at once to *Constitution* and discuss this with Preble." Captain Decatur rose, put on his jacket, and stepping past the surgeon and me, left the Cabin.

"How did you know there was something there, Mister Wakefield? I know

Edward mentioned about 'reading it in the light of a candle' and all, but what told you there was a message in the letter that would only appear by candle-light?" I could contain my curiosity no longer and remained mystified by the goings-on of the past hour and more. I looked at my discolored and slightly charred letter as if the secret would be revealed by my own gaze.

"It wasn't that it appeared by the candle *light*, Oliver; it was the *heat* of the flame that brought out the writing. You see, Edward had written another letter, dictated by Captain Bainbridge, it was, between the lines of his letter to you, in lemon juice! Of course, dry, it is quite invisible, as you saw, or rather, didn't see." He chuckled quietly at his joke and then became serious again as he continued his explanation. "When the page written in this manner is held to heat, the flame of a candle for example, the lemon juice turns brown and is clearly visible. Of course, you can only do that once, as the writing does not again disappear when the paper has cooled. I have heard that it was done frequently during the late War of Independence. And I am indeed sorry for the damage I have done to your letter. But see here, Oliver, it has not obliterated any of your brother's words; the letter as still quite readable!"

Wakefield stood and made as if to leave the Cabin. "Since we had to cut short our evening, would you, and Mister Stevens, should he be still be at large," again he stopped and chuckled quietly at his unintended play on words, "care to join me in a glass? I have managed to secure a most respectable bottle of Spanish port which I would happily open in celebration of our—your—discovery. What say you?"

"Oh, sir. Thank you. That would be most pleasant. I shall find James and invite him to join us." I once again followed the doctor out the door.

CHAPTER FOURTEEN

"Sir, do you think it possible that Commodore Preble might carry a letter with him to pass on to Edward through Captain Bainbridge? I would sorely like to let my brother know that I am well and in receipt of his own letter." I hesitated in asking this momentous favor (after all, I was merely a midshipman) after hearing Captain Decatur announce that Preble was taking *Vixen* to Malta expressly for the purpose of communicating with the prisoners in Tripoli, and leaving that very day!

"Have you written the letter, Oliver? I am sure the commodore will not mind a bit, as long as he is not forced to wait for you to pen the letter. Especially in view of your discovery." Decatur paused in stepping below after concluding a conversation with Mister Lawrence and Mister Morris. I had happened only to be nearby.

"Oh, sir. Yes, sir. I have only to add a few lines to it and it will be ready. Should I mention the . . . secret part of his letter?"

"No, Mister Baldwin. I suspect that the commodore will manage to convey to Bainbridge the fact that we deciphered it and are taking action. Now hurry along and finish your letter. I will put it with some other papers from *Mastico* which Preble has requested when I return to the flagship." Then Decatur disappeared down the scuttle.

Sending the letter to Edward—actually several were included from the first I had written some months ago to the most recent, finished only last night— lifted a heavy weight off my mind. I had also written to our parents to inform them of our, Edward's and mine, situation. Having once received a letter from Edward in captivity, my heart was now impatient for another, even though my brain knew one would be unlikely for a great while.

I watched as Captain Decatur was rowed, first to *Constitution*, and then to the *Vixen* schooner to find the commodore. After a brief visit with Lieutenant Joseph Bainbridge as he was taking his leave, he returned to *Enterprise*, smiling broadly.

"Gentlemen," he pronounced as he climbed over the bulwark, "we will be remaining here in Syracuse until the commodore returns, but then, I suspect, he will have employment for us!"

For a week and more, until *Vixen* returned with Preble from Malta, the air on *Enterprise* was filled with anticipation; it had taken less than an hour for Decatur's announcement to filter into all corners of the schooner. Officers and sailors alike were eager for action and speculation was rife as to just how the ship would be employed. The mids were, perhaps, the most creative in their estimation of how Commodore Preble would use us.

"I'll tell you what is going to happen," spoke Thomas one day, after keeping his peace for much of the guesswork in which we indulged. "You ain't got it right yet—none of you. Preble will order us to sail with *Vixen* and *Nautilus* right into the harbor at Tripoli and cut out that frigate. The schooners are the only vessels he's got what'll float in the thin water inside the harbor. He'll have *Constitution* and the brigs stand off and fire into the shore to make those pirate bastards keep their heads down while we race in there and steal *Philadelphia* right out from under their noses." Wheatley's smug look and confident manner made us all think he really might know something we didn't until Judd came into the cockpit and we told him of Thomas's plan.

"Somehow, I doubt the commodore would think a couple of schooners and the few deep draft ships he's got would be any match for the fire power surrounding that harbor. I heard there was more than a hundred guns along that shore and all mounted in castles and forts. We go in there with a few little schooners with twelve-pounders and we'd be blown to matchwood before we got anywhere near the frigate. My God, Tom, use your head. Even a landsman could see that hair-brained idea wouldn't answer!" Devon's look was one more of dismay than anger. He shook his head and added almost under his breath, "Stupid, just plain stupid!"

I smiled as Wheatley's expression changed from smug arrogance to dismay to anger. James giggled. Judd sat down at the table, and it was clear to all of us that he had put the matter behind him as he changed the subject.

"The other day, I was ashore with Lieutenant Morris and found a fine establishment which serves up a . . ."

"Damn it, Devon! Just who do you think you are? Mister 'I-know-it-all-midshipman' Devon, I'll warrant. What makes you so damn sure I ain't right about what Preble has in mind? You ain't got any better an idea than me," Wheatley interrupted. His fists were clenched and he half stood, leaning forward to be close to Judd's face. He had slitted down his eyes, and, from the way the muscles in his jaw bunched up, I was sure he was grinding his teeth in anger or frustration.

"Oh, Thomas, really. What difference does it make? None of us know what Commodore Preble has in mind for us—likely even Decatur. Don't get yourself so exercised over it. But use your head and think about what you say before you say it. It'll make you look so much less stupid." Judd sounded tired.

"Now you're calling me stupid? Devon, I've had enough of you insulting me. I'm calling you out." Wheatley stood up straight and, looking Judd right in the eyes, said, "I am at your service, sir."

None of us had an inkling of what he was talking about. At least, James and I did not. Judd looked at Thomas for a moment as if thinking of what to say.

"I think," he finally said, "that Captain Decatur would take a dim view of two of his midshipmen fighting a due. 'Specially since he's been involved in one himself. But if you demand satisfaction, sir, I will accommodate you."

A duel! I looked at James. His eyes were as wide as I suspect mine were, and his jaw was slack. Thomas and Judd were going to fight a duel! I could not believe it. James and I were speechless.

"As the challenged party, I have the right to choose our weapons, as well as the time and place of our encounter. I would like, I think, pistols. We will fire from forty paces. I will have to leave time and place for later as I have insufficient knowledge of this island to determine a proper locale. Unless you had something in mind?" Judd, a more serious look on his face than I had before seen, paused, then looked squarely at me. "Mister Baldwin, would you stand as my second?"

"Second? What do you mean, Judd?" I had no idea what a 'second' was and the confused look I wore complemented my words.

"It means you will step in for me should I be unable to fight. You'll take charge of the details of the affair and witness the event."

"Judd, I don't know anything about a duel. What arrangements? And as far as 'stepping in for you' goes, I have no great love for Thomas, but I certainly don't have a desire to shoot him!" *Or get shot myself,* I added silently.

All the while, James sat there looking horrified that his messmates were contemplating killing one another. Finally he found his voice.

"Do you both think this is really necessary? I mean . . . to go and try to kill each other? Why not wait a bit and see what happens? Who knows, one or both of you might get himself killed when we finally do get to fight—against the pirates! Then none of this will matter. Besides, Judd, we all knew Thomas was just spouting, just like he always does. Even I knew he had no idea what Preble would order us to do. Do we have to stand around and watch you two try and kill each other? Seems right stupid to me! The both of you . . . and don't challenge me on account of I called you stupid!" James, the youngest of us all, seemed suddenly to have the most insight of us all.

"Well, James, if you wasn't such a country boy, you'd know how the world of *gentlemen* works; that's just how it goes. And don't worry yourself about either of us calling you out; for me, I wouldn't waste the time—or powder and shot. Judd did, however, insult me, and I called him out. He accepted my challenge. The only way he can avoid me killing him in a duel will be by apologizing to me, in front of witnesses, for his insult." At first, a secret smile began to play at the corners of Thomas's mouth as he thought of Judd labeling himself a coward by refusing the duel.

When he saw that Judd showed no intent of apologizing, likely knowing full well the implication an apology would carry, the smile faded, and I think Thomas's face seemed a bit chalky. Now that he had spoken, there was no way out for him. It occurred to me that he might be having second thoughts, in spite of his brave words.

Come on, Judd. Apologize and let's be done with this foolishness. I have no wish to be your second or anyone else's. Here's a way out of this mess. Take it! My thoughts raced down two roads; one was very short and had Judd offering his hand in apology to Thomas. The other had the four of us standing in some remote field somewhere with pistols, counting paces and . . . I did not want to think about the possible outcome, especially if I had to be the 'second'!

Judd stood suddenly. *Oh, God! Here it comes. Judd's going to hit . . . well, I suspect that might be more agreeable than shooting pistols at each other.* I backed up, trying to get out of the way of the combatants.

"I will discuss this further with you, Thomas, when Mister Baldwin and I have selected a suitable field of honor. In the meantime, let us try to avoid crossing tacks with one another, as much as is possible." Without waiting for an answer, Judd left the cockpit. In the stunning silence that remained, we heard his footsteps fade as he went topside.

We all began to speak at once; James and me imploring Thomas to withdraw his challenge so as to restore peace to the cockpit, and Thomas strutting verbally about like a popinjay now that the immediate threat was past. He would have none of our pleas.

"You boys just don't understand this; it's a man's concern and not yours. Now be quiet while I enjoy thinking about shooting that scoundrel."

"We may be boys, as you think, Thomas, but Judd asked me to be his second which, I reckon, means you and I might be facing each other. Now, that just don't appeal! So like it or no, it appears we're all involved. And consider that *he* may wind up shooting *you!*" I was not about to be a party to his enjoyment of this dreadful turn of events if I could help it.

Wheatley stopped his bombast, shot a hateful look at each of us, James and me, and left without a further word.

"He'll never go through with it. He's a coward and will find a way to back out of it. Likely try to make Judd look the coward into the bargain." James spoke the very words I had been thinking. Apparently James had seen enough of Wheatley's less-than-heroic antics over the past several months to see through his bravado. But he did not witness the cowering Thomas that I saw mid-Atlantic in the teeth of a gale. I continued to hold my own counsel on that, but I clung to the hope that Thomas would repeat his performance this time and take, once again, the safe course.

A tense silence filled with furtive, scornful glances, hung in the cockpit whenever Judd and Thomas were there together; when they weren't, or when only Judd was there, the same antics and skylarking continued as before. Then, a week and more later, Decatur called the officers and midshipmen to assemble on the quarterdeck.

"As you no doubt observed, *Vixen* has returned with the commodore from his visit to Malta, and I have just come from a meeting with him. We have arrived at a plan to deprive the Bashaw of the use of our frigate which shows considerable promise. I will be taking the little ketch that Judd and Oliver brought in on Christmas, with a crew of volunteers, to Tripoli to burn *Philadelphia* to the waterline. Captain Stewart will support us in *Syren*, but will not enter the harbor there. I will be sharing this commission with the crew before we leave to ask for volunteers. I expect we will be ready in a week or less, and until then, would ask that you refrain from discussing it, either among yourselves or with the men." Decatur stopped talking but his eyes continued studying us, constantly moving as they had been when he spoke, covering each of us, lingering for a moment, then moving on. There were some moments of complete silence, and then it seemed as if every one of us spoke at once. Most, including yours truly, were requesting to be included in his crew. The captain smiled broadly at our enthusiasm, but committed to nothing.

The next several days were a flurry of action. We took on stores, water, and arms. Gunner Tarbox oversaw the stowage of combustibles on deck in *Enterprise* and taught several of us, James and me included, how to cut fuses and measure slow match to ensure a proper burn. Our marines spent considerable time sharpening their bayonets and repeatedly cleaning their muskets, overseen by their lieutenant and sergeant. Reliance Wakefield was busy with extra medical supplies and spent some considerable time with the various implements of his trade, sharp cutting instruments, called scalpels, forceps, and saws of different sizes and shapes. I found it unsettling to think of their likely use. The officers, Zeb Morris, William Hobbs, and midshipmen Judd Devon and Thomas Wheatley were equally busy, their actions overseen by First Lieutenant James Lawrence. With the anticipation of action, real action, and the preparations necessary, the two antagonists had declared a truce, or so it seemed to James and me. Captain Decatur, his presence required frequently on the flagship, spent little time in the schooner. I noticed a gang of local men working on *Mastico*, still secured to the pier where James and I had seen her some weeks ago. They were, I first surmised, getting her ready to be sold; then I recollected what Decatur had told the officers, that we were to sail her to Tripoli to attack the frigate and that heavily fortified harbor.

Several days later, Decatur had, during a momentary lull in our work, called First Lieutenant Lawrence, Judd and myself into his Cabin. Why he had included two midshipmen in his meeting baffled us, but summoned, we went. He was seated at his desk and rose to stand by the tiny window from which he could see the dock and *Mastico*.

"Gentlemen, I thought you would be interested in a development the commodore has only recently shared with me." Decatur looked from the window, turning to face the three of us standing in front of the table. "You two," the captain nodded in the direction of Judd and me, "are here because you brought in the prize and her captain. The papers from the ketch which Preble took to Malta for translation proved that the vessel we captured was indeed present at the assault on our frigate." He again looked out the window, then added, "And the captain, the Turk, was in the van of the boarding. It is most appropriate that the ketch be used to destroy the very ship she helped capture. Commodore Preble has ordered the prize be renamed and taken into the Naval Service. She is to be called *Intrepid* from this point forward, a name that will inspire each of us who sail in her to greater glory and honor." As he turned back toward us, his eyes held the fire I had seen more and more of late. I knew he chafed at his lines to be away on our mission of destruction, and the information he had just shared with us further inflamed him.

Without further discussion, we were dismissed from the Cabin. Judd spoke when Lieutenant Lawrence had gone his own way, taking hold of my arm as he did so.

"Oliver! What about that! That ketch was there when they took your brother's ship. I'd warrant that puts a new light on this whole situation for you, eh? Reckon you can't wait to get in there and hit those piratical scoundrels." His fire stirred my own briefly, and I smiled and nodded enthusiastically. He went off to see to his own affairs, while I stood where I was, thinking of what lay ahead.

Remembering the fear I felt when, after the fire on the prize ketch, we spied a ship closing on us. Knowing that with our scant armament, we would be unable to defend ourselves, I began to imagine our forthcoming commission. Sailing into a well-armed harbor and attempting to take a well-armed, well-manned ship of thirty-six guns seemed folly and a certain end to my naval career. And I had volunteered to the captain not once, but twice! Folly, sheer folly!

Happily, the tasks of overseeing the work we had to accomplish, our studies, and sleep made the time pass quickly. I had little opportunity to dwell on the precarious fix I had gotten myself into. Then, one evening, Decatur had all hands mustered on deck, and I knew our time was nigh. Even in the light of the late afternoon sun I could see the gleam, the fire that lit his eyes. He paced up and down the quarterdeck, smacking a fist into his open hand as he waited to hear Lawrence say, "All hands present and correct, sir."

"Men, Commodore Preble has given me—and you—an opportunity to secure honor and glory for ourselves and our country. I am taking the captured Tripolitan ketch, now called *Intrepid* and a unit of the United States Navy, which Mister Devon and Mister Baldwin brought in, to Tripoli to destroy the *Philadelphia* frigate, the selfsame vessel captured in a most piratical way by the corsairs of Tripoli this October past. We will not be cutting her out and returning the ship to our fleet; it would be nigh onto impossible and entirely too dangerous to make good our escape with the ship, even were we to succeed in taking possession. Instead, we will board her, kill whatever crew mans her, and put her to the torch. Who among you will volunteer to join in this most ambitious adventure?" Decatur's eyes seemed to glow even brighter than before and, as he studied each of his men, his fire instilled in each a sense of invincibility. To a man, every jack on the schooner's deck stood a bit taller, then stepped forward, indicating his willingness, his desire, to accompany his captain on this perilous undertaking. Even I was moved to volunteer yet again!

One, from a middle rank, called out, "Three cheers for Cap'n Decatur!" and was joined in lusty *huzzahs* that drew the attention of every craft in the harbor. From his face, the captain's pride in his crew was evident to us all.

Since there was a limited amount of space on the ketch, I puzzled over how we would ever put men enough aboard to accomplish our lofty commission when even the prize crew was crowded. I had thought a vessel of significant proportion, say, USS *Constitution* or the like, would be necessary to transport the large numbers required; certainly not a vessel smaller even than our own *Enterprise!*

Decatur stepped toward the eager sailors and, raising his hand for silence, spoke again. "You are to be congratulated for your zeal; I will be taking only sixty of you in view of the size of our ship. And six of my officers and midshipmen. We will be augmented by members of the *Syren's* crew who will join us by boat just before we attack. *Syren* will lay offshore of the harbor to assist us should we encounter difficulty beyond our capacity."

There was a sudden shoving and pushing among the men as those in the rear struggled to find room in the front ranks, thus ensuring their inclusion in the select sixty.

"Selection of the crew will be up to Mister Lawrence and his officers. You may rest assured he will choose those most qualified for this difficult undertaking." Decatur, his eyes still aglow and his jaw muscles tensing to a rhythm known only to him, watched the faces before him for several moments, then turned on his heel and stepped to the hatch leading to his Cabin. As he left, he ordered, in a voice loud enough for all to hear, "Mister Lawrence, you may dismiss our brave men."

How will only sixty men accomplish such a lofty ambition? That is a fully armed thirty-six-gun frigate, and anchored under the guns of a fortress! And how will we put even sixty men and six officers and mids aboard that tiny ketch? Where will they all sleep? Why, there was room for only Judd or me to sleep when we brought her in! Surely he does not expect to sail that vessel jammed to her gun'ls with so many! And what about provisions for them? I stood on the quarterdeck, exactly where I had been, and looked forward on *Enterprise*, seeing the men and thought they looked crowded on *this* ship. I could not imagine even half that number on *Mastico . . . Intrepid.*

"Oliver! Come on, boy! The first lieutenant awaits us in the gunroom to help him select the crew. We surely don't want to be left out!" Judd caught hold of my arm and nearly dragged me forward toward the hatch as he spoke. Again I considered the wisdom of volunteering for this, even as I stepped forward to do so.

By the time the ships' bells across the harbor chimed their four double *ding*s signaling eight o'clock and the start of the evening watch, we, or rather, Mister Lawrence and Mister Hobbs, had concluded the list of men who would make up *Intrepid's* crew. And Judd, Thomas, and I were, of course, counted among its lucky members. Mister Lawrence determined that James was simply too young to risk on so dangerous a commission (*I am only a few months older than he, am I not?*), and besides, somebody had to stay on *Enterprise* and assist Mister Morris, who would be acting as captain during our absence. The surgeon would, of course, go, as would our sailing master, Seth Cartee and Gunner Tarbox, along with some sixty others carefully selected from the schooner's crew.

"Thank you for your help, gentlemen. On the morrow, we will bring *Mast . . . Intrepid* alongside to load her out with provisions and munitions. We must be ready to sail on a moment's notice." First Lieutenant Lawrence dismissed us as he carefully folded the list and placed it in his pocket, no doubt to share with Captain Decatur that very night.

"Oliver, what say you to a bite and a glass ashore? I know of a fine establishment that serves a decent *porto* and not an unpalatable plate. Will you join me?" Judd spoke as we headed topside into the cool January night.

He was quite right; our supper was quite superb and, while I took it in some moderation, the *porto*, or port, as we call it, was sweet and dark with a fine rich aroma. It put me in mind of the finishing wine which I had found too sweet at the fancy dinner in Gibraltar. This time it seemed just right.

"What are you going to do about this . . . situation . . . with Thomas, Judd? You're not really going to fight him, are you?" Perhaps a glass or two of port inspired me to the question, but, after all, Judd had asked me to second him.

"Absolutely. And I fully expect to kill him! I chose the distance I did, forty paces, on account of he likely could not hit anything from that range. But I can. The more normal distance, you should know, for a contest with pistols is ten, sometimes twenty, yards. Even Wheatley might enjoy a dollop of luck at *that* range, but not at forty yards!" Judd's sudden change from frivolous and laughing to deadly serious added further impact to his words, as though any were needed. "You saw him shoot a pistol on *Argus* during all that practice we had coming across the Atlantic. He will be lucky to even pull the trigger, let alone hit me, before I put a ball through his heart! And good riddance to him, I say!"

"Is there no way to stop this? It seems so . . . wasteful that one or another of you should be killed or cruel hurt over you calling him stupid. I would even wager he knows he is! And I don't like Thomas any more than you or James does, but I don't reckon I want to see him dead." I took a forkful of something that had been quite delicious, but now seemed dull and tasteless, as I waited for Judd's response.

"I have heard that, should a commanding officer discover the plan before it is carried out and wishes to, he can order it stopped. But I suspect that Captain Decatur would be unlikely to, given that he himself seconded Captain Bainbridge less than a year ago right here in the Mediterranean; on The Rock, it was. If I recollect the story right, Bainbridge killed some English dandy just before they sailed for home in the *Chesapeake* frigate." He paused, chewing thoughtfully, then added, "April last year, it was. Or March. No, I'd say Decatur might indeed turn a blind eye to it." Judd smiled at me. I thought it an evil sort of smile. *He actually relishes the thought of facing Thomas Wheatley.*

While we continued to talk amiably over the remainder of our meal and managed even to laugh once or twice, our conversation had a strained quality to it, likely more on my part than Judd's; he was quite comfortable with the specter of facing Thomas Wheatley over loaded and cocked pistols. I wondered about that, too.

On the walk back, I asked him, "Judd, have you ever done this before?"

"Done what? Sailed an overcrowded boat into a hornet's nest of a fortified harbor to put an American ship to the torch? No, Oliver, I haven't." He slackened his pace not a whit.

I had slowed, anticipating a conversation might ensue, and had to hurry to catch up to him. He was smiling in the dark, knowing full well what I had meant and pleased at his ability to parry the question.

"No, Judd. I'd warrant not many have done *that*. What I meant was, uh . . . well, have you ever been in a duel?" This time he did stop and looked at me.

"Are you getting squeamish on me, Oliver?"

"No . . . well, I don't . . . it's just that . . . yes, I must be. I just think it's wrong for you to fight Thomas. Fisticuffs would answer just as well, would they not? And then nobody would be killed, at least."

Judd laughed. "If I thought he'd learn anything from fist fighting, I would not have called pistols at forty paces. No, Wheatley will only learn from being shot, and if he dies from it, then so be it; he will not have his newly acquired knowledge long. However, should I only wing him, think of the benefit to all who meet him in the future. Now, if you would rather not be my second, I shall find someone else who has the stomach for it, but we will fight a duel."

"I will act as your second, Judd; I told you I would and I shan't withdraw now. But I will continue to try to talk you out of it as long as I have breath."

"Save your breath, Oliver. It won't do any good. You know perfectly well I can not back out of this without apologizing, which I shan't do, and I would doubt that Thomas, even if he is a coward, which I do not, for a moment doubt, would withdraw from his challenge. He is too pig-headed by half for that." Judd began walking again, signaling the end of our conversation on this subject. "Now let us get back aboard and get a night's sleep; it will likely be a busy day on the morrow."

And he was quite right; the next day dawned with a flurry of activity, the arrival of both Commodore Preble and Captain Stewart's *Syren*, and the securing of *Intrepid* alongside our schooner. Most of the provisions, powder and other combustibles, and boarding arms were transferred to the ketch which, I noticed, had been furnished with a new and noticeably larger deckhouse.

CHAPTER FIFTEEN

Fortunately, the weather remained docile as the heavily laden ketch, in company with the *Syren*, cleared Sicily and headed just west of south toward Tripoli. *Intrepid* sailed with the wind abeam and all sail to the main t'gallant set; *Syren* struggled to retard even her usual stately pace to hold station nearby under reefed tops'ls, a single jib, and the spanker.

"Another fine day of calms and easy breezes. I surely hope this holds for us; boat lumbers along like a cathedral with all this extra crew and provisions." I stood by the weather mainstays as I watched the brig, a musket shot above us and obviously having difficulty going as slowly as needed, and hoped for the best.

"Would you rather we shipped fewer men to accomplish our task, Mister Baldwin?" Decatur stood behind me, for how long I knew not, but had quite apparently heard what I had just 'thought.' I had not realized I was actually speaking the words!

I turned, flushed at being caught in such unseemly words and saw him there, balancing easily to the gentle motion of the ketch, a smile playing at the corners of his mouth.

"Oh, sir! No, sir! I meant nothing untoward, Captain. Just that . . ." I stammered and fell all over myself trying to make right the impression I had created.

"I fully understand, Oliver. And you are quite right; *Intrepid* sails poorly indeed. However, we need her to fool the pirates in Tripoli, and we need these men, and more, to carry out our commission. Our Sicilian pilot, Salvatore Catalano—have you met him yet?—made the exact same observation only yesterday. We shall all pray for continued fine weather." Decatur grinned, shot a glance at *Syren*, and, stepping around several barrels and coils of slow match stowed on deck, made his way aft.

Chastened, but feeling less like a fool than I had initially, I remained at the weather mainstays and looked at the deck around me. All manner of casks, barrels, coils of rope and slow match, spare lumber, spars, sharp-edged boarding weapons, and men lay or stood on most every available spot. I knew that the hold, recently vacated by the human cargo the vessel had last carried, was jammed to the overhead with provisions. Already I had heard several of our marines complaining of the vermin that attacked them as they tried to sleep on top of the casks of provisions below; it was plain that whoever had cleaned the hold had made a poor job of it.

The four officers and three midshipmen aboard shared space in the Cabin, which had been designed for one or possibly two at most. Without question, the mids were left with barely enough room to stand when all were present, and we managed to find room to sleep by placing pallets on top of some casks and crates stowed in the passageway. The close quarters did little to improve relations between Judd and Thomas, but with Thomas being witness to Judd's daily pistol practice, I suspect he had little interest in further antagonizing the senior midshipman.

Each day since the third of February, 1804, when we departed Sicily, Judd had appeared on deck with several pistols; he claimed they were his own (a fact which impressed *me*) and, rigging several lines from the main yard's end, proceeded to shoot at suspended bits of wood and metal with remarkable accuracy. Each time he destroyed one, a seaman on the yard hauled up the line and replaced the target with another. His drill was methodical and lasted each morning for half an hour. On the first day of it, he, quite naturally, drew an audience, including Wheatley and me. With each splintered target, I watched Thomas become more agitated; finally he left, saying not a word to me or anyone else. On the two days since, I saw Thomas watching from afar, at least as 'afar' as was possible on a seventy-five foot vessel! Each time, his face seemed chalky, and I noticed beads of sweat on his brow. The rest of us, including Captain Decatur, found it an amusing diversion. I noticed a substantial amount of surreptitious wagering taking place among the crew and hoped that the captain continued to wink at the unlawful practice. I, for one, made plans to be near Judd when we boarded the frigate in Tripoli harbor!

Even at our slogging pace, we were off Tripoli on the seventh. Decatur had *Intrepid* drop an anchor after dark to the west of the harbor while *Syren* sailed off and on below the town's horizon. Almost immediately we had set our hook, the wind piped up and some nasty weather set in. The little ketch bobbed and danced as the seas quickly built, causing the captain concern as to our ability to cross the bar and gain the harbor.

He ordered our boat launched and Mister Devon, with the pilot, Mister Catalano, to reconnoiter the entrance. As soon as they reappeared from the darkness to come alongside, I knew we would not be going in *this* night; one man had put up his oar and bailed with his hat, and still the water sloshed midway up to the seats, while Judd and the pilot were soaked through and through. I was right; they reported breaking seas across the western entrance and the seas too rough to even get near to the eastern one.

Decatur ordered sail made and the anchor won. We stood offshore and found that the safest way for us to manage the seas and wind was to run off before it. We were too low in the water to risk even heaving to. After several days—they were days of absolute misery for all of us—we had been blown far to the east. And this was not even the *mistral*, the winter wind that blew from the north and made it so dangerous for vessels approaching the North African coast. Pumps were manned during every watch, and there seemed no dry area in the whole vessel. The Cabin leaked, making the officers quartered there testy and short; the hold leaked, as did the passageway we mids shared. By the time the weather eased and the wind veered, calming the seas, we were all a sorry lot, indeed. It took all of Decatur's powers of persuasion and his own fire to maintain calm heads and a sense of mission.

But, by the mid-afternoon on the sixteenth, we were once again lying to some five leagues from the eastern entrance to Tripoli's harbor. *Syren* was with us, disguised nicely as a ragged merchant vessel to allay the suspicions of any ashore who might spot her. The weather was fine and clear with an easy breeze, in marked contrast to our previous visit.

Decatur proclaimed his intention to "strike while we might and fulfill our commission." We would head immediately to the harbor entrance while the breeze was favorable. Under full sail, we left our larger companion and made for the harbor at Tripoli. Before we had accomplished half the distance to the harbor, it was clear to all that we would be at our destination—and clearly visible—well before dark.

"Mister Lawrence, we'll hand the t'gallants and take a reef in the main, if you please. Wouldn't do at all to let the Bashaw's lads catch a glimpse of us afore we were ready!" The captain's confidence and joy inspired all who heard him to catch his own spirit, and excitement and an air of almost gaiety invested the vessel. The men turned to with a will to shorten us down; their chatter and laughter belied the seriousness of our commission. But even under shortened sail, *Intrepid*, as though eager to meet her own destiny, forged forward, moving well in the easy seas despite the load of men and stores she carried.

"Mister Anderson, be good enough to stream a tops'l yard, one those spares there on deck, if you please. We must slow her down even more." Decatur shouted forward and watched as the bosun grabbed a few seamen who, after securing lines to the stout piece of timber, carried it aft and heaved it over the taffrail. The lines quickly took a strain and held the spar across our roiling wake, just before the small boat we towed astern. *Intrepid* slowed reluctantly, causing a smile to replace the frown on our captain's face.

Inexorably, the harbor entrance and nightfall drew close. To Decatur's and all of our joy, nightfall arrived well before the entrance. The wind began to drop causing, first, the drag to be retrieved and, ultimately, the reefs and handed sails to be shaken out.

"My God, Oliver! First we're tearing along too fast to suit him, and now we're barely rippling the surface. Perhaps he waited a trifle too long before he hauled in the spar. We may be sitting out here all night!" Thomas complained to me. He pointed ahead of us. "Look there, you can see the lights in the watch towers ashore. We should be in there, boarding that ship and firing her!"

"I suspect that Captain Decatur knows well what he is about, Thomas. And I'd wager we'll be boarding sooner than either of us expect." I left him and headed to the quarterdeck to take the watch with Mister Hobbs.

When I got there, Decatur and he were deep in conversation, so I moved to the leeward side and kept my own counsel. A smile from each to the other, and they separated, Decatur to the wind'ard side, his private domain, even on this little vessel, and Hobbs took a position near the helmsman. I joined him. He nodded at me but remained silent, as did I.

"Well, Mister Baldwin, are you ready for your first taste of real action? I expect this one will be a trifle warmer than when last we encountered the enemy!" Decatur spoke quietly to me, raising his voice only enough to be heard from the wind'ard rail where he stood, leaning his back against it.

Startled by his disembodied voice, I responded quickly, "Yes, sir. I certainly hope so, sir. I am somewhat nervous about it, though." I tried to sound confident, more confident than I felt.

"I am, too, Mister Baldwin. I am, too. You may not know that my own father commanded that splendid vessel during the recent unpleasantness with France; that makes it, in a small way, a part of me, my history, as well as my father's. And I am saddened to be putting our fine Philadelphia-built ship to the torch, but better to fire her than let that heathen pirate have the use of her.

"As you know, she was built and paid for by the upstanding and loyal citizens of our fair city, then given to the government. With your father a renowned cabinetmaker there, you likely feel as I do about burning such a fine piece of work as that vessel. Is his work in that ship, that you know of?" Without waiting for an answer, he assumed my agreement and went on. "Is it not a wonder, Mister Baldwin, that both our fathers had a hand in the history of that monument to our fair city? Perhaps you find that as unsettling as I do." Decatur stepped near and smiled warmly at me, trying, I think, to ease my worries.

"Oh, sir. I don't recall whether his was the shop commissioned to finish the Cabin and wardroom in *Philadelphia*; it surely could have been. I was only a boy of nine years when she was launched. I do recall seeing her before her masts went in, though. A splendid sight she made, especially in the company of so many other fine ships moored right close by." The memory was dim as, at the time, it barely signified to me. Now the ship's importance lay only in the fact that she had recently been the assigned station of my brother and was partly the reason that he languished in a prison. But I would most assuredly *not* offer that sentiment to Captain Decatur, especially as he waxed sentimental about his own father and the citizens of our hometown.

The wind grew even lighter, and it was nearly midway through the night watch when we carefully, now with Mister Catalano's steady and knowledgeable hand on the tiller, made our way into the harbor.

"Captain, a signal from *Syren*, sir. Cap'n Stewart asks us to wait for the boat. They can not catch us up." The quartermaster tucked his signal book under his arm, lowered his glass, and faced the captain, expecting as we all did, that he would acknowledge the lights and heave to. Decatur shifted his own glass from the harbor fortification to the barely visible cutter well astern, which held the ten men from *Syren* who were to make up our full compliment. It was apparent that Captain Stewart had waited too long before sending them after us and, even with the failing air, they would, as the *Syren's* signal had told, be unable to overtake us.

"If we wait, we will most surely lose this dying breeze and never get in at all without using the sweeps. Signal the *Syren* to recall the boat; we will proceed without them." He paused and, raising his voice a bit, faced forward. "The fewer the men, the greater the honor." His voice, as he no doubt intended, carried to the men amidships and, I think, filled them and the officers with an even higher sense of duty and the glory to be won from our success.

Judd, Thomas, and I stood forward of the quarterdeck, there was little enough room for Mister Hobbs, the pilot, and the captain, and I had been excused with the arrival of Mister Catalano to the helm. At the captain's words, we looked at one another and, in the pale light of the quarter moon, Judd and Thomas looked a bit wan; so, I suspect, did I. I hoped it was simply the moonlight. I seemed unable to stand still or find a comfortable position. Even though the night air held a delightful coolness, I became aware of moisture trickling down my collar and back, and my stomach seemed beset by a strange churning that threatened to move into my bowels.

"You men there. Only the watch on deck. The rest of you, below or lie down below the bulwarks. We need to look like a weather-beat trader, shorthanded." Lieutenant Hobbs spoke with a quiet gruffness to his voice that seemed to carry to the bow and inspired the men to move quickly. In only a few moments, barely ten souls were visible on deck, including the officers. When I looked at the quarterdeck, I was stunned to see Moors at the helm and standing nearby. Flowing robes and headcloths over swarthy faces glowed softly in the dim light, and I stared, elbowing Judd to look from our position behind the deckhouse.

"Oliver, you dolt! What did you think, for heaven's sake? We've not been taken over. That is Hobbs, there on the larboard side, and the tall one, that'll be Captain Decatur. The little fellow there at the tiller is Catalano. Those costumes, their darkened faces and hands, along with the few men on deck, are what we hope will act to get us close to the frigate. Now hush!" Judd's whisper was harsh in my ear, and I was glad for the darkness, feeling as foolish as I did. I tried to remain still, but it was not to be. I fidgeted and fussed. The longer we hid there by the deckhouse, the worse I felt. The sweat ran down my face in spite of the continual efforts of my right sleeve. More traced a course down my back, and my wet shirt grew cold against my skin. There was no question in my mind that I would soon either throw up or foul my britches, or both. I wanted to shout, make noise, something to break the tension, but with considerable effort, held my peace.

My personal problems were forgotten as soon as I peeked around the forward end of the deckhouse. We were coming, ghosting in the failing air, right

up to the frigate! I felt a chill run through me, and, without warning, my stomach heaved, and my mouth grew unspeakably dry, then wet, as if I had just
taken a drink but neglected to swallow. I knew I would be ill and hoped the
darkness would hide the effects of it. I swallowed hard several times as I pulled
my head quickly back into the cover afforded by the house. I knew I had begun
to tremble.

Judd sensed my fear; it wouldn't have taken a great amount of perception.
"Oliver, just concentrate on what Decatur and Lawrence told us before we came
in; no shooting, just cutlasses, half-pikes, and tomahawks. You will be with Captain Decatur and you with your fifteen men will take and hold the spar deck. I
am going with Lawrence below to the berthing deck, and Hobbs will take
Wheatley down to the cockpit and storerooms. Once we've got her, we set the
combustibles and powder aboard, set the fuses, and get out. No prisoners. And
for God's sake, remember the watchword, *Philadelphia*. It will be dark, and you
don't want to be mistook for one of them! It'll be over and done before you
know it." Judd's whisper gave me only slight comfort, but it did seem to take my
mind off the way I felt. I thought I could manage another peek and carefully
eased my eyes around the corner of the cabin. I would rather that I had not!

"Judd! Her guns are run out! That means they must be loaded. And there
must be men aboard to fire them. We've only got four little cannon. That castle,
or fort, looks close . . . real close, Judd, and I'd warrant there's guns up there too.
How're we . . . how can Decatur . . . oh, God! What's going to happen to us!" I
whispered back to him after I saw what lay ahead of us. Concern—no, fear it
was—colored even my hushed tones. I wanted to run to the leeward rail and
unburden my poor belly. But I remained in place, and Judd put a hand on my
arm to silence me as the pilot began shouting to someone in a strange language.

A voice from the frigate answered in the same tongue, and a short conversation ensued. The voice from the frigate did not seem angry, and Catalano's
voice sounded more weary than anything else. I noticed that Decatur was close
to the pilot's side. While I was unable to make out any words, I knew he was
speaking to the Sicilian, likely telling him what to say. I risked another peek
from behind the deckhouse. We were stopped scarcely fifty yards from the
frigate and directly under her guns! A look aloft showed the sails limp, hanging from the spars like clothes on a wash line; not a breath of air stirred. We
looked directly into the gaping muzzles of those huge cannons. One, should it
be fired, would be sufficient to blow us to matchwood; the half dozen trained
on us would leave nary a trace.

With an air of indifference, some men wearing the same Moorish costume
as Decatur, Hobbs, and Catalano appeared from the deck and climbed over the
taffrail, hauled in the boat we had towed for the past ten days, and disappeared
into it. Convincingly sloppy in their rowing, they carried a line from the ketch
toward the looming side of *Philadelphia*. The pirates sent out a boat, also with
a line, which met our boat, joined the two lines and returned, as did ours.

The line was passed up to the deck and our men, the American sailors laying along the side under the bulwark, began to haul us in toward our target without being seen. Quickly *Intrepid* was just below their deck.

"AMERICANOS! AMERICANOS!" The cry went through the frigate like windblown fire. Turbaned heads peered over the bulwark, looking down at us.

"BOARD, BOYS! BOARD 'em!" Decatur's shout galvanized us all into action. Suddenly sixty whooping American cutthroats, brandishing cutlasses, halfpikes, and tomahawks were swarming over our rail and then the enemy's. The flowing robes and billowing pantaloons I had seen on our men had been hastily cast aside. I have no recollection of leaving my position aside the ketch's deckhouse nor of climbing aboard the frigate; suddenly, I was there, on the enemy's deck right astern of Captain Decatur, brandishing a cutlass aloft in a death grip, screaming words, unintelligible even to me, at the white robed, black-bearded sailors before me.

More men followed us, and I was aware of Judd and Lawrence with a cadre of sailors flowing by me as they drove a large group of robed Arabs before them. Hobbs, his sword shining dully in the dim light, appeared, pushed me unceremoniously to one side, and neatly skewered a huge pirate through the chest. I had not even seen the man, so intent was I on watching our own men on the frigate's deck, and was quite nonplussed by the suddenness of it all. I did not realize until later that he had most likely saved my life. Hobbs put his foot on the man's chest to hold him as he withdrew his sword and, without a look back, rushed forward toward a hatch where some more of the pirates had disappeared. It occurred to me that he was still wearing his small glasses pushed down on the end of his nose.

The confusion and noise was overpowering: the clanging of cutlasses; the shouts, both in English and Arabic; the running, pounding feet; and the pushing and shoving as some tried to get away from us, while others pursued them. Some of the Arabs fought, swinging short curved swords and pikes at our men. I stood transfixed, trying to get my bearings and find Captain Decatur in the melee.

Out of the corner of my eye I glimpsed a figure, dark skinned and cloaked in white, rushing in my direction. He held one of the vicious-looking curved swords before him and swung it side to side as if cutting a swath through imaginary jungle growth. *Scimitar!* The word flashed unbidden into my brain, and it occurred to me incongruously as I turned to face my attacker that Edward had mentioned in his letter that the curved swords these rascals carried were called scimitars.

Clutching my own blade in both hands, I swung the cutlass with nothing more than instinct and luckily managed to knock his thrust aside. His blade hit mine so sharply that my hands and one arm vibrated in time to the ringing of my own steel. So startled was I by my success that I stopped, pleased with my performance. Prematurely, it turns out, as the man recovered instantly and came at me with renewed vigor, aiming a cut at my head. I ducked the blow and, with a still tingling arm, brought my cutlass up in a swinging, one-handed arc in the general direction of his chest, but with no target in mind. The man turned just as the edge of my weapon struck and, for his trouble, received a gash in his upper arm that immediately issued forth a stream of gore, black in the moonlight.

I had no opportunity this time to revel in this new display of my prowess; with a guttural utterance in his own language, my enemy acknowledged my success and hesitated, though for only a moment, his evil curved blade poised aloft for a death blow. But his hesitation gave me opportunity. I brought my cutlass, still in the air, back, rolling my hand over, and with it, the blade, just as Bosun Anderson had taught us, and, with all my strength, drew it down and across the point where his shoulder and neck joined. I was rewarded with a crimson fountain and felt the warmth of the unlucky wretch's blood splashing onto my arm and chest; some of it splattered into my mouth and the metallic taste of it made me spit, a gesture that, should the Arab have noticed, would have made me out stronger than I certainly felt. A surprised look crossed the man's face; his weapon dropped to the deck as his knees buckled, and he seemed to wilt before my eyes. He dropped first to his knees, then fell forward onto his face as his life's blood pooled at my feet, glistening and black.

Breathless, charged with the fire of combat and my own brush with death, I started aft in pursuit of Decatur and more opponents for my invincible blade! I realized that much of the din of shouting and clanging steel had subsided; indeed, there suddenly seemed only a few white-robed sailors on the deck, and they were rushing headlong for the far bulwark.

"Hold, men. They're done!" Decatur's voice rang out from the frigate's quarterdeck as the remaining Arabs leaped over the rail into the dark waters of the harbor, joining their mates, both dead and alive, who had preceded them. In the silence that now filled the night air, we could hear further sounds of a struggle drifting up from below, and I remembered that Judd and Thomas were down there, likely meeting the same early resistance we had met topside. Would that they might overcome it as quickly as we had!

As I reached the bulwark at the break of the poop, the silence became complete, signaling the end to the combat, and I sagged, suddenly quite exhausted and faint, against the waist-high wall. The sounds of men splashing in the water below me filtered into my brain, but did not signify; I could scarcely move my arms. They hung at my sides, the cutlass barely grasped in my limp hand. Without warning, a Saint Vitus' dance of trembling took over my whole being, and I felt hot tears coursing down my cheeks.

"Sir! Are you hurt, sir? You're covered in blood! Where is your wound? Doctor! Mister Wakefield, here, sir!" A sailor—I could not call to mind his name, though he was one of our Enterprises—faced me, wearing a most concerned expression.

"What? Huh? Blood?" I stammered, unable to focus my thoughts and join them to words. I stared at the man, uncomprehendingly, blankly. "No, I think I am quite all right." But his question caused me to look down at my own self to discover, shockingly, that I was indeed covered in blood; in fact, the front of my shirt, my arms, and my hands were black in the starlight. But nothing hurt; my shoulder ached as did my sword-arm. I noticed, without any emotion, that the skin on my hands and my neck was sticky. While I had never experienced the hurt of a sword cut, I assumed I would at least recognize pain in some part of me, even in my befuddled state. I repeated, "No. I think I am unharmed." I saw Reliance Wakefield, his white surgical apron showing dark blotches, hurrying toward us.

"Aye, sir. Glad of it. Must be someone else's gore all over you then. Quite a scrap, it were, eh, sir? I reckon we give 'em what-fer!" The sailor grinned at me and left. He exchanged a brief word with the medico, who changed course and headed forward where, presumably, somebody needed his services more than I.

"Get the combustibles and explosives up, lively there." Decatur's voice again cut through my fog and fuddle. Only slightly more aware of my own actions, I moved across the deck toward to where *Intrepid* was tied alongside. Already men were passing up casks and barrels, rope and slow match to willing hands in the frigate. I saw Lieutenant Hobbs and Thomas Wheatley directing the men who staggered under the casks and crates as they headed for the hatch. I wanted to catch up with Thomas, to see how he had fared below, but he was already heading back down to the hold carrying a coil of slow match.

More casks had arrived on deck and were being carried off, some below and many to positions on the spar deck. I saw Mister Lawrence overseeing the placement of one such cask near the mainmast and made my way to him.

"What can I do, sir? I am sure I have been assigned to a task, but can not recall what it was." I would have doffed my hat in a salute, but it was gone from my head, its absence unnoticed 'til this very moment.

"What? Oh, Baldwin." Lawrence looked up from the fuse he had cut. "My God, man! What happened to you? Did you see the surgeon? You are bleeding to death. Here, son, sit." He pushed a cask of powder over and gestured for me to sit down on it.

"No, sir. I am not hurt. That is not my blood. I am quite all right and looking for employment." I answered, trying to sound as unconcerned as my words and keep the tremble out of my voice.

"Oh, well, then. Glad to hear it." The concern vanished from his tone instantly. He became most businesslike. "You finish up with these men. We're setting charges around the masts that remain to destroy them along with the ship; no point in leaving anything those scoundrels might use!" He handed me a length of slow match and, stepping around me, disappeared into the darkness.

Luckily for me, Bradford was one of the men securing powder casks around the girth of the mainmast; I had little to do save hand him a length of fuse when he asked for it. Through the darkness I could make out others by the cannons topside driving nails into the touch holes on each piece. No one seemed to be shouting or even talking; they all went about their assigned tasks quietly and quickly.

"Are you about done, here, Mister Baldwin? I have little interest in remaining aboard much longer. That the rascals ashore have no inkling of our presence so far is extraordinary good luck; it would be folly to think they might continue in their ignorance." Decatur, the sword still in his hand glistening darkly in the moonlight augmented by a few deck lanterns, cast his gaze on the powder kegs secured to the butt of the mizzenmast as Bradford jammed the final fuse into the top of one.

"Yes, sir. I believe all is ready here. And we have already finished at the mainmast." I shot a glance at Bradford who nodded at me as he stuck his knife back into his belt.

"Then move your men to the rail at the ketch." He looked at me, for the first time, I think. "Great God above, Oliver. What has happened to you? Did Wakefield have a look at you?"

"Oh, no, sir. It's quite all right. I am unharmed, I think. The blood is not mine!" This was becoming habit now. Everyone seemed concerned over my well being! I smiled in spite of myself, enjoying the attention and concern. The momentary humor in the situation eased my agitation some, also.

"Very well, then. Leave one aboard to light the fuses and get yourself into the ketch." Decatur's concern over my health was short-lived indeed, and, having given his orders, he left without further comment. I did notice that the fire still burned in his gaze, and his focus and control over the entire situation seemed complete.

By the time I reached the bulwark, most of our crew had embarked in *Intrepid*; a few sailors and Lieutenant Lawrence remained aboard *Philadelphia*. Each held a lit slow match, and I could see several glowing points of light forward giving testimony to work they had already accomplished.

"Baldwin! Where's Devon? He ain't showed up yet. Don't let 'em blow the ship without him gettin' off!" I recognized Thomas's voice, and the concern it held, as he called up from the deck of the ketch.

"I have not seen him since we boarded, Thomas. He must still be below!" I called back and ran to the hatch leading to the berth deck.

"Judd! Judd Devon! Are you down there?" I shouted down the ladder. More fuses glowed in the dark up and down the length of the spar deck. I imagined I could even hear the sputtering of the powder-soaked cord! I called out again. "Judd Devon! The fuses are lit. If you're down there, come up, man! The ship's going to blow up!" My voice cracked, finishing my warning yell on a high note. There wasn't time to be embarrassed. A fire, set with our combustibles near the stump of the foremast, had started to burn brightly, and I could see tendrils of flame crawling across the deck as the pitch in the seams was touched.

"Just finishing up, here, Oliver. Be right along." Judd's voice floated up from the dark depths of the hole sounding as unconcerned and calm as ever he could.

"Hurry, Judd! The ship's took the flame forward and the fuses're lit." I threw one more warning back and hurried back to the bulwark where now, only Decatur and Lawrence stood. Fuses glowed brightly the length of *Philadelphia's* deck, and the flames I had earlier seen by the foremast now had spread to the fo'c'sle.

"Get yourself down there, Mister Baldwin. We must cast off at once, afore those ashore smoke our game." Lawrence took my arm and steered me toward the break in the bulwark.

"Sir, Judd . . . Mister Devon's still below. We must wait." I realized after I spoke that I was out of my depth in my words, but still, I thought, perhaps neither knew of Devon's absence.

"He'll be right along, I assure, you, Mister Baldwin. Now get yourself into the ketch!" Lawrence's voice was tight with tension, whether at the missing midshipman or the rapidly increasing chance of discovery I knew not, but I obeyed.

Then we were away, all hands, including Judd Devon, present and correct, lines cut and, with the breeze remaining nil, the sweeps were manned by anxious sailors who strained to put some water between the burning frigate and *Intrepid*. I realized there were still quite a number of powder casks and other combustibles on our deck and, as I felt the heat of the fire above us, thought of the devastation a single spark could create. Never in the history of naval warfare had a boat moved so slowly away!

Then the shore batteries opened fire. They quite obviously knew not where to aim as all they could see were the flames now reaching the mainyard on *Philadelphia*; the frigate was between us and the shore and sheltered us in her final role as an American vessel. Gradually, the distance opened, and, seeing that we were safe, the men gave three lusty *huzzahs* at our good fortune. In return, we received the fire from the shore batteries, now given a target!

Their aim was deplorable; only one ball found us, and that through the main t'gallant, touching neither spar nor line. Of greater and more immediate concern were the frigate's own guns which, because of the way she swung to her cable, commanded the entrance through which we must pass. Each was loaded and, though carefully spiked by our crew, now discharged as the fire heated the barrel, sending a ball flying across the harbor with reckless and sudden abandon. Those manning the sweeps were once again invested with inspiration and turned to with a will; *Intrepid* moved quickly into a building breeze near the harbor's mouth.

"Look at that, Oliver. The way the firelight lights up the splashes from the shore guns. The spray fairly glows in the brilliance of the flames." Judd, smiling broadly at our success and, I thought, his own survival, pointed over the ketch's stern as the spray thrown up by the shot from not only the shore guns, but also those of the frigate, was brightly lit by the flames behind them.

I still suffered from my trembling and was scarcely in the mood for Judd to wax poetic, thinking more on the narrowness of our escape. But I had to agree with him. "It is lovely to see, Judd. Especially as it's behind . . ."

BOOM! BOOM! Two thunderous explosions ripped through the night and sent flames and sparks into the darkness as high as the mainmast on *Philadelphia*. The men at the sweeps stopped pulling to look, and all hands stared open-mouthed at the spectacle astern as more explosions rent the night. In the light of the fires they created, we saw the mainmast—it might have been the mizzen—shoot straight up, burning like a rocket leaving a trail of sparks astern. We could hear the sizzle as it splashed into the sea alongside the now fully-engulfed ship. She was beautiful to behold; her lower gunports illuminated by the fire behind them, the windows in the stern castle equally bright, and the decks shooting yellow and orange flames skyward, the whole wreathed in billowing and roiling white smoke which reflected the flames' glow. Indeed, the ship had the appearance of the very gates of hell, at least the way I always had seen them pictured. I imagined Old Seth himself prowling the flaming decks of that inferno, gathering the souls of the unfortunates who, despite their dreams of paradise, would find a very different eternity!

"Judd! Look there. The *Philadelphia's* shore-side guns—they're cooking off! And right into the fort, there. The old girl's offering her own punishment to these barbarians! Look! You can see the shot landing in the walls by the light of the fires. I'd wager those rascals yonder must think we're still aboard and shooting back at them!" Now that we were quite safe from harm, and with a spectacle unlike anything I had ever imagined before me, I forgot completely about my former misgivings and returned to my old self, my limbs once again still. The walls of the city, lit by the discharge of their own artillery, formed a splendid backdrop for the brilliance of the burning ship, and the dark, still-unruffled waters of the harbor reflected each light myriad times, adding to the spectacle.

Safely out of range, Decatur let us remain where we lay to observe the vision of hell we had wrought. The breeze that would carry us back to *Syren* and, ultimately, to Sicily, was filling in.

"Mister Anderson, you may fire the rocket now, if you please. I would say we have accomplished what we set out to," Decatur called forward to the bosun who waited with the rocket we had brought to signal *Syren* of our success. With a *whoosh* it streamed straight upwards, leaving a short trail of sparks and exploding into a green star that hung for a second or two before burning out and falling back to the sea.

"There she goes!" Somebody soon called out from the waist of our little warship. We watched as *Philadelphia*, her cables burned through, drifted lazily toward the shore. She stopped, aground, and continued to burn, the occasional explosion deep within her adding to the conflagration. Then, with a breathtaking suddenness, the whole of the ship exploded, sending burning pieces of herself into the sky as high as the city walls. "Magazine's gone up," I heard several voices near at hand explain. I felt a thump on my chest, almost like I had been punched, even before the pieces of the destroyed ship fell back into the waters of Tripoli Harbor.

"Make sail, men. We've a breeze to carry us out!" Decatur was jubilant. Without seeing his face, I knew, as did every man aboard, that he was wreathed in smiles at our splendid success, and the honor and glory we had won.

Syren waited for us beyond the breakwater and her men gave us three mighty *huzzahs* as we hove alongside. The breeze that had carried us out freshened and carried us all the way back to Sicily.

CHAPTER SIXTEEN

" Twenty minutes? Impossible! I know we were there for an hour and more! We could've hardly fought those piratical rascals off the ship and set all the explosives and combustibles in even *that* time. But twenty minutes! I can not fathom why you would want to tell a tale like that! I was there, too, you may recall, Devon!" Thomas's attack had been provoked by Judd's quite accurate remark about the time we spent on the *Philadelphia* frigate. Judd ignored the outburst and continued.

"And you know, James, we lost not a soul. I believe one man, a seaman, was injured, not badly, by one of the pirates, but I find it quite remarkable that we came through our first encounter with nary a single loss. And they lost twenty killed, I heard." He looked at me, smiled, and added quietly, "Oliver got one by himself, you know." James gasped, and I could feel his stare.

That event had haunted me since we returned to *Syren*. I had barely smiled when we entered the harbor at Syracuse and every American vessel had cheered us as we passed. I had dreamt about it when I was able to sleep, and it still took very little to startle me. I knew James would clap on to that part of our boarding and bleed me for every detail. I was not ready for that yet. I thought the whole thing horrifying, still. I quickly changed the subject.

"Judd," I started before James, who had hung on our every word, even Thomas's, could speak, "what do you suppose Mister Catalano said to those barbarians to make them allow us so close, even send us a line?" It was something I had thought on over the three days of our return to Syracuse, and, try as I might, I could imagine nothing that would answer.

"Well, Oliver, I don't happen to speak Maltese or Arabic or whatever it was he was jabbering in. But I asked Lawrence the exact question you just posed to me. The pilot told them we were a Maltese trader just come over from the island and had lost our anchor in the storm. Aye, the same one that blew us off station before we actually went in. Asked 'em if we might tie up along side them over night so as to make the quay in the daylight. Pretty smart, you ask me, and I collect from what Lawrence told me, Decatur was the one concocted the tale! Lawrence also mentioned the pirates had noticed *Syren* out beyond the harbor and asked after her. Good thing Cap'n Stewart made her look more like a down and out merchant than a warship! Catalano told them she was a vessel called *Transfer*, one he knew the Tripolitans had just bought in Malta and which they expected to appear at any time. Told 'em her master was waiting on daylight to make the harbor. Reckon Mister Catalano can think on his feet as well as pilot a ship!" Even Thomas was silent and smiling as Judd concluded his explanation. And James sat open-mouthed, thrilled by our tales, and still rankled that he had not been allowed to participate in what he called "our great adventure."

"Our first lieutenant also told me—and this since we got in—that the commodore was overjoyed with our success and was writing to the Secretary of the Navy forthwith." Judd smiled broadly, then grew serious as he continued. "Catalano had told him that, based on the wind, tide and his skill, we could have cut out the ship and brought her successfully to sea, but Preble told him 'Captain Decatur carried out my orders exactly, which as I recall, were quite specific on that very subject, sir.' Reckon Mister Catalano won't be offering much more advice and counsel to our commodore real soon." Devon laughed at the lofty rebuke the Sicilian pilot had received.

Then he lowered his voice and added, conspiratorially, "Later, it was only yesterday, I think, Lawrence mentioned to Morris—I happened to be close enough to overhear—that Decatur was some put out that he wasn't allowed to bring the ship out. According to Lawrence, he was right sure he could have done it and saved the vessel from the torch. Reckon he puts a higher worth on following orders than seeking glory and honor. Or mayhaps he puts more faith in the pilot's skills than did the commodore. 'Course, as I recall, there wasn't a breath o' breeze when we took our leave from the frigate; likely woulda had a bit of difficulty *sailing* anywhere, let alone into glory and honor!"

"Well, Judd," I quite ignored his humorous remark, instead choosing to hear only his comment about Decatur's desire for glory and honor. I started off before I had even thought out what I would say. "I think Captain Decatur puts a pretty high worth on 'glory and honor' as you say. That's why he volunteered himself and his crew for the commission. And you heard your own self what he said when the quartermaster told him the men from *Syren* were unable to catch up outside the harbor." I tried unsuccessfully to mimic the captain's voice. " 'The fewer the number the greater the honor.' If that doesn't signify to you, I reckon I'm not likely to change your mind." I was quite sure I knew what had been in the mind of our commander throughout our mission and before.

"Sometimes, Oliver, just when I think you're close to becoming a man you say something like that and prove yet again you're still a boy—and think like one." Judd's expression matched his tone, and I recoiled some in surprise at the harshness of both. "What do you think this whole situation, the pirates, the capture of our frigate, the tribute our country, along with a large number of other nations, has been paying to those pashas for years, our very presence here in the Mediterranean is about? Honor, that's what! Our honor as a country, a nation. Our honor as men, and the honor of trading where we want and with whom we want. And if glory is gained in the pursuit of that honor, then so be it. But make no mistake, honor, our nation's and, indeed, our Navy's and, yes, our own as well, is very much what this is about. And do not forget, *young* sir, that you gained some honor and glory your own self in this business." Judd fairly spat out this last, especially the "young sir."

I sat stunned and quite speechless at the venom he directed at me, as did my colleagues. James's mouth hung agape, his eyes big as round shot, and he seemed to shy further away from the senior of us. Thomas displayed a tight smile, and I could only imagine what he thought. Likely grateful that I was the target of *this* broadside instead of him!

"I'm . . . uh . . . I . . ." I stammered as I searched for words that might undo the damage I had done. "Judd, you . . . uh . . . that is, I . . . didn't mean to sound like the captain is . . . uh . . . seeking glory or honor. I just meant that . . . well, it seems like glory just attaches itself to him whenever he does some grand thing. And I certainly can not find fault with acting out of honor, either, but . . . well, I reckon they do kind of go hand in hand, don't they?" I watched Judd's face to see if I had helped myself any. Out of the corner of my eye, I saw Thomas grinning broadly at my predicament.

"You will learn, Oliver, that there are those of us who take this business seriously, very seriously indeed, and will do, or undertake to do, whatever appears necessary to accomplish our country's goal. Very often, success in such an undertaking brings with it a dollop of glory, but usually, that is in the eyes of the beholder. Honor, however, comes from ourselves, our actions, and endeavors. And I can tell you, without a shred of doubt, that Decatur and all of us who sailed with him against those rascals will continue to receive glory from our efforts as long as people talk about it. And yes, the honor that goes along with it! And you should be grateful for it; it is not usual that a young midshipman on his first cruise is given the opportunity to bask in real honor, real glory." Judd stopped and looked at James pointedly. Then he looked at Thomas and said, "After all, on Thomas's first cruise, he never even left the Chesapeake Bay!" When Judd looked back at me and winked, I knew he was no longer angry with me for what I had said.

Thomas's face clouded over, his jaw assumed the familiar thrust, and his eyes narrowed slightly as he spoke. "*I* had no hand in where I spent my first assignment; was it up to me, I would have gotten assigned in a *fighting* ship, not some little brig with toy guns. And, *Mister Senior Midshipman* Devon, Lawrence did choose me to go on this commission, and glad to have me, I'd warrant. As should you be!" Wheatley finished speaking in almost a snarl.

Judd's eyebrows shot up and his brow furrowed. "And why should *I* be glad you came with us, Thomas? I don't recall even seeing you during our twenty minutes in *Philadelphia*. And I suspect you saw no action your own self, as Oliver did, or you'd have been crowing about it since we left the frigate. I can hardly imagine you having any interest in helping me or, I suspect, anyone else were I or they in difficulty. A coward wouldn't risk his own neck just to help a shipmate. 'Sides, were I to be cruel hurt or killed it might answer for you as a way out of our forthcoming engagement." Judd spoke so softly and without malice that, at first, his words didn't signify. But the quiet timbre of his voice spoke loudly of his feelings. I, for one, was quite shocked and when his import struck me, I was moved to speak.

"Actually, Judd, you would be wrong in that. It was Thomas who sent me to find you just before we left the frigate afire, while you were still below. I don't think even Lawrence or Captain Decatur knew you weren't in the ketch. Thomas did though." I looked directly at our senior messmate as I spoke, surprised at myself by my defense of such a loathsome character as Thomas Wheatley.

A silence hung in the cockpit for the space of several breaths. Judd looked at me and quite suddenly he stood up and shifted his eyes to Wheatley, who held his gaze without flinching. "I don't need the likes of Thomas Wheatley looking out for my hide, I assure you. And when I do, I shall surrender my warrant and go ashore for good! But thank you for your concern. Perhaps you're beginning to learn. But you can do your ship and us a service by just doing your job and staying out of my way!" Devon turned and took his leave in the stunned silence.

"That bastard! The scoundrel! I shoulda left his overblown arse right there in that damn frigate. Not said a word until she took the flame and them shore guns had us under fire. That's all the thanks I get for makin' sure we didn't leave him! Oliver, you still his second for our duel?"

I nodded, uncertain as to where this might lead us.

"Well, get us a place and time quicker than ever! I can't wait much longer to sight that rascal's heart down the barrel of my pistol!" With that, Thomas left the cockpit.

James was open-mouthed at the antics of our messmates. I suppose I was, too. I wondered what had come over Judd since we returned from the *Philadelphia* expedition; he seemed angry at all of us and quite without a shred of humor. Thomas was, in my opinion, justifiably roused after Judd's words, and I wondered at the outcome of their forthcoming duel, a duel for which I had yet to discover a place.

But it would not be immediately. Within a week of our return to Syracuse, *Enterprise, Vixen, Nautilus,* and *Constitution* were underway for Tripoli to effect a blockade.

With a fair half gale to speed us across the three hundred miles to the coast of that God-forsaken country, we arrived in good time and took our stations as assigned by Commodore Preble. The shallow draft schooners sailed off and on in the thin waters near the entrances to the harbor, while *Constitution* worked back and forth offshore of us, her guns ready to support any action we might encounter.

It was tedious work; long days of complete boredom, unchallenged by any, pirate or other, with an occasional visit from the *mistral,* the winter winds which would force us offshore far enough to avoid the fate of being blown ashore. These winds, which began in the river valleys of France and gained strength crossing the Mediterranean, would stir up the usually placid seas off the North African coast and send them crashing over the reefs and ultimately, ashore along with anything unlucky enough to be caught in their grip. They often lasted for days at a time. During these spells, life aboard the "Lucky" *Enterprise* was something less than comfortable for all hands. However, in spite of our almost constant case of the damps, most aboard were grateful not to be in the diminutive *Intrepid* for this commission.

During one of our forays offshore to escape the dangers of the mistral, we were quite overpowered by wind and wave and suffered the loss of our main topmast along with a large portion of our jibboom. Stays were jury-rigged to hold up the foremast, now unstable from the loss of the jibboom, and the topmast was cut free from the shrouds and running rigging that held it, swinging and banging into the lower mast and main yard. Worse, however, than the loss of these spars was the condition of the main deck; it leaked at a rate that required each watch to man the pumps for increasingly longer periods of time. With each wave that washed across us, the leaks poured water down onto those below, adding further discomfort to our misery. Then the carpenter, John Williams, announced to Captain Decatur that he had found two planks started and "beggin' yer pardon, sir, they be below the waterline of the barky."

This was a problem, more serious by half than the leaky decks; two planks that had separated themselves from their neighbors would likely open farther, leading to more and more water entering the vessel. Decatur and Bosun Anderson, along with Mister Williams, the carpenter, and Lieutenant Lawrence, looked at the offending planks and considered their options. Naturally, something had to be done quickly to stop or, at the least, slow the Mediterranean Sea from coming aboard. And once stopped, it was their considered opinion, shared with the rest of the officers later, that *Enterprise* would need the services of a naval shipyard to put her to rights. The immediate solution involved stuffing loose bits of cloth and dunnage into the gap. This had a positive effect on our buoyancy and enabled those manning the pump on the weather deck to make progress against the water level within.

"That'll hold her . . . for a while, anyway. Leastways, 'til another one lets go or these open farther." Bosun Anderson shared his cheery thought with me and James while we sheltered from the wind-driven spray lashing most of the length of the schooner's deck. "Then I'd reckon we'll be riggin' a *fother* under her belly. This old lady shoulda been heaved down, scraped, and refit more'n a year ago, 'ceptin' she wasn't on account of her bein' the only one out here what'd float in thin water."

Anderson saw my confusion and laughed when I asked him whatever be meant by his suggestion that we'd be "riggin' a *father* under her belly." To my surprise, it was James who spoke up.

"I know that, Bosun. Can I tell him what it means?" His excitement at actually knowing something about seamanship lit his whole being, and he fairly danced with impatience until he received a nod from Anderson, who now wore a bemused and slightly quizzical expression. "Oliver, it ain't *'fathering'* it's *fothering*. What it means is riggin' a sail under the ship and pulling it up snug with ropes, I mean lines, so that the water trying to get into the ship pushes the sail into the hole in the bottom." He looked questioningly at the bosun and broke into a grin when he got a nod from the surprised sailor. I guess I was just as surprised as Anderson and said as much.

"Where'd you learn that, James? From Judd or maybe Mister Williams, perchance?"

Now James's smile expanded even farther, and he seemed to stand straighter. "No, not from either of them, nor from anyone else. I *read* it in one of our books, Oliver!"

It was my turn to smile at my messmate. But the joy of accomplishment quickly gave way to the gravity of the moment.

"Bosun, will we make it back to Syracuse?" James's concern echoed my own. I shot him a look; *James, do you really want to know that?*

Anderson smiled at us, recognizing that our concern was born of inexperience. "Oh, you needn't worry yourself 'bout that, sir. We'll make it somewhere, prob'ly afore we get too low in the water to navigate!" His answer did little to mollify either James's or my concern. He did not say *where* or *how soon* it would be before we got 'somewhere.'

That night at supper in the cockpit, Judd informed us all that, as the temporary repairs seemed to be holding, we would sail to Messina, a port right on the northeastern tip of the island of Sicily, quite near to the Italian mainland. We would be hauled from the water and repaired, masthead to keelson, according to James Lawrence. With a bit of luck and the mistral easing a trifle, we should be under the lee of Sicily in two days and then into Messina in just another day or so after that. I guessed that the condition of our leaks was not so grave as to warrant an immediate rush to Syracuse.

"Reckon that'll be a right fine place for you to scout up a suitable location for me and Mister Devon to take care of our business, Baldwin. And since we're likely to be on shore for a month and more, I suggest, *Mister* Devon, that we get this matter between us settled." Thomas spoke evenly, emphasizing only to irritate Judd, which, by the look he got from Devon, he had succeeded in doing. James and I, now mere spectators in this ongoing *verbal* duel, looked quickly at one another and then concentrated intently on our meal. It took some considerable effort to maintain neutral expressions. The remainder of our supper was finished quietly with none of the bantering and skylarking we frequently enjoyed.

During the first watch the following day, the wind abated and veered significantly to the west; the seas began to moderate even before we tucked in behind the mountainous shelter of Sicily, easing the schooner's motion and, at the same time, easing the worried looks from the faces of Decatur, Lawrence, and Williams. Before supper was piped, we received a signal from the commodore in *Constitution* to heave to. Shortly thereafter, we observed a boat making for us from the flagship. Once alongside, Lieutenant John Dent clambered up our side and over the low bulwark.

"I am to ride into Messina, with you, Stephen, and see about expanding our fleet," he responded within our hearing to the captain's query. "Commodore Preble thinks we might be able to purchase or borrow some gunboats from the Italians there. He is taking *Constitution* back to Malta, where I expect he will be communicating with Bainbridge through the British."

Though spoken quietly, I heard this utterance with remarkable clarity, since the two passed me on the quarterdeck where I stood my watch with Lieutenant Hobbs. Immediately I thought of how I might communicate with Edward, but quickly pushed the idea from my head as silly. I still had no idea whether he had received my last correspondence and, further, I had written nothing new to him. Still, the idea of more letters between my unfortunate brother and myself floated around in my head, just below the surface like a waterlogged bit of jetsam, to show itself from time to time and raise the flicker of hope that I might again hear from him.

During the night watches, we could see quite plainly the fiery glow from Mount Etna as we sailed past the spewing volcano. The hands and I were entranced by the breathtaking display lighting the sky to the west of us, orange and red with occasional yellow sparks shooting skyward; while little, if any, lava actually came out, the splendor of the show more than made up for it.

In sharp contrast to our passage there, our arrival in Messina was unremarkable. Our repairs were quickly contracted to and undertaken by a competent and amiable clutch of Italian craftsmen. With *Enterprise* secure at the pier and the sounds of hammering, sawing, and ripping filling the air, along with shouted conversation in a marvelously musical dialect of Italian understandable to none of us, Lieutenant Dent went off in search of our auxiliary forces. I went off at the first opportunity, and at the urging of Thomas Wheatley, in search of a field of honor.

It took me some time, after our lengthy stay in turbulent seas, to feel comfortable ashore. The very moment my feet touched the dock I began to feel the familiar dizziness, as though the land should be moving but wasn't. I steadied myself on a piling, hoping the feeling would pass quickly, as Judd had promised. Gradually, I became used to terra firma under my shoes, and I discovered that Judd had been right; each time I came ashore, I found my "land legs" more quickly. But I still enjoyed, indeed, practiced, the rolling gait that would label me a seaman.

CHAPTER SEVENTEEN

"Are we ever going to get out of here and back into the action?" James spoke for most of us aboard the schooner. His question was not directed at anyone in particular so, having heard it almost daily for the past several weeks of our confinement in Messina, most of us gave it little notice, except Thomas.

"I would have thought you, of all of us, would be happiest here in the safety of Messina, tied to the dock, James." Since we had been in a month and more, now, heaved down, planks replaced, and refloated, Thomas had returned to his former, unpleasant self and, once again, James had become the target of most of the man's bile. "And in the event, we can not leave while we are waiting for Mister Devon and Mister Baldwin to determine a suitable location for our business. And I hope they get it done sooner than later! Unless they plan on delaying further."

I colored, stung by his remark. It was my task to find a suitable field of honor and, indeed, I had found several. However, in the fading hope of this "business" being forgotten, I had neglected to inform either of the antagonists of my success.

I spoke up now, carefully laying down my fork and knife next to my unfinished supper. "Thomas, I have found more than one location that would be suitable, as you say, but I have not shown them yet to Judd. I had hoped that I might do that this week, and then we could put this disagreeable business behind us." I spoke to Wheatley, but I noticed Judd turn suddenly at my words to stare at me.

He deliberately shifted his gaze to his challenger and spoke in a flat tone. "I welcome the opportunity to finish this, Thomas. I have been some distracted of late and apologize to you for being neglectful of my obligation. I will at once see what Oliver has found; then we can go out there, I will kill you, and it will be over. Though why you are in such a rush to meet your demise is quite beyond me." Judd's voice held a slight tremor, a result, I thought, of his effort at control.

"Bold talk is cheap and will not answer, Mister Devon. And that little quiver in your voice tells me you are not as confident of the outcome as you would wish me to believe." Wheatley stopped abruptly, clearly thinking. Then he rearranged his face into a smile and finished. "Once we are facing each other from forty paces and looking down the barrels of our pistols, we shall see just who will kill who!" Thomas threw down his fork and left, once again leaving a ringing silence astern. But his mocking tone had struck a chord in Judd. I could see our messmate react, and once again I despaired for Thomas' future, indeed, his very survival.

"Let us look tomorrow at what places you have seen, Oliver. I suppose it is best to get this unpleasantness over. Have you mentioned this to any beyond the cockpit?" Judd spoke after some considerable wait.

"No, of course, I have not, Judd. Besides, you told me it would be unlikely for Captain Decatur to stop it since he has participated in at least one duel in the past." I hesitated before proceeding. "Will you really kill him, Judd?"

"Oliver, you have seen me shoot; you have seen Wheatley shoot. What would you imagine to be the outcome of us facing each other at a distance of forty yards, hmmm?"

"Yes, but will you really kill him, or just wing him?" I persisted.

"That is something I will decide when I face him; but know that whatever I decide, it would be a simple matter for me to kill him." Judd's voice was soft and threatening. I saw that his eyes had grown hard and unforgiving, worse by half than when he lectured me on honor.

I withdrew into myself and directed my thoughts to other matters: Edward suffering in captivity, returning to the blockade, fighting the pirates, anything but having one of my messmates kill another, even one as objectionable as Thomas Wheatley. The other two, Judd and James, finished the meal in a silence broken only by polite small talk and instructions to our new steward, Augustus Goodbody. The meal finished, I stood to leave, planning to step ashore and visit a coffee house (called a *caffe* by the Italians here), where I had become known, and give myself time to ponder this nasty business and my own role in it.

"Oliver, a glass with you, if you please." Judd's voice held no rancor, no undertone of aggression. It was, in fact, friendly and welcoming.

"I had planned to step ashore, Judd. Would you join me rather than remain aboard?" I hesitated, then turned back to face him and tried to make my own tone match his.

"I suppose that would answer as well, but we must talk about this business hanging over us." Our senior midshipman picked up his hat from his cot where it had lain and, as I headed to the deck, followed me out of the cockpit.

Scarcely had we found a table in the empty coffee house and ordered, Judd, the special strong coffee he favored and me, a cup of delicious chocolate, than he faced me, a serious expression furrowing his brow.

"This dueling business is serious stuff, Oliver. I wish you would take it—and your own role in it—as such. It very likely will turn out to be a matter of life and death."

"You can not think, Judd, that I have done otherwise. I have done exactly as you requested of me in finding a suitable location for your field of honor. What more would you have me do? While I surely am not in favor of my messmates killing one another, I certainly realize the most serious nature of the affair." I studied my older colleague over the edge of my cup, trying to keep the distaste for his business out of my tone.

"I ask nothing else, save that you show me the fields you have seen and appear at the appointed hour to witness the event. As a matter of interest, has Thomas, to your knowledge, selected a second? We should know who it will be as he will need a witness as well." Judd stopped. Suddenly he smiled as a thought hit him. "And to take his place should he decide that dying by my hand is not in his best interest."

"Oh, Judd! How can you make jokes about this? You accuse me of not taking it seriously, yet you jest about something as serious as killing a shipmate, a messmate."

"Listen to me, Oliver." Devon leaned forward over the table and, after taking a taste of his thick, aromatic coffee, focused his eyes upon mine. "That boy—yes, 'boy,' and I know he's older than you—is a coward and, like many cowards, he is also a bully. I intend to teach him a lesson, a lesson whose time is well past due!"

"By killing him? What good will that do? Surely he will not have learned anything if he is lying dead on the ground." I could not believe he was serious.

"I am quite sure, Oliver, that Mister Wheatley is nothing but bluff and bluster. I suspect that when we actually establish a time and place for a duel, he will start to think of ways to avoid it. He wants nothing to do with facing me across loaded pistols. Recall, my friend, that he, like everyone else on *Intrepid* witnessed my little shooting demonstrations, which, you might as well know, I put on especially for his benefit." I nodded, having suspected as much. Judd continued. "I heard from several of our sailors that Wheatley was quite impressed and expressed as much to several. It could not have affected him in any other way when you consider that he is barely capable of hitting the water with a pistol fired from the deck. I have come to realize that he will go on haranguing us all about 'getting our business done,' but I assure you, Oliver, it is the farthest thing from his mind."

While not shocked at this revelation, I was mildly surprised; I had known for many months, since the storm in the Atlantic, in fact, that Thomas Wheatley was a coward. But *he* called out Judd, not the other way 'round. Why would he do that if he did not intend to see it through? He certainly could not have thought that Judd would back down from a challenge. Thomas, as the challenger, would have no choice but to let the events run their course. I could not imagine how he would manage to back out of it now. I said as much to Judd.

"I have not a clue, Oliver. But you mark my words. This duel will not take place. And should it, it will be only because Thomas is unable to find a fitting excuse or I decide teaching him a lesson is more important than . . ."

"How can you teach him a lesson by killing him?" I interrupted.

"I can not believe that you have not yet figured it out, Oliver. I do not intend to kill him, merely wing him to let him know he should think carefully before opening his mouth." Judd looked away, in dismay, perhaps, and lifted his cup to his mouth.

We finished our cups in quiet reflection, me thinking of how stupid I must appear to Judd, and him . . . well, maybe not thinking of how stupid I am in not figuring out his scheme. Our walk back to the schooner was also quiet, with Judd making mundane observations about various places we passed and me saying little.

As we entered the cockpit, James offered a game of dice or whist to either of us; Judd accepted as though he had not a care in the world, and I retired to my cot, where I spent a restless night fighting the images that marched in unrelenting reality through my reeling brain. Their chatter and expletives over their cards faded into the distance as I saw Thomas kill Judd with a lucky shot, then the reverse and, finally, Edward, still dressed in prison rags, appeared to take Judd's place in the field saying, "I can not let my little brother be involved in such unpleasant business. I will be your second, Mister Devon, in Oliver's stead."

I must have slept as, when I was rousted for our breakfast, I had to swim up from the depths of unconsciousness to the reality of a new day.

Our breakfast was interrupted by a great commotion on deck. As one, we threw down our utensils and charged at the ladder, fighting to be first to mount the steps. It seemed not to matter that Thomas prevailed, and we tumbled out of the hatch like puppies out of a basket, winning the curious and amused stares of our shipmates. The schooner *Nautilus* was approaching our pier and, from all appearances, preparing to tie up immediately astern of *Enterprise*. She was quite obviously damaged.

"Damn! Looks like she got herself into a scrap with someone. We missed another action, damn all!"

"Look at her rig; likely all shot to hell, it is!"

"Aye, and look at her forefoot, there. Took a shot or two there, I'll warrant."

The comments continued from our sailors as the schooner dropped her sails and ghosted alongside the dock smoothly, her lines handled by willing stevedores on the pier.

Within minutes, we knew in broad terms what had happened and, before the end of the morning, had all the details. Judd related it to us when he returned from a visit with Captain Decatur, who had gone to pay his respects and visit his brother, James.

"We didn't miss a thing, lads. *Nautilus* got herself beat up in a storm and then had the misfortune to run afoul of the *Syren* brig in the dark. Ran right aboard her, she did. That's what tore up the bow. From what Lieutenant Decatur, the captain's brother, told me, her rig got damaged during the blow. Lost her fore topmast and sprung her main top. As you saw, her rig's all ahoo, and Decatur thought they'd be dockside for a fortnight at the least.

"But *Syren* got herself a prize right after the collision. Took a *polacca* trying to scamper away toward the coast. The lads on *Nautilus* were right unhappy it wasn't them, but they were in no shape to get into a scrap with anyone. They will, of course, get shares of the prize money as they were right there when *Syren* took it."

"Where'd *Syren* take the prize, Judd? How come they didn't bring it in here along with *Nautilus*?" James voiced what had occurred to all of us.

"Don't know, James. I'd reckon they took it into Syracuse. Probably didn't see any reason to sail all the way here when they were only a day out of Syracuse. That'd be my guess." Judd stood, clearly ready to go on with his morning's duties, which included checking our powder and shot with Gunner Tarbox, a weekly occurrence in port. We all rose, following his lead, and left the cockpit. I headed forward to see to some work Bradford was doing on my guns.

Shortly before the dinner hour, when the crew had been called to spirits up and their meal, Judd found me still overseeing the work on the cannons.

"Let us go ashore, Oliver, and take care of that business. I have spoken to Lieutenant Lawrence and he has no objection."

No objection to our going ashore, or to Judd and Thomas trying to kill each other? I wondered. But I nodded, keeping my thoughts to myself, and obediently followed my superior to the gangway rigged in the waist and thence to the pier.

"Here is the first place I found, Judd." I spoke for the first time when we arrived, after a short walk, at a flat open place near the pier but unencumbered with the trappings of civilization, being as it was outside the limits of Messina.

"Aye, it might answer. But let us have a look at what else you have found. I collect you have other places in mind?" Judd said, after casting an appraising eye over the terrain and judging distances in his mind.

"Oh, yes! There are two other spots I saw; one is just a short walk up that hill." I pointed toward a nearby mound, hardly a hill, but in this land of mountains and cliffs rising out of the sea, there was scant land level enough to be suitable for our needs. And Judd had suggested a 'hilltop' when he instructed me on finding a field of honor.

"This is better. Yes, I think this will serve our purpose nicely. Enough trees to shelter us from those who might interfere and room enough to make our distance. Well done, Oliver!" Judd clapped me on the back as he turned, suddenly filled with enthusiasm, to march down the "hill" toward the town. I hardly shared his manner as I hurried to match his stride. He chattered with unmitigated good humor all the way back to the pier and smiled broadly as we stepped into the cockpit, where our meal was already on the table. I noticed that Thomas had taken his usual seat, not the one at the head of the table.

"Well, Thomas, Oliver has found a fine place for your undoing. It will answer well for our field of honor. What say you to tomorrow at the noon hour? Will that provide you enough time to find peace with your Maker?" Judd's wolfish smile at Thomas and his discrete wink at me left me somewhat relieved and hopeful that he indeed would only 'wing' his adversary.

"I would submit, Devon, that 'finding peace with one's Maker,' as you put it, would serve us both well. You seem not to admit that I might just as easily kill you as you, me. But, to answer your question, yes. Most certainly tomorrow at noon will do nicely. Then I can, for once, eat my dinner in peace." Thomas spoke quietly, his bravado diminished with the actual time and place established. The balance of our meal was eaten with a minimum of conversation carried out in subdues tones. James, his brow furrowed and the corners of his mouth turned downward, was particularly silent. I determined to tell him of Judd's plan when the opportunity presented itself.

I have little recollection of the balance of the day, though I am sure I must have performed my duties, even if in a perfunctory way. Sharing Judd's intent with James did, as I expected, ease his fears of one of us killing another, though he did mention the possibility of Thomas killing Judd. A concern, I agreed, though unlikely to become reality; I related Judd's thoughts on that to him.

The evening proved little more remarkable, though Lieutenants Hobbs and Morris quite suddenly invited the cockpit to join them 'in a glass' ashore. We found a table in a noisy but small *taverna* in close proximity to the docks.

"You lads seem some quiet tonight. Has not this lengthy stay in port restored your vitality?" Morris spoke to none of us in particular; I noticed that Lieutenant Hobbs nodded in agreement.

After a moment where, certainly I, and I am sure the others, struggled to supply a suitable response, Judd smiled at the officer and offered, "I reckon we're all a trifle weary of being confined, Mister Morris. What would likely put us into better humors would be a return to our duties off Tripoli, fighting those piratical bastards who hold our colleagues prisoner."

That was well done, Judd. I could not have managed that—even with my own brother as one of 'our colleagues'! I watched the two officers to see if Judd's response had found the mark.

"You young gentlemen have, no doubt, noticed that the repairs our vessel needed so desperately are about done. And *Nautilus*, I am sure, will occupy the time and talents of our workers. Captain Decatur has told us we will likely be underway for Syracuse to join up with the commodore and the others before the week is out. You will, I reckon, be getting your wish to 'return to our duties off Tripoli' sooner than ever you might actually want!" Hobbs spoke with a smile, whether at the prospect of going back to sea or at calling Judd on his comment, I had no idea. In the silence that followed his remark, the clatter of the public house, glasses tinkling, exuberant voices chattering in unintelligible dialects, and the boisterous singing of a small group in the corner, suddenly seemed overwhelming.

"So, should you have any business to take care of ashore, it would be prudent to get done with it sooner than later." Hobbs threw out this last and raised his eyebrow as he looked from one to another of us.

Oh, my God! He knows. Somehow the gunroom has discovered what is afoot between Judd and Thomas. I was startled at Hobbs' insight, though how he or any other not of the cockpit could have heard of our plan quite eluded me. *No, he doesn't know; he's just making conversation.* Perhaps more of a wish than a reality. I noticed, even through the gloom of the tavern, that my messmates had, to a man, raised their own eyebrows and sat with slack jaws as they considered the lieutenant's casual remark.

"Oh, sir! What business could we possibly have left . . . *ooooof!* Who kicked me?" James outburst was cut off by someone's well placed foot under the table.

"What James was going to say, I am sure, Mister Hobbs, was that we've been in for long enough to take care of any business we might have had ashore. Isn't that what you were about to say, James?" The mystery of who might have placed the kick was solved; Thomas' benign smile did little to erase the frown from James' countenance as he leaned forward over the table and reached below it to rub his bruised shin.

"Of course, it was, Thomas. You might have let me finish saying it my own self. I might also have added that anything left to do ashore could be taken care of on the morrow, and that we are all quite ready to get on with our commission." He directed his comment to Thomas, who nodded innocently, ignoring the petulant tone.

"Well, I am pleased to hear that, lads. We'll be back to sea before you know it. And to everyone's relief, I am sure." Morris smiled as he spoke and raised his glass. "Let us drink to our continued good health and each other, shipmates all." He swallowed deeply and, over the top of his glass, watched as Thomas, Judd, James and I followed suit. I wondered, as we drank to each other, which of us would be in less than 'continued good health' by this time tomorrow.

CHAPTER EIGHTEEN

B reakfast was again a silent affair, and we went about our morning duties, which, for James and me, included studies of our profession, with little heart. As six bells sounded, marking the hour as eleven, I made my way to the cockpit where I found Judd explaining to James and Thomas just how to find our 'field of honor.' I saw his case open on the table and a pair of pistols, the same ones he had used for his practice on Intrepid, laid out on a cloth before him. A small bag of shot lay next to them, and his powder horn had already been filled. I realized that both Thomas and Judd wore their dress uniforms, complete with dirks. It also appeared that they had brushed their jackets and blackened their shoes.

"So you are both clear on where you are to go?" Judd concluded his explanation and waited as his messmates nodded soberly. "James, I would like you to find Mister Wakefield and bring him there; he is sure to be needed." After a pause which included a telling look at Thomas, he added, "For one of us. And be sure to have him bring his medical box."

"What am I to tell him, Judd? Surely he will ask me why he should run off to follow the junior midshipman to a secret location. He will think he's on a fool's errand."

"Tell him only that one of your messmates has got himself hurt and needs his services. Then bring him with all haste to the hill I just described to you."

James nodded, clearly not convinced that the ruse would work, and rose to leave.

"Not now, James. Wait until we have gone, say until a quarter before noon. Then find Wakefield and follow on."

James sat down. His hands fidgeted, and he picked up the shot bag, weighing it, first in one hand and then the other. Judd glared at him. He put the bag down and began tapping on the table, shifting in his seat, and making little noises with his mouth. Thomas and Judd, by contrast, were, outwardly at least, as calm and unruffled as if they were to attend a party; certainly not fight a duel. I found myself to be closer to James' demeanor than theirs and poked my head into my sleeping cupboard seeking some article of great significance. Suddenly one of my responsibilities occurred to me.

"Thomas, Judd, listen here. As Judd's second, it is my duty to make a final effort to talk you out of this foolishness. You need not go through with such a drastic step over a silly remark. In fact, I can not even remember what it was that Judd said to provoke you, Thomas. But whatever it was, I am sure he did not mean it. Judd, why not apologize to Thomas and let us get on with our lives? Besides, think of how well we have all gotten along since this unpleasantness began. It seems as if the prospect of one of you killing the other has made us all better messmates." This last was more hope than fact, but I thought it sounded quite believable, and hoped they would too.

"I will accept an apology, Judd, should you be willing to offer one. For once, Oliver seems to be making some sense. Besides, I have no desire to kill you; if I did, I could just as easily have left you in the *Philadelphia* frigate to be blown to hell, instead of telling Oliver of your absence." Thomas sounded sincere, even to me.

Judd would have none of it; he looked at Thomas, his mouth a thin line, his eyes hard as iron. Then, quite without warning, he shifted his glance to me and smiled. "Did I not predict this, Oliver? He was full of bravado right up until the last moment, now he would like an excuse to be shed of it. Well, I think nothing will be gained by an apology; we will go through with this and you, my friend, will learn that a gentleman can not challenge another without facing the consequences. I will see you at the place I described to you. Come, Oliver; you will carry the pistols. I trust you have your watch?" Judd stood and handed me the box that, until he just mentioned it, I had failed to notice once again held its deadly contents. I patted my waistcoat pocket, feeling the bulge and weight of my silver watch and received a nod from my superior.

"As you wish, Judd," Thomas said. "I will be along momentarily. I am sorry you could not bring yourself to apologize to me. I hope that failure will not cost you too dearly." Thomas smiled, and we left him standing in the cockpit with a very somber James, who suddenly sat very still.

As Judd and I arrived at the hill he had chosen, he looked around and then, putting his hand on my shoulder, said, "Remember I told you I would not kill him. I intend to shoot him in his right arm. Hopefully, his aim will be less than true, and, at worst, I will receive only a scratch. However, should he get off a lucky shot, please see that people know that I died on a field of honor, and with honor. We will begin here, and you will count out the paces, then say 'turn and fire.' Wakefield will be here to attend to whichever of us is the less fortunate."

Suddenly I thought Judd seemed less confident than he had and wondered, silently, if he was having second thoughts about this business. I would have been pleased to call the whole thing off and once again offered the possibility to my principal.

"There is still time, Judd. When Thomas gets here, you have only to apologize and it will be over. I am quite certain he will accept your apology. And I would wager he will have learned his lesson."

"No. He will only learn his lesson, and remember it, if he carries a scar, a reminder, of his arrogance and stupidity. I am doing all of us, and his future shipmates, a favor by facing him. Fortunately, I do not feel imperiled by it." His face was a mask of confident determination and then he turned away, marching to the center of the field.

I withdrew to the sidelines and consulted my watch. Five minutes until noon; perhaps Thomas would not show up. James had also not appeared with the doctor. After the passage of what I was sure was several minutes, I looked at the watch again; still five minutes 'til noon. Had it stopped? I held it to my ear and heard the steady rhythm of its movement. I looked around the hilltop; no sign of anyone save Judd, still standing with this arms folded across his chest in the center.

Suddenly, I heard footsteps crunching through the undergrowth as they approached from below. Then Thomas' head broke the edge of the hill, followed by the rest of him. He walked straight to Judd and stood facing him.

"Mister Baldwin, the hour, if you please?" Judd raised his voice to a command level.

Again I consulted my watch. "Three minutes 'til noon, Mister Devon." I thought the formal seemed more appropriate, especially since he had used it first.

"Very well. Please inform us at the stroke of noon."

I watched the hands of the timepiece move imperceptibly around the dial. I shifted my glance from the face of my watch, the same one I had lost in Boston so long ago, to the two of them standing in the center of the field. I studied their faces and saw no sign of softening. *Surely Judd would apologize, and he and Thomas would shake hands, and we would all leave the hill, joined by James and Mister Wakefield as we made our way to a splendid restaurant for a celebratory dinner.* I glanced back to my watch. Suddenly, it was noon. How had the time gone so quickly? And still no sign of James or Mister Wakefield.

"Mister Devon, Mister Wheatley, it is noon, but Mister Stevens has yet to bring the doctor. Perhaps we might wait until they arrive." It seemed quite reasonable to me.

"We will begin. You may bring the weapons here, Mister Baldwin. Give Mister Wheatley first choice, if you please."

I walked slowly the ten or twenty steps to where they stood, still facing each other. Presenting the box, I opened the lid and showed its contents to Thomas. He shifted his gaze from Judd's eyes to the box. "This one will answer nicely, I am sure." He looked carefully at the pistol, and ensured that it was loaded and primed. His demeanor was quite different from that first time I saw him pick up a pistol on *Argus*.

Judd took the other, scarcely looking at it, he had loaded them himself, and turned about, his back to his adversary.

"If you are ready, Mister Wheatley, we will begin." Judd's voice held no rancor; in fact, it sounded almost friendly. And calm, I thought, considering what he was about to undertake.

"Aye, I am ready to gain satisfaction, Mister Devon."

"Mister Baldwin, you will count out twenty paces, if you please. Then, at your command, we will turn and fire."

"Judd, Thomas, please, will you not reconsider this business? Must this go all the way to one of you dying?" I made one final desperate plea.

"Begin your count, Mister Baldwin." Judd's voice was a trifle harder.

"Very well, then." I shook my head, resigned to seeing one of them hurt, or killed. "ONE." I probably shouted the first several paces. I thought I must be as nervous, scared, as they. *Where are James and the doctor?* FOUR. I was still shouting. I realized I had not moved from where I stood at the outset, now very nearly between the two of them. I hastened to the side of the field. *What would I do if Wakefield didn't show up?* SIX. I watched as my two messmates drew farther apart. *Maybe they will both miss. Forty paces is a great distance.*

My mind continued to reel and my glance shifted from Thomas to Judd to the edge of the hill where I hoped James and the doctor would appear. I continued to count.

FOURTEEN. *What if James had been unable to find Wakefield? Maybe he wasn't aboard and James is looking for him.* SIXTEEN. The two were far enough from each other and from me that I now had to shout to ensure they would hear me. SEVENTEEN. *Where was that fool? Why couldn't he carry out the simplest of orders?* EIGHTEEN. *Oh, God. Please come to your senses and stop this foolishness.* NINE-TEEN. *One more step and somebody is going to get hurt or killed.* Suddenly I found myself hoping that neither would hit their marks and that both would remain unscathed. TWENTY.

"You may turn and fire!" My throat was dry, and I am afraid the words were more of a croak than a 'command' as I had been instructed.

The two turned toward each other and lifted their pistols. Judd fired first, but only by scant margin. As his piece discharged, I saw, behind him and to the side, James' head appear over the edge of the hill. *Finally! Thank God. Where's Wakefield?* And then Thomas cried out and fired. His arm had been flung to the side by the impact of Judd's ball, and his pistol appeared not even aimed in Judd's direction. Judd remained unscathed, standing where he was with the start of a smile forming on his lips.

"Thank God! He missed." I said aloud. Then I heard a cry from beyond Judd. James' form had not broken the hilltop. *Where did he go?*

I saw Mister Wakefield kneeling at the edge of the hill. *Oh, no! Thomas' bad aim has hit the doctor!* But it was not he who was hit. The doctor was in fact bending over the inert form of my messmate, my friend, James.

"You damn fools! You've gone and shot this poor boy who had nothing to do with your foolishness!" Wakefield shouted at us.

Judd got there first, the look of horror on his face rivaled only by my own. My hand flew to my mouth, and I must have stopped breathing. It took a moment for the tableau to impact in its fullest and, when it did, I felt my stomach turn over and my knees grow suddenly weak. I knelt, as much to keep from collapsing as to be closer to my friend. When Thomas came to the scene, he, too, dropped to his knees, his own wound, though bleeding copiously down his arm, quite forgotten.

"Oh, my God! What have I done? James, James. Damn you! What were you doing there? Why did you show up then? Mister Wakefield, he's going to be all right, is he not?" I had never heard such concern from Thomas. The look he gave to Wakefield was truly pitiful. The doctor had opened James' waistcoat and shirt, both covered in gore, and was trying to staunch the bleeding in his chest. The surgeon's medical box stood open at his side, its contents spilling out of the drawers and shelves within, a result of his hasty search for the needed supplies. When he removed his hand, Mister Wakefield's arm midway to his elbow was red with blood. He looked first at Thomas, then at each of us in turn; I can not recall having ever, before or since, seen such a look of utter contempt and loathing.

James opened his eyes; they fluttered at first, then fixed on the nearest face, Thomas.' "Why did you shoot me? I had nothing to do with this." His voice was faint and it obviously took some effort to speak. "I think you have killed me, Thomas. I would have hoped to see real fighting against . . . piratical bastards." He smiled thinly, as though pleased he had at last been able to use the words he had been hearing for so long. "Now I will not."

Thomas touched James' forehead in the most gentle way and smoothed his hair. The young mid's hat had fallen off when he was shot, and his hair ruffled in the easy breeze, much as the grass did. "James, you will be fine. You'll surely see a fight with those pirate bastards. You damn well will! And I'll be at your side. I am sorry for all the bad things I said and made you do, James. You just let Mister Wakefield fix you up; you'll be right as ever afore you know it." Thomas looked searchingly at Wakefield. We all caught the barely perceptible shake of the doctor's head.

"NO, DAMN YOU! NO!" Thomas grabbed Wakefield' arm. The midshipman's eyes were overflowing. "You can't let him die, damn it. I didn't mean to shoot him! He just appeared over the damn hill at the very moment when I fired. Fix him! Stop the bleeding! You're a surgeon. Do it!" Thomas couldn't will it so and the doctor could do no more. James' life ebbed quickly and, with Thomas, tears streaming down his face, still patting the youngster's head, my friend, James Stevens, went limp, his head lolling to one side.

"He is quite beyond my help now, Thomas. But you are not. Let me have a look at that arm. You have lost some considerable blood yourself." Mister Wakefield took up Thomas' arm gently and began to examine the blood-stained shirt for the entry point.

"NO! You fix my friend. I am fine. Help James!" He jerked his arm back and, while I know it must have hurt mightily to do it, he made no sound or flinch.

"Thomas, hear me well, son. There is nothing that I, or anyone else, can do for James; he is dead. Unless you have some desire to follow him, you must let me stop the bleeding in your arm. Here, now, let me see." Again, Wakefield picked up Thomas' arm and, with a surgical knife, cut away the sleeve of his blood-soaked shirt. Thomas was unresisting and just sat next to the inert form of our shipmate, tears streaming down his cheeks, while the surgeon probed his arm for the bullet. In spite of what must have been excruciating pain, Wheatley never moved or changed his expression; his eyes seemed to be focused on a point a thousand yards away.

I stole a look at Judd. The horror I had seen on his face earlier had been replaced by a look of abject sorrow. I am sure he was thinking, as was I, that had he only agreed to the apology, none of this would have happened, and James would still be with us. The whole incident was playing in my head, as clear as if I had been watching it on a stage before me. Me counting, Thomas and Judd moving away from one another, then turning, raising their pistols, and James appearing over the hilltop. Judd's gun firing, silent this time, with only the flash of the primer and the fire and smoke from the muzzle offering testimony to the deadly missile hurtling out on its errand of destruction. It seemed to take minutes for the ball to find its mark, and I could quite clearly see the splash of blood fly up from Thomas' arm, thrown to the side by the impact of Judd's ball. Wheatley's pistol discharged in the same silent, exquisitely slow way: primer flash, smoke, then fire and smoke from the barrel. I saw Mister Wakefield's mouth moving as he shouted out what had happened, but heard no sound. And then Judd running, but slowly, as though through waist deep water. My own progress was no faster, and it took us forever to reach the side of our fallen friend. Thomas arrived, drifting to his knees in silence, not the screaming sudden arrival of the actual event. Mouths moving, but no words coming forth.

". . . back to *Enterprise* now. Come, there is nothing more we can do here." Wakefield's voice penetrated my conscious. I looked at him, uncomprehending.

"We can't just leave him." I must have spoken aloud as the surgeon put his hand on my arm, raising me to my feet, and he spoke kindly, gently.

"Judd will stay with him until I can send someone from town up to take care of his body. We will arrange to bury him here."

I followed Wakefield and a silent Thomas down the hill and back to the dock. It was a melancholy procession we made, all of us deep within ourselves. I took no heed of the stares Thomas' blood-soaked shirt and bound arm drew. Indeed, I barely noticed that the doctor had stopped and spoken to someone along the way. And then we were aboard the schooner. Still my vision was obscured; it was as if I were looking through a bit of gauze, and if I blinked my eyes enough, it might leave, but only for a moment. Rubbing them helped not a whit, and it was in this daze that I made my way to the cockpit, followed by Thomas.

He was still in a state of anxiety, and his tears continued to flow down his face, though he made no sound. His arm was tied in a jury-rigged sling to his chest. The bandage Mister Wakefield had wrapped around the wound was showing varying shades of crimson. It registered in my mind that he must still be bleeding. We both sat at the table, staring into nothingness. We were still in that state when Captain Decatur, followed by the surgeon, appeared in the doorway. Neither of us stood, but nobody seemed to notice, or at least care.

"Reliance, I think you might give them both a draught of something. Is Devon is the same condition?" Decatur's voice was quiet, barely penetrating my senses.

"I suspect he is, Captain. He should be appearing directly, as I have already instructed the local undertaker to collect the boy's body." Wakefield poked around in his box and produced a small bottle of powder. Without seeing him, I looked on as he stirred a measure of it into two mugs of water and handed one to each of us. "Drink this down, the both of you. It'll make you feel some better, I reckon."

Thomas and I did as we were bidden. I have little recollection of anything further that happened that afternoon. When I awoke, I was in my cot and Judd was standing at my doorway.

"Cap'n would have you in his Cabin, Oliver. Wants a word with you and Thomas. Best not to keep him waiting." His voice was hollow sounding and distant, not at all like it should have with him standing no more than a foot away from me.

I struggled up from the depths of my sleep, trying to focus my eyes, eyes which were all crusty and hurt, even though I had only just opened them.

"Wha . . . who . . . are you . . ." I finally managed to put thoughts into words. "Oh, Judd! I had the most terrible dream. You and Thomas had your duel, and I watched it happen! James got hurt from Thomas' bad aim. Judd, don't do it; apologize to Thomas and be done with it. It was a silly argument; don't let it come to killing each other! What does it matter?"

Judd became still, watching me with worried eyes. His voice, when he spoke was very quiet and gentle. "Oliver, you did not dream that. We did duel, Thomas got hurt, and James . . ." Judd looked at me and waited until I looked straight at him. "James is dead, Oliver."

I let out a gasp. My hand flew to my mouth as the truth, the horrible truth hit me like a shot from a twelve-pounder. I hadn't dreamed it at all. James really was dead and Thomas was wounded. It all flooded back to me, and I felt hot tears well up in my eyes.

"All right, Oliver. Try to get control over yourself. Get up and put on your jacket and shoes and go and see Decatur. I'd reckon that Thomas is already there." Judd handed me a small basin of water and a cloth.

As I left the cockpit, my eyes were uncontrollably drawn to James' cupboard. I saw his cot with several books left open where he had stopped reading them. I recalled him telling me how proud and happy he was to be finally able to read, and grateful to me for teaching him. God! It seemed so long ago, yet it was only a few weeks back when Judd and I had brought in the prize ketch. His spare shirt, wrinkled and stained, was lying across the foot of the cot, likely just where it landed when he had hastily changed to his best before bringing Wakefield to the hilltop. His sea boots, blackened but still showing the white stain of saltwater, stood neatly in the far corner. His chest remained by the table, and I realized, with a great sadness, that he would never be sitting on it at our mess table again, laughing and joking, or being the butt of Thomas' jibes. He was gone. I didn't cry this time. I think my tears had been used up, but I felt as though a great weight hung from my shoulders and another was on my chest, making it difficult to breathe.

The marine guard at the captain's door saw me coming and had already announced me when I stopped in the passageway.

"You may go in, sir. The captain's waitin'." He stood to rigid attention, the musket at his side gleaming dully in the yellow lantern glow. Seemingly without moving, he opened the door in front of me. I saw Thomas' back, one sleeve hanging empty at his side, standing before the captain. As I stepped in, I saw also that Reliance Wakefield sat to one side, a serious look on his face.

"Ah, our witness. Mister Baldwin, step in and stand there, next to the wounded Mister Wheatley. Are you sufficiently shed of your bout of emotional distress? I would like very much to hear the details, all the details, if you please, of the events of the afternoon and those which led up to them. Mister Wheatley has offered his tale, and I would now like to hear yours." Captain Decatur was not smiling; his face held a quite neutral expression, but his voice gave away his feeling. It was cold and sounded like it could cut, so sharp it was.

"Oh, sir. Yes, sir. I am quite able to speak." I struggled to get the tremor out of my voice. I had no idea what was to happen to me, or to Thomas and Judd, but I was quite sure it would not, could not, be good. "There was some problem between Thomas . . . I mean, Mister Wheatley and Mister Devon. It started . . . umm . . . well, I don't actually recall *when* it started, exactly, sir. But they didn't seem to get along too well. One day, maybe a month and more ago?" I shot a glance at Thomas, hoping for a nod, a sign, anything, and got nothing; he didn't even turn his head toward me. His face was ashen, and there was none of the defiance I had come to expect. "Yes, sir. I think it must have been something over a month ago when Judd . . . I mean, Mister Devon said something that Mister Wheatley took exception to and challenged him to a duel. Mister Wheatley challenged Mister Devon, I mean. I was asked to be Mister Devon's second and tried to talk them out of it, but they insisted I find a place for them to hold a duel. It wasn't 'til we got in here, sir, to Messina, that I actually did it. I showed it to Mister Devon yesterday and, well, he told me it would answer fine. Then he told Mister Wheatley and James about it and set the time." I felt the tears starting at my mention of James' name, and again pictured him appearing over the edge of the hill. My breathing sounded ragged as I struggled to maintain my "course to manhood," though I was beginning to have doubts about that as well. I struggled also to catch a breath.

Decatur waited patiently while I collected myself to continue the tale.

Finally, I caught my breath and picked up the story where I left off.

"They were supposed to be there by eight bells, sir, this noon." I hoped that my reference to 'bells' might soften his expression. It had no effect, whatever. "James, Mister Stevens, was supposed to find Mister Wakefield and bring him without telling him what was afoot. Mister Devon refused to wait for the doctor to show up and told me to start counting right at noon. After I had given each of them a pistol, of course. Which I did. To twenty. Then they turned, and Judd fired first, hitting Thomas in the arm. I reckon . . . uhhh . . . well, it looked like the ball from Mister Devon's gun made Mister Wheatley's arm fly out just as he fired. And, well, Mister Wakefield and Mister Stevens were just coming over the top of the hill. I think James was first. And he appeared just in the right place to . . ." I stopped. Again, my vision blurred and I could feel wetness on my cheeks. I choked, struggling for a breath. This was harder than I had expected.

"Yes, I think I know the rest. Very well, Mister Baldwin. Get control of yourself, now, and stop your blubbering. It will accomplish nothing. Do you have anything to add to what you have told me?" Decatur, his look unchanged, his voice still cold, studied me while I got control of myself.

"No, sir. I think I told you the whole of it."

"Very well, then. You may go. Mister Wheatley as well. I will determine what I shall do, and recommend to the commodore. We will bury your messmate on the morrow, prior to our departure for Syracuse."

I turned to leave at the same moment Thomas did, and we collided. For once, he said nothing. I think I mumbled an apology to him, the captain, and any within earshot, and then we were in the passageway and the marine was closing the door.

"What's going to happen to us, Thomas? And you? Do you think the captain will have us court-martialed? What if he does . . . what will we do? It was an accident. I mean your shooting James, not the duel. I know you didn't mean to hit him. Do you think Captain Decatur . . .?"

Thomas stopped my babbling with a harsh look, and the tone of his voice, when he spoke, showed me that the "old" Thomas was back. "Oliver, shut up. I have no idea what will happen. You might have put that part about an *accident* in your story to the captain. He might think I shot him on purpose." Thomas kept walking, not looking at me.

We found ourselves on the main deck of the schooner. Little knots of men stood around in the dark talking among themselves. The glow of their pipes and cheroots lit their faces. I saw some eyes shift and, with murmured words, they all went silent.

I followed Wheatley, having no better plan, and stood on the quarterdeck as he studied the harbor intently. I watched the reflections of the lights of vessels mingle with the dim lights of the stars above as they were disturbed by the course of a ship's cutter bringing officers in for a night of gaiety. The wet blades of the oars shone as they passed a vessel near at hand, picking up the lights from its deck. As the ripples from the passage of the boat died away, the little points of brightness again appeared in the water, winking and seeming to have life. Then as the water grew calm once again, the reflections became stationary, as still as the lights that created them.

I wondered what Thomas was thinking as he stood at the rail, his hand gripping then releasing the cap of it. I could make out his jaw clenching as the muscles in his cheeks worked.

"What are you going to do, Thomas?" I could stand it no longer.

"I have little idea, Oliver. I reckon it depends on what Decatur, or the commodore, decide to do to me. I doubt they, either one of them, have a problem with the duel, but James . . . well, that's going to be trouble." He shook his head and leaned forward, resting his elbows on the bulwark. His jaw gave me a clue to what he was thinking before he resumed. "Damn the little bastard, anyway. He couldn't get it right even to the end. And I had to be the one to kill him. Decatur didn't even inquire as to my own wound from Devon! I wonder if our captain would be all lathered up if it had been the great Devon what pulled that trigger. Decatur's had it in for me right from the start, right from that first time he had the midshipmen for dinner after we left Boston." He was musing, almost to himself. In fact, I wasn't even sure he recalled I was standing next to him.

"Oh, Thomas! Don't say such things! Of course Captain Decatur would want to know what happened had it been Judd who shot James. And he doesn't 'have it in' for you at all." I could barely believe that Thomas would so quickly seek another to blame.

"Well, at least with James gone there'll be more room in the cockpit for us, and more food, too!" I gasped aloud at his words, and he smiled in the dark, enjoying the effect his words were having on me.

Leaving him to decide what course he would follow, and to his outrageous ruminations, I went below to our quarters and found Judd sitting at the table staring into nothingness. He looked at me when I entered and raised his eyebrows.

I related our late conversation to him. His only reaction, that I could see, anyway, was to shake his head. His hands continued to be busy with something small.

"We are all diminished by the loss of our messmate, Oliver. While I realize that I had little to do with James' death . . . that it was little more than a tragic accident . . . I . . . we all must take some responsibility for it. Just as if . . . well, I know that had Thomas not challenged me, called me out, this would never have happened."

If you had apologized, even right before you two started pacing the twenty steps, it would not have happened. You were so convinced that Thomas had to be taught a lesson and that you must be the one to do it. My look must have given away my thoughts; Judd studied me for a moment.

"I guess you must think I am just as much to blame as if I had shot him myself, aren't you, Oliver?"

"No, Judd. But it would have been so much . . . easier . . . had you just apologized to Thomas instead of going through with that 'lesson' you had to teach him." My anger bubbled quite visibly to the surface. It only remained for Judd, now, to blame poor James, too.

CHAPTER NINETEEN

The following afternoon, *Enterprise* cleared the harbor of Messina and pointed her bowsprit into a short, wet chop, as we headed on a close reach due south to Syracuse. Little gaiety marked our departure; indeed, we were all quite sober and serious as we went about making sail to leave this place. We left James behind, finally at peace with no one to bear him ill, in a shady little cemetery in Messina.

The burial had been read by Captain Decatur and a local parson, a Romish priest, I believe, who, according to local law, was required to be in attendance. All hands, save a few left to mind the schooner, were present, each dressed in his best uniform. The officers and midshipmen stood to one side as the captain spoke of James, read from his bible, and offered a prayer for his soul. Then the local priest said all manner of things which I am sure were very nice, but to us, unintelligible, as he used not a single word of English. Each of the officers and then Thomas, Judd, and I threw a handful of dirt into the hole, beginning the process of covering our messmate. The two local gravediggers, who had stood a little away smoking cheroots during the ceremony, would finish. We left the burial ground and marched together in somber silence through the town and back to *Enterprise*. The whole affair seemed to take very little time.

A number of our sailors, tugging at a forelock, had come up to me to offer their condolences.

"Sorry about yer mate, sir."

"A right nice young lad, he was."

"Comin' right along, he were, sir. Mighta made a fine officer one day."

I am not sure whether any spoke to Thomas, but clearly, all hands knew most of the details of James' death. His role in the accident did little to enhance Thomas' standing with the crew, most of them having, at one time of another, felt the hostility that seemed to surround my colleague.

Thomas, for his part, went about his duties in silence. His jaw held its defiant cast, and his eyes were barely slits, an expression that encouraged none to engage him in conversation. Any words, orders only, that he uttered were spoken in a growl and received little in the way of acknowledgement.

None of us had received any further word from Captain Decatur as to what our future might hold. This uncertainty seemed to occupy all my thoughts not taken up by the performance of my duties.

I promised myself, no, I *forced* myself, not to despond. I would maintain a jaunty attitude, at least in the company of others. *After all, it was not I who* had shot my messmate. Indeed, was it not I who tried repeatedly to avoid the armed confrontation? But in the privacy of the cockpit or alone about the deck, the memory of James flooded back, and I discovered that my reaction to his death was quite another matter. Everything below reminded me of my friend, and, topside or aloft, I could see him clearly in my mind's eye as he went cheerfully about his duties.

I stood my watches with Lieutenant Hobbs as before; our conversation was limited to courses, sail trim, and other official subjects. I wanted desperately to return to the relationship with the officers I had previously enjoyed, but so far, it seemed that only the sailors were prepared to treat me, and the others, as anything but a pariah. As Judd and I sat down for dinner on the second day out of Messina—I had just been relieved from the watch by Thomas—I voiced my concern.

"Do you think Captain Decatur has told the officers to have naught to do with us, Judd? Seems like none of them will even talk to us."

"I have little idea, Oliver. But I quite agree with you. What I can't understand is why they would treat me, and you, that way. Thomas . . . well, I can understand that some might not want to keep company with him as he might be facin' a court martial, but we surely aren't. Doesn't seem to tally, in my book." His brow furrowed and his eyes got a distant look to them.

He really doesn't think he did anything out of the ordinary! As if fighting a duel with pistols at forty paces could be considered normal! I shook my head, quite perplexed at his attitude.

"Judd, do you think that facing a messmate at forty paces with pistols would not . . . might not . . . earn one a court martial?"

"Captain Decatur himself stood as second in a duel when he was last here, in '02 or '03, it was. Captain Bainbridge's brother—he's here in the squadron—fought some British fop. As I understand it, young Joseph Bainbridge, who was only a midshipman then, endured some insults in the theatre from this Englishman and then gave him a punch in the jaw. This, of course, earned him the right of facing the British civilian with pistols. He asked Decatur to second him and the captain set up the duel. I heard that their first shots proved nothing, and that neither would apologize. So they loaded their pistols again, and, after pacing off the requisite ten, I think, paces, Bainbridge killed the other with a shot through the heart. Decatur not only witnessed it, but he set it up, arranged for the place . . . everything you did for me, and more, Oliver. So I would think it unlikely that Captain Decatur would want to convene a court martial for *me*. Since Thomas killed an innocent, a bystander, if you will, a court martial might signify more in his case. And it would upset me not a whit were he to do so."

How can you sit there and cast all the blame on Thomas? I certainly have no love for him and, to be sure, it was him that shot James. But he wouldn't have been up on that hill dueling by himself! Had you apologized to him, the duel would never have taken place and James would still be with us. I reckon my thoughts must have been clear from the expression I wore.

"Oliver, when will you grow up and realize that in the world of *men, honorable men*, there are things that simply must be done. It is expected. And dueling is and, I suspect, will continue to be, honorable and not only accepted, but *expected* as well when the circumstances warrant it. And in the case of Thomas and myself, they surely did." Judd spoke quietly, but with a tone of frustration at, I assume, my inability to grasp the responsibilities of *men*, mixed with his growing impatience with me.

We finished our meal silently, each of us turned inwards. Immediately it was done, Judd stood, nodded to me, and left the cockpit. I was in my cot, thinking about how I was fast running out of friends because of my narrow views on killing one's messmate, when I realized he had left to take the watch. The night, the glowing sky over the volcano, still brilliant and colorful, held little interest for me.

The next morning, shortly after sunrise, I stood silently on the quarterdeck with Lieutenant Hobbs when the headlands of Syracuse were sighted, announced, and acknowledged. Hobbs did not even send me aloft to confirm it. By the time the watch would have been called to breakfast, we were shortening sail and making for the anchorage.

When I saw Preble's flagship dominating the harbor, my heart beat faster as the thought of a letter from Edward flashed through my head, and then an uneasiness came over me as I realized that the ultimate decision on our futures would soon be reached. *Syren* was also visible, and I could make out the little *Intrepid* secured to the brig's side. We made our number, fired a salute, and saw it acknowledged. Then flags whipped to the mizzen cro'jack yard on *Constitution*. I didn't need the signal book to read our number followed by "Captain repair aboard."

As soon as our anchor was set, Decatur had a boat lowered. "Mister Lawrence, see that the midshipmen remain aboard, if you please. And the officers are available should they be called as witnesses to a court martial." The captain's words as he stepped into the boat still rang in my ears, causing my stomach to churn with great enthusiasm.

I found myriad little chores to occupy myself while he was reporting to the commodore. I was sure that it would be some time before Decatur returned, since *Enterprise* had been away from the squadron for several months, and there would be a host of details to be gone over, as well as the matter of one midshipman killing another.

When I heard Anderson's pipe summoning attendants to the side for the captain's return, it seemed that only an hour had passed; in fact, he had been gone nearly all morning!

"Officers to the Cabin, Mister Lawrence, if you please." Decatur barely hesitated between the break in the waist and the hatch to his Cabin below.

"You wish the young gentlemen there also, sir?" Lawrence inquired of the back of the captain's head as he disappeared from view.

"We will deal with them after I have talked with the officers." And he was gone.

I hurried to the cockpit to share this intelligence with my mates, who still sat in stony silence at the table. As I repeated what I had heard, both looked at me with no more interest than had I mentioned it was raining.

"Why should you care about that, Oliver? Ain't likely nothing'll happen to you; you weren't holding a pistol." Thomas spat his words out of his mouth like they tasted bad.

"I think we're all in this together, Thomas. I wasn't holding a pistol and, to be sure, I didn't shoot anybody, but I was there as Judd's second, and that makes me a part of it." I stopped and looked at my adversary for a moment. Then I gave in to the temptation that lurked in my breast. "But I expect you'll likely come out the worst, since you did the killing." I was unable to suppress a smile as I said it.

"Aye, I done the killing. And you know, we all know, it was an accident. They don't court martial people for having accidents, you fool. There won't be nothin' what happens to me. You watch and see if I'm not right." His sneer and surly tone did nothing to hide the concern that showed plainly in his eyes. He clearly did not fully believe his own words.

So we sat, each wrapped in our own thoughts, and waited. Before dinner was piped down for the crew, a Marine knocked on the doorway to the cockpit, told us the captain requested our presence, and departed. As one, we rose, followed in the Marine's wake, and were summarily shown into the Cabin. The officers had already left.

Decatur spoke without preamble upon our entrance. "As you may know, I personally have no compunction about settling differences by dueling. It is an honorable tradition used for generations by honorable men. And I am imbued with the idea that it is an entirely appropriate activity for gentlemen. However, it would seem to go without saying that the participants only should be at risk, not the witnesses or bystanders. When others become involved, the event becomes less than honorable."

The three of us stood in a line in front of his desk at rigid attention, looking straight ahead. *Oh, God! Here it comes. He is going to court martial Thomas.*

"I have discussed your actions with the commodore and am in agreement with his decision; *Enterprise* will be returning to the blockade within the week and, Mister Wheatley, you will remain here. I will arrange for you to take lodgings with an acquaintance of Commodore Preble who, I am assured, will see to your needs and well-being." Decatur looked squarely at Thomas, who quickly exchanged the beginnings of a smile for a more sincere and serious face.

"I would be pleased to see to my own lodgings, sir. I would not want to trouble the commodore's friend. I have some money to pay for my keep, as well, sir."

"That will be quite unnecessary, Mister Wheatley. It is being arranged even as we speak. But I am sure your host will appreciate your willingness to defray his expenses on your behalf. And since you will be under confinement, there will be little else on which you might squander your funds." Seeing the look of surprise, then horror that crossed Wheatley's face, the captain continued, his voice still hard. "Remaining here while your messmates handle your duties, stand your watches, and essentially take your place will only answer if you are precluded from enjoying the pleasures that Syracuse has to offer. And there will be a letter of reprimand sent to the Secretary of the Navy for placement in your file." Decatur paused, watching Wheatley for a reaction. Save a stony, fixed expression and a grayish cast to his face, there was none.

"You other two," he continued, pointing a finger from each hand at Judd and me, "will, as I mentioned, take on *all* of Mister Wheatley's duties; you will stand his watches, handle his division, and slack not a whit in the execution of your own responsibilities while doing it. Having something to keep you busy will, perhaps, keep you out of trouble. I would suggest that, in the future, a different way of settling your differences might answer better than pistols. At least until you gain respect for the tradition." He stopped, returned his hands to his desk while he studied each of us in turn and then steepled his fingers, adding, "I hold each of you responsible for the death of your messmate, Mister Stevens. While Mister Wheatley actually pulled the trigger, you all were involved. It is indeed fortunate for you that, unlike the Army, the Navy has no laws against dueling, and neither the commodore nor I feel the need for any. However, there is no honor to be had in the killing of innocents. Mister Wheatley, you will collect your seachest and be ready to go ashore by six bells in the afternoon watch. You are dismissed." The captain dropped his eyes and began to shuffle some papers on his desk as we turned to march out. "One moment, if you please, Mister Baldwin. Stand fast; I have more for you."

Oh, no! Am I to join Thomas in the jail? I had almost nothing to do with James' death! In fact, I was the only one who tried to get them to call it off. What have I done? I am sure the color drained from my face; my knees certainly felt like they would no longer support me, and I put a hand on the back of a nearby chair to steady myself as I turned about to face the captain once again. The door closed behind my departing shipmates, leaving me alone with our commanding officer.

"I think you will find this to be of interest, Mister Baldwin. You might let me know if there should be any further secret inscriptions within." He extended to me an envelope on which I noticed at once my brother's familiar hand. I let out the breath I had been holding and was rewarded with a smile from him.

Oh, thank the Lord. A letter from Edward. Give it to me! I stood, rooted to the spot, momentarily uncomprehending. *Step up and take it, Oliver. He's not about to walk to you, after all.*

"Thank you, sir. Thank you very much. And I shall surely tell you if there is any secret writing in it. Thank you, sir." I stepped to his desk and took the proffered letter. "Will that be all, sir?"

"Yes, Oliver. Go and read your letter. I hope you find your brother, and my friend, still well." Decatur turned back to his papers, essentially dismissing me.

I turned, about to leave. He cleared his throat, stopping me in my tracks. "Sir?"

"Yes, Baldwin, one thing more, if you please. It may interest you to know that Mister Devon told me the details of your role in the unfortunate incident involving your messmates. It would seem that while you may be one of the youngest in the cockpit, you conducted yourself with a maturity, and honor, beyond your years. You may well turn out to be a fine officer one day."

"Oh, thank you, sir. That is very kind of you. I hope to 'turn out' as well as my brother." I brandished my letter, in case he had forgotten I had it.

Captain Decatur again smiled at me, nodded and returned his attention to the papers on his desk. I turned and was out the door before he could change his mind.

I knew the cockpit, where Thomas and Judd would be dining, would not be the place to read Edward's words, so I made my way topside and forward, to take my ease on the carriage of one of my long twelve-pounders. I was not very hungry either for food or their company right then. Carefully, I unfolded the precious letter, noticing as I did that my hands seemed to tremble a trifle.

> *My dear Brother*, he began, as he had the first one.
>
> Your brilliant stroke—or should I say *our* brilliant stroke—has had the desired effect; it has quite angered our captors and, I have heard, caused the survivors of your attack to wish they had died at your and Decatur's hands! According to our guards, the Bashaw was in a state, ready to remove the heads of any who appeared before him. When Bainbridge heard this, he smiled for the first time since our unfortunate grounding and subsequent capture by these barbarians.

I smiled myself at this revelation, but I felt my smile fade as quickly as it had arrived when I recalled the events of that fearsome night and my own, as Judd had put it, 'blooding.'

> Unfortunately, an additional result of your destruction of our late frigate was the removal of the officers, all of us, from our quarters in the palace formerly occupied by the American Consul to a prison in the fortress near to where our seamen are held. And, I fear, equally dreary to theirs. We have lost the right to communicate with our seamen and so have little idea of their condition at the present; it can be little worse than our own.
>
> Nothing you have experienced in your life, dear Brother, can let you imagine our apartments—if such a lofty name can be applied to a dungeon in the center of the fortress into which little light and

less air can penetrate. An opening high above our reach and covered in iron bars provides what little of each life-giving resource filters into the room. And while all of us, some twenty-five including the warrants, are confined in a single room barely large enough for ten, it is the other inhabitants which make it particularly distasteful. Apparently a collection of noxious reptiles had been ensconced here well before we took up residence, and they have not taken well to our intrusion. As a final insult, our rations have been reduced; but not our spirits, due largely to the bold action. We pray daily for further evidence of our fleet and, while hope for our release dwindles, the flame of hope burns brightly with anticipation of Preble again wiping the eye of the Bashaw. We have heard that the barbaric person has increased his demands for our ransom and tribute to his own self! Likely a further result of your brave stroke.

Prior to the destruction of our late ship, our treatment was humane, if not hospitable. We were even given fresh food, beef and vegetables, for our celebration of Christmas. I am given to understand it was through the efforts of Commodore Preble and more to Consul Nissen that this miraculous feat was achieved, and we are, all of us, indebted to the Dane for his efforts on our behalf. And to the commodore, of course, for his continued support. Capt. Bainbridge has received numerous communications from him that have included money for our comfort as well as several items of food and spirits which we hoard and consume on rare occasion. Some of these treats we managed to conceal from our captors and transfer with us to our current rude habitations. I have also received your letters by the same means, and you should know they are greatly appreciated. I am sorry indeed I can not be with you to share your tales and miseries. Your description of the attack on our late frigate was shared by all with suitable congratulatory comments regarding your own bravery and execution of your assigned duties. Again, I pine to be in your company offering you my own congratulations on your splendid performance!

We were only recently allowed a visit from a certain Midshipman Izard who, I am told, is from the commodore's Constitution and came ashore under a flag to speak on behalf of Comm. Preble to our capt. As a result of his visit, we will be allowed to receive supplies for the improvement of our conditions, but only through neutral vessels. Bainbridge mentioned the Bashaw will not allow boats of the Squadron to land, even under a flag of truce, unless it is to pay the ransom and tribute to that unscrupulous individual. We all hold to the hope that, as much as we would welcome our freedom, Comm. Preble will resist paying a single dollar to him. The only tribute that scoundrel should receive must be paid in iron from the mouths of the squadron's cannons!

After much discussion with Bainbridge and the others, we have concluded that the squadron must instigate an attack against the gunboats that seem to proliferate within the confines of the harbor here. Until they are destroyed, little can be done to breach the walls of this fortress, as the opinion seems to be that the afore-mentioned vessels will successfully drive off any but the most deter-mined effort to get close enough to be effectual. As a further detri-ment to that effort, it is apparent from our own misadventure that only vessels of the shallowest draft will be of use. Porter, our First, has opined that an attack from both the water—once you get through the gunboats—and at the same time, from the land side, would be most effective in bringing the forces of the Bashaw to heel. He believes that a force of two thousand would be sufficient and I am confident that Capt. Bainbridge has sent that information to the comm. through the offices of Midshipman Izard.

A particularly distressing discovery was made several weeks ago; it appears that these godless rascals have pressed our men into slavery and have them working on the construction of a fortress not far from the Bashaw's castle. I am given to understand by one of our guards who has some English (it seems to come and go as the spirit strikes him) that the fortress under construction was begun some years ago by merchant seamen, also the captives of these scoundrels. Indeed, we are told that the structure is commonly referred to as the "English Fort" in recognition of the original labor-ers. During the brief peace that civilized countries enjoyed with this unpleasant place, work stopped as there was no source of labor; all the captured seamen had either been killed by their treatment or their captors or returned after a ransom was paid. Now I am sure the Bashaw delights in a renewed supply of slave labor. We believe there are also a significant number of merchant sailors held in the prison who supplement our own Philadelphias.

I must end this as our messenger will be departing soon, and I will entrust it to his care. I am sorry to have to burden you with the depressing conditions we face, but you may rest assured, dear Brother, that we—all of us—live for the moment we will hear the bombardment of the fortress walls and the ultimate storming of the Bashaw's palace. So do not despair for me or the others; we are mostly of good spirits and in generally good health. I think of you often and hope that your employment is proving satisfactory to you and my old friend Stephen. Do not delay writing to our par-ents, should you have yet to accomplish that task. They will want to know that you are well as much as of my present circumstances. I will try to pen a note to you soon, and you should know that I and my shipmates continue to enjoy your letters. Cap't. Bainbridge's brother is also in the squadron, a fact with which I am sure you are acquainted, and writes to his brother as well, something we also share.

    With continued affection, I remain your appreciative brother, Edward Baldwin, Lt. USN

    P.S. You need not concern yourself about rereading this with a candle! EB

I looked around me as I let my hand drop into my lap. The schooner's rig and the nearby guns and deck furniture seemed fuzzy, and I wiped a sleeve across my eyes to clear them. I was surprised to find wetness along my arm, but my vision cleared, and I thought about what Edward had said.

The image I had held of him some months ago, dressed in rags, bound with chains, and starving again appeared, and this time it seemed even more vivid, more real. *Why would the Bashaw take out his anger on the prisoners? It was us who burned and destroyed his—our—frigate, not the men he held in his dungeon. I should talk about this idea of theirs about storming the fortress. But with who? I can't just barge into Captain Decatur's Cabin and suggest we attack. Mister Wakefield! He was the one who helped me last time. He'll help me, I'm sure. I must go and find the surgeon.*

I quickly read the letter for the second time and decided finding Reliance Wakefield was exactly the right course to follow. Before my resolve about approaching a senior with this matter weakened, I set off to find the doctor and share with him my brother's letter. I reminded myself to tell him that holding it over a candle would be unnecessary.

The schooner was innocent of the doctor; he had gone ashore, apparently while I and my messmates were standing to in the Cabin. While I stood by the bulwark in the waist, in the hope of spying him returning, Judd appeared, followed by Thomas. In spite of my knowledge of Thomas' fate, I started at seeing him carrying his chest. His expression gave nothing away; his eyes were not hardened nor was his jaw sporting its defiant cast. Judd nodded to me as they approached. Thomas appeared not even to see me, though he could hardly miss me. It appeared that his gaze was fixed on something about a cannon shot away.

"Mister Morris will accompany you, Wheatley, to ensure you are properly cared for in your new accommodations. Upon our return to Syracuse, I or he will look in on you to ascertain that you want for nothing." Lieutenant Lawrence's tone made it clear that he was not wishing our shipmate well. For once, Thomas said nothing, but rather stood mute, his gaze still focused afar.

Then Morris was beside us, attired in a full dress uniform complete with his sword, and the boat was alongside. Judd stuck out his hand.

"It will work out, Thomas. I doubt we will be at sea for long, and then you will be back in the midst of us. Bear up and be of good cheer. I know we've had our differences, but I shall miss you, if only . . . well, I shall miss you."

Thomas looked at Judd, took his hand and gave it a single shake. He then turned to me. "I guess now your guns will be the fastest, Baldwin, with me not there. You're not a bad sort, and I 'spect you'll do right fine, even with me not there to teach you!" He smiled, turned away, and picked up his chest to hand it into the waiting boat. For my part, I was speechless!

Finally, as the boat pulled smartly for the quay with Thomas and Lieutenant Morris in the sternsheets, I stepped up to the bulwark and waved my hat as I cried out, "Good luck to you, Thomas Wheatley! Keep well!" It sounded a trifle off, even to me, and, in concert with my own thoughts, I received a strange look from Judd, who then simply shook his head and walked away.

Neither of us went ashore that evening, though we had been given leave to do so, and supper was a quiet affair in the cockpit. We treated each other like strangers, in spite of the fact that we had been shipmates for nine months and had shared the same hardships, battles, and joys for those months. Later, when I realized I had yet to discover the whereabouts of our surgeon to tell him of Edward's latest missive, I took a turn around the deck, enjoying the cool night breeze and the familiar smells and sounds it carried from the shore, sounds and smells quite different from those we experienced in Messina. Still unable to uncover the elusive Mister Wakefield, I retired to my cot to fall asleep reflecting on the events of the past several days. My dreams seemed now to mingle the images of Thomas with those of my brother, and I awoke several times quite tangled in the bedclothes and wet with perspiration.

Two new arrivals to the harbor greeted us in the morning; a British brig of fourteen guns and an American schooner that appeared to be civilian in its character. Both had anchored close by the flagship, and, even as we watched, boats plied the waters between them and *Constitution* with some urgency. As Judd and I, now the sole occupants of the cockpit, took our breakfast, we found the strain of last evening gone and conjectured at length on the purpose of the two vessels.

"I'd wager that schooner is carrying dispatches for the commodore. Probably sent by the secretary himself." Judd spoke around a mouthful of fresh fruit which we had received from the local provender upon our arrival. "Were Wheatley here, he'd likely take exception to that, and claim he *knew* what the schooner is about." Judd smiled as he stabbed another piece of melon.

"What about the English one, Judd? What do you think they're about? I'd reckon they've brought intelligence to Commodore Preble about what those piratical rascals are up to . . . or maybe some communication from Captain Bainbridge." *And my brother,* I added silently.

The conversation continued with various hypotheses, each sillier than the last, until we heard a muffled cannon shot, followed by a commotion over our heads; a voice shouted down the hatch that "all officers're wanted topside."

Indeed, as Judd and I hurried topside, all were standing in the waist facing the quarterdeck where the captain and Lieutenant Lawrence stood side by side, their hands clasped behind them.

What was going on? What was the shot we heard? My thoughts were random and fleeting as I watched the faces of the lieutenants and Captain Decatur for any clue that might offer a hint to what was happening. Then Decatur spoke, as if in answer to my unuttered questions.

"The commodore has signaled 'all officers repair aboard.' I will take all save one of you with me. One must remain aboard *Enterprise* to maintain a watch." Decatur paused and looked at each of us. Finally, he made a decision. "Mister Devon, you will remain here to look after things in our absence. For the rest of you, dress uniforms at the waist in ten minutes." He turned and, leaving Mister Lawrence standing alone, stepped into the hatch and disappeared.

"Judd! I guess the captain isn't angry with you anymore! He wouldn't have left you in charge on the schooner if he didn't think . . ."

"You missed the mark on that, Oliver. It's exactly because he's angry with me that he left me here. I'd reckon something good is gonna happen on the flagship, maybe some good news or maybe he's gotten word about our prize money from *Philadelphia* or something. You mark my words, he ain't done with me yet by a long shot. Just because he sent Wheatley ashore don't mean this is over. I'd reckon the commodore told him to make my life miserable. He would've expected me to end the argument before it went as far as it did as I'm older, more experienced, and not a hothead like Wheatley. And you're too young to know what to do, even though you did try to stop it. Which, you might as well know, I told to Decatur in your defense." Judd's voice was hard-edged; I thought he even sounded a bit like Thomas would have. Of course, I already knew that Judd had mentioned my efforts to Captain Decatur.

"That was good of you, Judd." I offered. "Maybe he won't go as far as you think. We've both got to take on Thomas' duties; he said that while we all stood there in the Cabin. So maybe he left you on account of I'm too junior and he wanted the lieutenants with him." I smiled, hoping my words might make Judd feel a bit better.

"Maybe." Judd stepped away and headed for the bow as I went below to change my clothes.

CHAPTER TWENTY

Most of the officers and midshipmen of *Constitution* were lined up forward of the quarterdeck with those of the other American vessel, *Syren*, when the two boats from *Enterprise* hove alongside *Constitution*. Captain Decatur was piped over the side with due ceremony, and, in a moment, we all had taken our places with the others. Captain Robinson sent for the commodore.

When Preble appeared, he was accompanied by a British master commander who stood stiff as a ramrod next to him.

"Gentlemen, I have news, and Captain Bridgeston here has a message for you. Let us hear from the Royal Navy first. Captain Bridgeston, if you please." Preble turned to the Royal Navy officer, who took a half step forward and produced a folded paper from which he began to read. He still stood ramrod-straight and held the paper out in front of him at arms length. He reminded me of a painting I once had seen of a Roman senator, and I smiled secretly as I pictured him, not in the crisp blue, white, and gold uniform of the Royal Navy, but in a toga.

" 'To the officers and men of the American Navy Mediterranean squadron under Commodore Preble, Greetings.

" ' I have been informed in some considerable detail of your brilliant attack on and subsequent firing and destruction of the American frigate *Philadelphia* and commend you on your bravery and foresight. Depriving the Bashaw of the use of that vessel was most essential to our eventual success in curtailing the activities of his corsairs. Your courage and conviction are to be applauded. This adventure is surely the most bold and daring act of the age.'

"And it is signed, 'Horatio Nelson, Admiral. Off Toulon.'" Captain Bridgeston stepped back to his position alongside the commodore as he folded the paper again.

A murmur went through the assembled officers, the loudest being those of us who actually participated in the "most bold and daring act of the age." I grinned at the recognition we received from this hero of the Nile, perhaps the boldest and most daring of them all. I noticed that Captain Decatur was standing straight and tall, unsmiling and silent.

"Thank you for sharing Admiral Lord Nelson's generous comment, Captain." Preble smiled at the British officer and then faced us again. "The schooner that came in during the night is a civilian vessel chartered by the Secretary of the Navy to bring dispatches and orders to me from Washington and President Madison. Included in them is the following letter from the Secretary addressed to me:

" 'By dispatches sent to me I have learned of the destruction of the late frigate *Philadelphia* while lying in the harbor of Tripoli under circumstances of extraordinary peril to the parties that achieved it. I find, sir, that Lieutenant Decatur had command of the expedition. The achievement of this brilliant enterprise reflects the highest honor on all the officers and men concerned. He (Lieutenant Decatur) has acquitted himself in a manner which justifies the high confidence we have reposed in his valor and skill. The President of the United States has asked me to convey to Lieutenant Decatur his thanks for such gallant conduct and further requests that you thank in his name each individual of his gallant band for their honorable and valorous support, rendered the more honorable from its having been volunteered. As a testimonial to the President's high opinion of the brave and skillful conduct which obtained by all participants, he has requested that I forward and you, sir, deliver the enclosed commissions.' " Preble stopped and then looked squarely at Captain Decatur.

"Your commission, sir, is that of captain, United States Navy. You will do all of us honor by accepting it."

Another murmur went through the group, and Decatur took a step forward from where he stood with the officers of *Enterprise*.

"Sir, I can not be singled out for this honor without ensuring that those who volunteered to accompany me will likewise receive the recognition and honor they have rightly and equally earned with their own participation." The captain remained standing in front of us as a stunning silence fell over the group.

If we all get promoted, I thought, barely able to contain my excitement, *then I will be a lieutenant, and after only ten months a midshipman. Won't Edward be proud of me!* As these heady thoughts raced through my brain, I realized that the commodore was speaking again, this time in a somewhat quieter voice.

" . . . noble, sir. However, the secretary agrees with you and has forwarded suitable rewards for those who served with you." He stopped and consulted a list which he apparently had received with the letter. "All acting lieutenants are herewith promoted, effective immediately, to lieutenant. In addition, Lieutenant Charles Stewart, *Argus*, to lieutenant commandant. Midshipmen . . ." I held my breath, waiting for those words. " . . . are granted a monetary reward equal to one half year's pay."

I was crestfallen. No promotion. But, I consoled myself, six months' pay will certainly be a welcome increase in my often desperate financial position.

But our captain was not yet finished. He spoke quietly, but perfectly audibly to those of us who surrounded him and the commodore. "Sir, have you received word from the secretary concerning our being awarded prize shares from the destruction of the frigate? Surely the men who accompanied us are entitled to their just rewards as well."

A cloud passed across the commodore's eyes, darkening his look and speaking to either his frustration with the delay or his differing opinion. "That is an item which remains undecided at this time, Captain Decatur. But you may rest assured, sir, that, should the Congress see fit to decide favorably, I will forthwith inform you of that decision as quick as ever it is communicated to me." Preble spoke in a low voice as well, and, when he saw Decatur nod his head, he looked about him at the rest of the officers and again raised his voice so as to be audible to all. I took from his comment that he agreed that we were entitled to prize shares from *Philadelphia.*

"I have also been informed by our friends of the Royal Navy that my visit to Naples early in the late month has born fruit. The King of the Two Sicilies has agreed to grant me the loan of six gunboats and two bomb vessels from his fleet. These vessels will soon await us at Messina and, once brought to off Tripoli, will serve us to our advantage in attacking that city. It is my intention to leave on the morrow for Messina to collect these vessels and the schooner *Nautilus*, should her repairs be completed, and bring them to a position off the harbor of our enemy. Once there, we shall, as quickly as ever possible, begin a bombardment which will, should we be successful, reduce that city to rubble.

"It is necessary that these eight vessels be manned by our own sailors in addition to those Italians, some ninety-six of them, in fact, loaned to us by our ally, the King of the Two Sicilies. Of course, they will be commanded by our officers." He stopped and consulted another paper which he drew from his pocket. Then he listed the captains who would command the divisions of the gunboats as well as the individual vessels. I was thrilled to hear that Captain Decatur would command not only one of the boats, but a division as well. His brother, James, currently on *Nautilus*, and Lieutenant Lawrence, our own first lieutenant, would each be in charge of boats. The other three were given to an officer from *Constitution* and two others, whose names meant little to me, from the brigs.

"Each of the commanders will select those officers they wish to accompany them, along with some thirty seamen for each. We will join our comrades currently on station in the blockade and, with the Grace of God, offer those heathen scoundrels some American 'tribute' as a celebration, albeit several weeks late, of the independence of our great country!" Preble had barely completed his words before a great cheer erupted from the officers, joined quickly by a handful of seamen who had been lounging near at hand. I must admit, I was quite caught up in it and surprised myself with my own enthusiasm.

Then it was over. Most of the officers from *Enterprise* as well as the other ships clustered around Decatur, offering him congratulations and joy of his double promotion while we awaited the boats which would carry us back to our respective ships.

No sooner had Judd greeted our arrival on the schooner's deck than our captain addressed us.

"Gentlemen, when we take our position in the blockade and man the gunboats, it is my intention to have Mister Devon and Mister Baldwin with me. Mister Lawrence will take Mister Morris, and Mister Hobbs will temporarily command *Enterprise*. Should any among you have other thoughts, please let me know." No further words were necessary. He went below leaving us in silence on the deck. I am sure that each of us was deep in his own thoughts, recalling our attack on *Philadelphia* and relishing the thought of further retaliation against the Bashaw. For my own self, I wasn't so sure.

"What was he talking about, Oliver, taking you and me in a gunboat with him? What gunboat? Where are we going?" Judd grabbed my arm and whispered insistently into my ear. It brought me up all standing and I shook my head to clear it.

"We're going to take the squadron and a fleet of gunboats the commodore borrowed from some king and attack the fortress and the castle. Preble put the captain in command of one of the gunboats and told him to pick his officers and crew for it. He picked us as you just heard."

As we went below to the cockpit, Judd badgered me and finally drew from my still-addled head a detailing of the events that transpired on the flagship, including the promotions and money rewards. While I could not recollect the exact words used by Admiral Nelson to describe our attack in February on our late frigate, I think I successfully conveyed the feeling of his praise.

"Damme! I wish I had been with you. Did Decatur mention me, say anything that might make you think he was not still angry with me?" Judd's worried expression spoke more eloquently of his real concern than did his words.

"Well, Judd . . . no." I tried to think of something, anything to tell him. His face fell and his frown deepened. "But he did select you instead of one of the officers to go with him in the gunboat. That has to count for something!" I was pleased that I could come up with an answer for him, even a tenuous one.

"Aye. I guess that's something. It might give us . . . me . . . a chance to restore my honor in his eyes. Yes. Perhaps you're right. He could have left me in the schooner for that as well."

Judd took me over and over the events that took place on *Constitution*, and in the boat to and from, making me repeat words that might have reflected on Decatur's attitude toward him. Throughout our dinner, he continued to badger me, and I struggled to recall everything, even the tiniest detail of conversation and comment; I wracked my brain to come up with suitable answers for him. Later that afternoon, when we came topside, we saw that the flagship was making preparations to get underweigh, presumably to Messina to collect our gunboats and mortar vessels.

"You youngsters have anything to take care of ashore, I'd get it done sooner than later. I'll warrant we'll be gettin' our own selves outta here within a day or so, no more." Lieutenant Hobbs had joined us as we watched the flurry of activity on the big frigate. Judd and I shared a quick look, and I was some certain that the same thought ran through his mind as mine.

That's just what Hobbs said the night before Thomas and Judd fought their duel in Messina! Well, there's no duel to be fought now. I wonder what he's thinking. And Thomas isn't even here. Why would he say something like that?

"Likely be some warm action over there when the commodore puts it all together. I'd warrant the gunboats will make the difference. And I'd imagine the cap'n'll like as not want me in the scrap, bring *Enterprise* in close and show those rascals our own iron. You lads'll likely get a real taste of fightin' in this one." The older lieutenant smiled at us then gazed off into the distance, perhaps thinking about the 'warm action' he mentioned.

'A real taste of fighting' is it? What do you suppose he might think of the action on Philadelphia. *I'd call that one 'pretty warm,' at least from where I was standing. And as I recall, it was Hobbs who ran through that pirate right in front of me just after we came aboard! And without so much as a blink!*

"Maybe put an end to this blockade business, we hit them hard enough, right, Lieutenant? Maybe get our men off *Philadelphia* back from them as well." Judd spoke quietly, perhaps testing how Hobbs might feel toward him, whether he shared the captain's mindset or not.

"Likely won't change a thing, Mister Devon. Them pirates ain't likely to lay down and die just on account of we drop some shells and iron into their castle and town. And I doubt whether the Bashaw'd be real eager to give up the Philadelphias without he gets his damn ransom . . . and, like as not, tribute into the bargain. No, I think we might get his attention, is all. Mayhaps make it some easier for Preble and the consul . . . that Danish fellow . . ." He paused, thinking.

"Nissen," I supplied quietly in the silence, recalling the name from Edward's letters and how helpful the Dane had been to him and the others held in that miserable, rat-infested dungeon.

"Aye, Nissen. If they can convince the Bashaw that we ain't going away, and we're serious about destroying his town and his castle, he might back off some on his demands."

"Sir, what about these gunboats? What do you know of them?" I thought if he could offer some wisdom on them, it might be helpful to me in deciding whether or not I really wanted to go with Decatur.

"Well, Mister Baldwin, what I've heard is they are about twenty or so tons each with a crew of thirty or forty men. Carry a long twenty-four-pounder for'ard. Just one. Some of 'em, I hear tell, can carry another pair of lighter long guns amidships. And bein' flat-bottomed, they're not much seaworthy." He stared off into the distance again; neither Judd nor I said anything. "Damn near impossible to handle under sail or oar." He added, almost to himself and then, louder, to us, "Glad I'm sailing the schooner, I am. Yes, sir! But I'd warrant that the cap'n thinks right high of the two of you lads, to want you with him in the gunboat. Must think you can handle yourselves with the best of 'em." He smiled at us and walked away.

"Oliver, I feel much better about this whole business. Will you join me in a glass ashore? I think it would be right nice." Judd seemed suddenly a different man.

I nodded, smiling at the thought of returning to a more normal relationship, and soon, to a normal routine at sea.

Almost without conscious thought, and certainly without conversation, once ashore we set our course for the same *taverna* we had frequented when first we visited Syracuse, the very same one at which Reliance Wakefield had discovered the secret writing in my letter from Edward. That, as I thought of it, reminded me that I had yet to discuss with the medical man my brother's latest intelligence and recommendation. We found a table with little difficulty as it was still early for the local populace to be seeking their supper. Judd ordered a glass of the local brandy for himself. When the waiter looked at me, I flushed, hesitated, and nodded at him, indicating I would have the same. It seemed the easier course to follow.

"Judd, when the captain mentioned the prize shares he thought we were entitled to I was some surprised; I thought we only got prize money for the enemy vessels we brought in, like that ketch, *Mastico*." I was not just giving my friend and senior midshipman a chance to feel superior to me; I really was confused about the whole prize money subject. Devon looked at me, cleared his throat and took a breath.

"You're mostly right, Oliver. But if the vessel is destroyed and is of equal or superior power than the victor, like *Philadelphia* was, then we can collect our prize money. 'Ceptin' it'd be called 'head and gun' money, assuming we knew how many crew she carried and what her armament was. Which, in the *Philadelphia* frigate, we did. 'Course, with the little ship, *Mastico*, we weren't entitled to prize money, *shares*, it's called. The general rule is you don't get prize money even when you bring in a prize less'n it's sold along with its cargo. That's why we didn't get anything from the ketch; Preble took her into the squadron as a vessel of the Navy." Judd stopped and looked at me to be sure I was still with him. When I said nothing, he continued.

"Now, I suspect the problem they might be having at home with Decatur's claim for prize shares from the frigate is that she was an American ship, and our orders were to burn her. Not cut her out and sail her home. I'd reckon they in Washington look at it same as they'd look at us burning a building ashore. Of course, they weren't there enjoying the swordplay and fire the way we were." The image of that huge pirate coming at me with his ugly curved sword flashed through my mind. I shivered in spite of myself and shook my head to chase away the vision. Judd continued, unaware of my recollection.

"The cap'n says she was a prize, belonging to the enemy as she did at the time, and whether we took her or destroyed her, us and the others should get prize shares. The lads with Cap'n Stewart on the *Syren* brig also, since she was there to help us." He stopped and I saw his eyes shift to a point over my head.

"Well! You two certainly look serious. I do hope you're not planning any more duels! I suspect even *our* captain might take some umbrage at a second." Mister Wakefield's familiar voice was teasing rather than cautioning, and I turned in my chair to see him standing directly behind me, smiling broadly.

"Have you lads room for an old medico to join you? I really don't fancy eatin' by myself."

"Of course, sir. Please do." Judd stood as he offered the invitation, his action suggesting to me I should do the same.

The surgeon had no sooner sat than a waiter arrived with a glass (I had neither seen nor heard him order anything), and Wakefield took a deep draught of it. I thought it might be wine. Then he smiled, wiped his mouth and, looking first at me then at Judd, spoke.

"What did you young gentlemen think of the little gathering this morning? Hmm? Reckon you young lions are straining at your lines to get back across the water and into this scrap again, eh? I collect you were both in attendance?"

Silence.

"Uh, no, sir. Captain Decatur left me aboard *Enterprise*, in command, I assume, while the others went to *Constitution*." Even put the way Judd did, it didn't sound quite right.

"Oh, I see. He still hasn't put that little matter in Messina behind him, I take it? I would have thought, given his history, he might be some forgiving. Worry not, my young friend, I know our captain well, and I assure you, he will get over it. Eventually, even Mister Wheatley will be restored to grace. Though I surely do not relish the return of that disagreeable young pup to our midst." This last was barely audible, and I was not sure the surgeon even realized he spoke aloud.

He thought a moment, then smiled broadly at Judd, and, after another draught from his glass, went on. "I would suppose that Mister Baldwin, here, has regaled you with all the details of the morning." It was not a question.

"Yes, sir, he has. And I hope we can do those pirates some damage again when next we meet them. I thought it most generous of Admiral Lord Nelson to offer his congratulations to us on our 'adventure.' And splendid that the officers and midshipmen are being rewarded for our participation." Judd offered. Then, almost an afterthought. "And the captain's promotion . . . that was . . . grand, yes, a grand gesture by our Congress."

"Quite remarkable, I'd call it, that he should be elevated by *two* ranks instead of just one. I can't help but wonder if it's ever been done before that way. 'Course, now he's a *captain*, they aren't likely to leave him in command of a puny little schooner; no sir, something bigger and fancier will have to be found for him. Maybe even *Constitution*!" The doctor laughed; it started as a giggle and grew quickly into a full-blown belly-laugh, one in which we were drawn to join whether we wanted to or not. I, for one, could see nothing humorous, though I joined in the laughter. *Perhaps Reliance Wakefield had already slaked his thirst some before joining Judd and me.*

"Why would that be so hilarious, sir?" I asked when Wakefield had caught his breath and the attention of the others on the establishment had returned to their own interests.

"He's *barely* twenty-five years of age, and until this morning, was only a lieutenant, Oliver. Doesn't that strike even you as a trifle young to be com-manding the mightiest ship in the Navy?" He laughed again, though less bois-terously this time.

I considered the matter for a moment. "Sir, if I may, why should his age have anything to do with whether or not he can do the job?" *After all, look at me. I am barely fifteen and have already killed a man and taken part in 'the most bold and daring adventure of the age' . . . or something like that.*

The doctor considered me for a moment, undoubtedly deciding if I was serious. His brow wrinkled and two little vertical lines formed between his eyes. Then, quite suddenly, his forehead cleared, his eyes danced, and he smiled broadly. "Well, Oliver. I suppose you might have a point there. Look at you, after all. And young James Stevens. Was he not even younger than you?" I nod-ded. Wakefield grew serious and changed tacks. "I can not think of a more qual-ified commander for that or any other ship of the Navy than Captain Decatur. It just struck me funny that such a young man would be given such a respon-sible employment. But these are strange and different times and call for bold strokes to be taken."

Judd, thinking, I am sure, to turn the subject away from one that might strain my relationship with the surgeon, pointed across the room.

"Look there, gentlemen. Speaking of 'young,' is that not a midshipman from our flagship? Seems to walk with a certain swagger, for one so young." Judd aimed his knife across the floor to where a young man in the uniform of a midshipman, who looked about my age, was strutting toward a table already occupied by some of his mates. He did seem to *swagger*, suggesting experience and knowledge beyond his years. And, from what I could see of his face, he wore an expression of disdain, as though just *being* there was beneath him. We all watched him until he made a place for himself at the table. Then Wakefield turned back to us and laughed quietly.

"I do believe that's young Ridgely. Met him a few months ago, in less than glorious circumstances. If my recollection is correct, that *swagger* will turn into a *stagger* before he leaves this place. And that *will* be justified!"

We all laughed, this time genuinely, and continued to chat like old friends sharing a meal. Remembering my previous experiences and Wakefield's some-what caustic comment about staggering, I was careful about bringing my own self to that point. I did manage to suggest to him that I had a matter to discuss with him at his convenience.

"Tomorrow, lad, tomorrow. Once we are back aboard our little cockleshell of a ship, I shall be pleased to listen and offer whatever advice an old surgeon might have to offer. But, with your indulgence, I would wait until the light of a new day dawns."

And so it would be; and he would be quite sober by then, a condition that clearly eluded him now.

Our evening ended cordially, and was financially successful for Judd and me, as Mister Wakefield would hear nothing of us spending our own money. "You lads gave up whatever it was you had planned for this evening to amuse an old man; you must let me make that up to you."

It was only a matter of two or three days before *Enterprise* and the brig *Syren* won their anchors from the sandy bottom of the harbor at Syracuse and headed south to join the blockade with *Vixen*, *Argus* and, we hoped soon, *Constitution* and her fleet of gunboats. I was sure that Captain Decatur would be keeping a watchful eye on the horizon for *Nautilus* and his brother, James.

Boisterous weather and contrary winds met us only a day out but, other than delaying our arrival, did no damage to either vessel. We took our station as darkness fell just a few days past the anniversary of American Independence. *Syren*, under Captain Stewart, was assigned a station just off the rocks beyond the eastern approach to Tripoli's harbor. *Enterprise* remained to the west, in sight of *Argus*.

Lieutenant Hobbs and I were once again paired on the watch bill, and our quiet comments during the small hours of the next morning, as we guided the schooner off and on the coast, were interrupted by the hoarse whisper of a lookout.

"Quarterdeck! Vessel off the port bow. Might be a league distant. No lights that I can see."

A nod from Hobbs sent me scurrying forward and into the lower shrouds of the foremast, a night glass slung across my back. I studied the vessel from my perch on the ratlines and hastened back to tell Hobbs of my discovery.

"She appears to be a schooner, sir. Not unlike ourselves. I wonder if it might not be *Vixen* returning. Captain Hull did say he thought we were them when we came in last night. She surely did not have the appearance of one of those pirate vessels we have seen." I hoped I was not being overly optimistic; the arrival of *Constitution* and the gunboats would be most welcome in evening up the fight, when it came. Two schooners of twelve guns and a pair of sixteen-gun brigs would hardly be a match for dozens of Tripolitan gunboats, polaccas, and the few brigs the pirates held.

"Quartermaster, show a light to *Argus* telling her of this . . . never mind. I would reckon Hull's seen it, whatever it might be, himself. There's his signal lights now." Hobbs was watching our larger colleague through his night glass.

"Sir, yes, sir. That's just what they are. He also says 'Do not fire without my order.' Shall I acknowledge?"

"Aye. Do that. Oliver, you might have our forward guns manned, just in case. And fetch up the captain, if you please." Hobbs swung his glass forward and studied the approaching ship.

"Fetch me up for what, Mister Hobbs?" Decatur's voice was so quiet that it startled me and Hobbs more than had he shouted.

Hobbs quickly explained and offered the captain his night glass.

"I will just have a look myself, gentlemen." He strode forward and we watched him climb a few steps up the weather ratlines.

When he returned, he was smiling. "I think Captain Smith might take exception to being fired on by his own, gentlemen. That is clearly *Vixen* returning from wherever Hull has sent her."

"More lights from *Argus*, sir. '*Vixen's* number, it is, sir." The quartermaster was clearly pleased we would not be entering a contest just yet.

The captain retired below again, and the schooner fell in with *Argus* and ourselves. *Syren* remained barely visible to our west. The dark hours passed uneventfully. Dawn found us all close by one another in oily calm seas with sails slatting uselessly.

A signal came from *Syren* for captains to repair aboard. Of course, Captain Stewart had no knowledge of our captain's wonderful promotion; had he, the others would likely have come to *Enterprise*! Judd mentioned that to me as we watched our boat pull smartly for the brig.

It seemed barely an hour they were gone before the boat and our captain were again alongside the schooner. Of course, all of us stood expectantly near at hand, should Decatur have something to tell us, which he did.

"Well, we know now what vessels they have in the harbor, gentlemen. And it would appear to me that with the flagship's long guns, the gunboats Preble has borrowed from the King of the Two Sicilies, and ourselves, we can give them a right warm action. Captain Smith took *Vixen* right in and had himself a fine look." Decatur was jubilant at the prospects of a 'right warm action.' For my own self, I still was not so sure.

In the event, it would be a while coming; *Constitution* was not yet here and Mother Nature had different plans for us. The oily calm augured more boisterous weather, a black squall, I heard the men call it, and we were driven to find sea room away from the treacherous rocks and shoals of the Tripolitan coast. The shallow water caused the mounting seas to break, and the northerly gale threatened to blow us ashore unless we were able to claw our way into the safety of the deeps.

Two days into it, the flagship hove into view, towing a string of gunboats behind her. They were none of them faring well. *Constitution's* tophamper looked severely damaged even to my inexperienced eye; the gunboats seemed awfully low in the water and worked at their tethers in a most distressing way. Preble signaled us that he was headed for Malta to make repairs. It would be more than a week before he rejoined us.

CHAPTER TWENTY-ONE

By July's end, and still not a shot fired, the squadron was once again assembled within striking distance of Tripoli's harbor. *Nautilus* had come out just after the flagship left Messina with the gunboats, stopping at Syracuse to take in tow two mortar boats which would add nicely to our ability to provide our captain's 'warm action.'

The six gunboats and two bomb vessel were parceled out to the rest of the fleet; *Constitution* took in tow the two mortar (bomb) boats, while *Argus* took a pair of the gunboats behind her. *Syren*, *Vixen*, *Nautilus*, and *Enterprise* each towed one of the ungainly vessels and made their way to a position some two and one half miles to the north of the harbor, where we all anchored.

Again, Mother Nature conspired against us; not one hour had elapsed before the wind, which had been light from the east-southeast, shifted quickly into the north and threatened to blow us all ashore. The sea became alarmingly choppy, with the waves once again breaking into the low-lying gunboats. The signal was made to up our anchors and stand for open water. For three days the winds assaulted us, but to our great joy, it shortly had veered back to the east, which had the effect of knocking down the short steep seas. It would have been most awkward had we been forced to contend with big seas while we towed the small craft. Even so, our flagship suffered a split fore course and main tops'l, both having been close reefed. The shallow draft vessels, all the rest of the squadron, escaped unscathed. But our plans were again confounded.

By midday on August third, we were once again back on our stations a league off the harbor. It was a fine day with an easy, easterly breeze. Through the glass, I could see the rocks surrounding the harbor entrance; the seas were not breaking over them.

"Flags on *Constitution*, sir." The quartermaster studied them with his long glass for a moment, consulted his book, and offered, "Says, 'Come within hail,' sir."

"Bring her about, Mister Devon, and let us see what the commodore has in store for us. I'll warrant we'll all be most pleased with it." Decatur's eyes sparkled as he thought of what lay ahead. "It surely is time!" He muttered this last, giving voice—privately, to be sure—to the frustration most had felt with the delays in our attack.

Enterprise bore up, passed smartly through stays, and bounded off on the other tack to close with the frigate. Even the gunboat, still following obediently on its tether astern, seemed nearly as eager as the sprightly schooner as we narrowed the distance to the frigate. Judd had been restored to our captain's good graces, having been granted the privilege of standing watches, during daylight hours, by himself. It seemed a truly fine day.

As we approached the towering side of the flagship, Decatur became increasingly agitated, his body silently urging the little schooner to sail faster and more weatherly. His glance turned repeatedly to the vessel in tow, his scowl offering a silent curse at its deterrence to our sailing ability. His eyes glowed with the now familiar fire as he chafed at his lines for action and the honor that would accrue to us all. On the quarterdeck of *Constitution* we could see Commodore Preble demonstrating his own urgency; he paced continually, looking up often to ensure himself that indeed the smaller vessels were responding with alacrity to his signal.

"Stand to the harbor entrance, Captain Decatur, and there man your gunboat. As quickly as the others are ready, commence your attack. We will begin our bombardment immediately you are standing in." The voice, made tinny by the speaking trumpet, was not the commodore's, but it mattered not a whit to Decatur, nor any of us. The captain doffed his hat and made a bow in reply, giving the order to bear off under the frigate's stern. As soon as our rakish bowsprit was clear of the gig in its davits at *Constitution's* stern, he wore *Enterprise* around to "stand for the harbor entrance."

We were finally going to attack the castle and fortifications! Now that we were actually going to do it, I felt my stomach knot and noticed that my mouth was suddenly dry. It would likely be an hour and more before all the gunboats and schooners were in position and ready. An hour that I knew would pass all too quickly, and . . . I steered myself away from the timid thoughts and looked at my fellows on the schooner.

Why can't I be like Decatur? Look at him. He is positively delighted! Almost dancing with the anticipation of doing battle. I would reckon there's not a shred of doubt or fear in him. I looked around. *Judd neither.* Though by my own observation, Judd was certainly not 'almost dancing' with anticipation! But neither did he seem at all nervous.

It seemed barely a few minutes before we had rounded up to stays, brought the gunboat alongside on its tether, and begun passing shot and powder down to its deck. And then it was time for us and our handful of Italian seamen to take our positions in the little ship.

I had caught some of the enthusiasm exuded by my captain and colleagues, and, while not quite as exuberant as they, I was able to speak. While my stomach felt as though it had become quarters to a flock of butterflies, I no longer felt the need to remain close to the leeward rail. I consoled myself with the thought that, with our actions and my participation, I might help to speed Edward's release from the dreadful dungeon maintained by those barbarians. As we stepped down into our gunboat and prepared to cast off from the schooner, I found that my legs were no longer watery, and, while there *was* a slight, very slight, tremor in my hands, it seemed not to inhibit my abilities. I found myself looking forward to the excitement and danger of our pending action.

Hobbs, standing on the quarterdeck of the now shorthanded vessel, doffed his hat and shouted encouragingly to us. I saw that the same pantomime was being carried out at the other four vessels and watched the two ungainly mortar boats as they came toward us from *Constitution*, propelled both by oars and sails, but nonetheless struggling to make ground to weather.

Then, we were ready. The men of the gunboats and approaching bomb vessels offered up a quite spontaneous *huzzah* as we made for the harbor; I was surprised to find my own voice joining in with no lack of enthusiasm. A mighty roar gave voice to *Constitution's* jubilation at finally joining the fray as she fired her broadside into the fortifications around the town, signaling the start of the engagement.

Return fire seemed ineffective; only a few of the guns mounted in the castle's battlements responded to the flagship's offering and they were poorly laid. We pressed in, closing to a distance where our smaller guns and mortars could reach. *Argus* fired as her guns made the range, and I watched the shore carefully for signs of hits.

Here's your "tribute" to the Bashaw being paid, and handsomely, Mister Wakefield. Just as you wanted. I hope the barbarian takes it to heart! And soon enough we'll be offering more. I surprised myself at my own fierceness as I anticipated the moment when our gunboats would join in what would likely turn quickly into a 'warm action.'

Our orders required us to make up into two divisions of three boats each. We were in the second division under the command of Captain Decatur. The other boats were commanded by Mister Lawrence and an officer from *Vixen*, a Lieutenant Trippe. In the other group of three, all under the command of Lieutenant Richard Somers, were James Decatur from *Nautilus* and a lieutenant from *Argus* named Joshua Blake. Of course, *Argus*, *Vixen*, *Enterprise*, and *Syren* provided escort and shield for us as we approached the inner harbor, each firing sporadically into the fortified castle walls. The ships were all shorthanded now, but their fire appeared effective, judging from the bits of stone and debris which flew into the air with each hit. Once within the range of our own guns, we separated to our assigned sectors, and, at three o'clock in the afternoon, one of the mortar boats threw a shell into the town, signaling the start of our own attack.

Now suddenly, as though they had just taken notice of our approach, the enemy returned a hot fire, opening up with the rest of the shore-based guns in the fort as well as those in their own gunboats, which commenced getting underway from their moorings at the quay to attack us. It looked like there were dozens of them!

Our gun, as well as those of the other gunboats and the schooners, was firing as fast as the crew could swab, load, ram, and fire it. I watched as the Tripolitan boats drew closer; I counted nineteen of them and two enormous galleys. About a third of them kept to the east near the rocks, and another third moved into a position to the west. The remainder held close under the guns of the fort, apparently a reserve force, but that did not prevent them from firing at us. *Oh, my God! How can we succeed against such a force?* The butterflies gave way to a twelve-pound ball, and I eased myself toward the low rail of the boat.

With the splash of shot landing all around us, some close enough to wet our sail, Captain Decatur shouted for all the boats to attack the easterly grouping of the enemy and ordered our oarsmen to "Pull for all you're worth, lads!" The sails were adjusted to provide what little help they might, which wasn't much since we were headed almost directly upwind. Still the shot from the corsairs' guns splashed the water into geysers all around us. Had it not been so terrifyingly close and deadly, I would have reveled in the tiny rainbows and sparkle of the spray as each splash caught the sunlight.

As we stroked into battle, I looked around for the other boats. Somers' was making no headway to windward at all. He remained to leeward of us all and finally turned to attack some of the polaccas that were closing with him. In fact, only James Decatur's boat managed to fight its way sufficiently to windward to join in with our group. Blake seemed to be hanging back, and, while his guns fired, I could see that few of their shots told. Why he did not at the least assist with his division commander's attack on five of the enemy gunboats, which had stood out for him, I have no idea. But he did not, and Somers, by himself, fired repeatedly at point blank range, almost every one his shots telling. When the enemy turned to run under the guns of the fortress, Somers followed, firing all the while, but was unable to inflict any more damage on them than he already had.

A loud *thwack* followed by a shower of splinters and water and a definite lurch, almost a stagger, of our gunboat caught me unawares, and I grabbed onto the nearest support I could, which turned out to be Judd's shoulder, to keep myself from falling into the water.

"Careful, Oliver! You'll put us both into the sea!" Judd barely gave me a glance, and his tone was surely not that of one irritated at being grabbed at in a manner so undignified.

While we had suffered a hit, it seemed not to impede our progress; we continued to close quickly with a large Tripolitan gunboat.

Lieutenant Somers will have to carry on without me! No time now to keep my eye on him, I thought, surprising myself with my drollness, given the circumstances.

The enemy maintained his fire without restraint, but Decatur instructed all the boats with us, save Lawrence's, to hold fire while we closed; that vessel, which had suffered the loss of its lateen yard by an enemy ball, he ordered to lay back some and maintain as heavy a cannonade as they could manage.

As the Tripolitans drew closer, I suddenly realized it was our captain's intention to board them and so take the boats and their bloodthirsty crews captive. My experiences in our 'most bold and daring act of the age' passed quickly through my mind but did little to quell the growing anxiety that gnawed at my stomach and drew any remaining moisture from my mouth. My fear gathered me to its bosom in a suffocating hug, rendering me quite incapable of even moving. So held by my fears I was that I scarcely started when our first gun discharged, at Decatur's order, its deadly load of grape, followed by a load of canister. Immediately the others joined the fray, firing at their chosen targets. Again, our 'bold and daring' adventure and its stealthy approach to our object came to mind. This was certainly to be a horse of a different color!

Then we were alongside one of the pirate polaccas, grapnels hooked into the enemy's bulwark, and lines pulled tight to hold us cheek by jowl with them. Too close for the supporting fire from our colleagues or the bigger ships, we were on our own. I saw that one other of our number, at some distance from us was similarly engaged, though I could not determine which.

"MEN! Follow me! We will take them. Judd! Oliver! Take your men forward." Decatur's cry broke my chains of immobility. I was aware of Judd rushing by me, cutlass held aloft and pistol aimed to the front, shouting at the top of his lungs some unintelligible sounds.

"OLIVER! Come. Follow me. And cock your pistol!" I made out the words as Judd paused to rally me and our men.

Without a conscious thought, I mimicked his pose and followed, cocking my pistol as he had instructed. Ten or twelve of our sailors, armed with half-pikes, tomahawks, and cutlasses followed us, pushing and scrabbling to be first to gain the enemy's deck. Another group followed the captain, and the Neapolitan sailors, of whom we employed about six, remained in the gunboat.

Screaming and yelling in English and the unintelligible guttural invectives of our turbaned adversaries competed with the clashing of steel on steel and the sharp crack of pistols. In the background, I could identify, without looking, the flagship's steady, rhythmic broadsides. *Small comfort, that.* As I stepped over the enemy bulwark and onto his deck, a white-robed fellow with a dense, black beard and fiery black eyes rose up in front of me.

He held the same curved blade I had seen on the decks of *Philadelphia*, and his menacing posture stopped me in my tracks. He studied me for a moment and actually smiled. His teeth, stained and blackened, made the smile all the more horrible. I was rooted to the deck, unmoving even when he stepped toward me, raising his *scimitar* as he likely relished the joy of splitting me open.

"Shoot him! Shoot him, Oliver!" Judd's voice seemed far away as I faced this fellow who, though not a large man, was fearsome in his posture and intent, even at a distance of several steps.

As though underwater, I managed to raise my pistol, sight it as I had been taught, and pull the trigger. The fiery black eyes, the smile, and thick black beard disappeared in a wet red cloud as the man fell backward, dead by my ball taken full in the face. *There! Didn't expect that, I'll warrant!* I stood looking at him for a moment, perhaps a second, and then rushed past his inert form to catch up with Judd. My terror was forgotten as I gained Judd's side, replaced by the shock of my action. My shock, my horror, turned quickly to jubilation at my deliverance.

"Judd! Did you see? I shot that man! I killed him, Judd!" My excitement was tempered some by my realization that, once again, I had ended the life of a fellow human being.

"Aye, a fine shot it was, Oliver, and not a moment too soon. He would have killed you as soon as look at you had you waited. Split you stem to stern with that scimitar!" Judd shouted back, not looking at me; his eyes moved about the knots of men locked in combat. Almost without thought, he parried a corsair's thrust and, with a backhand stroke, laid open the man's chest to the bone. The enemy quickly lost his taste for the fight and leaped over the rail.

Around us the sounds swirled and clashed, combining their several distinct and identifiable ones into a single, continuous din, punctuated by the steady cannonading of *Constitution, Argus,* and *Syren.* It was confusing by itself, but added to the tide of white-robed Turks that seemed to flow in undiminished numbers amid the canvas trousers and blue jackets of the Americans, all fighting by now with spent pistol and cutlass, fist and tomahawk, it was astonishing to me that any of us landed a blow where we intended. But we did, even me. And presently, just as I struck a swarthy fellow with the butt of my discharged pistol, giving him a blow which caused him to drop to his knees, I heard the voice of our captain floating above the sounds of the dying fracas.

"They've struck, men. HOLD! We carried 'em!"

With surprising suddenness, the noise around us, the cries, the clanging steel, seemed to stop completely. The long guns of *Constitution* and the others continued their cannonade, now a barely noticed background noise. We stood panting, breathless, on the polacca's deck amid a dozen and more bodies clad in red-stained white robes which covered legs, arms, and torsos in contorted poses. Most were quite dead; a few moaned pitifully and stirred, not wishing to be heaved over the side to whatever fate had greeted their dead mates. The remainder, perhaps five of them, had surrendered and were herded in a group onto our gunboat. The polacca was secured astern and taken in tow, a prize of war.

Back aboard gunboat four, I stood amid my shipmates, numb with the emotions that coursed through me. The jubilation was gone; I was at times on the brink of tears while at others I wanted to shout out in glee. My twice spent pistol still hung in my hand, useful now as only a cudgel, and my cutlass, as innocent of blood as when I had boarded, remained firmly in my right hand, an extension of my arm. I watched without comprehension as our sail was unfurled and the oars manned, moving us in a direction that held no significance for me.

"Captain Decatur! Captain! Your brother, sir!" A voice from gunboat two, which I recalled was under the command of James Decatur, was carried by the scant wind to the ears of our captain. Turning, I spied the boat making for us from astern under sail and oars. That was the boat I had earlier witnessed attacking the enemy as we did. A midshipman (I recognized him, but was unable to call to mind his name) stood in the bow, hands cupped around his mouth.

"Avast heaving, lads. Shiver the sail." Decatur ordered us to wait for the pursuing boat, which quickly drew nigh.

"Sir! Your brother, sir . . . he's been . . . he got . . . shot, sir." The midshipman struggled to give voice to the dreadful words.

Our captain, who had come aft to better hear the messenger, stood quite close to me, and I perceived the fire leave his eyes, the fire that had glowed there so brightly since the commodore sent us on our way. Indeed, the captain's face seemed suddenly bereft of color, or even animation. His mouth was agape, and he shook his head slowly from side to side as if saying "No." With a visible effort, he recovered some of his composure.

"What happened, lad? My brother is not killed, surely?" Decatur stood in the quarter as the other vessel approached. Even though he shouted the words, the emotions that must have surged through him were plainly evident.

"Sir, I am afraid so, sir. He led a boarding party after the pirates struck, and their captain drew a pistol and shot him, sir. In the head. I am afraid he died most quickly. And I am sorry, sir." The report was given in a trembling voice, fraught with emotion both at the loss of the midshipman's captain and at being the bearer of such dreadful tidings. I was stunned at the horror of the treachery and the enormity of this tragedy. I glanced again at Captain Decatur; his shoulders were slumped, his head lowered, and he grasped tightly to a shroud as if unable to support himself without it. For a moment, I thought of Edward and what a devastating blow it would be for me were he to be shot.

"Sir!" our captain, after collecting himself, shouted to the midshipman. "Take our prize in tow, if you please. I will cast it off as we must make all haste and a vessel in tow would only act to slow us." As Decatur quickly gave orders, the polacca was set adrift, and our gunboat turned to move with alacrity toward the enemy. Our oarsmen, only moments before tired and spent with the rigors of battle, were now vital and strong, pulling for all they were worth, the quicker they might avenge our captain's tragedy.

The messenger had surely identified the enemy vessel captained by the treacherous villain who killed James Decatur and, after a chase of barely one hour, we were within a musket shot of it. During that interval, I noticed that I held no thoughts of butterflies or twelve-pound shot, beyond that which I hoped we would be pouring into the enemy. I had shaken off the terrors of my previous encounter, and, like our crew, was now intent on standing with our captain in his retribution. Judd, his eyes as hard as flint, and I shared a glance and a barely perceptible nod, confirming an unspoken agreement.

"FIRE!" Decatur cried out, and our cannon spoke with a mighty roar, sending a bag of grape into the deck of the vessel. Our vessel never hesitated, but continued its headlong rush straight into the enemy, propelled by men who drew their strength from their love for our captain and, without the exchange of a single word, had resolved, each in his own mind, to right this wrong.

With a resounding *crunch* of splintering wood, our gunboat landed alongside the pirate's polacca. Even before we heaved grapnels, our men were shouting their blood curdling yells and arranging themselves to board. Quickly we were secured alongside with hook and hemp, and then we were aboard them, scrambling over bulwarks to attack with pistol, cutlass, and hatchet. I spied a towering figure, cloaked in a white robe and holding aloft an enormous scimitar, standing on what I took to be the quarterdeck. He let out a mighty roar as our men landed on his deck. Without a word, Decatur made straight for him, armed with only his sword.

I and the others of our boarders fought the pirates with pistol and cutlass, halfpike and hatchet; we took it harder than in our first encounter, and I saw several of our men go down. Whether they were dead or not I could not tell, and I had little time to wonder as I fought side by side with Judd. We had both discharged our pistols, with some less luck this time, and used the spent weapons as bludgeons while swinging our cutlasses about us to inflict as much damage as possible. I wounded several who, after feeling the edge of my steel, backed away. Judd enjoyed some success as well, and I was aware of several of the white-cloaked demons lying blood-soaked at his feet.

We stood shoulder to shoulder amidships in the polacca, surrounded by Americans fighting like badgers against these scoundrels. I had broken the blade on my cutlass, striking it against the heavier blade of a native sword, and was saved from being split like a chicken by a thrust from a sailor's halfpike.

"I thank you, sir," I shouted to him as he turned to take on yet another opponent. The sailor grinned at me and waved his hand dismissively. As he did, Captain Decatur's long ago admonition to a young and untried midshipman flashed through one part of my mind. I recall actually smiling as I picked up a dropped tomahawk, very much aware of my surroundings, but hearing him say, "Oliver, *they* call you sir, not the other way 'round!"

As I straightened, my newfound weapon in hand, a snarling Arab thrust at me with a short, evil-looking dagger. Without a thought, I screamed something unintelligible even to me and swung the hatchet; he stepped back, his startled and confused gaze shifting between the gory, spurting stump of his wrist and his hand, which now lay on the deck, still clutching the dagger. Clearly, he had no further interest in the fight.

Caught up with a blood-lust I could scarcely believe, I looked around me, seeking another adversary. Instead, I caught sight of our captain as he parried with his sword a blow from the huge scimitar wielded by the giant corsair, the one I had earlier deduced was the pirate captain. So strong was the blow that Decatur's lighter weapon, like mine, broke off at the hilt, leaving him unarmed in the face of this great bear of a man. But for him, there was no convenient sailor to wield a halfpike in his defense.

A quick, though mercifully, poorly aimed stroke from the pirate left Decatur with a gash in his arm that flowed freely. He seemed quite unaware of it as he stepped toward his assailant, grabbed the scimitar and wrested it away from his attacker.

"Judd! The captain!" I rushed toward the polacca's quarterdeck, my dirk and hatchet, both bloodied, one held aloft, one at my hip, to attack. Judd was close on my heels.

The fighting continued all around the two captains, who now wrestled on the deck armed only with their strength of arm and will; the struggling officers, unnoticed by most, were only two more combatants in the melee. The noise was fearsome: clashing steel, shouts and curses in two languages, the *thump* of pike shafts banging off edged weapons and flesh, and the stamping of leather shod feet all blended into an unimaginable cacophony. I was unaware of the pounding of long guns, ours or theirs, though I am quite sure both sides continued their cannonade unabated. As we neared the quarterdeck, we had to fight a few of the white-clad pirates away; a single stroke with cutlass or hatchet usually convinced them to give way, that and the fearsome look we both wore.

As we neared the place where the two captains now wrestled on the deck, I saw happily that Decatur was uppermost in the intertwined pair. Then a white-clad arm raised a cutlass, perhaps one of our own he had snatched, to make a killing blow on our captain's unprotected head. My heart stopped as I witnessed what I was sure to be the demise of my captain, and I held my breath, too far away to do naught but shout a warning, unheard by any but those close at hand.

An American seaman, one I recognized as Daniel Frasier, with both arms rendered useless by cruel wounds, saw the deadly blow about to fall, and threw himself across Decatur's shoulders just as the lethal blade fell. The man absorbed the stroke intended as fatal to his captain and received a severe gash in his scalp for his efforts, but Decatur was unscathed. The sailor, bleeding profusely, rolled off the struggling captains and the Tripolitan, being bigger and stronger by half than our own captain, quickly turned the tables and had Decatur pinned below him on the deck.

He held him down with his body weight and one hand which grasped Decatur's throat; with his other, he drew and raised a dagger which he clearly intended to plunge in his helpless victim's chest. The captain, his face scarlet with the effort and lack of breath, realized what was about to happen and with his left hand seized the pirate's raised arm, holding the fatal plunge at bay while, with his right hand, he reached into his pocket.

Suddenly a shot, strangely muffled, rang out and the pirate captain crumpled atop Decatur. With some considerable exertion, Decatur rolled the lifeless body of the pirate off him and stood, a little unsteadily at first. In his right hand, hanging limply at his side, was the pistol our captain had secreted in his pocket and managed to twist around until it was aimed into his adversary's chest.

In seconds, it seemed, the splendid news of our captain's triumph had spread throughout the polacca. With the death of their leader, the remaining corsairs quickly laid down their arms and struck, having no wish to join their brothers, and their captain, in paradise. The polacca was ours, and the treacherous barbarian who had murdered James Decatur was dead, but at greater cost than any would have wished.

Seventeen Tripolitans had died in this single fight, including their captain. For our part, none were killed and four were wounded, including the captain and the brave Seaman Frasier who saved Decatur from the fatal cutlass stroke. Frasier, aside from the blood that poured forth from his head wounds, giving him a decidedly horrifying appearance, seemed unfazed by either his cruel wounds or his role in saving the life of our captain. Of James Decatur's crew, several of whom had joined our attack, two received wounds, neither life threatening. And, of course, James Decatur was, as reported, killed by the Tripolitan pirate.

As we climbed aboard our gunboat, those who were able saw to the prisoners, securing them amidships after removing anything that might answer as a weapon from their reach. The dead corsairs were heaved, with no regrets or ceremony, into the sea. Our wounded straggled aboard, making themselves as comfortable as they could wherever they could find some room. Judd and I, with the assistance of two sailors and overseen by Captain Decatur, gently lifted the body of James from the polacca and laid it carefully in the stern, near to where our captain would stand once freed from the enemy vessel. Then the grappling irons were retrieved, our sails set and the oars manned.

With the damaged polacca in tow, we made our way toward the flagship as those who were unwounded tried to ease the pain and stanch the bleeding of their less fortunate mates. Once again, both Judd and I had escaped without damage. Our captain, jacketless, with his wound wrapped in a piece of now-crimson linen that served only to slow the bleeding, had survived the encounter with his brother's murderer. He seemed, to Judd and me, to have regained control of both himself and the crew with the same quiet confidence and competence that had served him, and us, so well. Privately, I thought he appeared suddenly older by far than his twenty-five years and tired. I can not imagine the emotions I would feel were my brother to be taken from me in such a way; even though he was a captive held in unseemly conditions, he was alive, and I knew that I would see him again.

I looked around us, seeking to determine the fate of the others of our little squadron who had fought these villains. Most had disengaged from their combat; one had not. As I watched, horrified, I saw one of our gunboats go on board of a larger pirate vessel. I thought it might have been one of the galleys that we noticed earlier. Then, as the American sailors scrambled to board their latest adversary, I watched the two vessels separate to a distance where not a single additional brave sailor could join their comrades on the deck of the polacca.

I snatched a glass from a startled Neapolitan sailor and focused it on the fight. There was, I could see, a pitched battle joined on the pirate's deck, and there appeared many more white-robed figures than not.

"Judd, Judd! Look here. One of our boats is in trouble. Those men can not help but be overwhelmed by the pirates . . . there . . . look." I handed my messmate the glass, pointing with unwavering hand at the action unfolding a mere mile away. "Can we not help them?"

Devon took the glass and, resting it on a shroud, studied the drama before him.

"That could only be Lieutenant Trippe. He's one of the Vixens. And it appears you're right, Oliver; he clearly hasn't enough men to take that pirate. Why his own don't return to help I can not imagine." He continued to watch as Trippe and his handful of sailors fought savagely with the hoard of cutthroats on the pirate's deck.

"Looks to me like they're holding their own, Oliver. Seems like there's a passel of white robes either jumpin' or bein' thrown overboard." Judd described the action to me; what I really wanted was the glass so I could see for myself, but it appeared I would have to settle for his description. I watched with unaided eye and listened to my senior.

"Aye, appears Trippe might prevail, after all," he remarked with as much emotion as he might have used to comment on a change in the wind. "Hold now! He's gone down! Trippe has disappeared . . . can't see him . . . just a bunch of Arabs where he was. Now they're breaking up . . . my God! He's up. Looks like he got himself cut up some, but he's still fighting! I can't believe it!" Now Judd's tone was charged with excitement. I had never been otherwise!

"Look there! The gunboat's coming back alongside." I could see that without the glass, and Judd swung the telescope around, seeking the American vessel.

"Aye. Reckon Trippe'll hang on, long as they get alongside quick." Judd had measured the distance separating the two vessels with his more experienced eye and pronounced the outcome with some certainty.

Then, amid a faint clamor that sounded like cheering, the gunboat was back alongside the galley, and our sailors were rushing to the aid of their comrades. Without the glass, which Judd still held, I could tell little of what was happening aboard the galley, but now with three encounters with these devils behind me, I knew that the Americans would have a bloody fight on their hands before, and if, the pirates succumbed. A shout close at hand and flurry of activity drew my attention forward and stopped Judd's running description of the fighting. Lieutenant Trippe would have to manage without my help!

Barely a musket shot in front of us was our own Lieutenant Hobbs and *Enterprise* bearing away to unmask her weather guns for another broadside at the fortress. With deafening roars, seeming almost to be one continuous roll of thunder, the starboard side cannon fired in a rippling sequence. I had heretofore only experienced the roar of long guns from behind them; hearing their thunder close at hand from the muzzle end was quite a revelation! I shook my head in an effort to clear it. In the ringing silence that followed the broadside, Decatur bellowed to the schooner. Hobbs hove to and took us aboard. The two vessels, our gunboat and the prize, were quickly secured astern to join an enemy vessel captured by Lieutenant Lawrence and, of course, Lawrence's gunboat. No sooner were we aboard than Judd pointed out to Hobbs the situation in which Lieutenant Trippe found himself. There was a brief conversation to which I was not privy, during which Hobbs looked repeatedly through a long glass. Then, after some pointing and Judd taking a turn with the glass, they separated, Judd to join me in the waist, and Hobbs to continue with his duties on the quarterdeck. For want of specific direction, I had followed Decatur and some of the wounded men to the midships of the schooner, where a knot of men gathered. Some, watched by all eyes as they passed, had carried the captain's brother's corpse forward and set it carefully in a shady and protected spot.

Our first lieutenant looked some the worse for wear; he had received several wounds to his person. Reliance Wakefield, who had set up shop in the waist, was busy repairing the damage. Both had seen and recognized James Decatur's lifeless form; their eyes locked momentarily and then fixed on the captain's. It was apparent, even to me, even with no words spoken, that they grieved for his loss.

"Captain, please. Sit here in my stead so that Reliance might see to your arm. It appears a cruel wound and still bleeding profusely." Lawrence pushed the medical officer's hands away from his person and stood quickly upon seeing Decatur.

"No, no, James. But I thank you for your concern." Captain Decatur smiled at his first lieutenant and motioned Wakefield to continue sewing and bandaging Lawrence's wounds. "Mister Wakefield, when you have finished your ministrations to the first lieutenant, please see to those of my crew who have suffered wounds, some cruel, indeed, at the hands of the pirates. Then, should you have a free moment, you might have a look at my arm. I am quite certain it will keep until then. I shall be on the quarterdeck." Decatur turned to step aft and stopped.

He turned back to Lawrence and Wakefield and smiled fiercely at his medical officer who, for a moment, stopped squinting at the needle he was threading and glanced over his spectacles at the captain.

"We paid 'em some 'tribute,' Reliance, old friend. And I'll warrant, more to come!" A somber nod and a quick smile satisfied Decatur, who turned about again and left to resume command of his vessel. The slump of his shoulders gave away his grief and tired resignation, and his step seemed heavy.

"Oliver, I asked Hobbs to head over toward Trippe . . . see if we might be able to help him. I'd guess he'll be doin' that now. Less'n Decatur won't allow it. Hobbs knows Lieutenant Trippe, he is the little brother of the Marine lieutenant we had aboard *Argus*, you remember him . . . stocky fellow with a square face and hard eyes. You'll no doubt recall him as captain of our Marine detachment on the brig. Still aboard *Argus* far as Hobbs knows. He also thought that fellow tangling with the pirates will likely do alright; he's nearly as tough as his big brother."

We both jumped when our battery fired yet another broadside and was immediately echoed by the thunder of *Constitution's* 24-pounders. I saw noticeable impacts in the walls of the castle and fortress as stones fell and people scattered. The two brigs also paid tribute with telling success to the Bashaw's gunboats which had not retreated to the protection of the fortress's guns, now that most of the Americans were clear of them. They quickly turned tail in the face of this new onslaught of iron and started back toward the fortress and its battery.

"Signal from *Constitution*, sir, to all ships. Says 'Cover enemy approaching from east.' Shall I acknowledge, sir?"

"Aye, do so. Mister Hobbs, you may bear off some and we'll have a run at those devils coming out from the rocks, there." Decatur pointed with his good arm at a half dozen polaccas, still several miles distant, but now standing out from where they had remained during most of the engagement. Their striped sails ballooned out, and they each had a 'bone in their teeth' as they rode the freshening breeze toward the American fleet. "Load grape and canister, if you please, Bradford. Both sides." Decatur's voice carried easily forward to where the sweating gunner's mate was scurrying from gun to gun, filling in for missing crew and sighting each gun to ensure its shot would tell. He looked up at the sound of the captain's voice and waved in acknowledgement.

"Mister Baldwin, Mister Devon! You may take your stations for quarters, if you please. I am quite certain that Bradford will be glad of some help!" Lieutenant Lawrence, sewn and bandaged to the best of the surgeon's ability, was restoring order to our deck and taking charge of fighting the ship while the captain maneuvered us into position. The surgeon had shifted his attention to several of our sailors who stood, sat, or lay about his impromptu hospital. I noticed Daniel Frasier, the man who had taken the blow meant for Captain Decatur, lying on the deck in a widening pool of blood.

As Judd and I moved off to see to the guns, I stole a glance to weather to see how Lieutenant Trippe was faring in his own battle against the corsairs. Well, I hoped, as we were now headed off to deal with the new threat and away from Trippe's fight. I looked hard, barely believing my own eyes.

"Judd. Have a look, will you. Trippe must have prevailed. Looks like he's takin' the pirates in tow!" I was delighted that we had taken yet another of the enemy's ships. Perhaps now those barbarian devils might realize that Americans were not afraid of fighting them, even hand to hand!

Judd, already involved with his battery and too busy to look, waved a hand in response. I hurried on to the forward battery, where Bradford squatted behind the forward-most long gun. He had a pry-bar wedged under the carriage and another sailor stood ready to force the quoin further under the barrel, depressing its aim, should Bradford deem it necessary. The gunner's mate looked up as I bent over to sight down the barrel.

He smiled slightly and pointed at the next gun in line. Then he returned his attention to the train of the gun. His faced was streaked in sweat that had cut trails through the grime of powder coating most of him from the middle of his shirtless chest. A dirty bandanna was tied around his forehead and another loosely around his throat, and his bare arms were singed and smudged with the heat of his gun and the residue of his efforts.

"You may fire as they bear, gentlemen." Lawrence's voice carried clearly to the forward guns. As I looked over the bulwark from my position, now behind the second gun, I saw we were about to engage three polaccas that seemed well within our, and their, range. Slightly astern and to our weather sailed *Vixen* and *Nautilus*. It seemed the pirates were matched ship-for-ship; I wondered for an instant whether or not they would try to board us as was their habit. Perhaps, I thought, they might have learned that fighting American sailors hand to hand is an easy road to paradise, not to victory. Then Bradford's gun fired, a demand for my attention that would not be denied.

I stooped and squinted through the smoke, sighting my piece. Then, as *Enterprise* rolled up, I saw an enemy ship seemingly balanced on the top edge of the barrel.

"Fire!" I cried to the acting gun captain who immediately jammed his linstock into the priming hole. I stepped to the side as sparks jumped from the sizzling powder and burned down to the cartridge. With a mighty *BOOM*, the gun fired and hurled itself backwards, coming to rest at the limits of its breechings. While the limited crew I had clapped onto the tackles and waited for the swabber to ream out the barrel, I peeked over the bulwark to see what success I and Bradford had enjoyed.

The middle of the approaching polaccas had taken the brunt of both Bradford's and my shots; her mast seemed to teeter and the rigging around it was well shot up. I could tell naught about the effect of our loads on the crew, but it seemed reasonable to me that they should have suffered equally with the rig.

Now more of our sailors, both the undamaged ones and those less fortunate, bandaged and patched as well as Surgeon Wakefield could manage, took their positions behind our guns. Judd's guns spoke, followed quickly by those further aft, offering voluble testimony that we had most of our battery fully, or nearly so, manned and were pursuing a course that offered naught but disaster to the approaching Tripolitan pirates. *Vixen* and *Nautilus* echoed our sentiment, each scoring hits on one or another of the enemy ships. *Constitution's* deeper voice thundered all the while, maintaining a steady bombardment of the castle and fort. Farther to weather, I could see our two bomb vessels throwing mortar shells into the town, well behind the wall along the waterfront. *Syren* and *Argus*, standing off and on to our west, fired shot after shot into the castle itself, as well as into the polaccas which had sought the protection of the fort.

Of course, none of our efforts went unanswered; the approaching pirates, as well as those which had retreated, maintained an uneven counter fire at all of us. The sharp crack and subsequent deeper resonating echoes of the guns in the fort and castle bespoke their participation in our warm action. Some of their shots told, and, while *Enterprise* remained unscathed, we could see that our colleagues in the brigs and, more particularly, *Constitution*, suffered from the attention of the Tripolitans. But as I watched the skyline of the city against the late afternoon sky, I saw a spire-topped tower, a minaret, as they are popularly called here, spew a torrent of stone from its midsection, then teeter, and fall, leaving a void on the horizon. A brilliant shot from either *Constitution* or one of the brigs.

A faint cheer drifted to us, and a quick look told us *Vixen* had scored a telling hit in one of the polaccas; the enemy vessel's mast leaned precariously to leeward, then slowly, almost ponderously, toppled into the water. The sudden drag it created caused the corsair to bear off, nearly broaching, directly into her sister close aboard. The resulting chaos of spars, yards and cordage mixed with the entwined and broken oars of both vessels created a perplexing puzzle for the Arab crews to unravel.

The two remained tangled as guttural cries floated over the water to us. With the two of them snarled up in each other, we were presented with a splendid target. I tapped Bradford on his shoulder and pointed. He at once took my meaning, and we shifted our aim to the tangle of ships, spars, oars, and rigging. Judd's battery and the other guns aft continued to pour round, canister and grape shot into the remaining ship, still coming at us with a vengeance. Our consorts, *Vixen* and *Nautilus* continued their own efforts, firing on all three targets.

Our range had closed to what amounted to point blank; I could not imagine more than five hundred yards separated us from the two ships still on board one another. The third one, continuing to close with us, was receiving fire not only from Judd's guns, but also from the guns on *Nautilus*; *Vixen* continued to maintain a significant rate of fire on her first target, now combined into two. So far, none of the American schooners had received more than a ball through a sail, and, while each of us had received our share of the Tripolitan's attention, we all remained, for the most part, intact.

Decatur and Lawrence had adjusted our course so that our guns continued to bear and give us all the advantage they could. It told; suddenly the remaining polacca wore around and, with a poorly laid parting shot aimed at the closest schooner, *Vixen*, headed back the way she had come, toward the protection of the eastern breakwater, well within range of the castle's guns. Her captain apparently had no love for his brothers in the other two ships, as he left them to deal with each other and us and to find their own way to safety or paradise as their fates might decree.

Then, with a crescendo of shouts, gestures, and, though we were quite unable to decipher a word, curses, I am sure, those two got themselves separated. With their rigging and lateen yards all ahoo, they turned tail and, under the poorly coordinated but obviously frantic efforts of their oarsmen, straggled after their brother to seek the safety of the breakwater and the shore batteries. Paradise could wait!

"Hold your fire, lads! We got 'em on the run! They'll think twice about trying that again!" Lawrence's voice was gleeful. As we dragged our guns back from the bulwark, *Enterprise* hardened up and the sail-handlers trimmed for a course toward deeper water. A glance astern showed *Vixen* and *Nautilus* had followed suit.

Bradford, even more grime covered than he had been, stood erect next to his gun, stretched, and, wiping his face with a bit of waste, grinned at me.

"Any time you want to sail as a gun captain, Mister Baldwin, there'll be a spot for you on my guns!" His smile broadened as he looked me over. "Reckon you got the clothes for the job now, too! They won't let you into the gunroom in them!" His voice sounded distant, muffled, as it penetrated the ringing that still persisted in my ears.

I looked down; my shirt had somehow gotten torn from stem to stern, and one sleeve had been rent from elbow to wrist. My white trousers were filthy. My mother's face, wide-eyed in dismay at the state of my clothes, flashed into my mind as I thought of the time I would have restoring them to an acceptable level of cleanliness. I smiled in spite of it; Bradford had paid me the highest compliment of my almost-one-year Navy career! An even better one than the compliment Captain Decatur had paid me. I wiped a hand across my sweating face making the sailor laugh aloud.

"You got all that black mess on your face, sir. Take a look at your hand."

I did; both were filthy from the powder residue and the grease on the gun. Now that grime had mixed with the sweat on my face. I suspected I must look as bad as Bradford and laughed with him.

"Aye, Bradford. But you should see your own self. I can't possibly look as bad as you!"

Judd chose that moment to arrive; he was . . . well, not spotless to be sure, but he certainly bore no resemblance to either me or the gun captain.

"Well, I reckon we gave them a good . . . Oliver, what in the name of all that's holy have you been doing? You look like you were wrestling with a pig! And lost!" He started to laugh, and soon the three of us were joined by our gun crews as we guffawed and bellowed, slapped one another on our backs, and congratulated each other on the fine job we did against the corsairs.

CHAPTER TWENTY-TWO

O ur squadron, called off by the commodore while *Constitution* maintained a heavy covering fire, had reassembled outside the eastern breakwater before dark, and the captains were all called to repair aboard the flagship. Captain Decatur took with him to *Constitution* his brother's corpse, as well as the person of Daniel Frasier for further medical attention. Our surgeon accompanied his patient and the captain. We surmised that Reliance Wakefield felt he was unqualified to do more than stanch his bleeding and sew up a few of his wounds. He was particularly concerned about the deep, cruel hurt to the sailor's head caused by the Tripolitan cutlass. The prizes were transferred to the flagship as well, unburdening the smaller of us from the drag they created astern. Our bomb vessels and mortars retired also, to be taken in tow by the flagship. Finally, boats shuttled back and forth ferrying the Tripolitan prisoners, wounded and intact alike, to the frigate, as none of the smaller vessels had room to hold them.

As we drew close to *Constitution*, we could see that her rigging and sails were a good deal cut up by shot, and even from where we sailed alongside her, we could plainly observe that her mainmast had received a cruel wound, from a twenty-four-pound ball, according to the gunner, leaving a substantial hole nearly through the lower mast itself. I wondered how it continued to stand.

"I'd warrant we have their wretched aim to thank that the flagship wasn't more cut up, Oliver. That and the grape she kept layin' into their batteries from so close in. Commodore must have sailed to within three cable-lengths of the wall to do the level of damage he did! I wouldn't have wanted to be ashore and on the receivin' end of *that*, by God!" Judd stood with me as we watched from the rail the activity on the frigate.

With now several encounters with these scoundrels to my credit, I felt qualified to offer my own thought. "Aye, they must have suffered considerably in the fortress. Looks like *Constitution's* guns did more than cut up their walls and towers; seems like there's fewer houses poking up from behind the walls there. And I imagine the shells from the bomb vessels took their toll as well. I wonder how many they lost of their gunboats and galleys; I'd reckon it was considerable. Not to mention the several we all took as prizes!"

As I spoke, it occurred to me that Edward had been locked up somewhere in the middle of all that! *Oh, my stars! I hope nothing has happened to him or the others there with him,* I added with a twinge of guilt. *Would that he has remained safe throughout our bombardment!*

"Judd, where do you suppose they're keeping the Philadelphias? I mean, could they have . . . do you think . . . well, they'd be in a dungeon, somewhere, right?"

Judd took my meaning at once. "Oh, no, Oliver. I'd think the Bashaw would keep them locked up where they couldn't escape during the attack. I mean, think of the confusion and chaos that must have been rife there; would have been the perfect opportunity for those lads to make a run for it, given half a chance. No, I don't think you have to worry about Edward and the others. They likely heard it and maybe even felt the ground shakin', but I would wager they weren't anywhere exposed."

That eased my mind, and I hoped that our bombardment might make their captors consider giving up the sailors and officers from our late frigate. *Wouldn't that be glorious!* Then we could end this business and go home.

By the time Captain Decatur's boat returned to *Enterprise*, it was full dark, and the ships of our squadron tarried safely offshore, sailing off and on in company. Judd and I were taking our ease in the cockpit, having just finished our supper, when Mister Lawrence knocked once on the doorframe and stepped in, bending his tall frame through the opening and, so he would not have to remain stooped, took a seat at the foot of our table.

"Gentlemen," he offered as he sat. His somber tone warned us that our celebration of the day's events was done. "As you may have noticed, the captain did not return with his boat; indeed, he has sent word that he will remain with his brother throughout the night. But he also has requested that those of our officers who wish it join him in the flagship on the morrow to witness the burial at sea. As Lieutenant James Decatur was our only casualty of today's action, I suspect that Commodore Preble will personally commit his body to the deeps. And even though Captain Decatur implied that only those who wish to should go, it is my suggestion that not going might only show disrespect to a great man who has suffered an incomprehensible loss." He stopped and looked from one to the other of us, seeking something in our expressions.

I was about to offer to remain aboard the schooner to keep the watch so another might go in my place (I am uncomfortable in such situations) when Lawrence looked directly at me and, like a gypsy fortuneteller, read my mind. "He has asked Mister Hobbs to again keep the watch on *Enterprise*, since he was not in the action today, so as the rest of us might attend. You should both plan on accompanying us."

Well, that settled that! Uncomfortable or no, I would be there; I would not want to be thought disrespectful, especially as I held our captain in such high esteem.

As two bells in the morning watch signaled nine, we, the officers and midshipmen (I still had to remind myself that we were only two now with Thomas ashore and James . . . well, James gone now) assembled in the waist to be rowed across to the flagship for a disagreeable assembly. We wore our dress uniforms, including swords for the officers and dirks for Judd and me. I had scrubbed my skin raw to remove the grime from the previous day's activities and had found, to my great joy, that my dress uniform had suffered little since we left Syracuse; it seemed so long ago.

We arrived on *Constitution's* deck after a short and mercifully dry ride in the cutter. The officers and mids of the other ships were assembling with us. Under the direction of Mister Lawrence, we all took our places in ranks by ship and seniority. Standing on the spar deck with us, but forward of us, was the ship's company of the frigate, those, I assumed, who were not occupied with a watch. Commodore Preble stood at the foot of the mainmast talking in quiet tones to our captain. Both were dressed in their finest uniforms complete with their several decorations and swords. Near at hand, but closer to the bulwark, was a flag-draped sailcloth shroud in the form of a man. A large round ball could be seen at the lower end of the pall. I must admit to giving the damaged lower mast a more careful scrutiny than I might have under different circumstances, but in the event, it gave me exercise for my mind as well as an occupation for my eyes, save staring at my grief-stricken commander and his shroud-covered brother.

Then the commodore was speaking in glowing terms of our action of the day previous, using such words as "heroic," "glorious," "honorable," "gallant," and "daring." He gave the account of James Decatur's demise, emphasizing the treacherous behavior of the Tripolitan pirate who, through deceit and "inhuman behavior, cut down our brother-in-arms, the brother of our dear and valiant friend." I watched Captain Decatur during the commodore's speech; I saw no movement, recognition, or signal of acknowledgement during the whole of it. He stood ramrod-straight with an unwavering gaze focused somewhere distant. I imagined he was recalling memories of growing up with his brother in Philadelphia, standing up for him in winter snowball fights and uneven wrestling matches in the schoolyard, much as Edward had for me until he went off to the Navy. Of course, the Decatur brothers were closer in age than Edward and I and so likely had more time to develop a closer bond. I wondered, were I in his place, would I be able to maintain such a dignified composure.

At the appropriate point, Preble nodded to *Constitution's* bosun who, with his perfectly turned out group of eight sailors, lifted the board on which the flag-draped shroud rested and moved it some six feet to rest on the bulwark. As the Marine detachment presented arms, then fired a salute, the commodore read the words from his Bible, and the officers assembled doffed their hats in salute to a fallen comrade. At this point, Captain Decatur stepped to the rail and stood quietly next to his brother's body. He rested a hand on the flag-draped form, and, while I saw his lips moving, I could hear no words even though the ship was as silent as could be imagined.

When he stepped back and looked up, the board was tilted. From beneath the flag, to the accompaniment of a single muffled drum, the remains of James Decatur slid into the waters of the Mediterranean Sea with a soft splash. A dull *thud* from forward signaled a salute from Lieutenant Decatur's late command, *Nautilus*. Then it was ended. Preble shook hands with Captain Decatur, presented him with the flag that had previously covered his late brother, and, with a nod to Captain Robinson who commanded the flagship, gave permission for the hands and us to be dismissed.

It was a somber group that departed the *Constitution's* deck that morning; but under the gloomy exterior, and more noticeably in the midshipmen, myself included, was the satisfaction that we had exacted suitable payment for the death of Lieutenant Decatur, and the pride of acting with honor in the conflict. I would think the joy of our survival lurked within each of us as well; I know I certainly felt it profoundly and gratefully.

"Did you notice the commodore and Captain Decatur talking with Lieutenant Blake, Oliver? Didn't look to me like neither was congratulating him on the fine job he did yesterday!" Judd whispered conspiratorially into my ear as we waited at the break in the bulwark for the boat from *Enterprise* to come alongside.

I had noticed Blake, after the officers from *Argus* were dismissed, in deep conversation with Decatur and Preble, but Judd's comment took a moment to register. I looked around to see what he might be talking about. Then I recalled we had all seen Blake's gunboat hanging back as we went into the first action yesterday. He had been firing but, even to me, it seemed ineffective; I could remember none of his shots telling. Now Devon's remark made sense to me.

"Aye, Judd. I did see them, but it didn't signify. You think that's what was happening? That Preble was taking him to task for not fighting?"

Then the boat was there, and we were climbing down the boarding battens on *Constitution* with little chance to continue our conversation. Judd merely caught my eye and winked at me as we stepped into the boat.

Once back on the schooner, and having offered suitable condolences to our captain, Lieutenant Lawrence told us we would spend the day re-rigging our prizes from the lateen arrangement to a sloop rig. Battle damage would be repaired, and, with continued fair weather, we would fight again tomorrow. The squadron remained in close formation under short sail; after all, we had nowhere to go, and each ship would need only a minimum number of hands to manage her. Lawrence charged me and Bosun Anderson with overseeing the rig change to one of our prizes, still astern of the flagship, while Judd would assist Hobbs and Morris to manage the repairs to our gunboat and, time permitting, one of the mortars which had suffered a few stove planks.

"Sail! Sail! Comin' out th' harbor!" The cry from the masthead on *Constitution* was heard plainly aboard most of the squadron, and I think, without exception, every man topside stopped what he had been doing to look.

"They comin' out to fight us out here?"

"How many of 'em comin'?"

"They gonna get whupped again, same as yesterday!"

"Aye, worse, I'd warrant!"

That the men and ships were unready and, at that moment, ill-prepared to fight signified not a whit! We showed the pirates a thing or two yesterday and, by God, we'd do it again. Right now, should that be their choice!

But it wasn't the corsairs coming out; in fact, it was a single brig, quite small, and flying French colors, that left the harbor. Commodore Preble induced her captain to heave to alongside the frigate. While we could hear little of what transpired when the Frenchman went aboard *Constitution*, we did see some dozen and more Tripolitans walk or get carried into the French ship, which shortly left the flagship and headed back the way she had come, into Tripoli's harbor.

"Commodore Preble's sent the worst wounded back into that den of iniquity as a gesture of goodwill. Thinks it might make some difference to the Americans they're holding. Get 'em better treatment. Maybe even a few of 'em released."

When I heard Mister Hobbs, who had been in *Constitution* seeking some lumber for his repair efforts, tell Lieutenant Morris what had happened, my heart leaped; would Edward be among those released? Or if not, would he be a beneficiary of better treatment?

I had heard naught from my brother for some weeks, his last letter leaving me disheartened at the cruel treatment he and his fellows had suffered after our attack on the late frigate, *Philadelphia*. I dared not imagine what yesterday's event would lead to for them. Perhaps with the return of their more severely wounded brothers, the pirates might be moved to exercise compassion. Or not.

We found out later, when the Frenchman returned, that Preble had also sent in letters to the Prime Minister and the French Consul offering to negotiate once more with the Bashaw for the release of our comrades and establish a treaty between our two countries. Of course, the brig brought out no reasonable reply, causing the commodore to rail against the pirates in general, the Bashaw in particular, and to promise further punishment on the morrow.

True to his word, the dawn of August seventh found us shifting cannon from two of the more badly damaged Tripolitan gunboats to others and preparing for a repeat of our earlier attack. Each boat was crewed and commanded by the same men who had sailed on August third, except for James Decatur, of course, and Lieutenant Blake, whose absence was noted by Judd and me with a nudge and a telling look. The addition of the captured Tripolitan vessels gave us a fleet of nearly a dozen, with the brigs and schooners ready to add their own weight of metal to the considerable firepower of the smaller vessels. Since the wind had veered to the north-northeast, the commodore kept the flagship a greater distance offshore so that, should she be disabled by enemy shot, she would not be blown onto the rocks and lost.

Decatur's division attacked a seven-gun battery ashore, successfully dismounting all but one of the guns; *Argus* accompanied our attack and fired several broadsides at a small group of enemy gunboats that appeared ready to leave the safety of the inner harbor and attack us. Her shots told and dissuaded the pirates from launching a counterattack.

"Flags on *Constitution*, sir." A sharp-eyed quartermaster cried out over the din of our cannonading. "*Argus'* number shown. Says 'Investigate sail to north. Give chase.' "

We watched as the brig signaled her acknowledgement and wore around. *Syren* moved quickly to take her place, leaving *Vixen, Enterprise,* and *Nautilus* to help the other gunboats should they need it.

Suddenly a thunderous explosion rent the air, overshadowing the steady concussions of the bombardment. It took us a moment to discover that gunboat number nine, manned by a crew and officers from *Syren,* had taken a red-hot shot into her magazine and been blown up. Her entire stern, from amidships aft, was gone. We watched in rapt fascination as a midshipman, we could not make out which, continued methodically to help several men load the forward gun and then fire it. As the remaining section of the boat sank from under them, they offered three lusty cheers; then they joined their mates in the water, clinging to bits of wreckage until nearby gunboats found them. The men were promptly picked up by other boats and pitched in immediately to assist those crews. The heroic mid, it turned out, was son to a captured officer on *Philadelphia.*

Another one of us! I wondered how many of us were kin to prisoners of the Bashaw.

As the wind was now freshening, *Constitution* made the signal to withdraw. By dusk, all the gunboats were once again in tow and headed to the northwest. Our attack, while surely successful, had been more costly than the first. We had several men killed, both in the explosion of number nine and in number eight which took two twenty-four-pound shot through her hull. Several others of the fleet had their rigging cut up, masts and yards shot away, and sails rent by balls. To our credit, the fleet fired nearly fifty mortar shells and over five hundred twenty-four-pound shot into the town and castle. To my joy, there was no hand-to-hand combat!

As evening settled over us, lights appeared—two ships coming toward us from the north. It appeared in the dim light of a crescent moon and the stars that they both were rigged to t'gallants, cracking on a press of canvas to make all possible haste.

"I'm about fought out, Oliver. I surely do hope they might be friendly." Judd and I stood shoulder to shoulder at the windward rail, watching as the lights approached. I had to agree; we were still grimy from our afternoon's efforts, sweaty from the unrelieved heat, and we had both struggled to stay awake during supper. I did not relish the thought of further action now.

"I think they must be, Judd; doesn't seem like anyone's too anxious about 'em." I shot a glance past him at our flagship where there seemed to be no unusual activity or signals.

"Oh, thank God! Look! They wouldn't be doing *that* if they were about to attack us. There! You see? One of 'em's showing signal lights aloft." Judd pointed at the barely visible flicker of white light showing high up in the larger of the two vessels.

Sure enough, answering lights winked in the *Constitution's* rigging and then in each of the others' in turn, ours included. We made our way aft to see what was afoot.

"That'll be *Argus* comin' back. And from the look of things, I'd say she's bringin' us some help! Cracked on, they are, too!" Lieutenant Morris held a night glass to his eye, studying the approaching ships.

As they drew nearer, the signal book showed that the lights on the larger belong ed to the frigate *John Adams*. Word of her arrival spread through the schooner and the fleet quickly.

"Reckon another frigate'll be some useful here."

"Teach them piratical bastards a lesson, we will now, I'd warrant. Finish this business right quick, now." Bosun Anderson's voice rose above several others. He echoed the excitement we all felt at this new arrival.

The two ships sailed in company with us throughout the night, reducing sail to keep pace as ribald and joyful comments were hurled across the water between them and the others in the squadron close enough to be heard.

At daybreak, the captains were ordered to repair aboard the flag, and we waited, hove to, with breathless anticipation for Decatur's return and how Preble would use his new asset. It was not to be.

We were called to the deck upon Decatur's return, and he wasted not a moment before he dashed our hopes for the future.

"You all saw *John Adams* join last evening in the company of the *Argus* brig. She brought out to us all manner of supplies which have been sorely needed for many months. And additional shot and powder." This brought forth a murmur of relief and joy from each of us, as well as several of the warrants and petty officers who stood nearby to hear what they might of the captain's words.

He went on. "Unfortunately, in order to carry those so urgently needed equipments, she had to off-load most of her gun carriages to another of the ships which will be arriving from the United States directly. Indeed, a notable force, including the frigates *President*, *Congress*, *Constellation*, and *Essex* are on their way; they were supposed to have left Norfolk only a week or so after *John Adams* did." Decatur paused while we offered subdued *huzzahs* to this happy news. For some reason, Decatur did not smile in spite of the prospect of this desperately needed augmentation to our squadron and what it would mean to our efforts against the pirates. We soon discovered the reason.

"*John Adams* also brought orders. Commodore Preble is to be relieved by Commodore Samuel Barron as quick as ever the force of frigates arrives here. Barron is in *President* and will assume responsibility for the furtherance of our

James D. Nelson, MD
737 W. Allens Lane
Philadelphia, PA 19119

RECEIPT

No. 429538

DATE 9-20-06

RECEIVED FROM Mp Jennifer Aguca

○ FOR RENT
○ FOR

twenty - five

copay oV

$ 25

		○ CASH	
ACCOUNT		☑ CHECK	FROM
PAYMENT	25 00	○ MONEY ORDER	TO
BAL. DUE		BY Dr Jane Nelson	

DOLLARS

1182

cause once here. Commodore Preble is to return home once he has turned over command."

The silence was complete. Each of his previous pronouncements had resulted in comment, cheers, or at the least, smiles; now the whole of us was stony-faced and reflective. Preble was a hard man, a driver. But he was fair to a fault, a fine sailor and a brilliant strategist who was committed to achieving victory in this endeavor. Now he was to be nipped in the bud, short of triumph and glory; that would fall to another, the beneficiary of our efforts to date. *We* had wreaked havoc on this land and its barbaric ruler with a force short of that which should have been assigned, at some considerable cost to us. Now, in light of this news, it appeared the additional force would finish it *and* a new commander in chief would reap the harvest.

As one, the officers gave voice to questions, comments, and their opinions of this unpleasant turn of events. Even Judd and I joined in, though in notably more subdued ... ur voices were barely audible, even to us. The ... ir feelings for a moment or two, then he raised

... tention to offer a final salute to the town, the ... e squadron from the United States arrives. We ... oast directly, off-load the supplies from *John* ... boats with her seamen and small craft since, ... e unable to participate in any action we take. ... ll have a look into the harbor at Tripoli and ... attack the fortress and castle yet again." This ... *uzzahs* that issued forth from, not only the ... the throng of men who now, having heard ... p.

... s Judd Devon stood with me on the quar- ... Hobbs—we discussed the sorrow of this

... le won't be the one to finish this. When ... as commodore, Morris and Dale, I can ... l axe-grinding afoot. Preble's done more i ... them did for their whole tour! I can scarce under-stand why Congress would relieve him *now* when we are making our presence felt so keenly." Judd shook his head and looked aloft at our straining sails as we raced back to the coast of Tripoli. "You're shivering aloft there, Oliver. Mains'l. Have a look. Hobbs is expecting you to notice it!"

I glanced at the compass in the binnacle; we were right on the course Decatur wanted. I looked again at the sails; the fore tops'l needed to be braced around some, also.

"You there! In the waist. Man the fore tops'l braces and have a hand on the main sheet. Mister Cartee, the wind appears to have veered around some. See to our sails, if you please. Helm, hold to the course you were given."

We watched in silence as the hands heaved around to adjust the set of our vast amount of canvas. With the fair breeze still east-northeast, the commodore had lost not a moment in turning the squadron and heading back to the south to finish, if he could, what he so desperately wanted to finish. With some luck, the wind would hold until we arrived and then work itself into a southerly quarter.

"I could not imagine, Judd, that anyone at home could possibly know what is acting here; consider that we only made our first attack barely one week ago. And while the business with the *Philadelphia* was surely splendid and *daring*," I smiled in spite of myself as I recalled my first blooding in battle and the words of Admiral Nelson about it, "they have known about *that* a long time. Maybe they thought the commodore wasn't doing enough."

"Well, I'd reckon even those landsmen in Congress know that operations can not be accomplished during the winter and spring. And even in the summer, the weather at times can be damn difficult! It wasn't that Preble didn't want to attack sooner than last week; we couldn't. You were here. You recall how many times we were blown offshore just as we were getting ready to attack." Judd was getting some worked up.

Not wanting to upset him further, I nodded in agreement, muttering something like, "Aye, I was there too," and, noticing the quartermaster retrieving his chip log, walked to the slate to record our new speed. Judd stood at the rail for a moment, then made his way to the hatch and disappeared below.

When we made the coastline, it was nearly full dark, and the commodore signaled all ships to shorten sail and wait out the night in company. At first light, he signaled *Argus* to perform a reconnoiter of the harbor upon which Captain Hull embarked at once.

"Did you hear that? Sounded like cannon fire. Listen!" Lieutenant Hobbs and I once again ruled the domain of the quarterdeck, and he stood there listening, his head cocked to one side as he strained to hear again what he had just called my attention to.

"Yes, sir. I thought I heard something. Perhaps it was thunder, or merely the pirates practicing; they could certainly use it!" I was being incautious in my remarks to Hobbs, but our continual pairing on watch had opened an easy comradeship between us and caused me, at times, to offer more candor than I might with another.

"There. There it is again. I know that's cannon fire. I wonder if *Argus* is having a hot time in there." He stopped and looked around us. "Oliver, go tell the captain what we think might be actin' yonder an' see if . . . well, just tell him. He'll know what to do."

I was back in mere minutes, Captain Decatur close astern in his shirtsleeves and hatless. Now the cannon fire was more frequent.

"Quartermaster, signal to the flag, if you please. 'Firing in the harbor. May

I investigate?' Quickly now." Decatur paced the deck, one hand smacking into the other and the old fire back in his eyes. Every so often he shot a glance at *Constitution*.

"There! There's our answer." He stopped pacing and stood impatiently in front of the quartermaster as he looked up the signal flying from the flagship's cro'jack yard.

"Sir, the flagship says '*Enterprise* and *Vixen* to investigate and assist if necessary.' Shall I respond?"

"A simple acknowledgement will answer nicely. Mister Hobbs, make your course west a quarter south and call the hands to quarters, if you please." Decatur looked aloft, studied the sail we had set, then added, "And we'll have tops'ls fore and main and the outer jibs as well."

I passed Lieutenant Lawrence as we went to our action stations, his on the quarterdeck and mine at the forward battery. He shot me a quizzical look, clearly caught unawares by our sudden call to action. I said nothing, figuring the captain would tell him all quick enough.

"Sail! Sail headin' this way. Point off the leeward bow. Looks like a brig." The lookout pointed to the sail that had only then made an appearance from behind the rocks east of the harbor. Since Bradford had our guns well in hand, powder and shot out, and his crews working to ready them, I jumped into the foreshrouds to see what I could of the approaching ship.

"Sir! Mister Lawrence! It is *Argus*. And she's low in the water!" I shouted immediately what I observed and received a wave from Decatur, too deep in conversation with the first lieutenant to even glance my way.

The lookout, perched on the tops'l yard well above me, cried out again. "Deck there. Deck! Looks like *Argus* got some corsairs comin' after her." Indeed, there were two row galleys under sails and oars following the American from a range I took to be just beyond the reach of Captain Hull's stern chasers.

Enterprise bore off, sheets were started, and we picked up some speed as we closed to help our comrade. *Vixen* followed, sailing some lower so as to pass *Argus* between us. As we got closer, we could see clearly that the ship was riding lower than she should, and there appeared to be two steady streams of water shooting out from the deck, streams as thick as a man's thigh. Something was desperately wrong! I came down to tend to my guns, though I sorely wanted to remain aloft to watch the action.

"Stand by your matches, lads! Take the first of the pirates." Lawrence's voice blew forward as clear and strong as if he had been right with us. *Vixen* would deal with the other.

"FIRE! FIRE AS YOU BEAR!" Lawrence bellowed as the schooner eased her head down some, opening our windward battery. Bradford sighted the first gun, glanced at me and nodded.

"Fire as you will, Bradford." The words had barely cleared my lips when the sailor shoved his glowing slow match into the touch hole, and the twelve-

pounder erupted in thunder, jumping backward as it belched out fire and a great
pall of lavender-tinged smoke. It was followed immediately by at least three others. After that I could hear little and had not a spare second to watch what the
others might be doing. We fired steadily, creating a great cloud of acrid, sulphurous, eye-searing smoke that blew back over us. The men hacked and
choked, spitting and wiping their eyes, but never hesitated in working the guns.

"That'll do it, lads. Hold your fire. Looks like they aren't interested in playing today!" Lawrence's joviality carried forward as well as his command.
Indeed, the galleys, both of them, had hauled their wind and were making for
the safety of the mole and the guns of the fortress. Cheers, hoots, and ribald
epithets issued from our sailors and were echoed by the men of *Vixen* as both
the American schooners put about to accompany the slogging brig.

"You figure Hull run her onto the hard, Oliver? I can't think what might
make her start her seams like she must have done to take all that water." Judd
watched as the two streams continued undiminished from the vessel. We had
easily caught up to her and, under now reduced sail, kept a station on her
weather quarter while *Vixen* stayed comfortably to leeward. Judd and I stood in
the schooner's bow and studied the other ship.

I was suddenly aware of another presence beside me and looked up to find
Captain Decatur stepping onto the bulwark at the shrouds, a speaking trumpet
in hand.

"Isaac! What has happened? And what can we do to help?" Decatur
shouted to his friend on the quarterdeck of the brig.

"Took a heavy ball just below the waterline, Stephen. Couldn't get a sail
fothered over it fast enough. Got her stuffed with everything we can find below
and slowed it down a good deal. Reckon the pumps can keep up now. Got a bit
dicey for a moment there. Chased two of the bastards off; didn't have a taste for
taking any more of my iron than they did, but then those other two showed up.
I was startin' to think we were in a right pickle until you and Smith showed."
He pointed over his shoulder to *Vixen*. "Thanks for the help. Guess they didn't
fancy taking on both of you!" Hull waved his hat and returned his attention to
his stricken ship.

By the time we returned to the fold of our fellows sailing off and on to the
east of the city, Captain Hull had managed to actually get more water out of
Argus than came in. While not dry, or seaworthy for that matter, she was no
longer in danger of foundering. He sailed his vessel carefully onto a strand of
beach while the tide was about half out and set men to repairing what turned
out to be substantial damage to the planking. Though there was no hole
through and through, the water could flow freely in should the hasty repairs
made during the fight fail. By morning, *Argus* was refloated and ready to
resume her role in our attack.

That attack was delayed by a signal, which we spied flying from the French
consulate ashore; it requested a boat and officer to come ashore.

"I believe we may have gotten the bastard's attention; 'pears he wants to treat with us." Hobbs seemed saddened by this turn of events. I knew he craved more action and hoped the captain would put him in command of a gunboat for the next attack. Let Lawrence, still dealing with his wounds, stay aboard the schooner!

We watched as *Nautilus* sailed close to the harbor entrance and then sent a lieutenant from *Constitution* ashore in a boat bearing a white flag.

"I'd warrant he's carrying an offer of some kind for the Bashaw, and maybe some letters for Cap'n Bainbridge." Hobbs watched through the glass as the cutter made the mole and the lieutenant was met and escorted toward the castle.

Letters! I should have had one ready for Edward. He certainly knows we're here, but he has no way of knowing that I am still in sound condition. I will pen something suitable to keep on hand in case there is another opportunity! I berated myself for the failure, not giving ear to Mister Hobbs' commentary on the progress our man was making ashore.

Judd and I were eating supper when the word moved through the schooner like a breeze rustles the leaves in the fall that the boat had returned to *Nautilus* and the latter was heading back to rejoin. We left our fare where it sat and raced up the ladder to see whatever we might. I secretly held the hope that the officer might have brought letters from Bainbridge and others. No sooner had the officer been returned to the flagship when flags broke out from the mizzen gaff, "Captains repair aboard."

By the time Decatur returned, it was full dark of a moonless night. Had the boat bearing him not carried a lantern, they could have made our side quite unobserved, to the likely chagrin of Mister Morris who held the watch with my colleague from the cockpit. At midnight, I arrived to relieve Judd while Hobbs took over from Morris.

"Decatur had a whole packet of papers when he came back, Oliver. Maybe he brought you something from your brother. I reckon we'll know in the morning." Then Judd proceeded to tell me the information necessary to the watch and left me thinking, waiting in hopeful anticipation, that his words might be prophetic. The minutes dragged by; with each utterance from Hobbs, I hoped for orders to "go and tell the captain this" or "fetch up the captain, Mister Baldwin," but the words never passed his lips. Perhaps the captain would just appear as he frequently did during the night.

It was not to be; the watch passed quietly in uneventful boredom. When Mister Lawrence relieved us an hour and more before the dawn, there was little of consequence to offer him by way of information. For me, I went to bed tired enough to sleep, having convinced myself that, had the captain brought a letter from Edward, he would have sent it to me. Obviously, the officer sent to the castle brought only words for the commodore, and likely only from the Bashaw.

"Gentlemen," Captain Decatur greeted us as we gathered on deck at his request in the morning. "Yesterday, the commodore sent the Bashaw an offer—

quite generous, I thought—for the release of the prisoners and an end to this affair. The Bashaw rejected it out of hand, sending back the exact same demand he had made some six months back. As a result, we will continue to attack his city, the fortress, and his castle with vigor in the hope of bringing the man to his senses before his domain is reduced to rubble. *Enterprise* will not immediately participate in the first of our renewed attacks tomorrow night, as Mister Lawrence will be taking her to Syracuse for fresh water, vegetables, provisions and ball and powder. As you may have heard from Mister Wakefield, some of the men have begun to show early signs of scurvy, which, if left untreated, would result in serious reductions to our force." He paused as a rumble of comment passed among us.

What would Decatur be doing? And who was to go with Lawrence and who would stay with the squadron?

"I am sure you are wondering why I will not be in command; the commodore has asked that Captain Chauncey of *John Adams* and I reconnoiter the harbor to determine just where the pasha is keeping his gunboats now and what is the condition of the shore batteries. Chauncey's men will man the boat and the other schooners will remain near at hand during the time we are in the harbor. I have determined that Mister Devon will be of use to us, and he will, therefore, accompany me." Another pause, a rumble of comment. I looked at Judd in time to see him wink his eye at me as he struggled to maintain the decorum expected of him.

"Mister Lawrence will be returning as quick as ever possible with the necessary provisions and, with moderate weather, I would fully expect to see you all again within a fortnight."

"Boat ahoy! Boat approaching from leeward, sir!" The lookout's cry interrupted the captain's remarks and we all turned to see the cutter from *John Adams* being rowed smartly towards us. Judd took the opportunity to hasten below for some clothes to take with him.

We hove to the schooner and gave proper respect to the captain as he and Devon climbed quickly over the bulwark and dropped into the waiting boat. Somebody yelled out, "Good fortune, Captain Decatur!" but I did not see who it might have been. Then Lawrence set our sails and our course to the north for Sicily.

CHAPTER TWENTY-THREE

"Judd! Look who I brought back! A changed man, he has assured me," I shouted down to Devon as he stood in the sternsheets of *John Adams'* cutter, approaching us as we lay hove to a pistol shot from the frigate. I did not see Captain Decatur and part of my conscious wondered about that. But right then, I was more excited about having our colleague returned to us and was reveling in the joy of telling Judd Devon about it. I could see clearly the look of surprise on Judd's face and, with a sideways glance, the concern behind the smile on Wheatley's.

The squadron was still in place, now to the west of Tripoli. I learned shortly from Judd that, beyond the visit Decatur and others had made to the harbor, very little had happened because a northwest gale had blown for nearly a week and forced everyone to seek the safety of the deeper water offshore. The little ketch, *Intrepid*, had rejoined along with another brig, *Scourge*, both of which arrived laden with water and provisions. The brig had been a Tripolitan blockade runner captured during the previous season by *Syren* and before that, a French-owned vessel named *Quatre Freres* captured by the British in 1797. A fine trim looking vessel, it was thought she had been built in America.

"I thought you were to be held ashore for . . . well, a long time, Thomas. I am glad to see you back aboard. Hopefully, we can avoid crossing each other even though we are forced to live in close quarters." Judd pretended he did not see Wheatley's hand extended in greeting, and his tone belied his welcoming words.

I spoke up. "Judd, Thomas assures me he has learned from his mistakes and has changed. I have actually enjoyed his company for the week and more he has been aboard. And you may recall, I . . . well, we were surely not best of friends earlier. You will be surprised, I am sure, at the change in him."

Thomas looked from one of us to the other, but said nothing. He had started for the hatch when Judd called after him.

"Very well, Thomas; I will endeavor to start with the slate clean. But pray, how did you manage to get 'liberated' from your confinement? I really had not expected to see you this soon, barely six weeks from when we saw you ashore in Syracuse." The three of us headed below with Thomas actually offering a hand to Judd with his seabag, a hand which Judd declined.

"I reckon Lieutenant Lawrence had instructions from De . . . Captain Decatur to fetch me out. Must be he wanted my advice on how to finish this business!" Thomas smiled broadly as he spoke, deflecting Judd's invective before it came. "Actually, Mister Lawrence mentioned to me that the captain and the commodore had determined to end my sentence since it was convenient to return me to the ship and another hand would be welcome. Made me wonder if you two couldn't handle things without me!" He smiled and winked at me as he spoke. Judd's face began to contort with anger, and Thomas raised his hand, cutting off any retort before he could give it voice. He smiled more broadly at us both.

"I hear from the crew and Mister Morris you boys had a hot time of it out here. 'Specially that first attack you made with the gunboats. While I am sorry to have missed that scrap," Judd and I exchanged a look, "I might not have faired as well as you two since . . . well, that was then, and I have had time to think about things. I look forward to another opportunity to participate in some fighting with these devils!"

"Well, Thomas, you will not have long to wait; we will be attacking in the gunboats this very night. The captain is in *Constitution* even as we sit here and is planning the action with the commodore. By the way, I collect you have heard that Commodore Preble is to be relieved? I would wager that we will see considerable action now, at least until the rest of the frigates and Commodore Barron arrive."

"What are we doing tonight, Judd? We have always attacked in the daylight. Why at night?" I tried to keep the concern out of my voice, but my efforts fell short of the mark.

"You're not still afraid of the dark, are you, Oliver?" Thomas offered, but with a smile.

"No, Wheatley. And for your information, I never was! It's just that I . . . and I'd warrant you as well, have never fought at night." As I spoke, I remembered our "most bold and daring" attack on *Philadelphia* and put my hand up in resignation even before Thomas and Judd could remind me. "Yes, I remember last February. Well."

We all laughed, and Goodbody, our steward, appeared with dinner. In celebration of his return, Thomas rummaged in his seachest and produced a bottle of wine which he shared out to us, a token of his desire to be friends.

By nightfall, the squadron had moved closer to the breakwater in preparation of sending in the gunboats and bomb ships. And at midnight, the brigs and schooners towed them the rest of the way to a position where their cannon and mortars could fire effectively and, after manning the little vessels, cast them off to do their work. Again, Judd and I sailed on Decatur's gunboat, while Thomas went with Mister Lawrence on a bomb ship.

From two in the middle watch until dawn we fired and threw shells into the town. We could see the mortar shells when they exploded behind the walls of the fortress, but we received absolutely no return fire. It was as if the people had all left. I am not sure we did a great deal of damage in spite of the almost leisurely rate of fire we maintained. By six, the larger vessels had us under tow again, and we were removed to a safe distance away.

"That was certainly not what I had expected. Don't they shoot back?" Thomas commented as we sat at table for breakfast.

"Not only do they shoot back, Thomas, they generally send out their own gunboats and galleys to attack us. And then it often can get quite warm!" Judd replied with no rancor. "You just wait. You'll get your chance to meet these barbarians; we all have!"

"And they're as bad, worse, by half, actually, as the ones we met on *Philadelphia* last February. To me, at any rate!" I added in case he thought we had just been sitting out here carrying on a one-sided bombardment.

Two nights later, in the company of *Syren*, *Argus*, *Vixen*, *Nautilus*, and our own *Enterprise*, the gunboats and mortars again went in close to the rocks to bombard the town. This time, we received a heavy fire in return. At daybreak, *Constitution* stood in to within two cables of the rocks and laid down a withering fire of grape and round shot, targeting the enemy gunboats which had sailed out to attack our own vessels; there were thirteen of the hellish boats and galleys. Their fire succeeded in sinking one of the heathen vessels, disabling two others, and forcing the remaining ten to retreat to the safety of the mole.

Our flagship then followed the enemy to within a musket-shot of the quay, keeping up a hot fire the whole time, and attacked the batteries located on the mole. She actually hove to and held her position for nearly an entire hour while her twenty-four pounders hammered the shore batteries with over three hundred round shot and untold numbers of grape and canister. Preble did not restrict his fire to just the batteries; he poured five or six full broadsides into the castle and the town as well, with satisfying result. In the light of the fires started by the mortar rounds our bomb ships threw, we could see huge sections of walls and buildings that had crumbled under the onslaught.

Of course, the gunboat crews, no longer under attack themselves, were in perfect position to witness this remarkable display, cheering each new success with lusty *huzzahs* and ribald comments aimed at their enemy.

"We must surely be hurting them, Judd! No one could stand that bombardment for long without . . . well, maybe this will inspire the Bashaw to negotiate more reasonably!" I hoped!

"It's not entirely one-sided, Oliver. Look there. One of the cutters has taken a ball from the fort, it appears. They're sinking!" Judd shouted back to me over the thunderous roar of the pitched battle and pointed to a ship's boat (I recall it was one of those from *John Adams*) that was in complete turmoil and already awash to the gunwales. Men splashed in the water alongside and some clung to the wreckage. The firelight cast an eerie glow on the scene, bathing the unfortunate boat and the calm water in orange and yellow tones.

Then, as the first light of a new day began to brighten the eastern sky, the firing ended. The flagship and the fort battery went silent, and *Constitution* withdrew, picking up several of the gunboats as she passed. The brigs collected the remainder, and a cutter from *Syren* rescued the unfortunates from the sunken boat. In all, we lost three men killed and one wounded, all from the unlucky boat.

"Well, that was more like it. At least this time they knew we were shooting at *them*! Too bad about the men we lost, but all in all, a small price to pay. I'd wager we killed a damn sight more than three of them and did more than a little damage!" Thomas was positively ebullient as we returned to the schooner. Of course, none of the enemy shot had landed in *his* boat!

"You young gentlemen can have a day at leisure to rest, since we'll be staying on our anchors for the balance of the day," Lieutenant Lawrence told us as we dragged ourselves to the cockpit for some food. I was not even sure what meal we might find, so confused with fatigue I was! *Never mind the food. Sleep will answer best!* I found my cot and collapsed into it, asleep as I fell.

By dawn the next morning, August thirty-first, we had two new vessels in our midst; another supply ship had brought the squadron shot, powder, water and fresh vegetables from Malta, and a Spanish ship had come out of Tripoli with information, intelligence, and, I later found out, communication from our colleagues in captivity.

Since the supply ship had no word of Commodore Barron or the other American vessels said to be on their way, Preble waited a few days to see if they might appear—the additional weight of metal would be helpful—and then decided to launch yet another attack on the town and the castle. He was determined to bring the pasha to heel while he remained in command! When our captain returned from the flagship and planning the attack, he mustered all hands on deck and told us what would be happening later that day.

"Men, this might easily be the last chance we have to give our commodore his victory over these heathen devils. He has earned the honor, as have all of you, and it is only fitting that he be given the glory he is due, as you will be. We must bring the Bashaw to heel before Commodore Preble is forced to turn over his command. The attack we will undertake this afternoon will, with luck, beat down the insolence of our enemy, forcing him to negotiate and seek quarter, and return to us our comrades from the late frigate *Philadelphia*." I was sure Decatur looked squarely at me as he uttered this last, and my heart leaped with the hope that he was right! My mind, too, swirled with thoughts of Edward and how wonderful it would be to see him again, tell him of my experiences here, and take him home!

Won't our parents be overjoyed when they see us pull up to the house on Held Street and step down from a coach and four! Of course, there won't be time to send off a letter with the good news before we sail for home, so it will be a complete surprise! And to have the time with Edward, alone with no . . .

" . . . Baldwin's place in gunboat number four." The mention of my name jerked me unceremoniously me out of my imaginary visit with Edward and back to the deck of *Enterprise*.

What had I just heard? That Wheatley would take my place on my gunboat with Decatur and Judd? Oh, no! How could that be? Had I not acquitted myself with honor the past several times we had fought? Why would the captain do that? Thomas had only been back a few days and knew little of how things worked out there! He had barely been shot at! And never had he boarded one of their boats like I have, not once, but twice! And . . .

" . . . the schooners and brigs will approach closer this time and will be participating in the attack actively. We will keep more men aboard each to provide the ability to fight most of our batteries." Decatur continued his explanation of the plan while I continued to search my recent behavior to find the reason for being left out of what might well be our last attack. My delight at having Thomas back aboard the schooner had paled considerably!

When we were dismissed, I remained rooted to the deck, still lost in thoughts of my own inadequacy. I remembered nothing of my fears, my churning stomach, the trembling hands that had accompanied each previous experience on the gunboats. All I knew was that Hobbs was taking Lawrence's boat, now with Judd, and I was being left aboard the schooner with the first lieutenant while Wheatley took my place with the captain. I should have been relieved at this turn of events, but instead was bereft at being left behind.

"Well, I reckon we'll be some busy here aboard the schooner, Oliver. I am counting on you and Bradford to handle the entire battery. Since we'll be short-handed, you'll both be right busy, but I know you will manage just fine!" Lawrence was smiling encouragingly at me. I, on the other hand, stared at him, my incomprehension clearly visible in my blank look.

"Guess Cap'n Decatur needed two aboard he could count on since we'll be taking on the polaccas this time. Too bad the others in the gunboats likely won't be getting into a real scrap this time!" He didn't sound genuinely sorry about that, and, as he continued to recount Decatur's plan (which I had missed), I began to feel less like I was being punished for something.

Once again, as four bells sounded in the afternoon watch signaling two o'clock, the gunboats and bomb vessels were manned and sent off on their mission. I scarcely noticed, so busy was I with the preparation of our guns. I had assigned Bradford to oversee the forward battery while I managed those toward the stern, but Lawrence had made it clear to me that he would hold me responsible for the entire broadside, so after I had seen shot and powder laid out for mine, I stepped forward to ensure the forward battery was equally ready; I should not have worried. As usual, Bradford was perfectly organized and ready to fire either side as required, even with a short crew at each gun.

I was standing with the gunner's mate talking when the first bomb vessel fired its explosive shell into the fort, signaling the start of the festivities. I watched through the glass as the gunboats moved into position and saw that the enemy's polaccas and galleys were leaving the quay to attack. We were supposed to take on the enemy's boats, not our gunboats. Lawrence had not put the schooner in the right position to do that, and now I would miss that action as well! But, as I looked around me, I saw that *Nautilus*, *Vixen*, and the brigs would miss out as well; they were no closer than we were and well beyond the range of their guns from the polaccas and galleys. The gunboats had little choice but to turn and face the approaching corsairs; to continue toward the English Fort and the town would allow the enemy to get behind them and be directly upwind, clearly not an advantageous position.

Firing commenced and built quickly to a warm action between our boats and theirs. The bombs were now anchored and throwing their deadly missiles into the town, the fort, and the Bashaw's castle, receiving a brisk return fire from not only the castle, but from the mole, crown, and several batteries nearby. Neither we nor any of the ships with us were able to fire into the town; it was simply too far, and should we attempt to fire at the enemy boats, we ran the risk of hitting our own! It was, then, with a great sense of urgency that the three schooners and two brigs beat to windward in an effort to assist Decatur, Somers, Hobbs, and company with their attack, as well as have some action ourselves.

But then we watched the enemy's ships withdraw. As soon as our gunboats got to within pistol shot of them, perhaps remembering our previous encounters, the corsairs turned tail and retreated to the safety of the mole, under the guns of Fort English. Our valiant colleagues followed them in, firing grape and canister shot with telling effect. Suddenly, a hail of musket fire was unleashed from the battlements of the very fort I remembered Edward telling me that *our* sailors had built. They were not firing at us, rather at our gunboats, now well within their range. I was rapt at the events unfolding.

"Mister Baldwin, we will have a broadside at the fort, if you please. Stand by to fire as I bring her head up a bit." Lawrence's bellow from the quarterdeck interrupted my reverie, and I quickly stepped to my guns, noticing as I did that Bradford was ready and holding a slow match close to the forward most gun.

"Fire as you bear, men! Give 'em a taste of American iron!" Lawrence had brought the ship around, followed by *Vixen* and *Syren*.

BOOM! BOOM! *Syren's* guns roared out first, drowning out the rest of Lawrence's words and, immediately, Bradford's first gun echoed their shots. After squinting quickly down my barrels, I shouted, "Fire!" to my acting gun captains, and three more of our cannon spoke, sending their twelve-pound iron shot hurtling into the ramparts of the fort. I was now too busy to notice what our gunboats were up to as we maintained a hot fire of both round and grape shot.

The enemy boats were tucked in under the protection of that besieged fort and still firing, though sporadically and poorly laid. The musket fire had ceased but, in its place, the heavy shore guns had found our range as well as that of our gunboats. We filled the air with iron, fire, and smoke. In the easy breeze, the lavender-tinged smoke clung to us, as much hiding us from their gunners as it hid them from us. It became nigh impossible to see more than the barest outline of the fort; their own thick smoke obscured their battlements and flashed eerily with each discharge of their guns. I found, from watching Bradford, that laying my guns at the brightest point of the glow would produce the best effect, and soon we had silenced at least one of the batteries firing from Fort English. The American gunboats, I believe it was Somers' division which included Lieutenant Hobbs and Judd, continued to maintain fire into the polaccas and the fort, adding their considerable weight of metal to ours, *Vixen's*, *Syren's* and *Argus.'*

Further to the east, I could see glimpses of the other division of gunboats as they supported our bomb vessels, laying a steady fire into the castle and the batteries near to it. A deeper, more resonating voice announced that Preble had taken *Constitution* in close, closer in than were the bomb ships, and was entertaining the barbarians with broadside after broadside from his twenty-four-pounders. The presence of such a large target was irresistible to the enemy, and the flagship drew much of the fire away from our bomb vessels and the other gunboats. I suspected at the time that it was exactly what the commodore had intended.

We continued the action for what seemed only a short time, but when Lawrence called for us to cease firing and hauled his wind to bring *Enterprise* around on a course back to the north, I was surprised to see my watch said half after four. For over two hours, we had maintained a barrage of fire which surely told on the enemy. As the rising wind blew away the smoke, huge gaps appeared in the walls of the fort, the castle, and the wall around the town itself, much to the delight of all of us. Seeing that we had damaged the enemy to such an extent made the wounds to our own ships seem insignificant. While all the schooners and both of the brigs had sustained damage, it was mostly of a superficial nature to our rigs and sails. I am sure I was as grime-smeared as I had been when Bradford was inspired to offer the compliment, but hot, tired, and mostly deaf, I neither sought nor expected it to be repeated.

Weary cheers issued from each vessel and from each of the gunboats as we passed them towlines to haul them out. *Constitution*, visibly damaged from her foray off the castle, sailed by with one of the bombs in tow as well as four of the gunboats. I assumed they were mostly intact and included Decatur's as well as Hobbs' commands, as the gunboat astern of *Enterprise* carried no familiar faces. In the dimming light of the day, I counted and discovered that one of the bomb vessels and the brig *Scourge* had gone missing; they were neither with us nor were they with the flagship and the other gunboats. What had happened?

The fleet sailed in the rising breeze, a breeze which was shifting more and more northerly, to the same position we had occupied for days, well to the west of the fortifications and the town. We set our anchors while we knotted and spliced, hammered and nailed, and repaired our damage. The injuries to our vessels seemed more significant now than when we were still engaged with our enemy. Bosun Anderson and the sailing master were supervising a clutch of men aloft repairing falls and lifts and replacing blocks, deadeyes, and other parts of the rig. Our sailmaker had already pulled down the outer jib and the fores'l, which had both received a number of shot holes, the fores'l the worse by half. I knew that new or repaired sails would be bent on before the golden fingers of dawn overspread the eastern sky.

As I watched a gang of haulers on the main deck respond to Anderson's orders, heaving around on various halyards and braces as necessary, I wondered about Thomas and Judd and how they had fared. I knew several of the gunboats had taken hits to more than just their rigging. While neither was aboard, I recalled that one of the bombs was still missing, and Captain Decatur had yet to return to the schooner.

Perhaps they were in the group picked up by Constitution *and are still secured astern of the flagship awaiting a tow to us. I truly hope . . . .why do you care what might have happened to Wheatley? He took your rightful place with the captain and has most likely done some telling battle. You should be angry.*

But I was not; I was concerned about both my shipmates and offered a silent but fervent prayer that they might have escaped without damage. Supper in the cockpit, for just me, did not appeal, and I lingered topside, watching the other ships tend to their own wounds.

"Mister Baldwin, since it appears to be just the three of us this evening, would you care to join Morris and me in the gunroom for supper? I submit it will be more pleasant than dining alone in the cockpit." Lieutenant Lawrence stood behind me, a bemused expression suggesting his sincerity.

"Oh, sir. Yes, sir. That would be grand. I shall tell Goodbody that I'll not be dining in the cockpit. At what time should I arrive, sir?"

"About half an hour from now would be convenient. That will give you time to clean up some." Lawrence's voice seemed muted to my still-suffering ears, but the irony of his tone came through in spite of my own shortcomings.

I had touched neither water nor soap since we finished the engagement in Tripoli and was still, I am sure, a sight to behold. I remembered how I had looked after my last term as a gun captain and could feel my face flush, the spreading redness hopefully covered by the coating of dirt and grime that extended from my hairline to my collar and beyond.

"Yes, sir. I shall attend to that at once, sir. And thank you again, sir." I turned and headed for a bowl of hot water and soap along with a clean uniform. I repaired my considerably disheveled appearance within the allotted half hour and presented myself at the gunroom punctually.

"Mister Lawrence, sir. A boat from *Constitution* is headed this way. When we hailed it, the cox'n responded with *"Enterprise,"* so it must be Cap'n Decatur returning." The messenger stood stiffly at attention in the gunroom door while the officers studied him, chewing thoughtfully.

"I will be up directly. Ensure that Mister Anderson has called out sideboys, if you please." Lawrence stood and said to us, "Gentlemen, excuse me if you will. It would appear the captain is back." He strode purposefully out of the room, pulling his napkin from his neck and throwing it on the table as he passed.

Morris stood and announced he would join the first lieutenant. I took one more bite of the supper and, chewing it slowly, followed him, unable to decide whether my desire to greet the captain, and perhaps, my colleagues, was overshadowed by my unwillingness to be left alone in the officers mess.

"Welcome back, sir. It would appear you and the others of the gunboats accomplished a great success. I would expect the Bashaw would be more ready than ever to treat with us. And with more reason, perhaps. I think we taught him a lesson this time!" Lawrence greeted Decatur effusively, seemingly seeking credit for the efforts of the schooners and brigs.

"It was *Constitution* taught him a thing or two, Mister Lawrence. And no mistake. The gunboats and bombs certainly added their voice to the lesson, but the eleven full broadsides offered by Captain Chauncey, who again commanded the flagship, will be the telling stroke, no doubt. And it very nearly cost us one of the bomb ships; Robinson's vessel took enough shot into her to put her on the bottom of the harbor. It was only through fine seamanship seasoned with a good bit of luck that *Scourge* got to her in time to save the crew and pull the wreck clear. Lost not a soul on any vessel! A fine stroke of luck, indeed." Decatur had stopped and had caught up all of us on deck in his story and comment on the parts of the battle we had not seen. Lawrence asked him a question which I could not catch as I was distracted by a hand from behind me laid upon my shoulder.

"Some fun that was, eh, Oliver? You missed out on some right fine shooting. And who ever said those rascals don't shoot back? They most certainly did today!" Without turning, I instantly recognized Thomas Wheatley's gloat, even though he spoke barely above a whisper, and only loud enough for me to hear.

"I know they shoot back, I've been here all along, Thomas. Remember? And we took some shot aboard *Enterprise* as well. So did the other schooners and the brigs." I turned around to see his grinning face. He had apparently washed, but in so doing, had missed some of the dirt and grime from the firing and smears of it streaked one side of his face and his neck. I smiled at him, amused at his appearance; he thought I was sharing his *bon hommie* and threw an arm across my shoulders, leading me away from the others as he began to offer the details of their fight.

"Mister Baldwin, before you run off to share tales of gallantry with your colleague, a moment, if you please." Decatur's voice stopped me in my tracks, and I threw off Wheatley's arm to turn back.

"Sir? Yes, sir?"

"I think you might have an interest in this, Baldwin." Decatur held up something pale, scarcely larger than his hand. I could not make it out in the dim light of the quarterdeck lantern and stepped toward him.

"Yes, sir. What is that, sir?"

"Oh, just a letter from an old friend of mine you might enjoy reading." The smile in his voice was echoed by his countenance; he extended his hand with the letter, and I rushed to take it.

Edward! It's a letter from Edward! Where did it come from? Surely there were no messengers that came out during the battle!

"It came out with some other papers and letters the other day on that Spaniard. Been sitting on the flagship until Commodore Preble gave it to me just this evening. I hope all is well. I know Bainbridge is recovering nicely and, aside from a few cases of scurvy, I believe the rest are doing nicely, considering their captivity," Decatur told me as he presented to me Edward's letter; I could now see his fine handwriting in the dim light, and, as I took it from the captain, I could barely contain myself. I studied the outside as if I might divine the contents.

"Thank you, sir. Thank you. I had hoped for . . ." Decatur's laugh cut me off and he sent me along with a reminder to let him know of anything important Edward might have included.

The cockpit and my colleagues would have to wait; I had a letter from my brother and would read it now! As Judd and Thomas headed below after learning why I had been detained, I grabbed a lantern and made my way forward to sit again on the carriage of number one as I read my brother's words.

> My dear brother,
> It is my fervent hope you continue to do well in your employment, enjoying your profession and remaining unharmed in its pursuit. We have seen not only the evidence of you and your colleagues' visits, but from time to time, seen your ships and witnessed the splendid accuracy of your gunnery. From your past letters which never failed to mention your growing prowess with your battery, I trust some of the shot we recently received came from your own hand!

I stopped reading and searched for a date on the letter. *What did he mean by 'recent'? Had shots we fired done damage to the prisoners or their quarters? How dreadful it would be to have actually fired into the captives' quarters!* I found a date at the end, only a few days ago; it would have been written after our long night of firing during which we received no return fire, as well as the following attack.

> Your attack of the 3rd inst. was stunning! While I and my colleagues could see little of it, we were fully aware of the firing on both sides. Some of your shots told brilliantly in the fortress and castle and, we have learned from our warders, inspired the Bashaw to a fury previously unseen. It might also have been the loss of quite a number of his boats—we have heard variously numbers from two to twenty and surmise the fact is somewhere between the two.
> Your commodore and his captains, particularly my old and special friend SD, are deserving of great merit. One of the guards here mentioned, perhaps unintentionally, that several of the

Bashaw's gunboats were taken by boarding! If that is so, it is, according to the same source, the first time that any corsair has been successfully boarded and carried. It appeared to us, from his limited command of our language or any other civilized tongue, that these heathens have developed a new respect for American sailors. Bravo! And well done, Brother! You and your colleagues have taught them a valuable lesson and, we are sure, you will reap the benefit of it soon.

I smiled in spite of myself. Little did he know how right his prophesy was; already we had benefited from their newly acquired fear of being boarded by American seamen.

We applaud and cheer your splendid attacks and the success you are enjoying! They have, how so ever, taken their toll on the ones held in this God-forsaken prison. After the first attack extracted such a price and devastation on the surrounds, the Bashaw ordered the townspeople to assist on the fortress batteries as well as those on the mole. We understand that most refused, being more afraid of the American gunnery than the wrath of the Bashaw. You may have noticed that your next attack received little in the way of counter fire; there were simply too few men available to carry shot and powder to the guns. When we heard the third attack commence, we again rejoiced and celebrated. Until the guards took us all, men and officer alike, and marched us at sword point to the magazines to carry twenty-four-pound shot and powder to the guns on the walls.

Any flagging or shirking, which we all attempted with varying measures of success, was met with several strokes of the cat. Even against the officers. However, even with the prospect of a flogging staring us in the face, we all moved as slowly and clumsily as possible, dropping round shot and splitting open powder bags as often as we dared. Our delaying actions must have had the desired effect as at the next attack, they took only the sailors—the very same ones who had been pressed into building the fort from which they fired at you. And we have heard that they continued to move as slowly as possible.

In a strange irony, it might have been the better for us had we handled their cursed shot and powder! We received several American balls in our quarters during the firing!

I looked up, stunned at this revelation! *Oh, no! Exactly what I had feared. We have been firing into the very building where the Philadelphias are held. I must tell the captain so he can ensure we don't repeat that!* I went back to the letter, fearing the worst.

One twenty-four-pound ball, in fact, came through the wall in the small cell owned by the captain and covered the poor man with rock and cinders. It took us more than a little time to dig the unfortunate out, but we were overjoyed to find him nearly unharmed. A few cuts and bruises and a badly wrenched leg were his only complaints! Fortunately there were no serious injuries, else we would have feared for his life knowing the level of medical services we, any of us, are likely to receive.

The warders gloat that your forces have taken a great number of casualties in the various actions, but knowing how those same heathens try regularly to undermine our spirit and morale, many of us have decided that their estimate of the effectiveness of their guns, and the vessels those guns have done in, is some extravagant and mostly exaggerated. Pray tell me in your next letter how our brave sailors have fared!

Be certain to give my warmest greetings to your cap't., my great good friend from Philadelphia, SD. I have shared many of my memories of our youth with my colleagues here; there is little else with which we might pass the time. You were, I think, too youthful, or off at the academy, to share in the special times Stephen, his little brother James, and I spent chasing about in our fair city along with Dickie Somers and a few who chose to remain ashore. Of course, during the summers of the yellow fever, we saw little enough of one another as our families went in different directions to escape that dreadful disease. Though you were but a lad of 9 years, I am certain you recall the outbreak during the summer and fall of 1798. I was just starting out as a midshipman then and visiting our parents on a short leave from the Navy as I remember, and we, all of us, up and left in July for New Jersey. I left from there, as I recollect, to rejoin my ship; you all did not go back to Held Street until well into October. That was the summer the Mayor and both Mister Bache and Mister Fenno succumbed along with 3000 others. Dreadful, it was. Does that horrible disease still run rampant?

Enough of my ranting for now, you will think I have gotten a touch of the fever myself, the way I am going on. David Porter has asked my help with the young gentlemen as they continue to read their professional studies, and I must stop now to attend to that. Keep up your splendid efforts and with luck, the wearing down of the Bashaw, and the Grace of God, I shall join you sooner than later.

With the greatest of affection . . .

"Oliver! Where have you been? I been looking for you for the past half a glass and more! I must . . ." Thomas stopped as I looked up from Edward's letter, suddenly realizing he was intruding. Then he went on, barely a heartbeat later. "I must tell you my great good news! I am to go with Captain Somers on *Intrepid* when she is rigged as a fire ship! What do you think of that? I reckon De . . . Cap'n Decatur approved it on account of I ain't been out here as long as the rest of you and he thought I deserved it. There's going to be some glory there, when we blow the mole and his gunboats clear to hell!"

CHAPTER TWENTY-FOUR

H e stood there, breathless in his excitement, grinning hugely as he waited for my response. For my part, I could only stare at him. Part of my head was in the prison with Edward and another part of it heard Wheatley's announcement.

"I . . . think that's . . . I can't understand why the captain would assign that to you. Judd or I should do that. We've been here; we know the ropes." I was becoming less and less happy with his return; why couldn't he have stayed locked up in Syracuse?

"Oliver, I have more time in the Navy. And yes, you and Judd have been out here longer, due to my temporary 'holiday' in Syracuse, but I think the captain is trying to make amends for leaving me behind. I don't think our duel was all that troubling to him. Besides, Mister Somers *requested* me! And he is Decatur's closest friend; how could the captain refuse him?" His smile grew broader, whether in response to my reaction or to the prospect of the glory that would derive from the mission, I knew not.

"Let me finish reading my brother's letter, and I'll come to the cockpit directly." I had finished almost all of the letter; I wanted time to figure out the course I would pursue to right this wrong. He looked disappointed at my lack of enthusiasm for his assignment, but nonetheless, he left. I lowered my eyes to the letter, but saw none of the words; my mind whirled in stunned emptiness as I tried desperately to determine a course.

After rereading Edward's letter once, I stood, looked around us at the yellow glow showing from the lanterns on each member of the anchored fleet, and made my way aft with every intention of joining Judd and Thomas in the cockpit.

"Mister Baldwin, I collect all is well with your brother?" Decatur's voice stopped me before I had reached the hatch, and I turned to face him.

"Oh, yes, sir. He is quite fine and so, apparently is Captain Bainbridge, in spite of our firing into their prison! Not *our* firing directly; I recall he mentioned a twenty-four-pound ball entered the captain's quarters, so it might have been *Constitution*?"

"Lest you forget, Oliver, the gunboats all, or most, at any rate, carry twenty-four-pounders as well. So it might easily have been any one of them. Even number nine, from which, I am sure you recall, you and I managed to send any number of shot into the fortress." The captain smiled as he saw the look of horror which crossed my face, visible even in the dim glow of the 'midships lantern. "But fear not, no harm was done, at least of any lasting nature, and the Philadelphias are pleased we are reducing the Bashaw's stronghold, in spite of the depravations they must endure. I suspect, when Somers takes *Intrepid* in and blows her along with the Bashaw's entire fleet, they will be even more pleased. And perhaps *that* will encourage the heathen pirate to treat with us!"

"Sir, I know it is not my place to question, but why did Mister Wheatley win the assignment to sail in the ketch and not Judd or me? Have we not acted in a professional manner . . . and with honor?" I hoped my tone sounded less petulant than my words.

"Dickie . . . Cap'n Somers requested Wheatley, Oliver. I happened to mention him in conversation with Somers and others and remarked that he had acquitted himself well in our late action; for want of a different name, I must conclude that was the reason. I doubt whether Cap'n Somers is even aware of you and Mister Devon, beyond your names, of course. You both are fine midshipmen and will, in the fullness of time, make fine officers, I have no doubt. Fear not; neither of you have done anything to suggest otherwise." He studied me for a moment, judging my reaction, and then resumed his earlier posture by the bulwark, his back to me.

Well, that is your answer, Oliver. Just happenstance. There will be other times when you will go and likely that will make Wheatley wonder what he might have done wrong!

I stepped into the cockpit feeling much better as Thomas launched, again, judging from the expression on Judd's face, into a discourse on the brilliance of Somers' plan, and his role in it. Judd's eyes turned toward me and he winked, a half-smile playing at the corners of his mouth.

"Hold a moment, Thomas. Here is Oliver whom I am certain will want to hear of your good fortune. You must begin again so he hears all of it!" Judd stood as though he had just remembered something. "You will have to excuse me for a moment, gentlemen. I must speak to the first lieutenant on a most urgent matter."

His wink, unseen by Wheatley, spoke volumes: "Sorry about that, Oliver. I reckon you're the one stuck with him now!"

Thomas seemed not to notice Judd's departure and launched immediately into the story of how Captain Somers had selected him, above many others, to join the expedition into Tripoli's harbor. "I can only reckon that Decatur must have told him of my value in such a position! I am sure that any of the officers and mids in the fleet would have jumped at the chance to participate in such a daring move. I mean, think of it, Oliver; we're going to load the little *Intrepid* up with tons of powder and sail her right into the harbor. I can only imagine the bang that will make when we blow her to smithereens. It will be glorious!"

"It will blow you to *smithereens*, also, Thomas. Did you happen to think of that?"

"Oh, not on your life, young Master Baldwin. Your joy at my untimely demise must be short-lived, I am afraid. You see, we will tow a pair of fast cutters astern of us as we sail in. The fuses will be of sufficient length to allow us to row clear *before* the ship explodes. We, all of us, will be safely away to watch the destruction we will have caused from a good distance." He was putting on the accent of an educated person again, something I had not heard in some time. "I am sure the fireball and devastation will be of sufficient grandeur for it to be seen even from the safe distance where you will be." His smirk and false airs affected me not a whit; I merely smiled and nodded.

"When is this all to take place, Thomas? Surely it must be done at night to allow *Intrepid* to get close enough to do the damage you intend."

"Of course! I do not know which night it will be, Oliver, but I can tell you this, it will be soon. Preble is afraid he will have to turn over the command before he brings the pasha to heel and the next commodore, Barron, will win the honor of the victory. Cap'n Decatur and Cap'n Somers both think this might be the telling blow." He suddenly reverted to form, "So I would reckon they ain't likely to wait."

They did not; the very next morning the work commenced to convert the little ketch into a fire ship. No less than three ship's carpenters and six of their mates began pulling out bulkheads and decking to allow sufficient stowage for the one hundred barrels of powder that would be put aboard. I could scarcely imagine the explosion that *fifteen thousand* pounds of gunpowder might make; it would be devastating for any near at hand. It crossed my mind briefly that here was my very first prize about to be destroyed, and at the hand, indirectly, I suppose, of Midshipman Thomas Wheatley, of all people!

Well, I suppose better her than one of the schooners! And she had served her purpose well, bringing us alongside Philadelphia *and safely out again.*

The weather had turned sour again, but only briefly; on the afternoon of September fifth, Thomas rushed into the cockpit breathlessly, barely able to contain his exuberance.

"We're going tonight! We're sailing into the harbor and blowing up that piratical bastard's fleet this very night!" He practically shouted, causing Judd to start so badly, he upset a cup of coffee he had been drinking.

"Well, Thomas. Finally! You must be relieved that the waiting is finally done. And I think the moon will be dark tonight as well. Surely that will bode well for your mission. I wish you joy." Judd spoke as he wiped the table and his breeches, a thoroughly annoyed look on his face which only I noticed.

"Reckon the lack of a moon figured into the decision, Judd. Seems sensible to wait for it to be as dark as possible for something as important as this. We can not fail! Oh! It will be glorious to see that ketch blow herself to the devil and take those damn gunboats and polaccas with her! I must get back to overseeing the work on *Intrepid* so we can get the powder barrels loaded aboard. But I thought my . . . colleagues would want to know that your shipmate is about to sail into glory—and history. Along with Somers, the name of Wheatley will be remembered as the one who made the killing stroke and brought the pasha to his knees." He left as suddenly as he had arrived, and as breathlessly, consumed as he was with his own sense of importance.

"Can you believe the arrogance? 'My name remembered by history as the . . .' whatever it was he said. Never mind that we've been out here for three months pounding those bastards time and again. Never mind that we've been capturing their ships and destroying their forts and town! That self-focused imbecile! I . . ." Judd was sputtering in his anger and frustration. "I hope Somers doesn't let him light the fuses; he'd like as not miss! Remember how he could barely hit the water with a pistol? Why ever would Somers and Decatur think he could add anything to this commission?"

"Judd, calm down. There is nothing we can do about it now, and besides, Thomas does have some catching up to do. In that, he's right. Remember, you promised to start again with a clean slate when he came back aboard and forget about all the fussing and fighting that went on before Messina. Give him a chance for his own glory. Besides, maybe once he's seen the elephant, he won't be so impossible!"

"Seen the *elephant*? Oliver, what in the name of God are you talking about? Seen the elephant, indeed!"

"It's a classical reference, Judd. I learned about it in the Academy in Philadelphia. Has something to do with Hannibal and his elephants going through the Alps when he fought against the Romans . . . or the Greeks . . . or someone. I can't remember exactly all the details, but I think it fits here. But what I meant by it was that after he's faced the pirates, like we have, and done something grand, like we have, he might be a bit easier . . . well, he might be a better shipmate." *I thought* everyone *knew about 'seeing the elephant.'*

"Thomas was with us in February, Oliver, on *Philadelphia*. Remember? He likely saw the elephant then, if there was one around." He smiled and looked away as he muttered something I barely caught, but it sounded like he said, "I must have missed it my own self. But then, I was below decks most of the time!"

Judd and I made our way topside to watch the goings-on and studied with interest the preparations being made aboard *Intrepid*.

"I'd guess most of the powder's been put into the hold already, Oliver. Looks like they're puttin' something aft there, a box, it looks like. See it? Right on the quarterdeck, forward of the tiller. I wonder what that's about." Judd was pointing at the little ketch that was made fast alongside *Nautilus* where her captain, Lieutenant Richard Somers might keep an eye on the proceedings. Even though I peered through a glass, I could see nothing of our shipmate, who had had ample time to return to the fireship to "oversee the work" being carried out. I mentioned my observation to Judd.

"I doubt whether Somers would let him oversee the stowage of their rations, let alone the powder and combustibles." Judd snorted in disgust.

"Judd, they won't be taking any rations; they're only going to be gone for a few hours while they sail in and then leave immediately the ketch is fired." I couldn't believe that Devon actually thought it would be necessary for food to be aboard on such a short commission.

"Sometimes I wonder if . . . Oliver, you imbecile! That is the whole point of what I said; can you think of a less important job than stowing the rations that won't be there?" Judd's expression was one of amusement and bewilderment. He shook his head.

"What rations? I don't reckon we'll be takin' any food or drink in with us; takes up room we could fill with powder. Why would you think we'll be takin' anything like that? Too short a commission, by half, for that!" Thomas had come up behind us without making a sound.

"Thomas! You startled me! We were talking about something else, entirely. Nothing to do with your little foray tonight. I thought you'd be over on *Intrepid* or *Nautilus*, overseeing the loading." Judd spoke so disarmingly I almost believed him myself.

"Well, our boats are off somewhere, I think De . . . the captain's took one to the flagship, and I couldn't get there. But I'm sure Cap'n Somers has everything under control." He took the glass from me and peered through it for a moment. "There, he's already got them loading the combustibles into the box there on the quarterdeck. Just before we leave her in there with the fuses lit, we'll pour some whale oil around the deck just to be sure she takes the flame well. And when the fires reach the forward hold, all hell is going to break loose! Somers told me he's ordered near one hundred fifty fixed shells put in the hold on top of the powder casks. That ought to give those bastards something to think on, by God!" Our colleague was so caught up in his participation in this moment of glory that he was completely inured to anything we might say to him.

The remainder of the day passed with brave talk and anticipated glory to which we listened half-heartedly. I suspect that Judd hoped as much as I did that when this commission was ended, Thomas would get on with the more mundane aspects of our existence here. I don't think I could bear further self-aggrandizement from him!

It was while we were at supper, in fact, Goodbody had just set a fine pot of melted cheese in front of Judd to serve out, when the messenger from the deck watch knocked on the doorway.

"Mister Wheatley, there's a boat waitin' on yer from *Nautilus*. Said they was sent by Cap'n Somers. Might not want to keep 'em waitin' sir."

"Oh! Thank you, sailor. I shall be along directly." Thomas stood, grabbed up his hat and stuck out his hand to me. "Wish me luck, Oliver. This is going to be glorious!"

I took his hand and shook it vigorously. "The best to you, Thomas. I know you'll do splendidly and bring credit to *Enterprise* and all of us!" I actually meant it.

"I'll walk you up, Wheatley. See you off." Judd was now standing and, with a nod at me, followed our fellow out.

I wolfed down a few bites of supper, helping myself as I kept a wary eye watching for Goodbody, and, still wiping my cheese-covered lips with a napkin, went on deck to watch the proceedings.

Thomas was in the boat and just pushing away from our side as I reached the bulwark. Judd stood looking down at him, having just said something like, "Good luck," and Thomas was beaming back at us as he set off on his bold adventure.

"When are they actually sailing the ketch in, Judd? Does anyone know?"

"The talk is some later, after it's full dark. There's a small problem; a couple of the corsairs have been spotted by the western breakwater. And that's right where Somers intends to go in. Being observed would not answer at all; they've got to get in without anyone knowing, or the plan will fail."

Oh, dear. I hope they can do it! Having the commission cancelled or even postponed would make Wheatley impossible!

"I guess we might finish our supper then. I am sure we'll know when they actually start in!" I watched the boat carrying our friend toward the schooner, which remained about a long musket-shot away, the fireship still secured alongside.

Judd waved a final salute to Thomas and turned about, nodding to me and heading for the hatch. I followed, hoping that the cheese had settled to a new smooth surface to conceal my pilfering.

It must have been close to ten o'clock that night when *Enterprise*, *Nautilus*, and *Argus* won our anchors and escorted the heavily-laden ketch toward the rocks marking the western entrance to the harbor. Our batteries were loaded and run out; we were ready to attack any gunboat or galley we encountered while *Intrepid* sailed to meet her fate. I stood with Bradford in the lee bow, peering through the night trying to make out the ketch.

"I wonder how far ahead of us she might be, Bradford. Can't see a thing out here. I guess if we can't, neither can they. Maybe Captain Somers will just sail right through without a problem."

"Aye, sir. That would surely be my choice. And then we and the others just sail off and on out here to pick up their boats after they set the fuses. A right plan, it is. Simple! I like that!"

An hour later, the escort vessels all hauled their wind and hove to. No enemy had been seen or heard, and we had gotten this far unchallenged. I knew *Intrepid* and my colleague were now on their own, headed into whatever awaited them. All we had to do was wait, perhaps the hardest part.

"A light. A light ahead of us." The lookout, perched in the foretop, cried out in a hoarse whisper. While I could see nothing of him, I knew he would be pointing at it. I stared into the blackness ahead of us and thought I detected a single whitish glow moving as if someone were carrying it as they walked. Suddenly there was a blinding flash and an explosion like nothing I have ever seen before.

"My God! They blew it already!" Someone called out into the ringing silence that followed.

The ketch was clearly illuminated by the fireball; we could see a flaming mast, sails and rigging intact but wreathed in fire, soar into the darkness amid a shower of sparks and debris. All of us on deck were pummeled by an invisible fist, knocking some flat and causing others to merely stagger. The concussion of one hundred barrels of powder, one hundred fifty mortar shells, and various other combustibles detonating all at once was massive and shook the vessels from their waterlines to the tops of their masts. Then bits and pieces of the wreckage, fragments of shells, and burning scraps of sailcloth began raining down on us. *Enterprise*, being closer to the breakwater than the others, received much of the heavenly offering.

"Watch your powder bags, lads. Keep them sparks clear!" Bradford shouted out as I stood in shocked silence watching the glowing shards of what had been a fine little ketch fall from the sky.

"Keep an eye peeled for their boats, lads. They ought to be coming out anytime now," Lawrence's voice floated forward, followed quickly by our captain. Decatur took up a position in the bows, one foot on the butt of the bowsprit, and held a night glass to his eye. We could hear voices in *Nautilus* and the brig echoing Lawrence's command as others sought to find our colleagues as they made their way out of the harbor in the two cutters *Intrepid* had towed in with her.

"Do you think it worked, sir?" I spoke to Decatur's back as he studied the western approach with the glass.

"We can only hope, Mister Baldwin, we can only hope." He continued to hold his glass to his eye. "I would have thought Dickie might have lit his fuses a trifle early, but I guess we'll have to wait until they come out." Decatur spoke this last as though he were talking to himself and I barely caught the words.

Decatur's concern for the success of the mission seemed a bit excessive, even for him. Then I remembered Edward mentioning in his last letter that Somers and our captain were lifelong friends and companions. *No wonder he seems worried.*

"Let me know if you hear anything, Oliver. Listen for oars dipping, voices, anything at all. They should be coming out from about there." He pointed, his outstretched hand holding the glass, like an extension of his arm. "And keep silence about the decks!" Without further comments, Decatur disappeared into the darkness, leaving us all peering forward with hands cupped behind our ears.

"Show a light, forward, there. Give them something to row towards." Apparently the captain had decided that the risk of discovery at this point was outweighed by the need of our colleagues to find us.

"Sir! Listen. Do you hear?" Bradford grabbed my arm, his whisper edged with tension, the tension we all felt.

"Hear what? Do you hear the boats, Bradford?"

"No, sir. Listen! Voices and drums. Don't you hear it?"

Then I did. But the voices and the beating of the drums came from ashore, not from our fellows making good their escape. I called out to the quarterdeck with the information and received a "Thank you" and "Stand to your stations!" in reply. Perhaps the batteries ashore, now alerted to our presence, were about to fire.

They did fire, ineffectually, and in seemingly random directions. They could no more see us than we them, and their shots did little to dissuade us from waiting for the boats. Eventually the shore batteries ceased their useless firing, and we, all of us on three ships, continued to watch and wait in silence.

The dawn found us still hove to about a half-cannon-shot from the western rocks. I think not a soul in any of the ships slept a moment that night, waiting with failing hope of ever seeing our comrades again. A heavy air of melancholy had settled on all aboard as the realization struck home. Decatur had shown up regularly in the bow armed with his night glass, saying nothing to any of us, as he watched and paced.

With the light of a new day, exhausted men, diminished by the loss of our thirteen brave fellows, saw how the event had ravaged the face of our captain. His brow furrowed in consternation, his shoulders drooped, and the pall of futility hung about him like a great weight. The fire which had lit his eyes from the start was gone; now those demanding yet kindly windows to the captain's inner being were red-rimmed and withdrawn, underscored by dark shadows, once again giving him the look of a man of greater than five-and-twenty years.

"Show the signal to rejoin, if you please, Mister Lawrence. They will not be coming out. I must report to the commodore." Decatur stepped off the quarterdeck and took a position amidship, still occasionally turning his glass toward the brightening shoreline and harbor for some sign, anything that might offer some hope. Then, in company with *Argus* and *Nautilus*, we set our remaining sails and bore off to the west and our squadron.

EPILOGUE

"Did they ever come out, those men in the fireship, Grandfather? What happened to Mister Wheatley and your captain's friend, Lieutenant Somers?" The big eyes and concerned faces of my two grandsons made me think briefly I had offered more details of the events than I should have. But they had remained attentive for the entire story and deserved to know the end.

"No, lads. They were lost in what, to this very day, remains a great and melancholy mystery; no one ever discovered what happened. The ketch caused no damage to the gunboat fleet she had been intent on destroying, and the only surmise has been that Somers and his crew were discovered and boarded. Captain Decatur had told us that his friend had vowed not to be taken, and it was his considered opinion that they simply fired the ship and sacrificed their own lives to ensure that those hundred barrels of powder and the shells the ship carried would not fall into the hands of the enemy. We all knew how desperate the pirates were for both powder and ball. Your great-uncle Edward told me that Bainbridge had been taken to the shore to identify a half-dozen bodies that had washed up the next day, but they were so horribly shattered and disfigured as to be unrecognizable. And the ketch itself, or what was left of her, washed up later. No, I am afraid we will never know what happened that night." I saw brows furrow as the lads considered this, trying to make some sense of the story.

As they pondered, I again felt myself being drawn back to that time, now so long ago, when we saw the flagship's signal to return to port. It was a dejected and dispirited collection of sailors and officers who sailed into Syracuse Harbor some ten days later. Commodore Preble and *Constitution*, in company with *Argus* and *Vixen*, remained on station to continue the blockade and await the arrival of his successor. As our ammunition stores were very low, each of the departing vessels had off-loaded its powder and shot to the three which remained and towed the gunboats and bombs with us, to be returned to the King of the Two Sicilies. Now some of us, including *Enterprise*, would return to the United States, a prospect which filled me with conflicting emotions.

On one hand, I was overjoyed to be returning home after being away for over a year. I rejoiced at the prospect of parading my newly-acquired maturity before my parents and friends who had remained safely ashore in Philadelphia, and telling them of my adventures in the war. But rushing in like a wave thrusting up the shoreline, undermining the joy of my long anticipated homecoming, was the realization, the knowledge that we had failed in our mission, not only in causing the Bashaw to treat with us for peace, but more importantly, to secure the release of the Philadelphias. I felt this failure most keenly, knowing that Edward still languished in that heathen dungeon.

"Grandfather . . . Grandfather?" A small voice intruded on my reflection, drawing me back to the parlor in what I still thought of as my parent's home on Held Street, even though both had been gone for nearly thirty years. I looked down at the expectant faces. Timothy, my son's ten-year-old boy, wore a puzzled expression.

"When *did* you rescue Great-Uncle Edward then? Did you go back to Tripoli later?"

"Well, no. Tim. It was not until the summer of 1805, almost a year later, that the Bashaw agreed to a peace and released the officers and men of our late frigate to Commodore Barron, still in *Constitution*. I was not there, but I learned that the Danish consul, Mister Nissen, came aboard the flagship with a commission from the pasha to negotiate, and a treaty was soon drawn up and accepted by the Tripolitan potentate with certain conditions. One of the conditions was a ransom of sixty thousand dollars, which the commodore and our Consul-General in Algiers, Tobias Lear, approved, along with an exchange of their prisoners, your Great-Uncle Edward among them, for the ones we held.

"It was soon after the treaty was signed that the prisoners were marched to the mole, and *Vixen* sailed in to receive them. She received a salute of twenty-one guns from the castle which was answered by our flagship. It must have been thrilling for them, after they realized it was only a salute!" I smiled at the boys, hoping they understood the irony. "The Philadelphias were brought home later that summer in the ships of Barron's squadron, now no longer needed in those waters."

"Did I ever meet Great-Uncle Edward? I don't remember him." Benjamin, the younger child at just seven years, piped up.

"You were quite small, Ben. It's little wonder you don't recall my brother. You were not yet four when he passed on. And since he had accepted a position to teach at the new Naval School when it started in 1845, he lived there in Annapolis, down in Maryland. We didn't get a visit from him all that much." It was hard to reckon with the passage of ten years since that school began; it seemed only yesterday when Edward told me about it and that he would teach the young men how to be naval officers. And now he'd been gone four years himself.

Until they moved to Annapolis, Edward and his wife had lived here, on Held Street, enjoying the fruits of his thirty-year naval career, his own grandchildren, and a certain celebrity from having been in *Philadelphia* with Bainbridge, who had gone on to command *Constitution* during one of her most famous engagements in the late war with England. Edward, as well, had secured berths for himself in some well-known and successful ships during that war. Our father's cabinet shop had closed with his death, but still remained where it had stood since he built it, next door.

"Oliver, what drivel are you filling these young heads with?" Ann, my wife of nearly forty years, stepped lightly into the room. Her voice held the same good-natured chiding tone which she had used to correct my errors over most of that time. "Stephen and Sally will not let the children visit if you persist in telling them harrowing tales of your adventures. It'll likely give 'em the night terrors!"

It was a grand tradition that our oldest son's two children came for a visit each Sunday after services, stayed for dinner, and, after their parents joined us all for supper, returned to their home across the river in New Jersey.

"Oh, Grandma, it's fine. Grandfather has just told us of how Great-Uncle Edward was captured and put in a dungeon in Tripoli and they couldn't get out for two years and then he started the Naval School in Maryland. We liked it very well!"

"Well," my dear wife laughed, "I think you may have missed a few years there. You know that both Edward and your grandfather served in the late war with Britain. Mustn't forget that. In fact, your grandfather was with Commodore Decatur in the *United States* frigate when they took HMS *Macedonian* after a savage battle and sent her in to Newport as a prize."

"You didn't tell us *that*, Grandfather," Timothy, always eager for a story, said accusingly. "And what happened to Mister . . . I mean Captain Decatur? Have we ever met him?"

"The tale of the capture of *Macedonian* is for another day, Tim. Your grandma will scold me if I tell you that now. But as to Decatur, he, and I, did go back to Tripoli after the war, 1815, it was, when the pirates abandoned the treaty they had signed. Their brothers in Algiers and Tunis joined them this time. I was third lieutenant in the very ship Commodore Decatur had captured, *Macedonian*, on that commission. Of course, the ship now belonged to *our* navy. Decatur was commodore of the largest squadron ever assembled, fifteen ships, I think, and sailed the fleet right into the harbor at Algiers. When the pasha looked out of his castle at those ships there, he quieted right down and there was never a shot fired! The other heathen devils followed suit quick as ever you please. And that was that. We stayed for a few months and came home.

"It was just five years later, March 22, 1820, I shall take the date to my own grave, that Commodore Decatur was shot and killed by Commodore James Barron, the brother of the very man who had relieved Preble in 1804! A duel, it was, and over something trivial, a misunderstanding. Barron, who had demanded it, was wounded, but it was not mortal. Decatur's wound was, though, and he succumbed the day following. I attended his funeral in Washington, along with many of those who had served with him both on the Barbary Coast and in the war with England in 1812. All the members of the Senate and the House, the President, the Justices of the Supreme Court, and a multitude of other dignitaries were in attendance as well. A truly melancholy time; such a waste!"

A silence filled the room as I reflected on the event and my feeling of loss at the untimely demise of that great man, the lieutenant who turned a fourteen-year-old boy into a man whose character was tempered in the fires of conflict.

"Here's a somber looking group, if ever I saw one. Who has died?" Stephen's booming voice broke the mood, and I smiled as Timothy and Benjamin leaped up to greet their father, resplendent in his newly earned captain's uniform.

"Stephen, you startled us all. You're going to be the death of both your father and me, should you persist in sneaking about like that! Hullo, Sally, what a pretty frock. Come now and sit, supper is just ready."

BLOWING UP of the FIRE SHIP INTREPID commanded by CAPT. SOMERS in the HARBOUR of TRIPOLI on the night of the 4th Sept. 1804. Before the Intrepid had gained her Destined situation she was suddenly boarded by 100 Tripolines, when the Gallant Somers and Heroes of his Party, (Lieuts. Wadsworth and Israel and 10 Men,)

observed themselves surrounded by 3 Gun-boats, and no prospect of Escape, determined at once to prefer Death and the Destruction of the Enemy, the Captivity & a torturing Slavery, put a Match to trains leading directly to the Magazine, which at once blew the whole into the Air. Courtesy of USS Constitution *Museum.*

AUTHOR'S NOTES

While this story is technically fiction, the historical events are accurate and the ships and most of the people are real. The Baldwin brothers, Oliver's shipmates in the cockpit, and certain specific officers and sailors in *Argus* and *Enterprise* are creations of the author's imagination. The brothers Decatur, James Lawrence, William Bainbridge (and his brother), the Barrons, Commodore Edward Preble, and others existed and acted more or less as depicted in the events of 1803-4. They, along with several other officers, young lieutenants at the time, went on to further glory in the War of 1812. These include David Porter, first lieutenant on the ill-fated *Philadelphia*, Charles Stewart, captain of *Syren*, and Isaac Hull, who took over command of *Argus* after she reached Gibraltar. Later, Hull had *Constitution* during her well-known engagement with HMS *Guerriere*, the first significant victory for the young republic in the War of 1812. William Bainbridge, as Captain Baldwin mentions to his grandchildren, also had commanded USS *Constitution* in her epic battle with HMS *Java* off the coast of Brazil. James Lawrence is best remembered for his famous utterance, "Don't give up the ship!" which he spoke as his command, USS *Chesapeake*, was about to be taken by HMS *Shannon* on June 1, 1813.

Stephen Decatur, as a young lieutenant, did second William Bainbridge's brother, Joseph, in a duel in Malta in 1803 against the secretary to Sir Alexander Ball, the Governor of that island. Interestingly, the duel was fought at *four* paces, since Decatur felt that Bainbridge was such a miserable marksman as to be unable to hit a target at the more usual ten paces. It ended after each participant had missed with their first shot, reloaded, and fired again; the Englishman was killed and Decatur and Bainbridge shortly sailed for home as passengers in the frigate *Chesapeake*.

Decatur did die as a result of a duel with James Barron fought in Washington, DC, in 1820, the result of a long-standing feud between the two. Decatur had participated in Barron's court martial after the *Chesapeake-Leopard* affair in 1807 and had recommended Barron's dismissal from the Naval Service. Barron was, of course, not dismissed, and held that Decatur had insulted him during several later conversations. The two corresponded for several years about the incident, during which time the tone of each letter became more acerbic, more particularly those of Commodore Barron, and ultimately resulted in Barron's challenge, which Decatur reluctantly accepted. He named Commodore William Bainbridge as his second! The duel was fought at a distance of eight paces on March 22, 1820, at Bladensburg, Maryland. Decatur died from his wounds the following day and was buried in Washington several days thereafter with full ceremony and with every politician from the President to the most junior representative in attendance, along with many senior Navy and Army officers and countless civilians who had come to honor their hero.

Dueling was a common practice then, more particularly in the Navy, as by 1804 the Army had established laws against it. Later, so did the civilian world, but duels still took place and were considered an acceptable method of solving differences. The duel in the story between the two midshipmen, while fictitious, was representative of the several which actually took place during that conflict, including one involving two mids.

The raid to burn the frigate *Philadelphia* was carried out on February 16, 1804, just as described by Oliver; there were, in fact, fifty sailors, eight Marines, five officers including the surgeon, seven midshipmen, and one civilian, the pilot Salvatore Catalano, who sailed *Intrepid* into Tripoli Harbor that night. The notables among the officers and midshipmen included, of course, Stephen Decatur, James Lawrence, Joseph Bainbridge (brother of William, captain of the frigate) and Midshipman Thomas Macdonough, who found his own glory on Lake Champlain against the British in September 1814 (Battle of Plattsburgh). It has recently come to light that no evidence exists supporting the letter from Admiral Lord Nelson to the Americans describing their raid as "the most bold and daring act of the age." This legend apparently began in the 1840s with A.S. Mackenzie's biography of Stephen Decatur.

James Decatur, Stephen's brother, was mortally wounded during the August 3, 1804, gunboat attack; shot in the head, he died on board *Constitution* in the company of his brother. When told about the treachery that had led to his brother's fatal wounding, Stephen immediately attacked and carried the Tripolitan polacca. His hand-to-hand combat with the pirate commanding it and the way Decatur triumphed were properly described by Oliver. It is interesting to note that, for years, people ascribed the heroism of the wounded sailor who threw himself across his captain's body, and thus received the cutlass stroke, to Ruben James. Songs were written attesting to his act and at least two ships were named after him; it was not he, however. From contemporary medical records, Daniel Frazier has been proven to be the selfless sailor who saved Decatur's life and lived despite his grievous wounds. His act is generally credited to the devotion Decatur's men felt for him.

Decatur was promoted to captain by Congress subsequent to his action on *Philadelphia*. He was the youngest man, at just twenty-five, to hold that rank, before or since. Congress also voted him a sword and his all-volunteer crew received promotions as well as cash awards. The prize money he sought for his crew never materialized, a great injustice to the participants.

Stephen Decatur did assume command of *Constitution* shortly after the period of this story as Reliance Wakefield predicted, but in jest, to Judd and Oliver. He subsequently relinquished her to John Rodgers, his senior, but then in 1805, took command of the frigate *Congress* (36) which he held for some time. Of course, to his further glory, he was in command of *United States* (44) when she took HMS *Macedonian* in single ship combat in the fall of 1812 and sent her in to Newport as a prize, as Ann Baldwin mentioned to her grandchildren.

The ruling Bashaw of Tripoli, one Yusuf Karamanli, was, in the opinion of the United States, not the legal ruler of the country; that was his brother Hamet, whom Yusuf had forced out of the country in order to take the throne himself. But Hamet had exiled himself to Alexandria, Egypt, over one thousand miles distant. In an effort to end the hostilities, a small force headed by William Eaton, ex-U.S. consul to Tunis, was dispatched to Egypt to find Hamet, gather an army of Arabs and, after being transported to Derne by navy ships, march overland to Tripoli and storm the city in concert with a naval bombardment. Marine Lieutenant Presley O'Bannon, two naval officers, and some eighteen enlisted marines and soldiers made up the nucleus of the force which left Malta in the brig *Argus* on November 17, 1804, and arrived in Alexandria ten days later.

Eaton, after a lengthy search and dealings with both sides in a local civil war, found Hamet, and the party returned to the coast, only to be denied permission to board *Argus* by the Turkish admiral and governor of Alexandria. French interests there had convinced the Turk that the returning Americans were, in fact, British spies. Eaton and O'Bannon determined to make it overland to Derne, a distance of over five hundred miles. After enormous hardship and trial, the party, now swelled with the addition of Hamet's Arab troops, successfully attacked and carried that city on April 27, 1805. The *Argus*, still under Isaac Hull, and the schooner *Nautilus* were waiting there as arranged and supported the land attack with a naval bombardment of the city. Marine Lieutenant O'Bannon commanded a detachment of marines, twenty-four cannoniers, and thirty-six Greek mercenaries. Hamet Karamanli commanded an Arabian cavalry. During the battle, one Marine was killed and two wounded, one mortally; eleven Americans, including Eaton, were wounded. It was from this action that the Marine Hymn includes the words, ". . . to the shores of Tripoli . . . ." Of course, there also were Marines on almost all of the ships that participated in the blockade and bombardment of the harbor at Tripoli.

Yusuf Karamanli, having been told of the fall of Derne, sent his army with orders to retake the city. They attacked several times and, each time, were repulsed by the combined Christian and Arab forces. Both sides suffered heavy casualties, and all for naught, as during the fighting, Eaton received dispatches indicating that treaty negotiations were well underway and, in all likelihood, the Americans would have to evacuate the city. On June 11, 1805, the American frigate *Constellation* arrived with orders to that effect, and Bashaw Yusuf Karamanli's troops seized the opportunity to eliminate all the remaining local residents of the city for their disloyalty to the ruling Bashaw. While the action had little direct impact on the outcome of the war, most historians feel that the threat of an overland attack combined with the naval bombardment provided further inducement to the Bashaw to treat for peace.

Both Wakefield and Edward Baldwin make reference to the yellow fever outbreaks in Philadelphia. For nearly ten years, that often fatal disease did appear in Philadelphia during the summer. Of course, it would not be discovered that it was borne by mosquitoes until the construction of the Panama Canal many years later. Thousands, including many notables as mentioned in Edward Baldwin's letter (like the mayor of Philadelphia and the two newspaper editors, Bache [*The Aurora*] and Fenno [*The Gazette of the United States*]), fell victim to the dread fevers in Philadelphia and elsewhere.

Finally, there is no more information now than existed in 1855, when Oliver Baldwin tells his grandchildren the story of the fireship *Intrepid*, about what occurred that caused her to explode before reaching her target. Theories abound, including that the ketch had been discovered and was under attack; when Somers realized escape was impossible, he fired the ship. Others hold that a hot shot fired by a Tripolitan gunboat touched off the explosion. Whatever the cause, the outcome remained that all thirteen aboard perished with no discernable effect on the enemy. Bainbridge was taken to the shoreline the day following the unsuccessful attack to identify several bodies which had washed ashore; they were too badly burned to recognize even their nationality, let alone their individual identities. The other bodies were recovered by the Tripolitans within two days, and the floating remains of the ketch were found in the rocks several days after that. A memorial to Richard Somers and his crew, as well as to James Decatur and the other officers killed during the campaign, was established at the United States Naval Academy in Annapolis, Maryland, by their fellow officers.

All in all, Preble's squadron lost thirty killed and twenty-four wounded, two of whom subsequently died of their wounds. Edward Preble himself died of illness just three years after relinquishing his command to Samuel Barron, on August 25th, 1807, at the age of forty-six.

William H. White
Rumson, NJ
2002

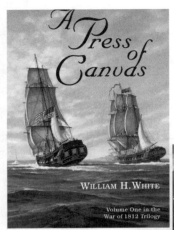

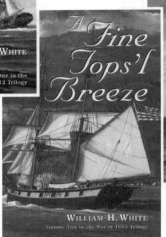

The War of 1812 Trilogy
By William H. White
Illustrated by Paul Garnett

A PRESS OF CANVAS, Volume One *Softcover, 5½"x8½", 256 pages*

A Press of Canvas, W. H. White's action-packed novel, introduces a new character in American sea fiction: Isaac Biggs of Marblehead, Massachusetts. Sailing from Boston as captain of the foretop in the bark *Anne*, his ship is outward bound with a cargo for the Swedish colony of St. Barts in the West Indies in the fall of 1810. When the *Anne* is stopped by a British Royal Navy frigate, Isaac and several of his shipmates are forcibly pressed into service on the *Orpheus*, actively engaged in England's long-running war with France. The young Isaac, naive and inexperienced, faces the harsh life of a Royal Navy seaman and a harrowing war at sea. His new life is hard, with strange rules, floggings, and new dangers. Then the United States declares war on England and Isaac finds himself in an untenable position, facing the possibility of fighting his own countrymen. A chance meeting with American privateers operating in the West Indies offers him a solution to his dilemma and a reunion with an old friend.

A FINE TOPS'L BREEZE, Volume Two *Softcover, 5½"x8½", 288 pages*

A Fine Tops'l Breeze, W. H. White's action-packed novel, continues the adventures of the newest character in American sea fiction: Isaac Biggs of Marblehead, Massachusetts. In the second volume of the trilogy, Isaac ships as Third Mate on the Salem privateer *General Washington* in February 1813. At the same time, his friends from the British frigate *Orpheus* and the Baltimore schooner *Glory* find berths on the American warship USS *Constellation* and, eventually, they wind up on the USS *Chesapeake* in Boston just in time for her disastrous meeting with HMS *Shannon*. Throughout the spring of 1813, Isaac and the *General Washington* roam the waters between Massachusetts and Nova Scotia, taking prizes and harassing the British. When the American survivors of the *Chesapeake/Shannon* battle are confined in Melville Island Prison in Halifax, the *General Washington* and Isaac play an important role in securing their freedom.

THE EVENING GUN, Volume Three *Softcover, 5½"x8½", 288 pages*

The year is 1814, the final year of the War of 1812. With the Atlantic seaboard closed by the British blockade, Isaac Biggs, Jack Clements and Jake Tate, fresh from their harrowing adventures in Canada, find berths with Joshua Barney's Gunboat Flotilla in the Chesapeake Bay. These swift and shallow-draft little vessels have become a thorn in the side of the British fleet and the British command is determined to destroy them. Barney's Flotilla is eventually chased up the Patuxent River to find temporary refuge in Benedict, Maryland, where Isaac falls in love with the daughter of a militia colonel. After several exciting forays against the British fleet, the flotilla must be scuttled and burned. Its men are called ashore to fight at the Battle of Bladensburg in an futile effort to halt the invasion of Washington, then are sent to defend Baltimore against the British siege of the harbor. Isaac, Jack and Jake witness the historic and horrifying bombardment of Fort McHenry from the outer harbor, aboard a British warship in the company of Francis Scott Key.

Written from the aspect of the fo'c'sle rather than an officer's view and through the eyes of an American, *A Press of Canvas, A Fine Tops'l Breeze* and *The Evening Gun* provide new perspectives and exciting stories of this oft-neglected period in American history. Tiller Publishing is proud to offer these carefully crafted tales as its very first fiction series.

> *By the publication of* A Fine Tops'l Breeze, *the second of his War of 1812 Trilogy, William H. White has taken his place in the charmed circle of writers of really good fiction about the days of fighting sail: Melville, Forester, O'Brian, Nelson, and Kent. Like them, his attention to the detail of ships and their hulls, spars, rigging and sails is meticulous. And, like them, his characters are not only credible, but memorable. He is a thoroughly welcome writer to this genre, which has brought so much pleasure to so many.*
> Donald A. Petrie, author of *The Prize Game:*
> *Lawful Looting on the High Seas in the Days of Fighting Sail* (1999)

> *Through Bill White's evocative prose, one smells the salt breeze and feels the pulse of life at sea during the War of 1812.*
> John B. Hattendorf,
> Ernest J. King Professor of Maritime History, U.S. Naval War College

> *"Sailors everywhere will rejoice in the salt spray, slanting decks and high adventure of this lively yarn of the young American republic battling for its rights at sea."*
> Peter Stanford, President
> National Maritime Historical Society

> *"A great read . . . a very engaging story with believable, honest characters . . . taught me a lot about this period of history . . . just fabulous!"*
> John Wooldridge, Managing Editor
> *Motorboating and Sailing*

> *The War of 1812 is a forgotten war. Few Americans recall much except there were some naval engagements and we won the Battle of New Orleans. Many don't realize that Washington was burned, let alone know about the battles on the Patuxent. Bill White has brought this neglected period of our history alive with all the drama, panic, and confusion that gripped Washington, Baltimore and the Chesapeake region as a whole in 1814. The description of the attack on Baltimore and the writing of the "Star Spangled Banner" humanize an event that we don't think about when we sing our national anthem. The War of 1812 and the sacrifices that were made to preserve our liberty will be better understood after reading* The Evening Gun. *An enjoyable way to learn history.*
> C. Douglass Alves, Jr.,
> Director, Calvert Marine Museum

About the Author

Mr. White is a former United States Naval officer with combat service. He is also an avid, lifelong sailor. As a maritime historian, he specializes in Age of Sail events in which the United States was a key player and lectures frequently on the impact of these events on our history. He authored three novels set during the War of 1812: *A Press of Canvas, A Fine Tops'l Breeze* and *The Evening Gun*, which make up the War of 1812 Trilogy. He lives in New Jersey with his wife of 36 years. More on William White and his books can be found at **www.seafiction.net.**

Photo by William H. White Jr.

About the Artist

Paul Garnett began drawing before he could write his name. He was a shipwright on the vessel *Bounty*, built for MGM's 1962 remake of "Mutiny on the Bounty," and his paintings have been published twice by the foundation which now owns the ship. His art has also been showcased on A&E's television program "Sea Tales"; the History Channel's "Histories Mysteries: What Really Happened on the 'Mutiny on the Bounty'"; and by *Nautical World* magazine.